Due Process

Vigilante Serial Killer—Justice Dispatched with Extreme Prejudice

Lyle O'Connor

The New Master of Crime Thrillers

Due Process

Vigilante Serial Killer—Justice Dispatched with Extreme Prejudice

Lyle O'Connor

The New Master of Crime Thrillers

Publication Consultants
Since 1978

PO Box 221974 Anchorage, Alaska 99522-1974
books@publicationconsultants.com—www.publicationconsultants.com

ISBN 978-1-59433-386-6
eBook ISBN 978-1-59433-387-3
Library of Congress Catalog Card Number: 2013939993

—First Edition—

Due Process is a work of fiction. All names, characters, places and incidents are products of the author's imagination or are used fictitiously. Any resemblance to actual events or persons, living or deceased, is entirely coincidental.

Manufactured in the United States of America.

Dedicated to Gena—Who shares my dreams and owns my heart.

Acknowledgement

My sincere appreciation to Walter Allen Grant, author, contributor, who guided my hand in this adventure.

Chapter 1

He who fights with monsters might take care lest he thereby become a monster.
And if you gaze long into an abyss, the abyss gazes into you.
—Friedrich Nietzsche

My Dodge Avenger purred down the highway as the sun dropped below the horizon painting the western sky bright orange; the vivid colors faded rapidly into various shades of twilight. I wasn't in a hurry; in fact, I had time to kill. I smiled, realizing my subconscious had provided the perfect pun. My rendezvous with Seth Poole was still an hour away; his time of reckoning was close at hand. Poole was employed at a convenience store on the outskirts of Salem, Oregon; a relatively short drive from where he lived. I'd been to his house before and over to the little store, but never had the opportunity to meet him in person, certainly not like we would meet tonight.

I exited the freeway and made my way down a winding country road to where Poole lived. Just past his dimly lit house I made a tight left turn onto a dirt road and coasted to a stop behind an entanglement of brush that concealed the Avenger from view. Out in this area houses were sparse and only a few spangles of light were visible through the gnarly old growth. With scarcely a sound I slipped from behind the wheel and pushed the door shut. Poole's house sat a short distance off the road and about fifty yards from the turnout. Leaves rustling in a chilly wind masked any noise I might have made on my way to his carport.

Over the next few minutes I opened the screen and knocked on the old Plexiglass storm door that opened into what appeared to be the original single-car garage; the carport was an add-on. The garage had been turned into a utility room and served as side entrance to his house. With no one answering the knock I assumed the house was empty as it usually was—Poole lived alone. The carport area was lit by a single overhead light inside the utility room which left much of the carport in darkness; this was to my advantage. Poole would enter his house from the carport when he arrived home. This had been his routine on the occasions I'd observed his customs and habits; nothing was likely to change tonight.

The magic hour approached. Poole was already on his way home and should be arriving within the next couple of minutes. I concealed myself in a dark corner of the carport and waited. "What if" scenarios played out in my mind—what if, what if, what if . . . Although I'd rehearsed my response to every conceivable situation, my emotions ran between apprehension and euphoria. When I spotted headlights peeking through the trees my thinking returned to normal and I put everything out of my mind except the job at hand. The wait was over.

Poole swung his EL Camino around at the driveway entrance, braked to a stop, and then roared up the driveway in reverse. The sound of heavy-metal rock music violated the night silence. For a moment I was concerned his back-up lights might illuminate the carport enough for him to spot me hiding in the shadows. I slinked farther back into my hiding place and waited. Poole turned off the ignition as the El Camino rolled to a stop. The radio went silent. I was thankful for the return of nighttime stillness—I didn't want any distraction when I confronted him. I wanted his full attention.

He turned off the headlights and emerged from the vehicle picking through a ring of keys held in his left hand. My single-word greeting, stern and commanding, carried an air of doom. "Poole!"

Startled, he dropped his keys on the concrete floor and began to back away slowly. Fear distorted his face. "What! Who are you! What do you want?" I moved from the dark recess of the carport into the shadows and then into a shaft of light from a naked bulb in the utility room. My handgun was now clearly visible to him. He continued to hurl questions at me. My response was deathly silence. I slowly brought my gun to the ready, sighting down the barrel at the center of his chest. His voice cracked as he cried out, "No! My God! Don't, don't shoot!"

Poole dropped to his knees with his hands cupped as if praying. "I'm begging you, man. I've never done anything to anybody! Don't kill me!" I remained silent as I took a few more steps toward him; I wanted Poole to meet his Grim Reaper face to face. He continued to plead for his life while I stood silently over him as judge, jury, and executioner. I drew within a few feet of the cowering, pathetic excuse for a man while leveling my pistol at his head. His cries meant nothing to me. From my subconsciousness came the question: Is there something I want to say before I pull the trigger? Nothing came to mind. In my opinion he didn't deserve the courtesy of knowing why I was going to put him out of my misery. He was a worthless scumbag who had ruined the life of another human being. An innocent boy, barely six years old, had been sodomized by Poole for his sick pleasures. Poole had a rendezvous with death; I was here to arrange the meeting. Sure, I knew whatever I did would not change what happened to the victim. There was no undoing what he had done. What it did mean was Seth Poole would never ruin another child's life. In the broader spectrum of my goals, it ultimately meant: chalk one up for Walter. That's one perp down and another half million or more to go.

The few seconds I held Poole at gunpoint seemed like an eternity to me. I doubt it felt much different to him. My pistol was intimidating. The .40-caliber Glock was fitted with a 7 ½-inch moderator that looked and worked much like a silencer. He was quiet now and his bowed head signaled he was ready to accept the inevitable. I don't know if I was thinking anymore or just ready to react when I felt a prompt to pull the trigger. No need to draw it out any further, it would serve no purpose. I hadn't come to torture him. I didn't feel any rush or exuberance. Thuup. Thuup. My gun blazed off two quick subsonic hollow-point rounds that could hardly be seen or heard. It was done.

This waste of humanity, known to me as the Poole Project, slumped to the floor. For a moment I kept my weapon leveled on him while I watched the blood flow from the wounds in his head. After a quick scan over my shoulders I lowered my weapon from the ready and removed the moderator. I holstered the Glock and picked up the spent cartridge cases. Cautiously, I slipped out through the dilapidated side wall of the carport and made my way through the brush back to my car. My mind was fixated on the event in the carport; I watched it play out over and over. It was like a kaleidoscope spinning from one picture to another and consumed my every thought. I had to snap out of it and focus on my departure.

Thirty-two-year-old Seth Poole lay dead. Although I could easily have accepted the blame for his untimely demise, it was much deeper than an opportunistic execution. He himself was the single most responsible person for his death. At least that's the way I saw it. Poole had committed a sadistic-heinous attack on an innocent young boy. It was that day that Poole unknowingly sealed his own fate in death. He considered himself as having paid the price to society for his crime, a statement he frequently repeated when questioned about his past. He had been sentenced to the Washington State

Correctional Facility at Walla Walla for too few years. He was cooped up with others of his own kind, away from general inmate population for his safety. His incarceration did not rehabilitate him and it ultimately did not make it safer for him. It only postponed the inevitable—his due. He championed the idea that his parole was the end of the consequences for his crime. He was gravely mistaken. I mean that literally.

I moved slowly through an overgrown hedgerow and onto the dark turnout. The Avenger sat quietly awaiting my arrival. I opened the car door slowly; its well-greased hinges were as silent as the night itself. The overhead lamp was disabled to allow easy access without being noticed. As I started the vehicle I realized no one was privy to what had happened. I turned on the headlights and slipped the car into drive.

Poole's house was a little over an hour's drive from my place. As the miles rolled up on the odometer, the tension that had built at the carport began to dissipate. As I drove toward home, somewhere during the route I distinctly heard the voice of a child whisper, "Thank you." I couldn't be sure how real it was, I never know anymore. Hearing it seemed reward enough.

It was unfortunate justice had not been served by the courts and matters had to be handled this way. What due process under the law should have been had become a mockery of justice and a flimsy bucketful of excuses for criminals' rights. Due process was now more of a provision for the miscarriage of justice than anything else. It was Walter's mission to put some *dues* back in *due process.*

I pulled the Avenger into my driveway, turned off the lights and engine and sat there thinking of how Walter had come to be. I wasn't a born killer; I was a made killer. I don't know how many times I've heard it said, "If that was done to my wife, kid, and so on, I'd kill 'em." Few ever do. It must make them feel better to say it and I'm sure they would like to see it happen but they don't have it in them to be doers. Justification for killing a sexual predator by a victim or a victim's family member is understandable if not widely accepted by a majority of people. No one blames someone who acts out in anger in these circumstances. It's personal, emotional, understandable, and to some extent acceptable in the eyes of the law. However, I am neither understood nor accepted. To exact a revenge killing after they've completed their prison sentence is not defensible. It is especially so in my case since I have no personal relationship with the victim or the victim's family.

I've never been a victim. I don't know what it would be like. I've never had a family member victimized in a heinous crime. I've never known friends or close associates who have suffered in this manner. My reason is entirely different. I tried for a time to justify my actions in a rational way that others might understand, but to no avail. For lack of better terms, I am a vigilante killer, and I accept that. I prefer to think of myself as freelancing in the justice system.

People kill people for many reasons: some lawful, some unlawful. Revenge, passion, rage, for their gods or country, the list goes on and on. In some rare cases the United States judicial system exercises power over life and death with a decision to execute. Regardless of what the reason is or if the reason is socially acceptable, killing goes on around us every day. I am not a homicidal maniac or a random serial killer. I kill with reason and purpose. I'm not ashamed of what I am or what I do.

Is it predestination, fate, or the will of one of the gods that propels my destiny? I don't pretend to know. I think of myself as playing my part in the here and now, that's all. Personalities are formed in the early stages of life and choices throughout life are made based in part on our personalities. I'm not talking about the cocaine-snorting Freudian crap spewed out by the "professionals" of our day but in layman terms, it's just the way we're wired. Maybe it's as simple as I never had a chance from the beginning.

After studying humans like rats in a cage, science still can't explain mankind's propensity for violence. Science can't predict who will become a violent criminal and doesn't have the cure. There are too many variables. It is a simple fact that each of us is a variable. You can make some sort of statistic from it if you like but it won't bring a conclusion, only a theory at best. The next brainiac comes along and uses those same statistics to disprove your theories and hypotheses. As for me, as far back as I can remember, I've always been inclined to choose my own path. I wasn't into doing what other kids did just because it was popular or because others did it: I did it because it was right for me.

Right and wrong or good and evil are concepts with very thin lines of demarcation between their elements. In different societies different taboos exist. In different eras different taboos have existed. There have been times when doing right was called wrong because boundaries lines were obscured. Elements of both right and wrong are equalized in some concept of fairness. Get over it. Life is never fair. A child is sexually abused and childhood innocence stolen, that is not fair. Not in our society and not in our era. But there is an emergence of liberalism that is obscuring the line within the justice system. A sense that crimes of this nature were treated harshly was "unfair" to the criminal and a movement emerged in the '60s and '70s to have shorter incarcerations and rehabilitate these poor lost souls so they could be productive members of society. Hogwash!

Victims of heinous crimes do suffer for a lifetime. Case after case demonstrates victims do not learn to live with what has happened. Fear, distrust, and the stigma of what occurred permeate their sense of security throughout life. In essence they have lost their lives. If the courts are unable to recognize what an offender owes, Walter will by execution.

I guess this is where my ideas differ from so many others. Crossing the line and doing what would be called socially wrong, was acceptable to me if it brought about the right that was being challenged. Right had to win. The police won't think so. To them it's a stat mounting against them. The media frenzy will capitalize on another scoop. Serial killer on the loose! Only a handful of reporters will even scratch the surface of the truth.

You might think I'm a right-wing religious zealot. You couldn't be further off base. I wasn't raised in any faith or religion. Good and evil to me are interchangeable terms with right and wrong. It's simply semantics, not religious beliefs. For the record, I admit I'm bankrupt in the area of religion. To me there is no god or gods. The Dalai Lama has the same power as Allah or Rah. Buddha, Lucifer, Jehovah, or Zeus—I believe in none of them. Wiccas casting spells, shamans and witch doctors with their hocus-pocus, have no power in my life because they don't mean a thing to me. Have I insulted all your gods yet? I apologize if I missed any of the headliners of religion. Nothing personal against those that practice or profess faith in something, it just wasn't for any of us in our household. Consequently, religion did not form any of my opinions on life.

I had a happy home life growing up. I admired my parents' relationship. I was never exposed to fits of anger by my parents, and child or spousal abuse was unheard of in our family. I wasn't raised in some clinically dysfunctional family. What I have become was not a product of my upbringing.

I was raised in a rural setting along the Columbia River Basin in Oregon. The ranch was literally nestled in the foothills of the Cascade Mountain Range. I roamed there freely as a child becoming a naturalist of sorts; I was inquisitive and left no stone unturned. It was paradise on earth.

There were dangers, of course. All variety of snakes frequented the barnyard and hillsides. There were rabid coyotes and feral dog packs in the area. Bears and cougars were spotted from time to time and presented an unpredictable danger. Then, there were the dangers from ranch animals and various pieces of farm equipment, such as tractors and mowers. I grew up knowing danger from many things. I considered it to be normal and routine exposure. What wasn't normal was harm suffered at the hands of another human. This was foreign to my world.

I was oriented early in life to the value of a weapon. I cut my teeth on a .22 rifle and .410 shotgun. The lure of shooting the big bores compelled me to shoot every chance I had. I became accurate and deadly. By my late teens, I was hunting everything from rabbits to elk. I was likewise doing most of the shooting on the ranch when it became necessary. Each year, we raised a hog and steer to butcher. It was one of my daily chores to feed them. They were absolutely dependent on us for everything and became very domesticated, but it was still the nature of the ranch that dictated their fate.

Generally, the first step in the butchering process was to put the gun to their heads and shoot. I was the shooter and I can tell you from experience it's not at all the same as hunting wild game. Shooting Bambi, even with all the personification we have given this cartoon creature, is still nothing in comparison to something you have grown an attachment to. The sense of attachment to something you have cared for, whether you knew from the beginning it was going to be butchered or not, attacks the emotions. Somehow, you have to overcome the reluctance to kill. I became a master at shutting down my feelings to carry out what was necessary.

The low spot of all the killing I had to do as a youngster was when my best friend Shorty mixed it up with a porcupine and got a quill in his nose. Shorty was basically a useless cocker spaniel for farm use, but he was my first dog and my friend. When the quill had worked its way up his nose and festered, it caused him to run a high fever that would ultimately kill him. My father insisted it was my dog and I bore the responsibility to decide how he would meet his fate. My heart sank and I felt deeply sorrowful when I aimed the shotgun in his direction. Shorty knew what guns did; he'd seen me kill a hundred animals. Friend or not, he knew my decision before the trigger pull. I could see it in his eyes.

A few weeks passed and I saw a porcupine slowly climbing a tree just a few feet from the ground. It was a young porcupine and I had no way of knowing if it was his quills that led to my dog's death and maybe it didn't make any difference. Using my bow, I took aim and stuck him to the tree. Looking back I'd say that was my first taste of revenge and I savored it.

The Avenger's engine cooled and it was time to retire to my quarters for a good night's rest. Seth Poole's encounter with Walter had gone as planned and another project awaited my attention. I wasn't born Walter but out of necessity I came forth. I am what I am, a normal average guy, that's all. Some people will see it differently and hate me for what I am. The criticism will not disturb me. Others, probably fewer in numbers and silent, will thank me for what I am. None will understand, unless you are like me, and maybe you are.

Chapter 2

Smooth seas do not make skillful sailors.
—African Proverb

Events happened during my formative years that had an impact on the way I saw the world. President Kennedy was assassinated. We were on the brink of nuclear war with the Cuban missile crisis. Vietnam, anti-war marches, political corruption, Black Panthers and race riots. Social upheaval, political corruption, Mafioso, and a nationwide epidemic in drug abuse; we devoured it as it was broadcast every night during our evening meal.

The United States Supreme Court swung the pendulum to liberalism by banning capital punishment for cold-blooded murderers. In my book, the decision to do something as callous as take another human life carried with it the consequence of forfeiting their life. Sadly, societal norms had greatly changed. I struggled to grasp the wishy-washy namby-pamby way society spewed out their "idealistic" utopist views. It was an unrealistic expectation for human behavior.

The judiciaries' decision to ban the death penalty nationwide and convert all death sentences to prison terms was based on their new interpretation of the United States Constitution's Eighth Amendment. They decided execution of a murderer was cruel and unusual punishment. In their opinion, it was a clear violation of the Eighth Amendment. Apparently, for 150 years, the Congress and Supreme Court had misinterpreted the law. Now, in 1972, the Johnny-come-lately Supreme Court judges discovered the proper interpretation. It was an insult that would not go unpunished. However, it was "We the people" that were penalized for their errors.

The lessons of life had transformed me from what I was as a child to what I am today. I did a tour in the military during the Vietnam War and once again found myself on the wrong side of public opinion. My book rapidly filled with ideas of mistrust for all politicians and government. They simply could not be counted on to do the right thing.

I tried my hand at marriage with my high school sweetheart but we were soon separated by military deployments. We matured, grew apart with different likes and dislikes, and eyed different futures for ourselves. When the divorce was final we said our good-byes. We never saw each other again. Somehow my memories of her are more romantic than real life, but that's okay, I prefer it that way. As I remember her now she is young, beautiful and frozen in time.

I wasn't much for barracks life; however, I did discover a remarkable kindred spirit in some of the troops. My first dorm roommate was with Sgt. Stone who I called "Stoneman." He was a Texican from what he referred to as the Armpit of Texas. It was a small dustbowl town in the Panhandle but the name escapes me. We spent hours jawing over the criminal headliners of the day. We reinforced each other's beliefs that consequences should be imposed that would probably never happen. My opinion was always the same. Annihilate them! Thin the herd! Execution was too humane unless it was done with a Ginsu knife over the course of a week or two. I wanted them to suffer excruciating pain. In my way of thinking, atonement was necessary.

Stoneman professed to be religious and expressed more compassion. "Give them a chance for redemption." In my way of thinking they didn't deserve it but I tempered to some small degree. Stoneman would regurgitate some hogwash he'd heard in church, "What if they were gonna find the Lord sometime in the future and execution takes that chance away?" My feeling was, "I don't care," but for the sake of conversation I offered a compromise. "If they are convicted they got ninety days for one appeal. At the end of the appeal time they swung on a rope." Stoneman agreed, if that wasn't sufficient motivation to find the Lord, most likely nothing in the future would ever make a difference.

Stoneman and I took the occasional jaunt out on the town for a little well-earned rest and relaxation. We'd hook up with a couple other troops and the crew would spend the night restoring our faith in humanity one drink at a time. The good thing about "the crew" was they were nearly as opinionated as we were when it came to the topics of serial killers of the day. Frequently we toasted our first drink of the night to Utah's firing squad that had sent Gilmore on his way to the next life. We dreamed aloud of forming a vigilante force, going inside prisons and getting some of these scum-bags. Someone in the "crew" came up with the idea of keeping a file on these convicts and at some later date, when all emphasis was off these slime-buckets, we would exterminate them. The plan was simple and I liked it. What a revelation, others believed like I did.

When my enlistment ended I returned to the ranch in Oregon. Most of my friends had left The Dalles for college, military, or employment. It was difficult to pick up where I had left off. Unemployment was high. Somehow, it was all a catalyst to seek a life elsewhere. By early, 1978, I landed a good paying job in Portland. It was aluminum factory work, repetitious, hot, and laborious. It wasn't exciting work but my future was there. It was a relatively stable and secure time in my life. However, I was distracted by only one thing, violent crimes. I was busy cutting out articles and alphabetizing them in a shoddy filing system.

Theodore Edward Bear, a liberal "lefty," was a brave sort in our midst. He was a college-educated Native American from a local Oregon tribe—a fact he never failed to mention when it was to his benefit. Bear was the kind of a guy who thought of himself as being smarter than everyone else at the plant. He looked down his nose at the common working stiff, even though he was blue collar. He may have had an above-average IQ, but he was lucky to get his boots tied in the morning. Nonetheless, Theodore, whom we called Teddy, mostly because he hated the nickname, could be very persuasive when arguing a point. Usually I didn't care about his psychotic drivel but there came a time he would be cast as my archrival and nemesis in debate.

Almost daily at the factory break room, Teddy engaged in debate. For a few years I avoided these gladiatorial events but when Teddy fired up on criminal rights, the need to vocalize my opinion surfaced. I put forth an effort to avoid a showdown with my antagonist, but irritation set in when he garnered a small group of allies to join in the debates. We referred to Teddy and Melvin Lowe as the Duo. They were two peas in a pod.

Lowe was a recent convert to Ted E. Bear liberalism. He was a Muslim transplant from Madagascar, who didn't fit in terribly well at the factory. Our expectations of workers in third-world countries were that they would be hard workers. Lowe put that misconception to rest. He came from a well-to-do family and didn't know the first thing about physical labor. His reason for coming to America was a mystery to us. I personally think he was a political activist, probably a wanted man, and a political refugee. That was just my theory.

Marsha Mellor was an ardent defender of both Bear and Lowe, not necessarily their causes. Regardless, she was their groupie. Marsha could be counted on to add nothing to the debate besides her vote of confidence in the Duo's position. It was inevitable that she would be tagged with a sarcastic nickname, and I'm pleased to be the first to have said it. Her lack of input and constant headshaking when the Duo spoke, favored the dynamics of a "Bobble-head." Yes, it stuck. Bobble-head became known far and wide; at least at the factory.

The Duo frequently tried to tag-team a debate. To me it was nothing more than a filibuster of stupidity. They considered themselves defenders of the weak and the poor. Loosely translated, it meant they were sympathetic to welfare proliferation, social activism, and the criminal's plight. I was not. In fact, I was insulted by their rhetoric. Mel was good enough to pay me a compliment on a number of occasions, calling me heartless and cruel. It was actually the highlight of my day. Further, I didn't argue his insult. I wore it as a badge of honor.

It was during this time I begun to vividly fantasize through daydreams and nightmares of rectifying the wrongs I saw. Villains had names, and thanks to the media's showing of film clips and the flashing of photos across the screen, my dreams grew more intense. The more I killed the better I felt, and the more convinced I became they deserved the punishment.

Regardless of how righteous I felt in my dreams, reality was quite different. Villains hitting the streets after a couple of years in the slammer and reoffending within months didn't sit well with me. The only remedy that rang true to me was "the fifty-cent solution," which was the price of a couple rounds of ammunition.

I was obsessed. I had become a media packrat, building files of newspaper clippings on criminal activity. Periodically, I went through and attempted to organize my files to make sense of what I was doing. These clippings were helpful to support my debates with the Duo. Memorization of statistics and details from these snippets came easy. I dwelt upon them daily much like a sports fanatic can quote statistics from their favorite team. A downside to gathering information was the feeling of frustration. Arguing with coworkers coupled with the injustice of the legal system weighed heavily on me. The penalties handed out to sex offenders, child kidnappers, and other violent criminals were more like inconveniences. I found myself at times ranting and raving when violators beat the legal system through courtroom shenanigans. At times, I might have appeared out of control to my coworkers, but more concerning, was the fact that I wasn't.

It was true—my behavior was escalating toward the socially unacceptable. I found it more difficult to keep my dream world separated from this insane world. I enjoyed the feeling of action and my innermost being was motivated to achieve something more satisfying than dreaming.

I praised the news media and despised them at the same time. Without them there would be little in the way of a constant catalyst to my behaviors. They saturated the airways with more and more graphic details of criminal violence. I both loved and hated it. I tried to limit my exposure from time to time, but that left me concerned with what I was missing.

The news media were not without their hypocrisy. Their insincerity ran deep. They abused their power to exploit victims of crime and sell their spin. I held them responsible, not for reporting the news, but for sensationalizing it. Horrific crimes always made the front page of the Metro sections but rarely were the trial results plastered on the front page a year or two later. People weren't interested in punishment—just the sensational nature of the crime. Nothing about the unjust plea deals being cut with the criminals or the early releases back into society. That was the real news. The media had been weighed, measured, and found wanting.

I started judo while in the service and played a couple years before turning to jujitsu in 1985. I enjoyed this activity for many reasons. I had felt it was giving me an edge over my frustration and a degree of self-control. By the early '90s, I found more and more people who were taking martial arts for self-defense. I was a class helper and frequently spoke with parents who enrolled their children. Without question, the number one reason for bringing their kids to the class was to give them a fighting chance against a violent predator. I was paired up with a younger man, Justyn Kase, who became a close friend. He worked the retail floor as a shoplift detective, which was a bit cowboyish in a rough-and-tumble sort of way. He was the first person I had met since the military I felt a comradeship with. He was hardcore when it came to violent criminals. He was the kind of guy that was looking for an excuse to unleash hell on the bad guys. I had already found one.

My personal contempt for the justice system continued to grow. Executions were few and far between with only a handful of states participating. Liberal newsmakers frequently covered the stories by presenting for the viewer a handful of religious zealots holding candles and singing or praying for the poor condemned murderers. Some states pushed forward with more executions while others stepped back from pursuing the deaths of even the worst offenders. A rise of anti-capital-punishment groups and civic organizations coupled with various religious activists fueled resources to overturn the death penalty. Lawyers had their own version of anti-whatever by driving the cost to execute so high through the "legal system" that it was less costly to let them rot in jail than execute them. If violent criminals actually rotted, I could have lived with it. But they didn't, not even close.

The Duo and I squared off many times from Robert Berdella to Arthur Shawcross. The results were always the same. No change. The villainous headliners all had one thing in common. They were serial killers who satisfied their bloodlust at another human's expense. They enjoyed the sadistic rape and torture of their weaker victims, and still the Duo advocated for their continued existence.

"We need to house and study them," Bear would say, "Psychologists and psychiatrists can help us to understand them. Maybe then we can prevent the next serial killer from becoming one." My response likewise remained the same, "All the doctors in the world will never understand or stop the next killer." Then abruptly I added, "They need to die." Bear, at this point, always appeared panicky. "Killing these people is not the answer! We'll never understand what makes them killers unless we study them."

It took many debates to realize what drove Bear and his cronies to know "why" with such an intense sincerity; it was fear. They didn't know what made a psychopath a psychopath. No one understood "why" or ever would, especially the professionals who made a living off studies and research. They produced books and lectured at universities and regurgitated their theories like they had the key to understanding. In the end, they offered nothing but excuses. They could not stop the next serial killer from appearing. I probably understood better than most. They didn't have a clue what made me tick.

Sounding like attorneys the Duo recited "excuses" as though reading from the criminal defense playbook. They regurgitated excuses but never put forward an answer. Diminished capacity because you're a raving loony from a nut bin, had a crappy childhood, possessed by demons, or because you've ingested drugs and alcohol until you don't know who you are or what you're doing, does not excuse criminal behavior—you are still guilty. I contended it is impossible to understand serial murderers, rapists, or violent criminals with a rational mind. It's a wiring problem and they need to be put down.

Teddy was an advocate of the "second chance" theory for violent offenders. He was passionate and always looking to blame something other than the guilty person. I favored a zero recidivism rate guaranteed by a firing squad. If sex offenders kidnapped, raped, or otherwise initiated a violent act on one of my family members, I would want them dead, not given a second chance. I knew others felt the same way. Society could not afford "second chances" to repeat these offenses. What about my concern for the offenders? I had none!

In 1966 Serial killer Richard Speck entered a student dorm and raped, tortured, and murdered eight student nurses in the Chicago area. He received the death penalty for his crimes. The story should have said "The End" but it didn't. The Supreme Court in 1972 added insult to injury when they ruled capital punishment unconstitutional. They went out of their way to commute all death penalties to specific incarceration times to serve. Speck received a sentence of fifty to one hundred years. The Court changed its opinion in 1976, reinstating capital punishment. The harm and revictimization to the families of the murdered nurses were already done. In 1991 Speck died in jail. Whatever consolation, solace, and comfort were garnered from Speck rotting in jail was momentary at best. What should have been a time of closure for the families was offensively interrupted. The Supreme Court's error was altered in 1976 but death penalties were not reinstated. Speck was not subject to the isolation of death row or having to face death looming over him. How hard could it have been on him?

Evidently, it hadn't been very hard. In early 1996, a videotape surfaced of Speck's horrible life behind bars complete with sex, alcohol, and cocaine. Even in light of this video, Teddy took opposition to the death penalty. Speck voiced his sympathy for his victims on the video, "It must not have been their day." What amazed me the most was Bear mirrored Speck in his compassion for the victims and their families. Was it possible Bear argued for what was inside him, as I did, for what dwelt in me?

Arguing with my archrival and nemesis would continue until I decided to leave the factory in 1996. I'd grown weary of their misguided mindset and tired of doing nothing about it. If I right the wrongs, I'll be a murderer in my own right and equally guilty of the same crime according to the law. The only exception—they are guilty criminals, not innocent victims. The difference is what makes the difference.

Judgment is coming at the hand of man, not some god. Civilized society can never survive without it. Try as they may to secure utopia, it comes by the aid of a barbaric monster hidden in the recess of society. They simply hate to admit the need for such a creature as Walter.

Chapter 3

The key to success is making your dreams come true
—Anonymous

What's the difference between a dream and a nightmare? My guess, the context of what the dreamer enjoyed was the greatest difference. Personally, I looked forward to sleep. It allowed me to enter the familiar territory of a dream world that I controlled completely. What was so special about my dream world? It was where imagination took on a nightmarish exercise of mental conditioning. Something I had come to appreciate.

Dream manipulation was a discovery I made as a child. Once I became comfortable with this fact that nothing was out of my control; dreamland was as enjoyable as a summer vacation. Things happened unexpectedly, like in all dreams, but I soon discovered how to make the challenge workout to my benefit. This has been a valuable tool in handling stressful and demanding situations with a certain confidence that only comes from experience.

I'm not sure when I had first begun solving problems in my dreams. I remember as a child facing the same nightmare night after night, over and over again. Oddly, I became so familiar with the dream I could anticipate what would happen next. When I became conditioned to the scenario I was able to weigh options and changed the outcome. I didn't win every bout in my dreams, but eventually I manipulated events until it worked out the way I wanted and needed it to. Once I was comfortable with the fact that I could think through the process, the frightened feelings and stress that initially petrified me, no longer bound me up in fear.

In my sleep I could recognize the recurrence of a specific dream when it started. I'd been there before in a previous dream, and I knew at some point I would need to react to a situation. This exercise conditioned my mind to produce a more desired outcome. I had lived through all the twists and turns thrown at me.

Eventually a dream would come to its end. There were no signs saying "the end;" nonetheless I would not dream the same dream ever again. When I had learned whatever exactly it was I was supposed to learn, the dream simply vanished. I enjoyed some of them enough to try and start the dream before I fell asleep but to no avail. When it was done, it was done.

Recurring dreams helped condition my mind by overcoming challenges rather than accepting the worst scenarios. They didn't start up as soon as one would end. There were months between dream episodes. I never knew when they would start, but I knew they would; it was a matter of waiting, not anticipating.

One of my favorite recurring dreams as a child was falling from the sky. I hear most people experience falling through the air or from a mountain or tall building; I fell in an old-fashioned wood chair. I don't know why I was in a chair but it always started out that way. The sensation of falling uncontrollably was scary at first. I remember waking suddenly in a panic, my heart racing, still feeling the sensation of falling until I realized I was in my bed. At some point I recognized the dream for what it was—a dream. From then on I no longer woke in fear. As strange as it may sound, I learned to fly that old wood chair! I enjoyed many dream world hours holding on to the seat of the chair. I shifted my weight to one side or the other and she banked perfectly. Sometimes it was nothing more than thinking as I flew and she responded to my desires. I didn't know the mechanism that propelled it and I didn't care. It was challenging and ultimately fun.

On my last flight I swooped down low over fields and brushed the tops of pine trees before making my descent to land. It was my first time bringing her in and as good fortune would have it a dirt runway appeared in a meadow. I slowed her up and brought the chair legs in contact with the ground. It was a little rough without wheels but the dust settled and I was alive and on the ground.

It was a harmless little dream that conquered height, flying, and ultimately the fear of death. It's humorous to think back about it today, yet I'm quite sure it was intended as training for my journey through the world I had yet to encounter. Looking back, I believe my life and who I was to become, had been predetermined. I have no idea how many lessons are embedded in my subconscious like this one. I don't recall them all now, but in retrospect I do understand how they have made the path I have chosen, or that was chosen for me, more manageable.

Not all my dreams were relegated to early childhood. During my days of camaraderie with Stoneman, I began to dream of ridding the world of child sexual predators, pimps, murderers, and the like. I thought the recurring dream was in part a response to our late-night conversations, which habitually turned into solving the problems of the world. I was never alarmed by the frequency of these dreams; I'd been down the path before. As usual, I grew fond of having them and welcomed their continuance. Perhaps the nature of the dreams would be alarming to others, but to me they were comforting in a special way.

My most memorable dream began with an old comic-book-type metro area similar to Gotham City. Tall dark buildings were hovering over the dimly lit streets. Shadows were cast on every alley and corner. I can still see myself wandering aimlessly down the mazelike city corridors, my eyes keenly observant. I was on a stealth-type patrol; at least, that was my recollection. I came to understand that my destiny was to counterbalance the criminal elements of this city. It would require a special skill set, imaginary skills formed by my dreams. Skills that today are second nature to me. I use them instinctively according to the situation.

Variations in these dreams were usual. This specific dream was different in escalation. Evil people challenged me, and my response rose to the level necessary to overcome their wickedness. There were rapists and child molesters that I caught in the act while at other times I faced pimps, pushers, gangsters, and street hustlers, preying on nameless innocent victims.

My job was clear. I was the White Knight to the rescue. Intervene and protect—that was my mission, my reason for being there. If violence was necessary I applied it with ferocity. Many times my intercession in a victim's defense brought death to the assailants, in a most brutal manner. It became ordinary and normal to kill.

Like all my recurring dreams, problems emerged. Multiple assailants or the progression to weapons by the criminals were commonplace. The ability to apply skills and problem-solve were put to the test. From a samurai katana to grenades, I was conditioning my mind to kill.

As my dreams were more and more successful, I took pride in their outcome. I felt heroic but sought no recognition of the fact. Seeing a victim safe or saved was gratitude enough. I suppose it could be said, I have a bloodlust for killing, and simply carried out those feelings in my dreams. It's just not true. In my dreams I could kill without emotion just like I learned to suppress my emotions when I killed a farm animal. However, one thing was very different. The farm animal was innocent of any wrongdoing. The predators I skewered, sliced, or otherwise dismantled, were the worst kind. Their sole mission was to cause innocent victims severe harm. They were attacking others, and when I stepped in, they attacked me. I had no problem with their disposal. As I look back on these episodes, I can see the value of precognitive conditioning. It has allowed me to expand my horizons. I've heard the motivational slogan so many times, "The key to success is making your dreams come true." When my dreams come true they will be a living nightmare for evil doers.

While I intensified my debating with Bear and Lowe, at night a sensation of pain and anguish would come over me in my dreams. Perhaps I brought it on by immersing myself in too many media clippings or watching the onslaught of new crime TV shows. All I knew was the feeling I connected to these criminal events, I loathe with a passion.

At times, deep in my dreams when the throes of agony baptized my every thought, I could hear whispers of a voice, only a word or two at first and very difficult to understand. This was unusual, new and stimulating. Never before had I experienced sensations that parallel auditory sounds. Identifying the voice was difficult; it was nothing I recognized from the past. A child's voice, maybe, I couldn't be sure. There was no rhyme or reason to the pain or auditory sensations and no particular frequency. While I was awake, fully cognizant, reading the news clippings, a sensation of pain would come over me. It seemed my dream world was merging with my consciousness. As much as I wanted to shrug it off as something generated by my mind, intuition told me there was much more to understand.

Maybe I sound a little crazy and perhaps that would explain everything satisfactorily if I were, but I'm not. Clarity came in the morning hours after I welcomed in the New Year with a bit more holiday cheer than necessary. I'd said goodbye to my work buddies and hopped a taxi for home. I tilted my head back momentarily to relax only to have my incoherent state disturbed by the cabbie. I staggered off to my doorway, fumbling around in my front pocket for the house key. Once inside I turned on the lights and plopped into the nearest recliner. Rather than passing out, as I should have in my drunken stupor, I was wide awake. I could see files and clippings strung out across the living room from coffee table to couch. I remember thinking to myself, "What am I doing with all this?" Then, I pulled the recliner handle up, raising the footrest, and pushed the chair into a supine position. Here, I intended to bed down for what remained of the night.

I may have dozed for a while, I can't be sure. A brilliant light flas| me; it was painful to look at. My eyes squinted closed. I awoke bent daybreak, only a trace of light shone from the hallway. Surn somehow the only visible source of light was responsible, I returned to my state of slumber. Suddenly the intense light appeared again. I was conscious yet unable to move. The wind howled and dark ominous clouds rolled across the horizon. A field of apparitions swayed violently like grass on the rolling tundra upon which I stood. I had plunged into a stormy dreamlike state the likes of which I had never before experienced. Lightning flashed, obliterating all darkness momentarily. I awaited the thunder that never followed. Each flash became more intense, more blinding. Black and grayish clouds swirled above me like a giant vortex. In the distance a ghostly silhouette came into view. As it drew closer I could make out the outline of a young child five or six years of age.

This apparition was fully clad in white and did not speak or look in my direction. It was two-dimensional, although similar to a still photo, it appeared alive, yet the affect told a different story. The eyes were dark caverns of lifelessness filled with pain and sorrow. My intuition told me an unnatural and horrific event was responsible for the vacating of both heart and soul. I felt helpless and anxious as it stood motionless before me.

In the distance, a slight vestige of pleading or supplication could be heard like a wave reporting the sea. I recognized it as cries, filled with pain and sorrow. It was somehow familiar to me, something that I had experienced before. My anxiety turned to sadness. Was it a harbinger of this child's fate? Was this the foreshadowing of something I could still do something about or was it relegated to the past?

I asked the apparition, "What does this mean?"

A child's voice answered, "These are many." The apparition looked out over the field and again said, "These are desolate cries and desperate prayers, without remnant of hope and long dashed by the lack of miracles."

With that I startled awake. My thoughts were immediate. What was this nightmarish dream? In past dreams, I was accustomed to acting in some way to fix the problem. No such problem had presented itself this time. This dream had a different relevance, one I had to pursue.

From the first night the child apparition appeared to me in a dream it became a continuous presence; a familiar spirit if you will. There was increased intensity in these sensory perceptions to a degree it forced me to question my own sanity.

"Am I mad?"

I would have to say to myself, "No! I suppose not." Although I assume all insane people think they are not. Mere questioning one's own sanity cannot be the test. If I admit I'm Insane, then all is explained. I can rest easy knowing I need medication.

"Do I hear voices?

The answer is clearly, "Yes," a voice that has transcended my dream world.

"Do I hallucinate?"

"No, not really." Maybe it is a gift, a very special gift. A gift that will make your blood run cold and your hair stand on end.

As time progressed, the area of sensory perception became more vivid. I was cognizant of what I was seeing and what I had felt. The painful visualizations surfaced at times when I read my collection of clippings. They were, what I believed to be, momentary glimpses of what a victim experienced at the hands of a predator. What was still perplexing was what, if anything, I was to do with this awareness?

Review of my media collection was a daily task. Usually the voice was quiet while I read the articles. I came across an older file, one that I have read a hundred times when pain and fear coursed through my being. The file to me was one of many but somehow it was a gateway to understanding. I set the file aside, sat back, and mused upon these things. Prompted by sensory perceptions I fell into a trancelike dream. The familiar childlike apparition flashed before me. Moments or hours later I opened my eyes to find a medieval scene before me. To my left, high upon a grassy hill, a black stallion with heavy armor pranced back and forth. Mounted upon the stallion was a knight, himself adorned in black. He appeared fearless, sitting tall on his steed holding a lance glistening in the sunlight. He was a crusader, the embodiment of a righteous evil. At the bottom of the hill were thousands of ghostly beings, neither male nor female, taunting the knight to charge. My familiar apparition appeared at my side pointing at the people, whose foul stench represented the nature of their being. A child's voice loudly reverberated across the sky, "These are the souls of those who are guilty of unthinkable atrocities against humanity."

Alone, the black knight stood against these beings. What chance had he? I thought. It was clear, regardless of the outcome, the knight would take the field in combat. His armor-clad steed grew anxious; snorts of lightning emanated from his nostrils and the pounding of his hooves was as the sound of thunder echoing across the barren plains. Chills ran down my spine as the knight began his descent to the field below. The knight's heels sank into the flanks of his trusty mount, urging him forward. Reaching the flat land of the battlefield, the knight leaned forward simultaneously lowering his lance to engage. His fiery stallion responded instinctively to his master's commands.

I watched the knight, with unwavering courage and valor; assault the line of filthy souls. He did not slow in his advance. The knight's gallant steed bowled through and over many; his lance punctured and collected even more. Regardless of the continuous onslaught of apparitions entering the battle from all sides of the field, the knight drove forward. No end in sight. It was then I realized my role in this drama.

I woke with a new perspective for the purpose of my existence. It was far more than being a bit player with a cameo appearance. It was playing a lead role on the stage of life. I would vanquish the villain or die trying.

The visualizations of the victim's faces I've seen were very personal to me. Faces filled with grimacing and pain while others were flat and emotionless. Innocence and hope lost at the hands of wicked people satisfying their lust. Victims' voices cried out to me. Not to me alone, but anyone who would come to their aid. Regardless of what manner of diversion I engaged in, the sensation of their torture I could not escape. It was more graphic than words could relay, more horrific than a mind could bear.

My memory is intact. All that I dream will become a predator's nightmare in reality. I will find comfort in my resolve and act accordingly. Some people deserve to die. By their own actions they have lost their right to live. It's an emotional response, I agree. Since when is this argument strictly academic? But then again, perhaps fate had predetermined their consequence even before I was born and I wasn't given a choice as to the role I would play. I will make them pay the natural price for their transgressions. For I know and understand the common emotional feeling that drives the natural man. That's where Walter comes in.

Chapter 4

I have never killed a man, but I have read many obituaries
with great pleasure.
—Clarence Darrow

Everyone loves a park and every town seems to have one. Some are small historical landmarks whereas others are recreational, complete with ball fields and tennis courts. Many have outdoor concert stages, unpaved hiking trails, and nature areas. Smaller communities and urban neighborhoods have developed parks that focus on traditional family areas complete with picnic tables and playgrounds. All parks have one thing in common—they lend themselves to criminal behavior. Why do you think they are so often closed in the evening? Could it be the potential criminal activities?

Two blocks from my Portland suburban home lies a bike path that links a maze of arteries throughout the city. These urban conduits winding through neighborhoods and parks emptied out into the city's main retail and industrial areas. Few people are truly aware of criminal behavior occurring along their favorite bike path or in city parks. Some areas along these urban arteries are more dangerous than others. Getting to a park nearly always requires passing by or through these unsafe areas.

I have been an avid hiker my entire life. I've hiked on the Pacific Crest and Oregon Skyline trails. I've taken treks on Mount Hood, Broken Top, Three-Fingered Jack and the Three Sisters wilderness area. Hiking of this nature requires some conditioning training if one wants to enjoy it. When you live in Portland, or any other city, this can be a challenge. The options are to drive many miles to remote areas to walk on trails, take a daily trip to a local gym for some cardio, or use the city bike paths and parks. Pathways seem to be the best option. Why not—they are free for the use and close by.

My first jaunt on the bike path was immediately uncomfortable. Vagrants in some areas, hoodlums hanging out in others, it wasn't as pleasant as I'd hoped it would be. At other times there was very little activity on the path. This added likewise to my anxiety. Too quiet for too long and my hackles started to rise. I felt both alone and watched at all times.

My jujitsu throwing partner, Justyn Kase, and I developed a close friendship. Best of all, we thought a lot alike. I let him know what I felt about the bike path. I was delighted to hear his input. "Why don't you carry a gun?"

I thought out loud, "A handgun would be nice, but city laws against carrying concealed would be problematic. I couldn't afford the consequences. There is nothing like being an honest upright citizen carrying a pistol for personal defense and catching a felony offense for it."

Justyn had thought about this before and answered, "Well, I'd rather be in court explaining why I had to shoot some scum-sucking criminal than him being in court lying about why he killed me."

Sound logic, I thought.

"You want to borrow one of my guns for a while and try it out?"

"Yeah, why not, I guess that's the answer."

"Brother, I have a short-barreled hammerless .38-caliber revolver that'll work well for packing."

I considered the consequences, but couldn't say no, the idea was perfect. No one other than Justyn was going to know I had it, I'd probably never use it, but just knowing it was handy would be very comforting.

"Yeah, I'll try it." I'd no sooner agreed to packing when I'd dismissed the idea as nothing more than talk. The next morning I was awakened to Justyn hammering on my front door. He delivered as promised the revolver and included a box of hydra-shok ammo as well. I didn't particularly care for that style of hallow point in a .38 but then again, I wasn't really going to be using it to shoot anybody. Worst-case scenario in my mind was to brandish the pistol to ensure my safety. I loaded the revolver and tucked it into my fanny pack. I was ready to get some fresh air.

I hated wearing that style pack. It was difficult to maneuver the weapon in and out of easily or quickly. I found myself incredibly conscious of the gun and felt any casual observer or passerby could tell I was packing. I tried keeping my hand inside the pack but that was awkward. Regardless, it solved the problem of carrying concealed and abated my concerns about a negative encounter.

Walking the paths was for the most part scenic, relaxing, and therapeutic. The path I enjoyed the most passed by an elementary school before entering a patch of woods. It was a warm summer's day in 1994 that left an indelible image seared into my memory of that path.

I mapped out a course that brought me back to the school in about an hour's time. I was just nearing the school on my way back through the wooded area when I caught a glimpse of someone ahead of me on the winding path. As I drew closer I could see two people scuffling and the sounds of muffled voices. My hand slowly slipped into the pouch with my gun. It was clearly trouble of some sort. As I went through a shallow depression and across a footbridge I lost all sight of the trail ahead. I reached the top of the steep incline and no one was in sight. My hackles rose on edge.

I'm like a lot of other folks in that I didn't want to get wrapped up in some domestic dispute. On the other hand, I didn't like the looks of what I saw. I slowed my pace as I approached the area of the path where the people were. Over the creek embankment I could see movement. It was the flash of colors from clothing but I was unable to make out what was happening. Suddenly a muffled yell from a female broke the silence. I eased the weapon from the pack and made my way through the brush. I counted on the noise the people were making to mask my approach.

As I broke through the thicket a man was semisprawled above a woman, pinning her to the ground. He jumped like a startled alley cat, landing on the far side of the woman. His eyes darted about looking for an avenue of escape. With my gun brandished at the ready; its stainless steel frame glistened in the sunlight. I glanced toward the bloody-faced woman who was sobbing hysterically to the point of hyperventilating. Her clothes were torn from her upper body and steeped in blood. She gathered what was left of her blouse around her and slowly made her way to me. I wanted to help her but I didn't dare take my eyes, or gun, off the assailant. Adrenaline, traversed my veins instantly causing my heart to beat rapidly, yet time seemingly stood still. My thoughts raced, I was in a near panic.

The perp was silent and awaiting my next move. Game over, I thought. I could shoot and ask questions later. The victim either won't care if I plug this guy or not remember the chain of events that resulted in his death. I can always say he reached for what I thought was a weapon and fired in self-defense.

Now what? Knowing the potential for an escalation on my part, I hastened the victim to move behind me. I watched the attacker, intently trying to discern what he was thinking, but I drew a blank. The one and only thing I was certain of was one flinch, and I was more than willing to crack a primer on him.

As the victim regained composure she made her way to the trail side of the bushes out of view of her attacker. I wanted to maintain visual on her but heavy underbrush made it impossible. She was obviously frightened beyond reason and why wouldn't she be? Her serenity had been stolen. A near miss with death would do that to anyone. Nonetheless, she was the only lifeline out of the predicament.

I can't be sure how long the assailant and I remained locked in a motionless state, but in psychological time it was an eternity. No sooner had my adrenaline begun to ease when my hair stood on end at the sound of, "Kill him." The thunderous pulsation of a voice rang out a second time, "Kill him! This is destiny." An apparition appeared behind the detained man pointing a finger in his direction, "Kill him! Kill him!" I dared not respond. How could I without bringing attention to myself in front of the apprehended assailant. Yet, I noted he sensed something was near him he could not see. The ghostly figure was of a blonde female in her late teens or early twenties. Her hair was long and waving, yet there was no breeze. She was dressed in a bright white light making any clothing indiscernible. Her eyes were glowing reddish embers, a reflection of her inner being. She was displaced from another dimension in time to interact with the present. I wanted to appease her; I was more than willing to oblige her. Subconsciously I was hoping the guy would give me a reason to terminate his worthless life but justification was necessary.

The victim had flagged down a pair of boys riding by on bicycles and sent them for help. The sound of one, then two police vehicle sirens, faint at first, grew louder as they drew near. I knew they'd arrived when the sirens went silent. It was a relief to hear the sound of police radios in the distance and the rapid footsteps approaching the embankment. The spirit-being faded away, but her voice resonated in my ears, "This is destiny." Still distracted by the apparition I was barely aware of the first officer to arrive. "Put the weapon down," he repeated over and over. Complying, I laid my revolver not far from the perp and raised my hands above my head. Secretly, I had hoped he would make a lunge for the pistol and meet his doom. He looked but didn't bite. Additional officers swept by me, taking Lewis Pohle into custody.

Officers confiscated my weapon at the scene, but I knew it wouldn't end there. Doing good never ends up right. I may have stopped a rape or murder, but I also violated the law and I knew it. I had rehearsed in my mind, if I was nabbed for the unregistered firearm or carrying it without a conceal carry permit what I might say or do. What I really wanted was an opportunity to tell a jury, "I did it and I'd do it again!" Whatever punishment came my way, so be it. But now, my brilliant defense was made complicated by the fact I actually brandished the pistol to intervene in a criminal act. This would not be rewarded in the judicial system as one might hope.

The victim, Estelle Hertz, made a gesture of thanks to me while the field interview was in progress. The cops seemed conflicted. On the one hand they knew I stopped a worse scenario from occurring. On the other, they could not condone an armed citizenry taking matters into their own hands. I was transported to police headquarters, interviewed, and given a receipt for my gun. Hours later, at the conclusion of interviews with detectives I was provided a ride home. On and off over the next few months I had the opportunity to repeat my story to the detectives and District Attorney about what I observed and my course of action.

I saw Estelle on a couple of occasions during some of the questioning. Rehashing the story only served to deepen her emotional scars. Maybe in a therapeutic environment it pays off to talk about events like she suffered, but interrogation techniques are less than comforting to a victim. Reliving the events may produce a more stable case for police and prosecutors but it drove Estelle into a shell. I didn't understand what was wrong with the facts of the case in the first go-around. Maybe I didn't know all the facts but what was there to know other than, "Pohle was guilty."

At one of the police interviews I met Mr. Hertz. He was an intimidating presence. He was lean and muscular. His stature was a good six feet plus. He was leathery, tanned, with cold steel-blue eyes that squinted almost closed. His hands were massive and powerful as he shook my hand. He appeared calm and collected yet I sensed an underlying short fuse. He didn't talk much and I suspected that was his personality, yet when he did speak he was undoubtedly sincere. "If I'd been there we wouldn't be here today," Mr. Hertz remarked. He didn't have to repeat himself to make a believer out of me. The attacker, Lewis Pohle, may not have gotten lucky the way he had hoped the day he assaulted Estelle. On the other hand, Pohle should thank his lucky stars he had the misfortune to cross my path instead of Mr. Hertz's.

There were the usual grand jury indictment hearings. What a goat rope! The fact that we had to appear three different times was certainly an indicator things were going poorly for the prosecution. Lewis Pohle retained a well-known defense attorney. How could an indigent hoodlum like Pohle afford a high-profile class act like Ruben Darroe? He had the prosecutors stymied. Darroe was capable of presenting a serious challenge to a cut-and-dried case. Something seemed amiss. Perhaps someone else had a vested interest in how this trial turned out. It was not so much about the players but about the end-game results.

Darroe was a master at dragging a case out. He knew the odds shifted to his favor the longer he stalled the actual court date. In small-town America, a crime like this would be big news for a long time. In metro areas like Portland, the media would move on quickly to the next sensational crime, and they did. The prosecutors had cases piling up; they needed to put this behind them. Pohle himself had a checkered past, having accumulated multiple convictions in his adulthood. Some were minor thefts and trespassing charges, but other convictions demonstrated a concern for his base nature, that is, assault, public indecency, lewd and lascivious acts, and voyeurism. None of his convictions had caught much jail time and with Darroe at the helm, Pohle hoped to continue his run of good luck.

The trial preparation drug out for months. The defense filed motion after motion to dismiss various items of evidence or testimony. Attorney Darroe referred to me as a "racist" because the defendant was Louisiana Creole. His roots were Dominican and Louisiana French. I could not have cared less. It is an insult to play the race card. In my description of Pohle to police and in deposition I referred to him as black. Well, he looked black to me. You know, like with dark pigmentation of skin. It wasn't racist, it was a fact. But Darroe found another use for it; a ploy to discredit my testimony.

Darroe seemed to have a grudge against me right from the beginning. He made accusations of vigilante activity on my part. His statements were unfounded but it didn't stop him from spouting them out. Prosecutors preferred for me to disregard his actions and accusations but his deception was difficult to ignore. Darroe wanted to see me bite the bullet for having an unlicensed firearm, being unlicensed while carrying concealed, brandishing a firearm, and assault with a deadly weapon, thereby muddying up the water for court testimony. Darroe was quick to point out I violated his client's civil rights repeatedly and if this behavior went unpunished by the courts, it would encourage more people to take the law into their own hands. I thought "what an excellent idea."

Pohle was unable to make bail himself and whoever was flipping the bill for Darroe was not so inclined for Pohle. So he hunkered down and awaited the game's outcome at the pretrial facility. Estelle Hertz was mending physically. The vicious assault had left very little physical damage. The same could not be said for her mental and emotional state.

Tuesday, 2 May 1995, I was notified the case reached a plea agreement. Prosecutors felt the best course of action was to accept the assault conviction and ask for a steep sentence. I showed up early for the disposition of the case. I had hoped to talk with the Hertz family but they were mysteriously absent. The judge read the plea agreement then levied his decision. Lew Pohle would receive a whopping three-year sentence with some stipulations for when he was released. He was credited with time already served and placed on probation for the remainder of the sentence. This dog-and-pony show was over.

Defense Attorney Darroe had worked the miracle he was hired for. It was an exceptionally baleful miracle and he was proud of it. He did more than defend his client. He went out of his way to revictimize the victim. Darroe stooped low and I held him personally responsible for this miscarriage of justice.

Pohle didn't have a reason for his criminal behavior on the bike trail. He didn't have to, Darroe made one up for him. He hired a staff of former lawmen to conduct their own investigation. They left no stone unturned in the backgrounds of the Hertz and me. He wasn't protecting the rights of the accused—he was fabricating a fantasy world and robbing the victim of her opportunity for a fair trial. In my book, Darroe was no better than Pohle and my book was about to be the only book that mattered.

I stood as the judge exited the court room. Other attendees were quietly filing out and soon I stood there alone. "Kill him." The voice of the apparition came to mind; I could no longer argue with her. She was correct, I should have killed him. I named the spirit-being Destiny since she had become my travelling companion. I got the impression her past was blocked from her and she had no recollection of who she once was. Having no memory might serve, in some cases, as a definition of heavenly existence. For me the question was clear. How could I follow Destiny's direction?

In the aftermath of the mock justice I disdained the fact that I had not shot Pohle when I had the chance. Logic told me one thing and Destiny another. Pohle would come back to haunt me, and I him, before it was finished.

There is no mystery about what Pohle was doing that day on the bike path. I knew what he was capable of and he was still the same man. He would strike again. He might learn to be clever, but he was incapable of becoming wiser.

I began with a new fervor to reorganize my files and included additional violent crimes, such as home invasions. I spent more time making personal notes from true crime shows that indicated what either police look for at a forensic scene or mistakes criminals had made. I frequented used book stores finding a treasure trove of books on forensics and crime scene investigations from police academies. It was clear, "the devil was in the details"—or was it just me in the details? Common sense sprinkled with a little understanding could take someone a long way.

At the time, I knew most of my neighbors since I had bought my home. The house was a 1,900 square foot split level. The area was relatively crime-free and many folks had lived in their homes most of their lives. It was located on a large city lot just off NE 122nd Avenue and NE Sandy Boulevard. Every summer we had a block picnic party which set the pace for future gatherings with neighbors up and down the street throughout the summer.

Harold Horn was one such newcomer to our area in 1994. As a crime reporter for the *Portland Trumpeter-Gazette*, he had my full attention whenever he spoke. He was a superb storyteller as well as an accomplished feature writer. I could tell his writing was constrained to facts while his stories took on an air of heavy embellishment. He was a bit egotistical and liked to toot his own horn. He elaborated on police investigations as if he had actually participated in the case. We all knew it was bunk but he was a really good storyteller and they're hard to find.

Harold chose to be on the side of law enforcement although it always seemed he could have been just as involved from the other side. Sounding the horn on breaking news is every reporter's focus, Harold was no different. As news reporting took more liberties in the way they covered information, he found more and more creativity in his abilities. Harold's claim to fame in the metro area was covering what he referred to as "stale dated" cases. Crimes that were a year or more old and going to trial were lost to the public's consciousness. He was in a position to breathe life back into the coverage just like it was a new scoop. He was ingenious with his feature articles covering whatever aspect of the "trial" he wanted to present. People loved them in a morbid way. He related many times how personally satisfying it was to cover a trail or plea deal, then editorialize it to whatever conclusion he wanted his audience to come to.

Harold took a particular interest in the Hertz case, mostly because of my involvement. I kept Harold up to date on my dealings with the judicial system while he returned the favor from his perspective. Pohle was an unknown character to Harold. So many names and so many faces made it hard to remember an insignificant moron like Pohle. On the other hand, Darroe was a well-known name to Horn. He shared with me what I thought were ridiculous courtroom antics credited to Darroe. I doubted any judge would really allow such dramatics in a courtroom, but I was soon to be proved wrong. Horn said Darroe was so well known for his shenanigans, he and his colleagues referred to courtroom antics as Darroe-isms, a quip of sorts to an evolutionary Darwinist theory of survival of the fittest.

Horn had watched Darroe perform in person. According to him, the courtroom action was nonstop. He bullied and intimidated victims and witnesses during testimony, making every attempt to cause an embarrassing moment that he could capitalize on. He recounted many of the trials where Darroe had successfully represented the alleged bad guys and got them off or got them ridiculously less time in jail. Before the plea deal was reached in the Hertz case I wouldn't have believed it possible to pervert justice that efficiently; I was wrong.

Harold was outspoken and opinionated. He wasn't shy when it came to relating his thoughts about Darroe.

"They ought to just shoot him too," Horn exclaimed.

"Harold, they don't shoot the criminals, why would they shoot the lawyer?"

Harold stood firm. "He's as guilty as those he gets off. They are bound to go and do it all over again."

Strong words, I thought, definitely strong words from a guy who's been more involved than most people ever want to be.

What I liked most about Harold was his love of talking about the details of a crime. I looked at it as another resource for learning the ropes of investigation. I don't know how much of what he said was true but certainly the way he obtained information intrigued me. We spent hours in my backyard drinking brewskis and talking about the cases of the day. Harold would many times fill in the history on a case and predict the outcome before a trial concluded. It was uncanny how informed he was on crime and how well he understood the flow of the trial.

Harold helped with a great many debates. I was armed with information better than any coworker who wanted to discuss the topic. Unfortunately, my time at the plant was to be short-lived. I could not tell anyone what I was contemplating. Coworkers would be mortified if they had a wannabe killer in their midst. It simply is not in people to be supportive of that type of person. Harold would have been conflicted, himself being a crime fighter of sorts. This was a secret I had to keep to myself.

Harold provided guidance in some of his trade secrets for gathering article information. He introduced me to the public records systems at the courthouse, which he frequently used when he was breaking a story. Often the alleged criminals had lengthy records or other "newsworthy" information available in the archives. He taught me the meanings of words used in trials that aren't common terms, at least not where I worked at the aluminum plant. I asked and he answered. If he couldn't answer he helped me find an answer.

I focused my attention on violent sexual crimes. I considered them the lowest of the low. Hours that I used to watch crime shows on TV were replaced with intense Internet searching. I was amazed how much information was at my fingertips. I was encouraged to read comments by regular people on the news articles covering violent sexual assaults, kidnapping, child molesters, and child abusers. "Fry 'em," "String them up," "Euthanize the wacko!" Wow, regular people thought like me. They'd never act on it but the mindset was there.

I learned to discriminate when it came to labels like "sex offender." A nineteen-year-old high school senior boy got involved sexually with a fifteen-year-old sophomore girl because they thought they were in love. I don't look twice at that case. It might have been the same label but it was not the same thing I was at odds with.

Every news article I'd read that had a comments section said the same thing. Every interview I'd seen with family members said the same thing, "I'm not satisfied until he/she is dead." People were sick of the arguments for convicted criminal's rights. Victims would struggle a lifetime dealing with their pain of memory. Many I read about went off the deep end in drugs and alcohol, developed PTSD and other psychological issues, and still others committed suicide. While the perp sucked down sodas and watched Disney movies in a halfway house paid for with tax dollars. A walk in the park on a warm sunny day convinced me it was time to take care of business.

A couple years later as I scanned the news articles I ran across a second time Darroe represented Lewis Pohle. The newspapers carried the story, "Elderly woman assaulted in Wood Village." Lewis was not a smart criminal. He left fingerprints, semen, and a witness who could identify him at the scene of the crime. Darroe, who I considered truly to blame for this present crime, cast his trickery once again by swaying the courts away from prosecution in favor of hospitalization. Low IQ and a history of psychiatric problems was the basis of Darroe's defense. The prosecutors opted for psychiatric care with a civil commitment and some assurance Pohle would be secured away for at least a little while. A little while was exactly what it was. Pohle was hospitalized in a psychiatric facility and spent about a year institutionalized. The psychiatric sentencing review board granted discharge to an assisted living facility while compliant with his medications and with his illness in remission. I thought, Walter, this is your cue.

I can't describe the feeling I had the morning I woke up to read Lewis Pohle's obituary. It seems he died an unnatural death. In my book, however, a Rock River Arms AR-15 .223 semi-auto 20-inch barrel with a GemTech Halo Suppressor sounds like natural causes to me, or at least in Pohle's case.

The assisted living facility from its outer appearance looked very hospital-like. I don't know if that was intentional or if it was just an old hospital that was converted. The grounds had a fenced area with a few trees more or less central to the yard. Plastic benches and chairs were dotted about the yard for leisure, and a paved pathway encircled the yard. It was nestled away from the main streets and against a hillside laden with heavy trees and underbrush.

Walter spent a few days bird-watching in the area. Perhaps looking a little nerdy; with a pork pie hat, casual wear, and a set of binoculars, he was quite the sight. On a couple of occasions he spoke with people that were on nature walks or cutting through the wooded area, which was difficult to traverse because of the underbrush. Most visitors, however, didn't stray from the beaten pathways through the area. The living facility fence line was well marked and posted. There was evidence others had trod that direction before, though it was doubtful they had the same intention I had.

Springtime brought out the best in nature; likewise it brought the facility residents out in the yard for long periods of time. Plenty long enough for me to get a bead on Pohle. I've always enjoyed trying new things and new ideas. A long-range assassination was a newly devised plan that required a special purchase of a specific type of weaponry. But hey, Pohle was worth it.

It was Sunday and a heavy mist hung in the air, a cloudlike canopy, blocking the sun. I made my way the short distance to an area I had scoped out earlier that would conceal my presence slightly more than 100-yards from the treatment center yard. I packed the short-barreled rifle in a guitar case reminiscent of the old Chicago gangster days.

Near the crown of a hill I carefully spread out a non-reflective space blanket and hunkered down behind a rotting log covered in Oregon grape foliage. Spreading the bipod and leveling the weapon in the direction of the yard I could see clearly through my scope, even with these flat light conditions. Nine o'clock rolled around and the sun was struggling to burn away the cloud cover. The yard door opened and two residents proceeded into the yard. The staff member hooked the door open and made her way to the benches, drying them with a towel she was carrying. Pohle came to the door briefly, and then returned inside.

Anxiety piggybacked on my anticipation. Pohle appeared in the doorway again, this time he stood motionless with his arms crossed. My shot was lined up, but it wasn't the shot I wanted. I could hit arm bones and ricochet the bullet away from a vital organ or hit him in the shoulder and knock him back out of view from a second shot. In the distance was the murmuring of a voice, one that was familiar but of no concern. Destiny was nearby.

Lewis moved from the doorway to a lawn chair but he wasn't alone. My scope showed clearly he was unknowingly being escorted into the yard by Destiny. As Pohle sat down, Destiny gestured by opening her arms as if to say, "Here." He sat back and propped up his legs. He appeared comfortable and content. Zhoop . . . Zhoop. Both shots struck center mass; if he wasn't dead he would be sorry he wasn't. Quickly I removed the bipod and placed the rifle, bipod and spent casings into the guitar case. Hunched over I gathered up the space blanket and stuck it in my jacket pocket. It was time to exit stage left.

This was not a high-profile case but reporters would be interested to make it into more than it really was. People would react critically to the killing of a psychiatric patient, but to me he was no better or worse than the next rapist or murderer. If the police found exactly where I was during the shooting there would be some level of forensic evidence, I suppose. However, not enough to track or trace me or even put me under the microscope. I've made that as difficult as possible.

It was Walter who pointed out to me how much pleasure can come from reading an obituary. It marked a new day in my life that allowed me to enjoy walks in the park again. The obituary was small and probably insignificant but the reporters went hogwild for this kill. Some writers speculated with terms like "vigilante" and "revenge killing" while others capitalized on the string of run-ins with the law and courts, making their feeble attempts to analyze the "causes" of this poor soul's demise. I think he's dead because Walter killed him. That's all.

Chapter 5

We are so accustomed to disguise ourselves to others,
that in the end, we become disguised to ourselves.
—Francois de la Rochefoucauld

A life can be taken and no one can stop it if the person taking the life is willing to trade his own to succeed. I determined I was such a person. The decision to pursue my intentions would cost me my existence, at least the one I had known. I would, out of necessity, live anonymously among my neighbors, alone and without friends. I dare not bring attention to myself; it would be counterproductive to my goals. I am willing to sacrifice everything to appease justice. What were my intentions? To extract vengeance in blood by the bucketful.

It has been a long and confusing road to this point. I've reflected on it often. Now a light shines at the end of the tunnel. The path before me is clear, illuminated by Destiny, for I know her well. No longer do I surge with rage at the judicial system's many failures. It is behind me now. I feel at peace. I continue to hear the cries of suffering souls; I feel their pain. It is a penetrating motivator. Whatever resolve I could not attain by my own understanding, apparitions have guided my footsteps. I realize I have been chosen.

A springtime rally was held in Portland to stop vigilante violence. I followed the development of these activists' agenda and noted a strong leaning toward sex offenders. Specifically, the new sex offenders' registry. I passively roamed through the crowd listening to speakers bemoan the actions of ordinary citizens who had grown weary of sex offenders living anonymously next door in their communities and acted out in some negligible manner. As the social militants lamented their grief-stricken woes I was overcome with emotion.

Attendees may have thought I was moved to tears by their stories, but that was hardly the case. I couldn't care less about these perverts bemoaning their unfair treatment. I heard the cascading of voices crying out in unison for vengeance like the roar of a waterfall. The voices were loud and deafening coming from all sides around me. I was impacted by the flashing of mental pictures of violent sequences and shocking perversions with members of the small crowd as I passed by them. If I could believe these visualizations to be true, I was in the midst of an unholy alliance.

The files I have collected over the years have spoken to me in their own special way. Long ago I'd concluded the punishment didn't fit the crime. Violent criminals did too little time and within months of finishing their hitch were back in jail with another violent crime notched in their belt. I planned to put an end to that cycle.

Sexual offenders were never really off the radar but have carved out an anonymous life in the general population. We have been assured they would be watched closely by the authorities, but how can we believe that? How can a known sexual predator kidnap children and sexually abuse them for years before being discovered if they were so closely monitored. I don't accept the excuses of too large caseloads for these probation officers to do their job. That's nothing more than window dressing. If it is true, the judicial system is to blame for giving communities a false sense of hope that they are protected from predators returned to the street. It is all a testament to the failure of the system that "watches" these offenders.

It is not just my perception that sexual offenders are not punished sufficiently. The correctional system that once punished violent sex offenders now spends more time and money rehabilitating and educating the inmates. Are sex crimes the product of the undereducated or the poor? It is as much a problem with the rich as it is with the poor. The problem is wiring! No amount of mind-altering drugs or rehab will fix it. The lawmakers have worked hard to remove emotion from the law but the issue remains emotional for the victims and their families. These criminals have ruined the life of another human being and in some cases many lives. Taking the law into my own hands, vigilantism, is my only answer. I will be the human element of the law and launch a private war. It will be measured in body count. Then maybe the lawmakers will hear. Until then vigilantism is the only way.

I grew weary of arguing with the likes of Lowe and Bear on my breaks at work. It solved nothing and changed even less. My understanding of a spiritual dimension seeking justice prompted me to action on their behalf. My memory of Darroe's treatment of Hertz frequented my thoughts while the video of Speck revictimizing so many families served to reinforce my intentions. The tables had to be turned. Violent sexual predators would become victims of their own doing, and maybe not just their kind, but other vile criminals as well. Every judge or jury that thinks violent acts against the innocent can be measured in a few years is wrong. These are life-changing attacks that have profound ramifications for the victims and their families. Who says punishment and vengeance must be separated as if they are two distinct goals?

My father's passing in the mid '90s left the ranch to me. I struggled with the idea of working the ranch, but I had other things on my mind. I had removed myself from rural living by taking up residence in a metro area; it would be difficult to go back to the ranch. I had plans and they conflicted with ranching or a full-time job of any kind. It had started as a thought, an idea, and now I was driven. It was time to take up the gauntlet; I had no choice. If I believed in God I might think the ranch was a sign from the Almighty to deliver me from the temptations I now faced. Nah, if it were a sign from God, it was to sell the ranch and use the money to support my hunt. That was more believable; if I believed!

The ranch was an easy sell. Wheat, alfalfa, and pasture land with a house and barn was a sought after commodity. A picture of independence was coming together. I'd lived debt-free with the exception of my Sandy Boulevard home. The sale of the ranch provided the finances to buy something outright in cash. With plans in mind I started looking for something in a transient-type environment. A mobile home community would be convenient and affordable. I was about to become trailer trash.

I located a 1972 Brookwood mobile home with everything I wanted and had looked for. The structure was a 24-by-40-foot two-bedroom, one-bath with a carport and storage shed. The well-maintained yard bordered a nature preserve in the Johnson City area not far from Interstate 205. The move was about twelve miles south of my N122 residence, but in a city like Portland it was far enough that I'd probably never see any of my old neighbors again.

My N122nd Street home eventually sold and brought in a pretty penny. My inheritance, the sale of my home, plus the money I'd saved while working at the aluminum plant left me debt-free with plenty of money in the bank to finance my new lifestyle. Life was looking good. I said goodbye to Harold and friends in the old neighborhood. I left the impression I was going to travel the country and see the world I'd inherited. There would be no expectation by them to see me around. I followed suit with the plant saying goodbye to friends and coworkers. Thankfully I don't have to put up with gerbil-brained chatter of irresponsible frivolity anymore. I felt liberated!

Over the past few years I'd developed some simple resources. My love for an old 1957 Chevy half-ton pickup that Dad had given me. My second vehicle was a black 1995 Dodge Avenger. It was bland, low profile, and paid for in cash. As it turned out, it would be key in facilitating my plans. It blended into any area of the city.

The next thing I had to work on was me. I wanted to stay in the background, like a spider hidden in a hole; exposing myself just long enough to snatch life from a victim. My plans involved being seen—if you can be seen, you can be identified. The real question was: What did I want people to see?

I was in my mid-forties, non-descript at five feet nine inches, and average weight. My hair was light brown with a touch of gray appearing throughout. I have worn a goatee for the past fifteen years. My facial hair was brown but fading to a yellowish white, and looking scruffy in recent years. The easiest change would be to shave the goatee. It grew back quickly enough to provide an incognito appearance when needed. I intended to be clean shaven whenever I worked a project. A little bit of hair dye and presto, I'm a new, younger man. The hair dye rarely keeps my hair dark brown very long, the old grayish stuff is soon in full bloom again, thus hiding my identity. Eyeglasses, the inexpensive black framed type purchased at discount stores, were added to further conceal my appearance.

My façade adapted the Clark Kent look without the hidden superpowers. My research would require me to get close to sources from time to time and what better way than a news reporter or writer. It's a profession easily recognizable by almost everyone. I decided to present myself as a freelance feature writer for a major syndicated magazine. It didn't really matter which brand name I used. The important thing, it legitimized my connection and interest in the case. No one was likely to suspect I had anything other than professional curiosity. They would never suspect an investigative reporter of gathering information for raison d'être.

The area of clothing was a challenge. I was a factory worker. Casual dress to me was a jungle-style fatigue shirt, T-shirt, and denim pants. Flip-flops or tennis shoes are in style every day as far as I'm concerned. If it's really cold I pull out a hoodie.

It was necessary to fit the perception people may have of a seasoned middle-aged reporter. Casual professional I call it. I opted for long-sleeved polo shirts with a blazer when weather dictated, chino pants, and comfortable loafers.

Clean shaven with a little hair dye and black framed glasses, I had a new appearance without a new identity.

I honed my interview skills, adapting the Harold Horn methodology. It was basic tracking groundwork for a news scoop. Pulling all available documentation on a crime from courthouse records and reading transcripts provided viable interview opportunities. Some courthouses were run a little more strictly than others, an inconvenience at times. But, since anyone can view a case, I could not be denied access.

The Internet was a rapidly developing resource. Websites were beginning to pop up aimed at hindering criminal behavior by informing the public of convicted sexual offenders and violent criminals' whereabouts. I made it a tool of my evolving craft. Most website information files are easily accessed without any personal info being gathered from the inquiry. There was a chance my computer might leave a footprint on a website and be traceable. But there were ways around that as well. Simple fixes such as the purchase of the most recent cyberware designed to hide your IP identity were available. It seemed there was always someone developing a new way to trace IPs while at the same time their counterparts were developing new ways to disguise your computer identity. If Johnny Law caught up to me, they wouldn't need my computer to convict me. There would be plenty of other evidence. I just wanted to stay off the suspect list.

Many of the cases I researched included depositions and testimonial evidence. It was easy to spot hostile witnesses simply by reading their statements. Through people finder websites I was able to identify where many of these witnesses lived. Criminals might try to avoid the same cities or the same states where they'd committed their crimes. But hostile witnesses almost never left the area. They were often common folk that became involved in the case by no choosing of their own and tended to stick it out where they were.

I remembered reading a Portland case of so-called "vigilantism." The police reportedly responded to an alleged rape in the early morning hours in the Sandy Boulevard area. A female victim was discovered unconscious and bleeding at that location. The suspect was a twenty-nine-year-old neighbor of the victim and was also discovered at his residence bleeding profusely. Three other men were taken into custody as well for assault on the alleged rape suspect. The leader of the vigilantes was the husband of the rape victim.

I put my skills to work. I was able to locate all the people involved in the case except for the rapist, who was convicted. The husband, wife, and two others involved had all remained in the Portland area. I pondered on what story they had to tell. Collectively, the men remained hostile toward the perp. None of them regretted having retaliated. None of them equated their actions with vigilantism. All were aware the criminal was released from incarceration after three months and felt they dished out the only real punishment the guy ever received. They generally felt wronged by the system, but offered to have another go at their punishment for the perp, if it could be arranged.

I wanted to create more than a false identity for my façade. I created an alternate personality and gave life to it. My name's not Frankenstein but I think I know what the old doctor must have felt like when he yelled, "He lives!" I'm not psychotic; I'm crystal clear with what I'm doing. If I'm caught you won't hear me sniveling about it or claiming insanity. Others might say I am but I believe emphatically it needs to be done.

Plenty of people put on a façade every day. I've met and known many of them. Maybe it's when the boss comes through the factory door or at church with family; there's plenty of façade to go around. People don't want you to know who they really are. Half the time they don't even know who they really are anymore. Criminals are well versed in this manner of adaptation. They want the real person cloaked until the last possible minute. How many times have I heard it said, "I thought I knew him," only to learn later that person was a scam artist or a pedophile? They can't believe it because they were duped. They thought they knew the person; what they knew was a façade. I am the same way.

As part of my new me I wanted a name to present. Clark Kent wouldn't work; it had been used and besides I was a far cry from a superhero. I needed something viable. My mind raced back to what Irene, a friend and coworker, bluntly said after she listened to me spout off, "That's your alter ego speaking." From then on, Irene called me Walter Ego teasingly. Now, a year later it dropped into my mind from nowhere, only it sounded like Irene's voice speaking. Walter, my alter ego, is my "wannabe" me. I liked his ideas better anyhow.

Walter E. Goe, there are others by that name, but none can lay claim to being more unique than my Walter. He is a chameleon. His ability to blend with his surroundings, adapt to people, places and things is uncanny. He is predatory by nature. He is uniquely adapted to visual hunting. A skill developed early in my life and bequeathed to him. He is pitiless. His emotions are contained when he kills. More importantly, he kills that which is reviled by mankind; insects without natural predators that would overrun the world if it were not for Walter.

Forensic sciences have advanced by leaps and bounds over the past few years. Keeping that in mind, I went about making my preparations as carefully as I could. I didn't see the need to make tracking me easy. I used common Latex or leather gloves to handle everything from business cards to weapons. No latent fingerprints. It wasn't rocket science either. Forensics might be able to identify that a suspect wore Latex gloves or even the type of printer used for the cards, maybe. But they would be no closer in knowing who the suspect was or where the printer was. I wanted to keep it that way.

Since my plans involved interviewing people I prepared, in advance, the spiel I would give at the time I presented the business card. People find it hard to listen to you ramble through an introduction and read the business card at the same time. It's diversionary and it works. People divide their attention and remember less of what you're actually saying than if they were able to focus on the introduction.

I used common products that could be obtained in any city. Nothing weird that police could use to easily track me. Without a criminal record and with no direct connection to my targets, I would not be on anyone's radar. Regardless, I worked diligently to keep my identity hidden.

There was no one single or perfect weapon for Walter. His weapon of choice would be whatever worked best in the time of need. I knew how to shoot so it was more natural to use a gun, but I would use anything to accomplish my objective. Gun shops and gun shows helped me become familiar with what was on the market. When the time came to acquire a weapon I turned to the newspaper first. Private purchases from want ads were the most discreet way to go. Close second places to the want ads were gun shows out in the boonies. Cash purchases with no strings attached. No ATF forms and no gun registrations, just what I liked.

Portland area gun shows were heavily regulated, whereas the small community-based shows were a bit looser, as were some of their participants. I counted on these facts for buying opportunities. The first weapon I settled on was a .40-caliber Glock. It handled well and operated smoothly. Most importantly, it had the right karma.

I continued my search for weaponry at rural gun shows, I came across a seedy-looking vendor who struck up a conversation like a used-car salesman. He had ammo, clips, and parts for everything but not one assembled weapon was on his table. We made an arrangement to hook up and go through what he had at his house. He convinced me that a spendy little moderator package he had picked up along the way would work much like a silencer to reduce noise and flash. He presented a smooth-bore barrel saying, "No rifling's to trace with this." I think he knew what I wanted to do.

"It'll get you in trouble 'less you get permitted for it," said Mr. Seedy. I acted interested in what he had to say. "Did you get a permit?"

"Nope, don't need one 'cause I don't own one of these gizmos," pointing at the moderator package. Seedy winked and smiled. His few straggly teeth showed through his shabby beard as we traded "gizmo" for cash. I didn't have to ask if there would be any record of the transaction.

I was the proud new "non-owner" of the moderator. Seedy said, "You might wanna try subsonic rounds. That'll make that there gizmo purr like a kitty." By that I assumed he meant quieter and picked up a box of ammo. If I got caught with the hardware on my Glock and a magazine full of subsonic hollow-points, it would probably be because the police had connected me to a string of killings and not because I didn't have a permit for a "gizmo."

It was time to build a toolbox for work. A small knife was a great tool for a host of applications but there existed a need for a larger knife with at least a six-inch blade. What if I had to gain entry into a house? A glass cutter, yes, maybe—what about a set of bump keys? Licensed locksmiths act like they're the only ones that can buy bump keys. I bought my set online and I wasn't asked any questions. Bump keys could open almost any residential door lock or dead bolt within seconds. It would prove to be a good investment.

I laid out a set of guidelines that would hopefully keep me off the police most-wanted posters. Getting to know the perp personally would be a mistake. It could create a link between us that I wanted to avoid. Some contractors like to befriend their mark and weave a web around them. Not me. Keep it superficial. My real preference was not to know them at all. The same was true about anyone I interviewed. Why become involved personally—it is a mistake.

In a target-rich environment, the rule of engagement is "any target of opportunity." That rule would require modification. To be opportunistic would be a disastrous course of action for what I was planning. Far more thought and planning was required. The down side, some might get away. As tragic as that might be, it was the way it was.

The finances were set. I had moved away from the old neighborhood, started a new life, and was no longer working the plant. I had plenty of time to devote to my projects. I was practicing with my pistol at the range daily.

In my opinion, there was nothing worse than a killer who was a lousy shot. It might be construed as cruel and unusual punishment and I'd hate to be accused of that.

Besides weapons practice, projects required planning. Who, where, when, and how were the guts of the project. These things required the most time. I was becoming comfortable with who I was, the new me, Walter. Like an actor auditioning for a part, I wanted to do more than just act like Walter, I had to become Walter. At every opportunity that presented itself I played Walter like it was a dress rehearsal. I began introducing myself as Walter. I wanted it to feel natural and flow.

I remained aloof in my new neighborhood, making every effort not to meet neighbors. The less I knew about them and them about me, the better I liked it. Summer was rapidly approaching. The sensory perceptions were growing strong with the Dover case clippings. Destiny was in my ear prompting me to act. I had many questions concerning Dover—most would never be answered. He would be dead and Walter would be responsible. It was off to Seattle to begin my recon of the target.

Chapter 6

There are a thousand hacking at the branches of evil
to one who is striking at the root
—Henry David Thoreau

It was the beginning of a beautiful summer in the Seattle area. Only one thing in my way of thinking could improve it, my first project coming to fruition. The "who" was easy, it had already been decided. Destiny watched over my shoulder making a big to-do over the news clippings involving one man's name. Even worse were the voices disrupting my sleep. The voices were always with me, but recently they had increased in frequency and intensity. If I was going to get any rest I had to kill this guy, and I had to kill him soon.

Regardless of how harassed I was by dimensions of a spirit world, I refused to go off halfcocked. It was bad business. Every project had a plan. That was something I was proud of. It wasn't haphazard or random but well planned, methodical, and to be performed with precision. In the military we called it a recon. The success of the follow-up mission, usually a search and destroy, depended upon the value of the recon. My reconnaissance left no stone unturned. Statistically it was undefeatable.

Benjamin Dover was more than just the target of my first project. Just the thought of killing him was stimulating. I didn't think it should affect me that way but it was inspiring and enjoyable. Dover, a child rapist, had lived too long already. He had a price to pay and I was going to collect on it.

It was fair to say I took an interest in Dover before Destiny put in her two cents' worth. Destiny didn't verbalize her feelings often but relied frequently on gestures and some form of telepathy. I trusted those things that were transmitted to me to be honest and truthful. Dover had made it to the top of my short list. In some sense he was the same to me as all the others I'd compiled notes and clippings on. I knew something of his history and what I knew I didn't like. Prodded by sensory perceptions and the need to right the wrongs done to innocent victims, I pursued my project with zeal.

I didn't feel the necessity to meet with or greet him on a personal level; however, it was a technique I would employ if need be. Who he was as a person didn't matter to me. If he had gotten on with his life after incarceration, if he was gainfully employed making a new future for himself or just being reunited with his family and enjoying their love and support, I didn't care. He should never have lived past his sentencing day.

Everybody had a story and my target was no different. Benjamin grew up in the southern suburbs of Seattle. His parents were both employed in the aircraft industry and had provided Ben with a stable home environment. It was a normal, working, middle-class neighborhood and family. Sometimes you hoped to put your finger on something and be able to say "That's what went wrong," but frequently it was just not there. More often it was as simple as a wiring problem for which there was no fix or cure. In Ben's case there was nothing remarkable about his upbringing.

His physical appearance was perhaps an issue for him. He was small in stature not unlike thousands of other kids his age. He was regarded by classmates to be reclusive. Benjamin followed in his parents' footsteps. After graduating from high school he landed a steady job at the aircraft plant. He worked around women in the workforce but never really dated. He was twenty-seven-years-old with no personal life outside company picnics and parties. He was a loner.

It was at one of these company picnics that Anita Mandalay met Benjamin. Anita with her young son in tow attracted the attention of Dover almost immediately. She saw stability and kindness in Benjamin, two attributes she was looking for in a relationship. She made it easy for Ben to become involved. She made him dinner and showed herself capable of being a wife and mother to him. She didn't want to do the dating scene; she wanted a husband who would provide for her and her son. This was just the type of relationship Benjamin looked for as well. Avoiding the social environment was what he was all about.

Initially, Benjamin was exceptionally loving and good to her son. A ready-made family seemed to suit him just fine. Ben always brought candy or a toy for the lad when visiting Anita. Within weeks Benjamin was staying every night at the Mandalay residence, and it seemed right. Whatever went wrong went wrong quickly. Psychobabblers would later state their case in court for leniency, blaming everyone from his parents to the school system for his "undersocialization" that caused his lack of self-control. In the end it was just another meaningless excuse.

The history making Ben the man of my dreams was ugly. He took his live-in girlfriend's little boy and repeatedly sodomized him. He was caught and incarcerated. End of story as far as the judicial system was concerned. The aftermath of such a debased event as happened to this youngster was rarely taken into consideration. By all accounts he was a smiling, curious four-year-old who loved to explore the world around him. He colored pictures and when he could escape the house into the backyard, he would wander for hours, bug to bug, dandelion to clover, all the while sporting an awestruck smile. He was full of life, full of innocence, and happy. Ben changed that forever.

Anita worked outside the home in a retail store. She worked an evening shift starting at 4 p.m., finishing up around midnight. Ben and her son got along well together. Anita was delighted when he volunteered to baby-sit while she was away—it just seemed natural for Ben to accept the responsibility of care for the boy. Court records indicate it was only a matter of weeks before Ben began to fondle the youngster. With each passing day Ben escalated his behavior until he began sodomizing the child. The boy never said a word to his mother. Why? No one knows.

Anita, who suspected nothing, had not noticed the personality changes in her son. He was now withdrawn and played by himself in the house. Anita was wrapped up in her new life with Ben and might not have known anything was wrong if her son had not become sick. Anita took him to a doctor and an evil was exposed. Plenty of evidence was noted from anal bleeding and scar tissue from what appeared to be sexual activity. That's where it came unraveled for Ben.

Prosecutors seized the opportunity to avoid a messy trial by offering Dover a plea deal. According to them, it was still a felony conviction for Dover and since he had no previous criminal convictions, jail time would be minimal. In their view they were "saving" the victim and family the "embarrassment." Dover copped a plea to a lesser felony charge which carried three years in the slammer and five years of useless parole. The courts slapped other punishments on him, like months of self-reflection therapy and a taxpayer-funded meditation group led by a swami.

However, from my perspective, the plea deal was unfortunate for Dover. He would have been better off if they had locked the door and thrown away the key. But now, he was out of jail and subject to Walter's retribution. It was a great opportunity to employ techniques I have put together for this purpose. His parents had not moved from the Renton area despite the ill-gotten fame. The court documents showed strong support from his immediate family members and unless something had occurred, this wasn't likely to have changed. He was an easy target to locate and set up on to watch. Anita was also easy to find. She had continued her residence in Seattle. Evidently she had never married and lived alone on the north side. She frequented a behavioral health center not far from where she lived. On a couple of occasions she took a young boy from this facility on afternoon outings. I suspected then, this was her son and everything wasn't working out well for him. I had to take a chance, I had to get closer.

I needed Walter to contact Anita. I chose a day after her visit to the behavioral center to approach her at her home. After introducing myself and providing the usual business card and rationale for my visit we got down to brass tacks.

"I'm doing a piece for a major news magazine on victims of crimes five and ten years after the courts decision. I'd like to review what happened in your case?"

Anita began to sob uncontrollably. Her grief knew no consolation. Eventually, she choked out her remnants of anger, "He spent a couple years in jail, that's all, a couple of years." I gave her time to collect her thoughts and proceed as she was able. "He ruined my son's life." She couldn't see it but I recognized her broken spirit. She was burdened with the feelings of guilt and her life was but a shell of what it could have been.

She was angry at Benjamin and it spewed out freely. In the end, she blamed herself for putting her son in danger. I took notes intermittently as she talked. She seemed eager to answer questions and filled in the gaps historically. She said her son has been in treatment multiple times for depression, requires mood-stabilizing medications, and continued to be withdrawn. She knew Dover was "out" but had not seen or had contact with him.

"I wished he had been raped to death in jail." These were sentiments I'd read many times before from victims' families. They want vengeance and ultimately a day of reckoning.

Before departing, Anita asked, "Is it fair, that's what your article should ask, is it fair?"

I felt a little depressed I wasn't actually writing a feature piece for some rag, but I hoped what I had to offer would give her peace—Ben's head on a serving platter.

Some might be concerned for Benjamin. It appeared his family continued to love him. They were supportive and kept in contact with him. His life certainly was a tragedy and likewise took its toll on family members. It might sound callous to say, so what, but so what? He was responsible for his actions and I couldn't care less about him.

I was in position to cause Anita some much-needed peace of mind. Soon, she would receive the good news of Ben's death. It would be especially comforting to know he didn't die a natural death but was murdered. To help ease her pain it would have given me considerable pleasure to let her know his fate was already decided, but that would've been foolhardy. I thanked her for her time and for sharing her feelings with me and said goodbye. It was time to locate Benjamin.

Seattle was nearly 300 miles north of my Portland home; this had its pros and cons. When a serious crime is committed, police and their profilers usually look in the neighborhood where the crime was committed. If it is discovered down the road that a serial killer is on the loose, law enforcement will focus their attention where they determine the first kill took place. In theory, most serial killers do start close to home where they are most comfortable. In my case it would be far enough from my residence to insure an extra degree of safety.

This presented some logistical issues to be overcome. Fortunately, a high school friend lived in Kent, Washington. From his Seattle suburban home I would establish a base of operations. He bought my reasons for being in the Seattle area. As far as he knew I was gathering information for a story about the aircraft industry. It was a dull and boring subject that wouldn't stimulate any conversation.

He seemed to think little about the frequency of my trips and enjoyed our time reminiscing. It saved me the expense of a hotel, but even more important, my name would not appear in hotel registers anywhere in the Seattle area. The less paper trail the better I liked it. I found most of my reconnaissance paying off quickly. Another plus for living locally was I had as much time as I needed to get the project finished.

Ben was employed at a Mom and Pop's music store in a rundown strip mall in White Center. This old suburb of Seattle was a lower-income area with many older homes and apartment complexes. Maybe better than that, people kept to themselves and minded their own business for the most part. People can, if they were of a mind to, stay in the recesses of a city like Seattle and go undetected their entire life. In this scenario, what was good for Ben was likewise good for me.

I needed to have "eyes on" before assuming a more difficult role. As Yogi Berra once said, "You can observe a lot just by watching," and watching was one of the things Walter did well. The street view of this strip mall with an L-shape design appeared to be to my advantage. Plenty of parking was available on the lot in front of the stores. This was indicative of an older mall which was common years ago to provide lots of parking spaces. I suspected at one time it had been very busy. Now it was used mostly by commuters parking their vehicles and carpooling or using the mass transit system.

To avoid detection one must avoid obvious and conspicuous locations. The area surrounding the parking lot provided good cover. A major intersection was located at the south end of the lot. Adjacent to the front of the lot was a busy bus stop. People frequently milled around the front of the mall killing time waiting for their bus. This was all to my advantage. Blending in was something I did well. The more people and the busier the area the more difficult it was for someone to note my presence. Isolated terrain features created difficulties for getting close to a target. And I liked to be close. Close enough to feel their presence. Close enough to hear their last agonal gasp for air.

The mall was surprisingly busy with all the storefronts sporting a business of various designs. A large Chinese restaurant had the anchor position of the mall nearest the main avenue. Next to the restaurant was an embroidery shop, a surplus dollar store, a martial arts studio, a couple of independent insurance agent offices, and a small community resource center located on the lengthier part of the mall. The music store had a prominent position being nestled in the corner of this L. It was flanked by a flower shop and a day-care center.

Because my recons were sporadic and Dover's work schedule fluctuated, I became concerned when he hadn't shown for work in a couple days. I paid the little store a visit asking for Ben. He had been terminated. People thought very little of straight-up questions. Concocting elaborate schemes usually didn't pay off any better and it was hard to remember the script. The young punk rocker working the music store provided me with more details than I asked for. Dover was often stressed out, tired and sleepy with a constant tardiness on the job. He was a skilled laborer with a good education and felt society was terribly unfair to him and he didn't seem shy about making the accusation. The consequences he continued to encounter for being a sex offender were in his eyes unfair. I turned my observation to his apartment.

It was time to close the loop. It was midmorning, sunny and warm. Down a dimly lit corridor of the aged apartment building the small stature of Benjamin Dover could be seen on the move. The service door, which he apparently preferred, emptied out into a shaded parking lot hidden from street view. His vehicle was parked near the rear of the lot away from other resident's vehicles that usually crowded near the door. Like clockwork he was going about his normal routine. I suspect he thought he was sly, but I saw him differently. His destination was a well-known park that catered to families with young children. His activities were also known to me. And far more sinister than perhaps the common person expected. I've made a life out of studying sexual offenders and I'm in tune with their thinking matrix. I knew what he was thinking; I was there, watching closely.

Today was no different other than that he was now unemployed. He drove a short distance to a local Safeway, purchased a bag of candy, and then proceeded to the park. The park was relatively small, a community type with plenty of swing sets and monkey bars for the little kids to play on. Spotty patches of shade trees covered the park benches that lined the paved path circling the children's play areas. It was picturesque and disarming in many ways. People felt isolated from danger here, yet it sat not far from any of them.

Dover's trip to the park might seem like a harmless venture, but sexual offenders were never harmless. They might be opportunistic, acting out on impulse or actively seek to manipulate their way into a safe environment to prey upon the innocent. Dover was no exception, he reeked of predictable treachery. Regardless, his present state of mind was not my interest. I wasn't here to build a legal case against him. I had come to settle a score from his past. Dover was guilty of the worst kind of betrayal, violating a child's trust. The consequences were devastating. In my court, there were no negotiating terms or mitigating circumstances to consider. The penalty of death loomed closely for Ben.

Dover could have parked in the lot for patrons but he chose a spot a block away in front of a large apartment complex. He was being deceptive. He casually strolled to the bike path entrance and into the grounds. It was interesting to watch him. He was paranoid, looking over his shoulder frequently, coming to a halt if others on the path were gaining on him. But when he sat on a bench and watched the children all his attention was on them. He didn't look around; he was almost spellbound with a sheepish little smile. I watched as he spoke with children playing and offered candy from his Safeway bag. What was wrong with this? He was a child sex offender.

He spent the remainder of the day in the park. In the late afternoon he drove to a Jack-in-the-Box where he spent more than an hour in the play area eating his dinner. From my vantage I could keep Dover in view. Dusk was approaching and knowing his routine I made a beeline to his apartment complex. As usual there was no one present in the back lot. I parked my vehicle in an adjacent lot out of view. I slipped on my latex gloves and jacked a round into my .40-caliber. The moderator fastened tightly just like it had the many times I'd rehearsed it. I sat back and waited. My hat cocked at a forward angle like I was napping as darkness approached.

The parking lot lighting illuminated near the apartment but back by a row of shade trees where Dover liked to park, it was of little value. His car came into view as he pulled off Ambaum Way, and as anticipated, he backed into his favorite spot far away from the apartment building. The cab of the car flashed bright for a moment as he lit a cigarette then leaned his head back on the seat.

As I prepared to meet Mr. Dover for the first and last time, Destiny passed before his car. Dover sat up momentarily and appeared to look in her direction. Maybe he did; maybe he didn't. I'll never know if she was visible to him.

My anxiety was beginning to build. I recalled my way of controlling my emotions on the ranch when I had to kill one of the animals. A technique I called "switching channels." It was a mind game to close out my emotions and it worked. I could do this kill without feeling anything, just as with the animals I killed, except I liked the farm animals.

Dover was a worthless piece of humanity. He might have changed his ways, repented of his sins, found god, or been enlightened by Confucius—it was irrelevant. It didn't change what he had done and wouldn't change the outcome of his day.

I looked about as I exited my Avenger. No one was in sight. My eyes continued to search the cars and apartment windows for any sign of people that might see the transaction take place. My Glock with the moderator attachment seemed longer than I thought it would be. I covered it loosely with a thin jacket with the butt facing forward and placed it under my left arm. It only had to be veiled for a few minutes. Dover sat relaxed, smoking a cigarette, with his left arm hanging limply out the driver's side window.

"Yo!" I announced my presence. I didn't want to startle him approaching from the back left corner of his car. Destiny, who decided to accompany me against my wishes, moved along the passenger side. I didn't have time to watch her right now; my focus was directed to my target.

"Hey buddy, my battery is dead, do you think I could get a jump?"

Dover leaned forward and looked me over for a moment, "What's it worth to you?"

I probably looked like an easy mark to him. Nerdy and casual business dress was out of place in this environment. "Hey, everybody's got to pay a price." In reality, I was addressing his payment.

Dover smiled, took a long drag off his smoke and said, "Ten bucks will get you rolling."

"Absolutely," I said with a big smile as I turned in the direction of my car. "It's right over here," all the while scanning the area for passersby.

I heard the ignition of Dover's car as I moved toward the back of his car. He looked out his window in my direction, probably just in time to catch the small flash from my .40-caliber in the corner of his left eye. Thuup. The temple shot spun him around. Adrenaline coursed through my entire body. He shook and kicked like he was having a seizure. I found it difficult to contain my own exhilaration. Thuup, the second round hit in the back of his head. His twitching stopped. Both shell casings were in plain sight and soon in my pocket. I walked directly to my car, only looking about after I was back inside my Avenger. No one seemed to notice. The moderator along with subsonic rounds had done their work. Quiet and effective, it's the way I had planned it. I inched my Avenger forward without switching on the lights until I turned onto the street.

I don't know what I expected to find in the newspaper about the incident. It was two days before the article appeared buried beneath three other killings that had taken place and was evidently insignificant in comparison. A child kidnapping by a mother's new boyfriend who was a known sex offender took top billing in the metro section. It was followed by a lengthy article about a shootout at a tavern frequented by longshoremen that had left two dead, and a Samoan street gang committing a home invasion that left one man beaten to death.

The Dover article stated he was found by a "passerby" who contacted the police. According to unnamed sources there was speculation Dover was involved in a drug buy gone bad. Where do they get these ideas? Then again, I didn't know Ben all that well. Maybe he did have drugs in the car, I don't know? According to police the area was well known for drug dealing. I would rather they had speculated he might have been shot because he was a child rapist. The only way that would make news was if I confessed, and that wasn't on my agenda.

I said my goodbyes to an old friend I would probably never see again and made my way home to Oregon. I thought about the project during the drive back to Portland and found myself smiling a lot. After a couple of days' rest

I busied myself with destroying any file material that might link me to the deceased. I started a fire in the wood-burning stove and placed the evidence in the fire. Briefly, the apparition of a very young child appeared before me looking into the blaze at the burning file. I knew this child from many of my dreams. I pondered the idea, having never met Anita's little boy, if this could be him coexisting in some sort of alternative time dimension. Perhaps because of what had happened, the soul and the human shell had separated. If so, could my actions be a path for reunification of his being?

As the fire roared, the sound of a fleeting choir of voices could be heard. In their voices was the sound of joy. As the file vanished into a charcoal dust the voices grew silent and the apparition disappeared.

I still think about Dover from time to time, it's something you don't forget. I wouldn't have it any other way. Is it just an obsession getting the best of me or is there a greater purpose? It was quiet at my home for a couple of days, and then, the sound of a distant voice could be heard. It was familiar yet somehow different. I couldn't make out the voice or what was being said, but I knew it would become clear soon. I looked forward to it.

Chapter 7

He paid the price society required. But it wasn't society that was victimized
—it was a school girl
—Walter

Any hope of a prolonged Indian summer was fading. A scattering of red-and-gold-tinged leaves mingled with the green; the approaching new season with shorter days and cooler nights would soon coat them in autumn colors—characteristic of early October in Oregon. I have full appreciation for the breathtakingly picturesque countryside and fertile Willamette Valley where lush grapes and berries grow. Small local wineries dot the valleys and hillsides, converting nature's best into deep fruity-tasting full-bodied nectar of the gods. I'm not a connoisseur by any stretch of the imagination but I do enjoy the sweet-red libation found here in Oregon. Trips over to the Pacific coast from Seaside south to Depoe Bay are relaxing weekend ventures I take to maintain whatever level of sanity I possess.

Regardless of how easily one can become distracted by the scenic beauty, evil is never far away. Not that I'm counting bodies but I am conflicted by the fact that more people are convicted of violent sex crimes in one year than I will be able to tag and bag in my lifetime. I've been at this for a year and outside of ensuring a zero recidivism rate of a choice few, I've made no headway at all. So much time is devoted to research and reconnaissance I can't make any progress; if anything, I'm falling behind. I've managed only a few kills since the summer of '96 and I'm feeling frustrated. I have to date left a small number of bodies across Oregon and Washington, making sure to keep my projects as far away as I can from where I live in Multnomah County. Make no mistake about it, there are plenty of targets available in the Portland area but by keeping them widespread I felt it might keep me from being caught. I'm also a realist; someday I'll either make a mistake or fate will put me in the wrong place at the wrong time. Regardless, until that day comes, I will continue to apply justice my way—Walter's way.

To my benefit, police investigating a murder in their area may not link it to another killing in another state or county, especially when the person killed had a viable list of potential suspects. Victims and their families will certainly top the list of possible killers. Friends of the victim or victims' extended families head up the next level of suspects. It would take police time to eliminate that potential. Only latent fingerprints or other forensic evidence could link me to the murders. Part of my job is to ensure that doesn't come easy. Otherwise, the fact that I had no known association with any of the deceased would keep me from being a suspect. If and when I am identified I will continue the cat and mouse game until I'm behind bars. I could stop now and maybe avoid ever being detected, but why?

There wasn't much I could do about the long planning phase. A properly executed project meant a safe outcome at the completion. What could I change to be more effective? Up to this point I've pretty much dropped targets where I found them. I've avoided the messy business of hauling bodies around or trying to hide them in shallow graves but any business can be refined. The goal will be to construct a new timeline to include disposing of the body in some way to make an investigation more difficult. Confusing timelines and changing modes operandi buys me more time. Perhaps even never to be found. A perp that up and disappears is not unusual. Every state sexual offender's registry has hundreds listed as noncompliant. In most cases it means they're not living where they're supposed to be. Authorities will put out a warrant on them, but if it works out my way, well, it'll never be served.

Dover was my first kill. It hardly made the news. I was disappointed. To homicide detectives it was probably an irritant to have an unsolved murder but it wouldn't be their first cold case to shelve and did they really care about Dover? In Spokane a couple months later I put down another scumbag. Would the detectives in Seattle and the detectives in Spokane make any connection? Outside the coincidence that they were both convicted sexual offenders, was there anything else that tied the case together? Only if there were some reason to tie ballistics together could they make a connection.

My first kill in Oregon was a guy I capped off Interstate 5. I left him right there in the carport bleeding. Would detectives make the connection to a serial killer? Did anyone really care that he died? Next was a slime-bucket I put down in John Day, Oregon. I guess townsfolk cared about that killing.

They didn't care about the victim but rather the unique ambience of their little community being shattered when the project culminated. Small towns don't handle it well when someone gets murdered. That's one of the pleasures of living in a small community, big-city stuff like murders just don't happen every day. If those folks had known what he had done they would have hung him themselves. But it was kept quiet. The local newspaper was superficial in their coverage and Johnny Law wasn't letting anything out. So people didn't understand and remained very much afraid.

For the past couple of weeks I'd been traveling from Portland over to Highway 101 to get the lay of the land for what would be my next project. The target area was Neskowin, an unincorporated beach-side vacation hamlet thirty miles south of Tillamook. With only a few hundred residents it was just the type of place I'd like to avoid for a project.

Strong sensory perceptions associated with this old file started the ball rolling. I felt the pain associated with the crime and saw what I believed to be the victim in my dreams. My clippings were insufficient to provide valuable information concerning the whereabouts of Mr. William Loney. This criminal was a Canadian-born naturalized citizen and I was concerned I'd be making a trip to British Columbia to settle the score. But even a nebulous fellow like Loney, once out of prison, couldn't hide forever.

My life it seemed had become a series of road trips to conduct interviews and visit courthouses in neighboring cities and states. I should have invested in KOA Campgrounds and then I could at least have used them freely. Early on I purchased a 1994 thirteen-foot Casita Patriot compact camper that was easily pulled by my Avenger. My '57 Chevy pickup could have more easily pulled it, but I wanted my personal vehicle left out of it. Trying to keep a low profile meant holing up in small campgrounds a distance from my areas of interest. The Patriot made that easy to accomplish.

Mr. Loney was seemingly a man twenty-years-old one day and thirty-nine the next day. I knew the absence of personal history was mostly due to his incarceration. Taking the life of a seventeen-year-old girl that he raped and sodomized caught him a murder rap. His lawyer had him copout to a lesser charge and was sentenced to twenty-five years in the plea agreement. Not a bad strategy; jury convictions for these heinous crimes generally carry a stiffer sentence than the run-of-the-mill plea agreement. That's why they call it "plea bargain," because it's a good deal for the perp. Good behavior in jail counts for something as well, netting about twenty percent of the sentence being knocked off. In Loney's case he spent seventeen years behind bars. For those in society unaffected directly by this rape and murder, it may seem a sufficient sentence. He paid the price society required. But it wasn't society that was victimized—it was a school girl. Not only had she been brutalized to death by Loney, her family and friends also had someone they loved stolen from them. No number of years would be sufficient for them. Not even the price of death would be enough, but it would be a heck of a lot closer. Further, it didn't sit well with Walter either.

Taking my time and going through the usual steps to prepare was important. They might have been a waste of time in the end, but you couldn't tell unless the steps were completed to begin with. Unfortunately, due to the plea agreement in this case I would have to resort to other resources. Plea agreements often lacked testimony, something I commonly used to establish names of witnesses and family for interviews. Further complications arose from this being a juvenile victim case. Much of the information was difficult to obtain and names were often just initials. In this case there would be no interviews.

With a vast number of people-finder sources available on the Internet it was possible to track down the location of a subject or a last known residence. Personal information such as age range, phone numbers, and others living at the location could usually be obtained as well. There were any numbers of ways to track someone and obtain viable information.

In the Loney case the Internet had provided just the lead I needed on the last known residence. My file photo from the old clipping would provide some assistance in identifying the mark, but it could not be counted on since so much time had elapsed. Next stop would be Neskowin for reconnaissance.

The rolling spruce covered hills along the pristine coastline made this a popular beach-front. It had scores of vacation rental homes and resorts for thousands of travelers who swelled the summertime population to more than two thousand people. It evidently was also a great place to stow away from society, or at least Loney thought so. Being off the beaten path, most visitors came for the scenic beauty never noticing those around them. In Loney's favor was the fact that his crime was far in the past. Few if any in this area would remember hearing of him.

I set up observation on his home, a secluded beach-front cottage. He had landed a full-time job as a live-in manager for a property management group that had rental cabins along the beach. It was apparent to me Loney had started a new life in Neskowin. Not bad for a felon. It was certainly better than the fate of the high-school girl when he killed her. He was married now, with a newborn child. His wife was much younger than Loney, maybe in her early twenties. She commuted to Lincoln City for work. I can't speak to her wages but she was able to take the baby with her to the office each day. None of that was of any real concern to me, just unfortunate. Meanwhile, Loney was free to do the handyman chores with the cabins, rent vacancies, and take care of various little boats and kayaks stored on the property. It was a pretty sweet deal.

A few more preparations and I would be ready to go. With my Avenger I visited junkyards frequently looking for parts. Some of the folks that run these bone yards don't make much off what they sell so they let you do the labor, like removing a bumper, tailgate, or a license plate. Switching license plates for a project is handy in keeping a low profile. In the remote event that someone was suspicious and took down the plate number off my vehicle it would be useless in identifying me as the owner.

The morning was brisk the chosen day of the event. The coastal communities would almost assuredly be near-deserted. It was the off season but even then some folks liked to get away from the hustle and bustle of city life for a few days of relaxation.

I pulled into a roadside parking area above the cabins and watched for the daily routine to begin. Mrs. Loney with baby in hand departed on time, driving their only vehicle south. Bill wasn't out and about yet. I had dressed for the occasion. Casual slacks, turtleneck sweater, rain slicker and chukka boots. I always felt like a moron until I slipped on the black-framed glasses and vintage charcoal gray Stetson fedora. I was no longer assuming a role; I was Walter, 100-percent.

The sun made its appearance warming the air only slightly while a mist clung to the ground. The radio announcer called for a cool and disappointing fifty-five degrees for the high. It would have to improve some for that to happen. On the horizon loomed a wall of dark clouds preparing their assault on the coastline.

Loney strolled out of his cabin with broom in hand. He didn't look like a man in a hurry to get the day started. It was, however, routine. He swept the porches of cabins one after the other as he worked his way to where the boats were stored. I made my way across the hard sand to the back of the boat-storage shed. I could hear movement inside but nothing distinguishable. I looked about to the parking area; there was no one in sight. The impending storm might have deterred beachcombers for the day. That was good news for me, bad news for Bill.

Six cabins sat side by side facing the beach. Whoever had built them had the foresight to put up privacy walls between the cabins' sandy yards leaving the view open to the beach. The walls were a wood slat construction running twelve feet from the cabins and stood more than five feet high. The design allowed wind and blowing sand to pass through them, yet obscuring the view of neighbors from each other. Inside the yard were an outdoor grill, picnic table, and lawn chairs. Other than looking weathered it was reasonably nice.

I walked to the nearest cabin and knocked loudly. I already knew cabin number one was the only one occupied. It was rented by a middle-aged couple. I continued knocking until I heard the storage shed door open.

"Can I help you?" Bill shouted.

"I'm looking for the manager."

Bill closed the door behind him, "Well, you found him."

"I'd like to rent a cabin for a night, I'm meeting friends tomorrow in Depoe Bay and I'm just early getting here."

Bill nodded. "One hundred twenty-five dollars a night. Do you want to see the unit?"

"Hey, that's great."

Bill opened number six that I had been knocking on and gave me the tour. It was certainly sufficient for my needs. Of course, all I needed was a quiet place to shoot him.

Bill asked, "Where did you park?"

I pointed to the parking lot by the road. Bill pointed to his cottage and the road leading past it to the cabin parking area. "Pull'er on down there, it'll be a lot easier for you."

It doesn't feel right, something is wrong, I thought. At this point I'd not touched anything inside the cabin. If I needed to I could abort and no one would be the wiser.

"Are you putting the rental on a card?"

"No, I rather use cash when I can."

Bill nodded again as I pulled out my wallet to pay him. I guess if I wasn't asking for a contract he wasn't offering one either. "Do you need a receipt?" Bill asked.

"Just a waste of a good tree," I jokingly replied.

Loney smiled and proceeded to the front door pointing to the door key on an end table. I slipped on my black ultrathin leather gloves and closed the door behind me.

Bill went back in the storage shed as I made my way through the sand to my vehicle.

Destiny was awaiting me there. Somehow I knew I was on the right track but my feelings of confusion were puzzling me. As I sat there in the roadside parking area my concerns were soon put to rest. It was people! A man and woman showed up apparently to check on a rental cabin. If I had killed him in the unit upon my exit they might have seen me and sounded the alarm upon finding the body. It was a risk I hadn't really planned for but should have.

The visitors left and Bill slowly strolled back to the storage shed. This was the largest outbuilding on the beach measuring somewhere around twenty feet wide and thirty feet in length. The windows were maybe six feet off the ground, serving some purpose other than to see in or out of. I drove my Avenger past the area for parking and on to the parking pad alongside the shed. Quietly I exited my car and made my way around to the front storage-shed door. Opening the door, I found Bill sitting in an old office chair behind a makeshift desk of plywood and wooden crates. With feet propped up he looked relaxed and enjoying a magazine. "Problems?" he said as he closed the magazine and pushed it under the plywood cover.

"No, no, I just have a couple questions."

Taking his feet down, Bill leaned forward and replied, "Shoot."

This was awkward. Shoot was exactly what I wanted to do. He must be a flippin' mind reader! Not yet, not yet, I kept telling myself. Not yet.

"I'm a feature writer for a travel magazine and I'd like to get some pictures of Proposal Rock. Can you give me some ideas?"

Bill thought for a moment, "You could rent a boat, swing out in the ocean and get some shots."

"I've never driven a boat. Do you think I could do it by myself?"

Shaking his head in a manner indicating no, he chuckled, "It would be suicide."

Wrong! I was thinking homicide, not suicide. "What about some cliffs in the area, maybe overhangs or something where I could get some good shots?"

"There are some steep cliffs a couple miles from here," Bill said pointing south.

"Time is of the essence I think. Any chance I could rent your services for an hour or so to guide me? The rain is going to hit soon and I'd like to get the photos as the storm is approaching. I think they'll turn out well."

Bill thought for a moment before answering, "I suppose so."

"Does a hundred dollars sound right?" I asked.

"Sounds right to me, let's do it."

I pulled a hundred from my billfold handing it to him and into the Avenger we went.

"Where's your camera?" Bill asked.

My reply was quick, "In a bag in back." I thought to myself, is he getting concerned?

Traveling south a short distance we turned off the main road into a parking area. Remote, no other vehicles, I was feeling right about this place. A short hike found us standing on a promontory overlooking basalt cliffs and an increasingly turbulent sea. The wind was whistling through the trees; undoubtedly that's all Loney heard, but there were voices too.

It was somewhat unnerving to stand with no barrier between me and the 150-foot fall into the water. I hoped Bill didn't feel the same way. I set my bag down and began to pull items out, one of which was a large black steel pipe 1-inch thick. I had filled this pipe with cement and named him "Thumper" for obvious reasons. I pulled out a small tarp partially concealing the pipe while Bill continued to look out over the beach area toward Proposal Rock. He began to point out different landmarks when he fell forward on his face. His eyes were glazed and blood trickled from his nose. Walter had introduced him to Thumper. With a creased skull above the right ear, he didn't utter a word. Perhaps he no longer was able to. He rolled onto his stomach and I brought down the pipe again at the base of his skull. I don't know if he was still alive when I pulled him to the edge and rolled him over the cliff but it didn't matter. He was dead the moment he got into my car—he just didn't know it.

The stormy sea swallowed him quickly into its frothy brew. His body would be carried far from the base of the cliffs by storm's end. Even if someone thought he had ventured into the water, the Coast Guard search and rescue teams were not likely to set a course in this storm. I loaded my things back in the bag. Kicked a little dirt over the blood trail on the outcropping and figured the storm would take care of the rest.

Back in the Avenger I looked around at the deserted parking area and relaxed for a moment. This was not how I had planned to kill him. In a way it was tragic—I mean, I had tossed Loney in the drink with a hundred dollars of mine in his pocket. Otherwise, it seemed to go well and I believe he felt the brunt of his punishment with the help of Thumper.

I spent the next couple days in Tillamook while the storm pounded the coast with plenty of wind and rain. I watched the local papers to see if any articles surfaced on Loney. Evidently, he never surfaced either.

Whatever the authorities thought about his disappearance is a mystery. Without any evidence that he was murdered he will be labeled another sex offender on the lam. I thought about the young widow, Mrs. Loney, having the hardship of a love taken away. Then there is the baby deprived of its biological father. How unfortunate for them. This project has caused more reflection for me than most. I question myself as to how I am different than he was. Loney had deprived a loving family of their daughter two decades ago. I deprived a family of their loved one. Does that make me like him? I think not. He killed an innocent young person—I have killed a guilty person. I blame the justice system for allowing this error to go uncorrected for so long.

I've accomplished what I came to do. Loney has passed on to whatever exists for him next and a hidden timeline for the murder has been created. Enough reflecting, I'm more than satisfied with the outcome of the project.

Chapter 8

A predator for prey is expected. A predator for predator is not.
—Walter

Everyone holds the power of choice. Everyone must accept responsibility for his or her own actions in life. There are no exceptions to the rule. On this, Walter and I agree. It is irrational to believe you can be saved from your own bad decisions and stupidity. There are no excuses, only consequences. As Walter would say, "I am that consequence." And believe me, I've seen the results. It's not pretty but it is the last consequence some scumbags will ever know.

With Walter, all the excuses in the world won't change the scale of justice. Defense attorneys love that Freudian crap because they can spread it like fertilizer to grow "reasonable doubts." Walter doesn't buy it! Pointing fingers at moms and dads to explain aberrant behavior is the basis of a well-fertilized defense argument. Perps make decisions to commit criminal acts of violence on innocent persons to gratify their own seething lust. You can choose to believe regurgitated psychobabble spewed out at trials if you like. I hold violent predatory criminals accountable for their actions. Defense attorneys are con artists, selling juries excuses like their counterparts of the Old West with their snake oil. It's only a tactic; there is no legitimate defense. None!

Victims, more than anyone, should be willing to bring this behavior to an end and break the mythical cycle of abuse. I say mythical because it is overplayed by lawyers on behalf of the criminals. Oftentimes there is no support for this hogwash the defense is selling the court. It's a ploy to blame someone other than the only person responsible for the crime. Unfortunately, it's gone in favor of these perps too many times. That's why they band together in activist groups with lawyers at the helm. Its society's biggest betrayal and worth far more than thirty pieces of silver.

Someone needs to step up to the plate. That's where I come in. I'm a pinch hitter! What family members might have done with audacity and opportunity, I do voluntarily without fear of consequence—vengeance is mine! Offenders of violent crimes must die if crime is to be reduced—there is no alternative.

One of my victims, in a rather hyper verbal state, related how he wished he had killed himself rather than rape a little girl. But he didn't! He raped the little girl and tried to hide from his crime. His tears met my gunpowder. As with my ill-fated friend, suicide is never opted for by any perp, so I help them along.

Yes, I'm advocating suicide as a far better choice than subjecting another person to violent sexual abuse. When perps do choose to commit such an act against someone, they should not be so naïve as to think a violent reaction is far away. They should expect it, not whine and cry about the unfair consequences they receive from a judge and jury. It's nothing in comparison to what I have in store for them when our paths cross. Predator for prey is expected. Predator for predator is not. I am not supposed to exist, but I do.

One thing I had decided from the start of this venture was to keep my projects at a distance. I did not want to get to know them on a personal level. I felt no inclination to befriend them or get close to their personal lives; it wasn't necessary. What I hadn't planned for was a situation involving a long-term platonic relationship.

Latisha Hughes and I had worked the factory together for many years. She was single, never married, and in no uncertain terms ever wanted to be. I was content with having loved once and lost and moved on with my life. We went out to a few events together, but that's where it ended for both of us. However, we had on numerous occasions discussed the problems of the world over a brew or two and actually solved most of them, if that can be believed. Unfortunately, most folks would never go along with the cures, so we kept them mostly to ourselves. It was this friendship and perhaps my views that brought into my world a set of circumstances demanding my personal involvement and a solution to Tish's problem, a solution only Walter could administer.

Bang! Bang! Bang! The pounding sound on my front door ricocheted off the walls as the afternoon was rudely interrupted. Since I never invite anyone to my house, I carefully opened the door not knowing what to expect. I was momentarily taken aback to see Tish holding a young female in her embrace. Mia looked up from Tish's shoulder, her face grimacing with pain, and sobbing uncontrollably. Tish appeared upset and angry, asked,

"Can we come in?"

Startled at her appearance and tone, I swung the door open, "Sure, of course."

Mia Payne was a casual acquaintance of mine. That is to say, I had met her on a couple of occasions. Mia was a newlywed of about six months. Her husband, Macon, I hadn't met prior to their marriage. He was a polite and well-mannered young man that left me with the gut feeling he was putting on the dog for someone. There was something more artificial and counterfeit than genuine but I couldn't put my finger on it.

She brought to the new relationship not only herself but a cute little six-year-old daughter, Barbie. Her father from the former relationship might have blessed her with his DNA but had brought little else to the table. The relationship was never made official and soon they drifted apart.

Mia composed herself as best she could as she sat on the ottoman facing me. Tish sat near her on a recliner holding Mia's hand and absorbing her tears. It was a struggle for Mia to open up. The pain was overwhelming. She didn't seem to know where to start. She was hesitant, but with coaxing, blurted, "Macon is a felon. He did time in the state pen at Salem." After a long pause it became easier for her and she continued. "He was involved with some other guys, they were all really young, and they were caught red-handed committing house burglaries. Macon was driving the car when they caught him. All the stuff they took was in the trunk."

Mia knew the story from the beginning. She was involved with a church ministry which had brought her in contact with Macon while he was incarcerated. Weekly religious meetings opened the door to begin their relationship. They started corresponding and talking on the phone frequently. At the end of his nineteen-month stint he was ready to move his relationship to another level. In Mia's mind it was all behind them and buried in the past. Less than a month after discharge from Corrections they were hitched in a private ceremony. They were at this time six months into their marriage and had developed an ugly secret. Mia continued to beat around the bush. I found it interesting but felt the worst was yet to come. Why else would Tish bring her here?

I tried hard not to have contact with any of the folks from the factory but I let my guard down with Tish. It was a mistake. I had given Tish my address sometime back at her request. It seemed the normal thing to do and abnormal to conceal it from her. However, I never suggested or encouraged her to drop by, nor did I expect her to. It must have been my lucky day. Bad luck, that is. I suspect she chose me because I was the most trusted person of anyone she knew and further, I was a man, which offered a degree of safety for what was going to be revealed. Regardless, I was chosen to become the recipient of Mia's bad news.

Macon watched Barbie while Mia worked an evening job. According to Mia, Macon loaded the little girl into his car and went for a drive while Mia was at work. He stopped by a liquor store purchasing a four-pack of wine coolers then proceeded to a "scenic" spot to enjoy the beverages. Or so it would seem. He gave Barbie a couple of sweet and fruity wine coolers, which she downed. When she became woozy from the booze and nearly passed out he sexually assaulted her with his finger. More might well have happened if it wasn't for Barbie becoming sick from the alcohol and vomiting profusely in the car. He drove her home, put her in the shower, and washed and dried her clothes. Except for the stench, he managed to clean up the car before Mia got off work.

Macon picked Mia up that evening and, when asked about the foul odor, confessed. However, Macon's hope for a concealed lie amidst the truth failed miserably when Mia talked with Barbie about the incident. She hadn't been as drunk as Macon thought and remembered the parts Macon left out. When Mia confronted him on the accusation, he lied and denied anything of that nature had occurred. Seeing Mia wasn't buying, he quickly pivoted to a new position of weeping and crying about how sorry he was. In truth, Macon was no doubt sorry, sorry he got caught, not sorry he did it. I'd heard enough.

Mia went on with her story, although she really didn't need to. I was busy planning a project, vaguely hearing what she was saying. I snapped out of it enough to hear her concluding the story with packing up her daughter and leaving for her mother's house.

"Mia called me frantic," said Tish, still holding Mia by the hand for comfort. After meeting up with her at Mia's mom's house the two of them tucked Barbie into bed, Mia and Tish both giving her hugs and kisses before finding a place on the porch they could talk privately.

"We haven't slept a wink all night," Tish said. "There's no reason to go over it again and again. The story is the same."

Tish tried to get Mia to take Barbie to the hospital and file a report with the police but Mia was adamant, she did not want to involve the police. Tish had hoped I might talk some sense into her.

"Mia, take it to the police." My response was everything Tish expected

She promptly refused. "Macon is still on parole. A parole violation would put him right back in jail and he'd hate me."

I will admit sometimes I just don't understand people. This was one of them. "Why do you care if he hates you? Don't you hate him for what he has done? Don't you want him in jail? Isn't that what he deserves?"

Mia sat back, "I don't know, it would devastate him. What if he killed himself?"

Well she had a point; it would take care of the problem and save Walter the hassle.

"I'm not worried about him, Mia, he's a big boy and he's responsible for what he has done."

Mia's tears were gone and she sat soberly fumbling with a wadded-up ball of Kleenex. I thought for a moment I'd gotten through to her.

"He told me he was leaving Oregon and he would not bother us again."

My response was coarse, "Is that all you want? Just gone? He'll go somewhere else and he'll do it again if you don't do anything."

Mia sat quietly without responding. Tish continued to hold her hand while I looked into her eyes and awaited the next opportunity to coax her in the right direction.

"He mentioned Australia," Mia said looking at Tish. "He said he was going to Australia. He's probably on his way already. He was really scared of what would happen if he stayed here. Besides, I can't put Barbie through a big court ordeal."

His leaving solved Mia's immediate concern but it wasn't the full measure of an answer to the problem. It would be up to Walter to resolve it permanently.

I was through trying to talk her into something she wasn't going to follow up on. Mia continued to talk, an attempt to justify her feelings, but she didn't have my interest. I was angry Mia would not show the proper care and concern for her daughter. I toyed with the idea of telling her to hit the dusty trail but that would not make matters better.

Hindsight being 20/20 it was easy to see Macon had been grooming Barbie from the beginning of their marriage. Mia recounted having observed Macon's behavior at home that sparked the initial concern. Macon, the loving new dad in the picture, made attempts to bond with Barbie, or so Mia thought. Macon would go into the little girl's bedroom at bedtime and give her a back massage. What bothered Mia was his manner of stroking her back, over her buttocks, and down her legs. Although it raised a concern in Mia, she thought she was just being overly protective and dismissed it. Macon ingratiated himself in Barbie's eyes by giving her treats and privileges Mia frowned upon. Again, Mia did not want to derail her new husband's good intentions of being a father figure and stepped aside. Then the straw that broke the camel's back. This was unforgivable. Yet, she didn't want to involve the police.

Mia felt partly to blame for what happened and a criminal trial might bring that out. To me it was just another child sexual abuse case that would never be reported. She was another parent who didn't know right from wrong and it was wrong to allow the crime to go unreported. Under the guise of protecting her child she would allow for more victims to follow. Macon would seek a lair in some out-of-the-way place where he could hide what he was, then resurface to victimize another child.

Mia asked, "Can you pay him a visit just to see if he's left yet? If not, maybe you can encourage his packing and leaving."

Now I'm an errand boy! Getting involved would be a mistake. Ted E. Bear was right, I can't just kill everyone. In this case I might end up a suspect! I could feel my judgment becoming clouded, not because of Mia, but anger over what had happened to this little girl. Personal involvement was against everything I believed in and planned for. I was playing with fire and I knew better. Shaking my head as I sat back I reluctantly responded, "Okay, I'll do what I can."

At the door Tish gave me a brotherly hug, whispering, "I'll give you a call."

Great, I thought, more involvement. "Tish, let me call you. I don't know what all this will entail."

I saw concern sweep over Mia's face. Looking toward her I called her name, "Mia, hang tight. Let me handle it, okay? I'll help him be out of your life forever."

"What if something goes wrong?"

"I'll call you, if there are any problems, I'll call, I promise!" Mia gently hugged and thanked me.

I turned my attention to Tish once more knowing how she is. "Give me a chance and I'll make sure he's gone."

Tish responded, "I know you will." With that Tish and Mia made their way to her car.

I spent the night pondering my foolhardy decision to become personally involved. Why didn't I insist she go to the police? Problem solved! But I knew why, I wanted to kill him. He was a predator and he was not going to change. Formulating a well-thought-through plan and executing it was time consuming. Time I didn't have for this one. I would have to act first to keep him from going on the lam. I could not let him escape but what I was contemplating would be far chancier than what I had done previously. To make matters worse, no sensory perceptions were guiding me this time, just the natural feelings of anger and a desire to rid the world of another perp. To further complicate my thought process my target this time was not a convicted sex offender but a hearsay offender. I would have to tread lightly.

I decided it would be better to arrive at the front door unannounced than to call ahead. If he was still there he might try to hide or run and that wasn't one of my solutions to the problem. Arriving at his house I pulled up in plain view of his front door. It was a small ranch-style home with a living-room front window. My persistence at ringing the doorbell paid off when I heard him unlock the door and open it a smidgeon. The door moved easily as I nudged it with my foot. Macon was walking away with his back toward me when he grumbled, "What do you want?"

"I just want to talk for a bit."

Stillness filled the air as he ignored my request. I moved to a couch and sat patiently. Macon wandered in circles around the house for a few minutes; it seemed much longer. He appeared disheveled and anxious. His eyes showed signs of a lack of sleep and were filled with fear. He was moving rapidly from room to room looking for something but it was obvious he didn't know what. He was lost. Occasionally he picked up something and jammed it into a suitcase that lay open on the coffee table before me. I made attempts to calm him for the better part of an hour and offered to drive him to wherever he needed to go. I wanted him to know I was there to help.

Mia had taken her car, which was his only form of transportation. With no place to go and very little pocket cash to get there, he sat on an opposing couch and began to cry. He admitted to me what had happened with Barbie but spared me the worst details. It was probably nothing more than curiosity but I wanted to know, why? At first he shrugged his shoulders, unable to form a viable answer but everyone knew why they acted the way they did. As I sat patiently he slowly began to unravel the clues. The long and short of it was simple, he blamed his parents. Both his parents had utilized Macon and his two siblings in sex orgies with other adults. He said he had two sisters who were engaged in drugs and prostitution. He credited their behavior, as well as his own, to the abuse inflected on them by his parents. He recounted vividly one night how a visitor clamped a vise grip on his finger and squeezed until blood came out from underneath his fingernail. Then the sadistic visitor sexually assaulted him while his parents were present. I would have to know more about this. If it was true there were a few more people I'd like to kill.

"Macon, how could you turn around and do the same sort of thing to another child?"

At first he made some excuses how it wasn't the same as what happened to him. Then breaking down again he cried out, "I hate it! I'd rather kill myself than do the same thing to another kid."

That bothered me. Most people by now would be sympathetic—not me, he was lying. In fact, nothing indicated he had tried to stop himself at all. Contrary to his feelings, the feelings he was now sharing with me, he'd gone out of his way to devise a plan to damage Barbie's innocence. There was something egomaniacal with this line he was giving me and I was not buying it. Macon continued to stumble through a maze of half-truths and distorted thoughts, unable to accept responsibility for what he did. I knew he knew why, he just couldn't admit it. He eventually composed himself, washed his face and combed his hair.

"My mother passed away while I was in jail."

I, of course, thought, one down, and two to go, but kept my wits about me and my comments to myself.

"My dad lives about an hour's drive away."

"Do you ever see him?"

"Not often, but we get along okay."

"Is that where you want to go?"

"I'd go to my sisters, they live together, but there won't be any room. My dad lives alone, there's plenty of room for me there." Macon was now looking more relieved.

"I'll take you to your dad's if you want?"

Macon paused briefly before answering, "Sure, that'll give me some time to get some things worked out before I go."

"Where are you going?"

I saw Macon's eyes dart around the room like a con man checking to see if anyone else could hear him, "I'm not sure but it'll be far from here." How noble on his part, I thought. He told Mia Australia; it's all part of the game. Oh, he'll flee the state. He'll end up in California or Florida or somewhere like that doing the same thing he did here. And what's this about his father, the person he said was responsible for him being the way he is. I don't know what to believe.

"Doesn't it bother you, knowing what he did and allowed others to do to you and your sisters?"

Macon replied in a soft voice, "Yes, but he's still my father and it was a long time ago. When I was in jail, he was the only one who came to visit. He put money on my books so I could buy things I needed. He's always been there for me."

"Macon, if it works for you to stay at your dad's house, just lie low for a while and get your ducks lined up before you go."

He nodded in agreement knowing he would have to put a plan together. Macon was still on parole—if he ran, he violated his parole and would be returned to jail if caught. The drive passed quickly as he rehashed details of his and his sisters' early family life. I was nauseated by what I heard because on some level there was truth in there. Walter would get to the bottom of it.

My plan would expand in scope and difficulty if Macon's story rang true. Regardless of the mitigating factors that jurors took into account, I was not forced to consider them. Namely, Macon was absolutely to blame for what happened to Barbie. I was not conflicted between right and wrong in this case, only saddened.

We reached a shack of a house Macon called his father's home. We pulled onto an overgrown path of a driveway that led to a lean-to roof off the house. An eerie tree-branch canopy covered the roadway that hid the house from view. The house was dark and foreboding. I immediately felt uncomfortable here. A single light appeared as the front door opened. The small stature of a man could be seen peering out. I assumed it was Macon's father, since he had mentioned the old man lived alone. As Macon came around the front of the car the old man invited us in straight away. As we entered the door, Macon introduced me to his father, Phil Payne. I extended my hand in greeting and followed Phil and Macon inside; the house was as shabby inside as it was outside.

Phil appeared much older than his stated age. His beard was gray and straggly, and his hair had been shaved to a crew cut. He looked emaciated and smelled of rotting clothes soaked with perspiration. His denim pants and a once white T-shirt had given way to various stains of brown and yellow a long time ago.

I sat with Macon and Phil in the dimly lit front room. Macon wasted little time explaining what had occurred with Mia and Barbie. This time he went to greater lengths with the sordid details. I watched closely for his father's reaction. Phil became restless. His eyes darted back and forth from Macon to me. Macon confronted Phil, "Dad, it was the same things you did to all of us kids." Phil never raised an objection to what Macon said. His only response to any of it was, "I don't remember." As Macon talked, blackened shadows formed in the hallway's recesses, I could hear them groaning and see them reaching outward toward us. I became tense, wanting to engage these apparitions as they slowly crept into the living room. A white blinding light appeared from behind me. My reaction must have been noticeable as Macon and Phil gave pause to their conversation and cast a glance in my direction. Destiny stood in the room, her arm outstretched toward the hall and not a shadow in sight. Macon, smiling, asked, "Are you falling asleep?" I apologized. It seemed like the quickest way out rather than explain what I saw. Not that any of them would have believed me.

As Macon continued his conversation it turned from accusation to planning. Macon was dead set on leaving. Getting up the money to go was the big thing.

"Macon, why don't we get some rest tonight and hit it fresh tomorrow," I said. "We'll have better ideas if we can sleep on it." In all honesty, I was biting at the bit, the place gave me the heebie-jeebies and I was glad to escape.

It was at this point I realized the truth to the adage, "The family that preys together, stays together." Macon and Phil were two peas in a pod, preying on society. I also realized I was getting a bargain price on this kill, so to speak, two for the price of one. Preparations for a well-executed project usually took weeks. To pull this off, I only had days.

I fell into bed exhausted. My mind was turning a hundred miles an hour. How to do it? When should I strike? I've killed before and felt nothing. What would I feel this time? Would it be harder? Did both deserve to die? If so, who did Walter kill first? Where were the voices that help guide me? There were too many what-ifs to plan for and too many questions demanding an answer.

Mia was eager to hear if Macon had left. I related some aspects of our discussion but I seriously doubted he would be able to come up with the funds to make it happen. I mentioned Phil and Macon were planning a less costly move to Canada which seemed to please Mia. She continued her clear message that she never wanted to see him again; I felt confident she never would. Further, after she was sure he had left the country she planned to petition for divorce. That was perfect.

I kept daily contact with Macon, driving out to visit him. He was growing more anxious to leave. I was growing more anxious to kill him.

"Can I catch a ride with you?" Macon asked.

"Sure" I answered "Where to?"

Macon had secured a vehicle. He didn't tell me the details of how he came by it but his plan was to get it roadworthy for a long trip. Phil had warned

Macon not to mention to anyone where they were planning to go. My time for action was growing shorter by the minute. I took Macon to his sisters' home where he picked up an old station wagon. I followed him back to Phil's house then hung out while Macon worked on the car.

Not only did Phil look old and worn down but his house and property mirrored his appearance. On the property, brush had taken over what was a small field. The property had been fenced at one time with hog wire fencing, some of which was still visible amidst the brush and attached to trees along the field perimeter. Twenty yards out from the house sat an old-fashioned river-rock well. It was characteristic of decades earlier when this patch of ground was viable. It was complete with the rotting remnants of a water bucket tied to what was left of the cross member. I was inquisitive and asked Phil about it to which he replied, "Hardly any water ever in it. It's bone dry now. Too many people pumping water out of the ground around these parts." Stacks of old bleached plywood and various size boards were leaning up behind the house and piles of firewood dotted the backdrop. To add to this tinderbox, summer's heat had dried the brush brittle.

Macon was making frequent trips from Phil's to his sisters' trailer house. He was liquidating property he and his father could sell using his sisters' place for their yard sale. Macon, trying to be cautious in my presence, mentioned to Phil they had cleared nearly everything out that they wanted to get rid of. Keeping tabs on their progress and advancing my project were paramount.

While Macon was busy with the yard sale I had plenty of opportunity for small talk with Phil. "Phil, I know you're not telling anyone where you're going and that's a good way of doing it. Breaking all family ties for just you and your son must be hard?"

Somehow this question triggered an unexpected response. Phil spoke frankly with me. "I have to make it up to my boy. I did a lot wrong to him and his sisters."

"Are you talking about what Macon brought up about being used for sex orgies?"

He fell silent and gazed toward his backyard. He walked slowly to the rock well as I followed close by. We stood together looking into the well. Phil cleared his throat. "I was strung out on booze and drugs. Twenty years of booze and drugs." Typical excuse, I thought, and meaningless! After pausing for a moment Phil continued, "I just couldn't stop it. I wanted to. I just couldn't. It didn't happen all the time, just sometimes." Once or a hundred times, I thought, what's the difference. I was convinced without a shadow of a doubt he needed to die. He might not be able to sexually abuse a child anymore because of his health or age. Maybe he was no longer a threat to society. I was killing him for what he'd already done. He was responsible for the damage he did to at least three children and I suspect more, although that was never clear. I couldn't stomach listening to him any longer or I'd kill him right then. "See you guys tomorrow, Phil." I walked to the car while Phil stood near the rock well gazing into the void.

I stopped in to say a quick hello to Macon at his sister's place. Macon said the sale was going well and he planned to work it straight through and move as much as he could in the next day or two. That signaled to me it was becoming a now-or-never situation.

Monday rolled around and as expected Macon headed to his sisters' place. I gave it about fifteen minutes before pulling into Phil's driveway.

I heard Phil holler through the open door, "Macon's at the girls' place."

"That's okay, Phil; I wanted to see if you wanted to sell that ol' rock well. I'd like to have it, unless you've got other plans for it?"

I could see Phil at the door scratching his chin and thinking.

"Well, let's see."

Phil smiled and led the way to the backyard. Leaning up against the well, he said. "You've been a good friend to my boy, how about free?" Unfortunately it was a deal I'd have to pass on. Phil didn't own the property and it wasn't his to sell; besides he had a use for it after all. Thumper crashed into the base of his skull. I swung the steel pipe again and again as Phil lay out cold against the well. I don't know if it killed him then or if the plunge headfirst to the base of the well did him in but I was certain he was finished. I really didn't care as long as he was dead. I leaned over the well and watched for any signs of life but there was none. It was a productive morning already and it had just started.

I drove to meet Macon at the yard sale. When I pulled up Macon had just about finished loading his car with the remnants of the sale. He gave his sisters a couple leftover items he didn't want to take with him and said his goodbyes.

"Hey, I'll follow you home and help with the items in your car."

"Thanks," Macon replied. "If there's something you want, it's free." What a giving family. My dad used to tell me, "Doing good is its own reward." That's what I was all about; doing good for good's sake.

I chatted briefly with his sisters until he finished sorting the trash he wanted to keep from the trash he planned to leave. After a few minutes he had finished his task and jumped in the wagon.

"Let's go."

I nodded to him and addressed the girls with one parting statement.

"Macon's other car is in better shape. More than likely he'll take it when he goes."

"What other car? I thought he only had the station wagon."

"Trust me; he'll be well taken care of." The gullible girls wanted to believe everything would work out for the best. As we talked, both sisters made comments that they knew what was up, at least to some degree, and that Phil and Macon were leaving for an undisclosed destination. I was satisfied it would be awhile before they became concerned. I jumped in my Avenger and followed Macon to Phil's house.

We pulled off into the dry and dusty drive leading to the house. Macon was already out of his car when I pulled up behind him. He walked to the back of the wagon and opened the tailgate. I followed with my Glock neatly concealed next to my side. If need be I was ready for action. Macon pointed to where he wanted to stack the items then entered the house looking for Phil. I'd moved a couple items from the car when Macon emerged from the house. He didn't say anything but with a puzzled look on his face, proceeded to the overgrown backyard and field. I followed a short distance behind as he ventured out farther into the field.

I continued behind a safe distance so as not to cause him alarm. From the corner of the house the well area was a twenty-yard shot, one that I had practiced many times. I lifted my left hand up for a brace as I took aim. Macon was making his way toward the rock well all the time looking toward the tangled wood and brier. Thuup! The first shot struck him in the back. I approached quickly, Thuup. Thuup. The next two shots blew blood and brain matter out onto the ground.

This was a nasty mess, not the way I wanted to work. I pulled Macon up and dropped him in the well. It was early evening and I would have a majority of the night to apply the cosmetics as needed. I had brought a bag of lime to pour on the bodies to minimize any smell of decomposition if the larger plan didn't work out effectively.

The pairs of latex gloves worn for both kills were tossed in the well. Trace forensic evidence that might be in the gloves would soon burn. A woodshed stood near the back of the house. Some gnarly old chunks of wood not fit for the small woodstove in the house were piled alongside the shed. I carried a dozen chunks to the well to conceal the bodies and poured an accelerator of old fuel and oil on them. Black smoke rose from the well but the bonfire was concealed.

The ground was dry and hard. Boot impressions were difficult to see but I had been in the house many times and that was a forensic concern. I scooped up any visible blood splatter and used a piece of brush to whisk the ground to cover my actions. Next I busted up a few pieces of the old plywood and put down the well. The glue in the plywood made for a hot fire. The smoke turned to a light gray as the big gnarly chunks turned into deep burning coals. This would be an all-night babysitting job and maybe the next day too.

My schedule allowed for me to make a phone call or two so I began with Mia. I kept it short and sweet, "He's gone."

She sounded sad. "Do you know where?"

"No, and I don't want to know."

"What if the parole officer comes around looking for him, what do I say?"

"First, don't mention me at all, Mia. If you want to tell them he left you or whatever that's up to you but don't involve me. I've done my part."

"Okay," she muttered.

She might not have been happy with her decision to put him out of her life but it was a decision she could never go back on now.

I slipped by the sisters' home and let them know Macon and Phil had left. They were pleased Macon got away without any problems. They couldn't care less about their father.

"The police will probably come around looking for Macon. If you're smart you'll let it end then and there with 'We don't know where he is and don't expect to hear from him.' Don't even mention me; I've helped him all I can."

They were both prostitutes and druggies. They were used to contact with cops and not talking. They agreed it was the best course of action. I promised to bring the station wagon back from their dad's house since I knew they didn't ever visit him. That was fine, they said.

I parked my Avenger about a quarter mile from Phil's place and walked the rest of the way to the house. Wearing my latex gloves, I emptied the wagon of all the belongings and placed them inside the home. I shuttled the car to the sister's trailer the next evening, arriving about ten minutes before the taxi would arrive. I'd arranged for a cab to pick me up at eight o'clock. The sisters were either gone or asleep; in any case, no one came out of the trailer so I left the keys in the ignition and had the cabbie drop me at a driveway leading to Phil's house. Under the cover of darkness I walked back to the Avenger and it was off to stoke the fires.

How long can someone be missing before it is noticed? Reclusive people like Phil or me, probably a long time. Macon's parole officer might discover him missing after a couple months and issue a warrant, maybe. His soon-to-be ex-wife was glad he was "missing." If he was a no-show for court, the divorce was automatic. The sisters were happy he had slipped through the cracks and was making his way to the Canadian border. They were not going to raise a concern that might impede his getaway. There was nothing for the media to sensationalize if it was discovered they were missing.

Just a couple more things to take care of and I'd feel better about my involvement. Phil's house wasn't Phil's, it was a rental. The landlord posted an eviction notice on the door. It wasn't a month later that all the worldly possessions Phil and Macon had were being loaded into a trailer. My guess was it was headed for the dump.

The rainy season began in September. I drove by the house one last time. It looked like a bunch of hippies had moved in. Throwbacks from the sixties complete with tie-dyed T's, long hair, and that sort of thing. Any evidence that might have been there was contaminated so badly it would hold little value, except perhaps for two charred bodies in the well. As long as the bodies weren't discovered, I was in the clear. No crime was suspected, other than Macon's skipping his parole requirements.

I felt good about what I had done, although those that fail to understand will consider me horrible. "You killed people you befriended." I did no such thing. I was never their friend nor were they mine. I'd done what I set out to do, dispose of the worst kind of criminals and escape detection.

I kept tabs on Mia to oversee any interest that might arise over Macon for skipping the country. As I was wrapping this up I decided to swing by and check in with Mia. She told of a parole officer who stopped by. Seemed he was interested in the details of Macon's leaving the state. The officer was aware of the filing for divorce and asked for a call if Macon contacted her. Mia produced a business card from another officer from the Multnomah County sheriff's department. Detective Brandon A. Ware was investigating missing persons as part of some type of criminal task force.

Mia said, "I told him the truth." What truth! I thought.

Mia went on after a short pause, "I told him he ran from the state and was never coming back because he didn't want to go back to prison."

"Did you mention me?"

"I didn't talk about anyone but Macon," Mia said as tears began to well up in her eyes.

"Okay, okay," I responded, giving her a hug and reassuring her it was the right thing to do.

A flatfoot snooping around for a missing person, a task force for missing persons, seems strange to me. I never heard of such a thing. But then again, I live in a world filled with strange things. Apparitions and premonitions I know to be true that guide my destiny and bolster my courage.

I decided to make a quick trip to the sisters' home and see if Detective Ware had made an appearance there. With their past criminal history they were not likely to warm up to answering questions from Ware. Arriving at their trailer it was clear they had moved out. Where to? I could trace them down, I suppose, but why? It was time to leave it alone and get back to the work at hand. As Walter would say, "There are other fish to fry!"

Chapter 9

There is no greater fulfillment than hunting a human predator that is equally armed with cunning and intelligence. Once you have done so, you will never care for anything less.
—Walter

Growing up on a ranch had taught me the value of game trails when moving through dense brush and trees on Oregon hillsides. Every couple of days, my chores included saddling the horse and checking on cattle and fence line. Growing up on a working ranch I learned the natural cycle of life, living, and survival. Understanding animal behavior, both wild and domestic, was a skill taught mostly through observation and experience.

Game trails were cut across the terrain over decades, perhaps centuries, by one animal following another back and forth to food and water. It was not uncommon to see tracks of deer and other wild creatures after a rain or in the soft dust ridges of a trail. They also served as camouflage for predators to stalk and ambush their prey.

Outdoor enthusiasts, as well as predators, use urban biking and hiking trails pretty much the same way animals use game trails. I can't begin to count the number of violent criminal and sexual offenses that occur each year on urban game trails. Despite what is commonly believed about the safety of bike trails; statistics tell a different story. Heavily wooded and isolated areas along these trails cater to predators and harbor a far greater risk than most people think.

It bugged me that nearly eleven years before a predator had been working in my backyard, so to speak. I remember thinking to myself at the time I'd like to run into him in the act and put him down like a rabid dog. All I needed was a little justification and I could whack him, or so I thought. I now know that would never have happened. I wasn't ready then. A lesson I learned the day Lewis Pohle crossed my path. In Pohle's case every opportunity presented itself and I didn't cap him. An exercise in futility as it turned out when he was released seven months later for time served while awaiting trial. If I had pulled my Roscoe and plugged him, I would not carry deep inside the feelings of guilt that I do for the elderly woman Pohle violated. Now my only solace is the fact Pohle will never rape again, thanks to Walter.

My recollection of a bike trail predator first surfaced eleven years ago after a middle-aged woman riding a bicycle narrowly escaped an attack. Her description of the attacker was a young man in his twenties, light brown skin, medium-length straight black hair, five feet ten inches to six feet and 160 to180 pounds. Soon after this event news reporters followed up with a second report that evidently occurred a week prior to the first one making the headlines. It too was a failed attempt on another would-be victim along a bike trail. Coincidence? Not likely.

People love their freedom and hate to let anything interfere in their lives. I understand that, but it is more than laws that take away our freedom. Predators, through fear, take away our freedom as well. Park or trail warnings have little effect on people's safety; only a few folks take heed and then not for long.

When the story broke it was the talk of Portland. Some talked about it out of fear, others talked about it out of concern, but few were dissuaded to give up biking and hiking the trails. A few days passed before the attacker struck again. This time he was successful. Similar descriptions emerged and police were now asking for the public's help: "Call Crimestoppers or your local police if you see someone on bike trails that matches the description." I have to give it to the Portland Metro Crimes Bureau—they were hot after this guy. Now with everyone alerted and watching, the fourth attack still occurred. This time it was a sixteen-year-old girl and once more he was successful. He was becoming an effective predator.

Police were quick to ensure that the local newspapers made a big front-page splash when the attacker was captured. Peace and safety had returned to our community, as if there were only one predator in Portland. The attacker, twenty-year-old Morey Leicester, was found less than a mile from the attack, where he was living in a tent.

It was no surprise when the media didn't cover Morey's plea deal. It was old news. He served nine years in jail as a first-time offender and due to his predatory nature he was listed as a Class III offender on Oregon's sex offender registry.

When people rely on laws to protect them they fail to understand the law. Laws were designed to punish offenders, but more commonly now; they are used in an attempt to rehabilitate. They don't protect anyone. Sexual offender registries serve as nothing more than false hopes to appease society's call for justice. No perp will be stopped from committing another sexual offense just because his name is on a registry. Never! It's a false sense of security.

At home my attention was drawn to his file. The sensory perceptions caused me to feel the fear and pain experienced by the victims. I could hardly remain sitting upright from the agony it brought upon me. I winched backwards and heard the noise like a roaring wave of voices crying out, "His time." The feelings of hopelessness subsided as I refocused my attention on the clippings I'd compiled on Leicester. He topped my short list of candidates for execution.

I'd known for some time of apartment buildings being used to house a very special clientele. Some metro areas purchased more than services of a halfway house. They went the extra mile with taxpayer funds to permanently house sex offenders at no cost to the criminal. Talk about discrimination. Bank robbers, drug runners, and murderers didn't get the same freebee—why did sex offenders? Some probably thought this was a great idea. I didn't. It was another case of misguided justice. The liberals argued it was a better solution than having them living in residential areas. Walter argued that they shouldn't be alive at all. That's Walter for you.

I learned of these apartment–halfway houses by noting a number of sex offenders being released to a single address. I'd made it my business to know where complexes like these were located. I referred to these apartments as high-risk locations. I'd spent hours observing and documenting behaviors around these facilities.

Morey was a resident of such a facility. The complex sat in an older Portland neighborhood near the Beaverton and Interstate 5 confluence. It wasn't a low-rent district per se, just an older part of the city with many well-built middle-class-type dwellings. The twelve-apartment two-story facility appeared to model a military barracks of the early fifties from the outside. It was an unlocked halfway house that utilized a pass system for its residents to come and go. Not exactly freedom but nonetheless a pretty standard operating procedure, monitored in a very substandard way. Still, it wasn't going to be easy getting close to the target.

Walter sported a little heavier jacket due to the lower temperatures, normal for November in the Pacific Northwest. The plan was to make quick work of this project. Christmas was just around the corner and I wanted to get into the spirit of the season—what could bring more joy to the world than the fresh December kill of Morey Leicester? His victims would undoubtedly be ecstatic.

It was necessary to make a positive identification of my target. It would be boots on the ground, tailing residents, until a positive identification could be established on Leicester. My assumption was that with the passing of a decade, Morey's appearance hadn't changed enough to make it difficult to determine whom to stalk.

Each morning, Monday through Friday, residents gathered outside at eight o'clock to smoke. I didn't know if Leicester was a smoker, but I'd start there trying to make a positive ID. My vantage point for this observation was an old red brick Christian church. There was no designated parking lot, just a small dirt field and curbside parking around the church. It was easy to blend into these surroundings with my Avenger. A few of the cars hadn't moved in weeks, others came and went frequently. Most important was the view. It was a clean, straight shot at the back corner of the halfway house where the "smoking circle" assembled.

There were a couple of very dark-skinned men that could be eliminated as the target immediately. The other guys, well, I needed a closer look. Not much activity went on around the complex on the outside of the building. When daily passes were issued residents began to filter out. One man caught my attention as he left the compound walking slowly down the sidewalk toward a corner convenience store. My Avenger rolled in quietly to the rear parking area. I sat for a few minutes and watched the front door. With my .40-caliber strapped under my jacket I made my entry to check things out. I instantly came face to face with the man I was following. His now visible red blazer caught my eye first. A fast glance at the name tag revealed his name as Ryan. The arrest records I had on file showed Leicester at five feet eleven inches. Ryan wasn't any more than five feet six inches. It was back to the drawing board after a hot cup of coffee.

Driving back to my observation area I passed two fellows exiting the complex gate. Both had potential. They made their way to a bus stop and waited about fifteen minutes before a ten-thirty bus arrived. In this urban jungle buses made frequent stops and if you tried to tail one you might be picked out by a discerning eye. I decided it best to lie back as far as possible and try to pick up the scent later. I followed loosely, keeping the bus in sight. At its major hub downtown the bus emptied out before I was able to park and watch. Tomorrow would be another day.

At home I kicked back and watched the evening news. Sometimes I wondered why it really agitated me when I heard one report after another of murder, rape, gang activity, home invasions—man there was no end to it. I was ready to turn it off, remote in hand, when an interview with a sheriff's department detective caught my attention. Sergeant Brandon A. Ware was investigating a homicide of some nature but I didn't catch the details. My interest was stirred with this older-looking gentleman with a drab suit jacket and matching tie. There was something familiar about him. Something I recognized. I searched my thoughts momentarily before the light came on; this was the "Missing Persons Task Force" officer who had come to see Mia Payne. My interest now piqued. Ware was a homicide detective. The MCSD must be stretched awfully thin if they had him looking for a missing person.

Early in the morning I renewed my observation of the apartment. I looked over the smoking group closely to see if I could ID Leicester. Some of the men wore hoodies pulled up, others had skull caps on. To make this guy I would have to get up close. I drove about a block south of the bus stop, parked, then strolled to the Plexiglas bus stop to wait. Like clockwork one of the men from the previous day approached the waiting area. "Hi" I chirped. The fellow nodded in my direction.

"It's my first time taking the bus here, do you ride it much?"

"Yah, some," he replied.

"Is it usually on time?"

"Always."

I already knew this was not Leicester. From an old description I had and a more recent picture, this guy didn't even come close to matching.

"Any sites to see along the way?" I asked.

"With a sigh he answered, "Trees, lakes, and parks, that's about it."

We continued the casual conversation over the next few minutes. I pressed the point of finding a secluded area along the route where I might enjoy my privacy. Eventually he offered up something of value. "One place along the way is probably good. I got a friend, Mo, he goes there, I guess he likes it."

"Point it out when we pass it, will you?"

"Yeah, sure."

I sat back and waited for the bus. If Mo found a nice secluded place, he was up to no good, assuming Mo was Morey.

My new acquaintance pointed out an old park a couple miles from the halfway house. It was imperative I check it out before the recon proceeded further.

The park sat to the north side of the roadway overlooking an undeveloped hillside. The well-nourished fir trees in the park were so dense, sunlight scantly penetrated through them. My reconnaissance of the park showed it was little else than a nature trail through the heavily wooded area. No playground equipment, facilities, courts, or ball fields. By park standards it was small, encompassing about a city block. Its main feature was a winding pathway dotted with park benches. My probing here convinced me Mo would like a park like this.

My focus changed to where my stakeout would be centered on, the park's only bus stop. Early the next morning I made my way to the site for the observation. I eased my Avenger up to a prime location with a clear view of the bus stop. I awaited with anticipation the arrival of the first bus of the day.

Casually sipping coffee I perused the local interest stories. Nothing really caught my eye until I spotted "Police Eye Vigilante Killings" written by my old friend Harold Horn. It was a rehash of a recent murder with Horn's speculation on the motive. He always fancied himself a detective and this was his way of living it out. The problem that faced me was that he was very close to the truth.

I sat very uneasy as I read the article. Horn quoted Detective Ware in an interview on the recent killing, "We are looking into the possibility of this murder being linked to other recent homicides." What others, I thought, as I slipped down a little lower in my car seat.

How was this recent murder Detective Ware was working on being linked to other killings? Was it my work he referred to? I suppose I should be thankful they were on the wrong track on the latest homicide but it offended me they might attribute my work to someone else. Hopefully, they weren't looking to hang another murder on my collar, one I didn't do. At times I wished I had an inside ear to police activities. I'd like to know if they've turned up any other perps I've eliminated or connected the dots to the Washington projects. I feel myself becoming more nervous and glancing out my car window in all directions. Not because I'm afraid of being caught; because I haven't killed enough yet.

Horn went through the recent crime emphasizing what was apparent to him to be motive. The man killed in the Portland suburbs was a sixty-year-old retired Catholic priest, according to Horn. The priest had a known history of allegations of sexually abusing children in his parish. He was defrocked and sent away for treatment but never charged with the multiple rumored crimes. The motive in Horn's mind was clearly "revenge." He based this loosely on the historical allegations and the fact someone emptied a full magazine into the priest. Had I known about this man of the cloth before his killer got to him, I might have been the responsible party they were looking for. It was the end of the article that had my curiosity the most. In his interview with Detective Ware he stated he had "a person of interest" they were looking for. Was it me? Horn said it was possibly a deeply religious male in his early twenties. I can only hope they buy Horn's profile, I'll be in the clear.

It was after 5 p.m. before I knew it. I spent many hours today thinking this current project through. It wasn't a smart move to kill this guy while the heat was up, but the alternative was to wait and see what happened. I could change projects, maybe cross state lines and hit somebody in a new area. That would take time out of my busy schedule to devise. And that means time was being wasted. The value I saw in this "person of interest" was a more confusing picture for police. I really didn't want the new shooter to get credit for what I had accomplished. On the other hand, if they picked this shooter up, it'd cover my tracks for a while.

Three days passed and I was still perched watching the little park from my car. The main traffic in the park was bike riders and joggers, and then not many. This was a perfect spot for criminal activity. All predator animals selected their prey—so did predator people. People got a false sense of security because predators didn't constantly attack. That was true, because they were like animals. They attacked when they needed to feed. It was not every day or all the time but when they struck, their prey would be isolated and defenseless.

Predator animals worked game trails because their selection was convenient just like bike paths and park trails. They didn't expose themselves to unnecessary risks to bring down their prey. That behavior pattern was never more evident than with human predators that had been to the Big House for a previous selection and conviction. They were far more cautious and cunning the next time around and there was always a next time.

Harold's article set off a barrage of media articles on vigilantism over the next few days. The reporters were singing to the choir and the people were eating it up. The media were fickle, not really supporting the idea of vigilantism but not dispelling it either. A lineup of psychologists and various disciplines in therapy were adding motive and rationale to the frenzy. Criminal rights advocates were putting in their two cents, readers were writing letters to the editor, everyone had something to say or add; all very sensational—and useless.

I was at my park stakeout for a week and the fervor had not let up. Most of the media opinions didn't amount to a hill of beans to me but I had to be concerned. Joe Citizen might start looking around and report a suspicious person. It could be a lucky break for Detective B.A. Ware. It was something to be considered. Besides, sitting here at the park wasn't paying off. I started to make a plan B for this project. At home I laid out the file, information, and notes I had collected in some hopes of discovering a new or overlooked clue that would get things moving. The news flashed its lead story, "Twenty-one-year-old held in connection with priest's murder." The story was scanty on the news hour. The alleged assailant, Darren Deed, was believed to have known the victim and was apprehended attempting to flee the Portland area.

No way! This was the "person of interest" Ware was looking for? This snotty-nosed kid was all amateur. The only possible connection with any of my work was the victims were child molesters. It wouldn't take long for Ware to sort this out.

Another week passed before I would get a break. The media had put this story behind them and moved on to newer happenings. As for Portland communities, the threat of vigilantes taking the law into their own hands was swept away by Deed's arrest. Street gangsters battling over drug turf topped the headlines once again and the media were off and running in another feeding frenzy.

I had a lot of respect for Detective Ware. He'd been around. You got the sense he was old school about law enforcement. His interview answers with the media gave the impression he was pretty tight lipped and serious. There was no room for questions he chose not to answer and he did not elaborate on questions he did answer. His press release was exactly that, a release of information he wanted out, that's all. I'd like an opportunity to meet him. On the other hand, it was best I didn't.

Monday was a classic fall day. Portland was well known for its wind and rain. Doubtful anyone would use the park for a stroll on such a blustery day. The transit bus pulled up as scheduled and a lone figure dressed for foul weather pulled a hood up over his head as he exited. He proceeded into the park as the bus pulled away. I waited a few minutes to watch for any unusual behavior. As I prepared to face the elements the hooded person turned around from the height of a small knoll and appeared to look about. It was a fast scan and then he was on the move again over the hill and out of sight. When he turned in my direction I had him framed in a pair of binoculars; a quick glimpse of the subject's face and I was 90 percent sure this was my target. I flanked the man's movement staying well hid by the hill, bushes, and trees. Most people watched behind for movement and toward the front in the direction they were moving but didn't watch their flanks closely. It was there on the flank I felt most comfortable.

I caught fleeting views as we moved through the park until he vanished from sight into the brush. I moved slowly in his direction, I wanted to see what he was up to. I dared not approach too closely for fear of blowing my cover. As I crept closer I heard rustling noises in the brush that I was unable to identify what was happening. I backed away slowly and took refuge in a thicket, squatted down to wait it out. Something was going on here and I was determined to investigate it.

Psychological time passes slowly. A minute can seem like an hour when anxiety interrupts the hands of time. My wristwatch showed fifteen minutes had elapsed since I concealed myself in the brush but the pounding rain made it seem much longer. I kept still as I watched the park visitor work his way through the brush to the pathway. I continued to watch until he was gone from sight. I decided it best to sit out the tailing and put my efforts into finding the reason for his visit. It's an instinct, nothing more, but instinct hasn't failed me yet; I rely on it heavily. I'm unable to explain why or how I can tell when I've seen something that is very wrong; a gift or a curse, I don't know.

I moved into the brushy area the mystery man had vacated a few minutes earlier and found with little difficulty the area he had rustled around in. The ground was heavily saturated from the rain but in one small area I could see a number of leaves showing a light brownish dryness mixed in with darker wet leaves. This area had recently been disturbed. Had I waited until later, the leaves would have been soaked and the area unremarkable. I probed the ground until I heard a sound of something crinkling under my latex-gloved fingers. With as little disturbance to the leaf cover as possible I slipped out a brown nylon ripstop stuff sack frequently used by backpackers to keep their gear dry. I carefully opened the bag revealing a revolver. Maneuvering the pistol in the bag I could see it had rounds in the cylinder.

I removed the rounds, placing them inside my coat pocket before rewrapping the gun and placing it back in the hole it came from. I scooped some leaves over it and left it much the way I'd found it and made my way back to my Avenger. My sixth sense told me this man and I were destined to meet, perhaps soon.

The weekend passed without any sign of the park visitor. Editorial comments were appearing in the newspapers concerning Deed and the defrocked priest he had allegedly killed. The media, being the bleeding-heart liberals they were, had Deed convicted of vigilantism in the public arena before the formal charges were levied. People wrote letters to the editor expressing their outrage at the epidemic of priests abusing children; very few letters were critical of Deed for taking the law into his own hands. It was another meaningless debate.

Anna Sasins, an independent feature writer, caught my eye. According to the newspaper profile, Sasins had extensively covered human-interest stories as an investigative reporter for some of the top newspapers in the Pacific Northwest. Unlike other writers that aligned on the side of liberals and denounced vigilantism, she focused on Deed's action as a result of a failed legal and religious system. Her point was clear and I was in agreement with her conclusion. The church organization protected itself—not the innocent child in their care. Mr. Deed, if guilty, was well within his rights. At least that's the way Walter saw it.

Friday morning rolled around and I began to second-guess my chances of making the park observation work out. The eleven-o'clock bus pulled up and a lone figure stepped off. The man moved quickly into the shaded park before stopping to look behind him. I could see it was Mo. I stepped from my Avenger with the Glock tucked under my jacket. With the moderator on it was easier to carry it short distances tucked away under an arm inside my jacket than fitting it into a holster. If opportunity knocked, I was ready to rock 'n roll.

I flanked his movement as before, this time with the intention of making a close encounter. Leicester moved into the brushy terrain as before, I made my approach. I could see him on his knees in the area of the hidden gun. Ten feet from him I stopped. I could tell he had heard my approach; he was still. I called out, "Leicester."

He fumbled for something between his feet then stood upright.

"Morey Leicester, step out here."

With his gun partially hidden behind his leg, he shouted nervously, "What do you want?"

I stepped through the brush while drawing my weapon; he quickly brandished his into an old fashioned Mexican stand-off. I stepped forward slowly and closed the gap between us. With our weapons nearly touching I heard the clicking noise of dry fire from his revolver.

I dropped the rounds from his revolver on the ground in front of him. "On your knees! On your knees! On your knees!" The command finally resonated and Morey whispered, "No." His gun fell to the ground behind him. "I'm sorry, it was a mistake." For what it's worth, I agree he's a sorry individual.

I'm not sure what mistake he was talking about, I suspect he made a lot of them but again I had to agree a mistake was made. For his crimes, he should have been locked in a dungeon and the key thrown away—he should not be walking the streets nine years later. I couldn't change what he had done but I could change the court's mistake and Morey's future.

Not that it made all that much difference to me but insincere contriteness mixed with a lot of begging for your life was always a nice touch. But, as I've said before, it didn't make any real difference.

"Did the women beg you to let them go?" He bowed his head and slowly shook it from side to side as memories ran through his mind. Now I know he understands my presence. "How about the teenage girl, what did she say? Did she beg you to let her go?" He didn't answer. I raised my voice, took a step closer, and demanded, "I want to know, did she beg you not to rape her? Did she?"

Morey's head sunk lower. His stare was distant as if reliving his victim's pleas.

A symphony of angelic voices began to cry out from above the treetop canopy. I knew it was time. Thuup, the .40-caliber ripped into his forehead. I placed three more rounds into his head making a bloody mess for crime scene investigators to contend with.

With the past couple of kills I had done my best to hide the bodies. Mo Leicester I left purposely where I killed him. I wanted him found with his gun near his side with his fingerprints all over it—a convicted predatorial multiple rapist who did his dirty work on urban game trails in the parks of Portland. The press would have a field day with it. They'd resurrect the history and cause concern in their own special way. Instead of charges, Deed would probably get a medal for ridding the world of the priest with a passion for young boys. Certainly, Deed was in line to gain God's favor.

From my actions the press would be quick to exonerate Deed as a serial killer. How could he be, he was locked up tighter than a drum. If Deed kept his mouth shut, he might walk a free man, you never know. If he got off, that was fine with me. I didn't hold revenge against him. He was violated and the perp got away with it. If Deed did kill the priest, he made two things perfectly clear—revenge is what every victim wants and he wanted to ensure it never happens again to anyone else. The priest would never harm another child just like Mo would never rape another girl. It was a 100 percent guarantee.

I didn't know what Morey was planning to do in a secluded area of the park with a handgun but statistically, the next time around, the victim would not have lived. It was something they learned when given a few years behind bars to think about the next time. In any case, he was dead. It didn't matter what he was going to do, Walter killed him for what he had done a decade before.

Back at my home I cranked up the wood-burning stove. A peace settled in as I warmed myself. I didn't have a Yule log or chestnuts to roast, just an old project file to burn. Things were shaping up to be a very merry Christmas after all.

Chapter 10

When the legal system failed, I factored myself in as a consequence.
That's what I was—a consequence.
—Walter

It has been said so many times after a tragic event occurs to a child at the hands of a parent, "It should be illegal for some people to have kids." I couldn't agree more. The problem, however, is it's impossible to know who should and who shouldn't have children ahead of a child abuse event. But it sure screams reasonable to me, once it has happened, such people lose their right to have kids. They simply can't be trusted with the life of another child.

Child abuse comes in many forms. Whether the psychiatric community identifies emotional abuse or neglect as the cause of abnormal behaviors or the religious community identifies the sin of sparing the rod and spoiling the child is all irrelevant to Walter. It is when I read of excessive physical abuse that involves violent torture or sexual abuse that it becomes my interest.

Over the past year and a half I've followed a case that my old friend Harold first reported on in his crime log at the time of arrest. Quickly forgotten about by most, I watched to see if justice would prevail. Feature writer Anna Sasins covered the story in historical depth. She profiled the family in a human-interest piece. Taking Horn's and Sasin's articles I sat back in my recliner and listening carefully to my thoughts, found a channel of communication I didn't fully understand, but the message was clear. A war horse of unnatural white stood before me with knighted vesture dipped in blood on the horn of the saddle. A voice beckoned me, "Adorn yourself and join in battle." To the voice I said, "Have I not engaged the enemy many times?" As the last words slipped from my lips, two dragons screamed in the distance. The voice cried, "Ride, hesitate not, for it is the dragon's time to die." Quickly removing the royal robe from its resting place, I draped the mantle over my shoulders and mounted the steed. The voice cried, "Ride, ride!" I could hear the echo of the command as my eyes opened in the comfort of my home. I was now sure legal justice would not prevail in the case.

The Medford, Oregon couple that Horn and Sasins wrote about was jailed for aggravated child abuse and child endangerment of their five-year-old daughter. One thing reporters know, the uglier the facts of a case, the more the readership. Horn was straightforward with the facts without the grotesque hype whereas Sasins looked for an angle to accentuate a specific point she wanted to make. Something she referred to in her writings as the "human interest" side of the story. As for me, I loathe the media's reporting. My preference would be to never have known such bizarre crimes occur, yet I immerse myself in articles of this nature. I may be a killer, but I don't kill innocent children. I kill for good, I don't kill the good; I'm good at it because I can do it without reservation.

Mona Lott was a drug-abusing whiny crack whore who wasn't able to take care of herself, let alone a child, but she had one regardless. She was the product of a well-to-do-family with a historical background. The Lott family had migrated from England to America before the colonies were formed and helped settle Virginia. By the time the War of 1812 rolled around they owned a large tobacco plantation and had a great deal of clout. From there the pioneering spirit took hold and they followed the sunset to the west coast. Mona's grandparents and parents enjoyed the benefits of the industrial revolution in California while Mona pursued being a junior pharmaceutical major near colleges rather than in them. Something went badly wrong with the gene pool when it came to Mona. Her parents said it was the drugs, but was it really? The question always prompts a second—which came first, the chicken or the egg?

Her live-in, off-and-on-again boyfriend, Owen "Icky" Moore was reportedly the biological father of their little girl, Vanessa. No one is quite sure how Icky got his nickname, only that he really revered its connotation. He, unlike Mona, came from a seedier environment. His parents were dysfunctional alcoholics that spawned a large family in Detroit, Michigan. His brothers and sisters, to their credit, rose above their upbringing and made something worthwhile of their lives. Icky took the path of least resistance. His siblings attended local schools in their neighborhood; Icky attended reform schools and similar institutions. For most of his teenage years he was incarcerated at youth facilities. At nineteen he could no longer be held as a juvenile and was released back into society. Sasins says she spoke with family members who described Icky as a bully who regularly got into fights with other kids. One sister complained it was impossible to keep a house cat with Icky around. He was incredibly cruel to animals, stabbing them with sharp sticks and choking them to death. They were not surprised to hear the law finally caught up with his cruelty.

Icky's lifestyle brought numerous run-ins with the law, mostly bar fights and trespassing beefs. He enjoyed hanging out at bars, picking up hookers, and drinking on somebody else's dime when he could intimidate them. He secured labor jobs working in residential construction. Something about his work habits or reliability always seemed to come up that caused him to be sent down the road.

At twenty-seven Icky met Mona, a skinny girl with low self-esteem, and seemingly a boatload of money. Mona's loving family enabled her lifestyle, making provisions for her every need. Her car and trailer house were bought and paid for by the Lott family. Her parents would have preferred her to live at their home but she was found to be untrustworthy and they thought it cheaper to pay her to stay away. At twenty-four she met the man of her dreams, Owen Moore. It was into this relationship a little girl was unfortunately born—bad luck for Vanessa, pure and simple. Mona and Owen never officially married; to do so would have cost them government freebees, but they were nonetheless in love.

Hospital records submitted as evidence during the trial helped piece together the first known facts of the case; however, there were previous injuries before the June 1999 visit that alerted hospital medical staff to the child abuse. Police and Child Protective Services acted promptly and took Vanessa from their home. This began an investigation that resulted in both Mona and Icky being jailed for inflicting injury on a child and child endangerment. Mona's parents, although sympathetic, could not bring themselves to post the hefty bail and Icky didn't have anyone who cared enough to admit they even knew him.

The defense team was headed up by none other than Ruben Darroe. Whoo, whoo! The big top was in town; let the circus begin. I remember well his shenanigans in the Hertz case with Lewis Pohle. It had become commonplace for this imaginative lawyer to exploit legal loopholes and make a mockery of the court proceedings. I felt it was my duty to follow this case and insure justice was served. With Darroe at the helm, it was likely I would have to mete out the final touches of punishment.

The little bit of graphic information I was privy to brought me great pain. It was literally physical pain that wrenched at my innermost being, only to be replaced by rage when the pain subsided. The thought of these two parents walking on the charges because of Darroe's trickery disturbed me in ways I'd never known before. In all likelihood I was already notably disturbed. When the legal system failed, I factored myself in as a consequence. That's what I was—a consequence.

Vanessa was savagely tortured at the hands of her parents. They were responsible for multiple bite scars on her torso, buttocks, and genitalia. I say "they" because there was plenty of fault and blame to go around. According to medical evidence reports, the bites she suffered mutilated her genitalia and caused permanent disfiguration of her breast area. She also bore signs of recent battery. Mona had taken Vanessa to a hospital emergency room because she was having difficulty breathing. This was Vanessa's first trip to a medical facility since she was three. Mona must not have been thinking clearly; the initial assessment alerted hospital staff to the physical abuse and started the wheels rolling. X-rays further revealed cracked ribs that explained the nature of the breathing problem. When Vanessa was asked about the scars and bruising, she would only say, Daddy. She was placed in the State's custody. Mona and Owen were jailed.

Mona held her tongue and refused to rat on Icky for the trauma Vanessa had endured. It was clear from her initial interview she was at minimum guilty of neglect. She allowed the little girl with severe wounds to go untreated and the abuse unreported; to my way of thinking she shared an equal if not greater guilt.

In court, Darroe raised concerns about Owen Moore's civil rights being trampled on and the excessive force used by arresting officers. In deposition Moore asserted his innocence by pointing out that Mona, during their on-and-off-again relationship, had other men in her home. He implied that in his absence, Mona herself might be responsible. Vanessa, for a five-year-old, was barely able to communicate. Mom, Dad, yes, and no trumped her vocabulary skills. Mostly she threw tantrums and uttered noises when in want or need. Court-appointed doctors concluded she was severely traumatized with impaired social skills for her age.

Criminal proceedings were delayed multiple times. Darroe and prosecutors jockeyed motions around and amended charges. There was psych testing and challenges to testing results followed by more psych testing. First break for

Darroe's case came after careful examination by court-appointed doctors who without reservation declared Mona not competent to stand trial. It is odd to me that various definitions of incompetence are in use because neither the legal system nor court-appointed experts can agree on a single meaning in the context of criminal law. The psychologist report found Mona "cognitively deficient, which impairs her ability to supervise, protect, and care for her child." She was in their opinion emotionally unstable and unable to participate in her own defense. Mona would not stand trial. She would be placed under mental health supervision which did not require hospitalization or further incarceration. She would, however, lose all custodial rights to Vanessa.

The second break came shortly afterwards in the form of a plea deal. What the State could prove beyond a reasonable doubt and at what expense became the pivotal points of the case. It was set to be a very costly trial, Darroe would see to this. Perhaps someday he'd pay for the harm he had done.

Prosecutors offered a single count of felony assault and battery on a child with a minimum of seven years incarcerated. It was a stiff sentence but Icky had history and it didn't play well for him. Justice was served or so the saying goes. Owen would serve at least two thirds of his sentence before being eligible for parole. I marked the date on a laundry list of names that I hoped to see again. Arguably justice had not been served. Owen Moore destroyed a life he helped create. It wasn't his right. Anything short of paying with his life was simply too lenient.

Icky had a nasty reputation for being cruel and inflicting pain. Mona knew he was ruthless and prone to violence, but she didn't care enough for herself or her daughter to change the scenario. She lacked something natural inside. Maybe her continuous drug abuse fried her wiring harness; I don't know and I don't care. It was no excuse. Mona was responsible in one way or another for all that had happened to Vanessa. If it were the drugs that made her a living zombie, then she bore the responsibility for taking the drugs in the first place. She needed to pay for a life destroyed. The shell of a human that was left as Vanessa was not at all who Vanessa would have or could have been. That is tragic.

Mona instantly qualified for social security now that she was "incompetent." She played the welfare role before. People like Mona didn't deserve to have a second child. Mona was still an unrepentant drug abuser. She would have no problem finding a needle-sharing sperm donor again. What bothered me the most about Mona was that she was remorseless. She had no compassion for her child. If she had she would have stopped trying to protect her lover long ago. I don't claim to understand the dynamics of someone like Mona. I don't have to understand to pull the trigger.

Mona was easy to locate. I felt she was comfortable in the Medford area where her circles of lowlife drug-seeking friends were, and I was right. Like most people she had a telephone; she listed it as M. Lott. No question in my mind it was her. The question really was how do I make contact? Maybe a straight-up call from Walter, but how would it go? "Hello, I'm Walter E. Goe and I'd like to schedule some time with you for an execution." No, that wouldn't work, even on someone as brain-dead as Mona! But an interview might, especially if was sprinkled with some cash.

Mona was not uneducated—she was, according to the psych doctors, mentally fried. She had swum in the pool of drugs for so long I was going to have to hurry in order to kill her before she did it herself. I placed a call the next day to Mona from the Southside mall just outside Portland.

"Hello," She answered.

"I'm calling for Mona Lott."

"This is Mona."

"My name is Walter E. Goe. I'm a feature news writer for a national news magazine. I would like to do an article on your mistreatment by the justice system."

As I was giving my sales pitch she interrupted, "Ah, I don't think so."

"Mona, I think your story is worth telling. You were not treated fairly and you should not have lost custody of Vanessa." Mona did not respond.

"Seriously, I'll pay two hundred dollars up front for your story. If my editor likes the workup, there'll be a big payoff for you when we publish it."

"What do I have to do?"

"I would like to keep this quiet and private until we have the story copy ready."

"Okay."

"I'm in Seattle, but I can fly in tomorrow, we can meet somewhere and put some ideas on paper."

"Okay, but I don't have a car to meet you."

"No problem. Is there somewhere close by, a city park or place you know well?"

"Kornbreads is a nearby buffet, we can meet there."

"Excellent, I'll give you a call when I get into town tomorrow, say, early afternoon if possible and we'll schedule a time for our meeting."

Mona replied, "Okay," and hung up the phone.

Of course I was in the Portland area since that's where I lived, not Seattle. Driving would take me a few hours at most. I called Kornbreads in Medford and asked for the address. I located a nearby hotel, The Privacy Inn, on Biddle

Road and booked a room for a couple of nights. The parking area was a horseshoe layout that wrapped around a small strip mall, Kornbreads, and the Inn.

It was early spring and temperatures were dropping into the low forties at night, warming to midfifties and sixties during the day. The weather allowed me to wear a turtleneck sweater, chino pants, penny loafers, and a light overcoat that went nicely with my homburg fedora that I wore slightly tilted to the left. As usual I shaved my goatee, had my hair trimmed neatly, dyed my hair a light brown and completed my disguise with black-framed glasses. All that was left to do was pack a few essentials for the trip, .40-caliber, tool box, latex gloves, and a change of clothing, just the essentials.

The next day I contacted Mona from a nearby gas station. I never use my cell phone on the go. Calls can be traced too easily when the police start snooping around a corpse. Mona sounded excited about our meeting and said she would be at Kornbreads around 3 p.m. Minutes before our scheduled meeting I pulled my Avenger into Kornbreads parking lot as far from the diner door as possible in a corner position. My intent was to watch for a lone female and note the direction from which she approached. I didn't know this diner; it might have outside security cameras in the parking area. No sense getting sloppy.

Less than ten minutes passed when Mona came walking up Morrow Road. After she entered the diner I waited another ten minutes before getting out of my car and heading for the front door.

I scanned the area for any security cameras inside that might be visible. Anyone who might notice would only assume I was looking for someone I knew. Mona was seated at a booth facing the door and saw the cue. She lifted her hand with her palm facing me in a simple gesture, I'm right here. I walked directly to the table and extended my hand as I inquired, "Mona?"

"Yeah."

"I'm Walter, very pleased to meet you."

We exchanged greetings and I sat down opposite her, opening my card case. An authentic-looking business card for a well-known magazine popped up. She took the card and gave it a casual onceover. I went into my spiel the moment she took the card.

"I want to make this as painless as possible."

She smiled and replied, "Okay."

Mona went through some of the history and the things Icky had done to her and Vanessa. Tears welled up at times as she talked about her fear of Icky. I, in turn, was sympathetic and consoling. "I wanted him to stop, but he wouldn't. There was nothing I could do." After nearly an hour of this dribble, I called a halt to the interview. She was making me sick with her sniveling. I suggested we finish up tomorrow. Mona was agreeable.

"How about the money you promised?

I could see by her expression she was not bashful about the request. Under my note pad was an envelope containing four fifty-dollar bills that I had prepared while using latex gloves. I let it slip out from my notepad and pushed it to her with the pad like it was a drug deal going down.

"I'll call around noon, if that's alright with you, Mona?"

She replied, "Noon is good," smiling ear to ear and clenching the envelope tight.

Mona folded the envelope into her pants pocket and slipped out of the booth. The hook was set. After saying our good-byes I walked south and around the back of Kornbreads. I rounded the building, then back north to my car. I arrived at the Avenger in time to watch Mona walking west on Morrow Road. I pulled off my hat and glasses as I watched her. When she was almost out of sight I started the car and drove slowly in her direction until I saw her walk from the street into a small four-plex apartment building.

The next day I placed the call; we set the time to meet for 1 p.m. I drove down Morrow Road and parked at a graveled crossroad near the entrance to her quad. Mona exited the bottom floor apartment nearest the street and proceeded toward Kornbreads. I now knew where she lived. I waited until she cut across the street into the parking area of the diner before pulling out onto the road. Parking my Avenger out of sight of the diner, I eased out and met with Mona. We finished up a few questions I had on how the courts and legal system screwed her before turning the conversation to the local area.

I asked, "Since I'm here for the rest of the day, I'd like to see some of the local sights. What is there around here to see?"

"What kind of things do you have in mind?" Mona replied while gently running her hand over the top of my hand. Sometimes you don't have to be a mind reader to know what someone's thinking. I decided to play the hand that was dealt. Mona wasn't attracted to me because I was good-looking; she was attracted to me because in her eyes I looked like Ben Franklin, lots of them. Not moving my hand I responded, "Well, I was thinking historical landmarks, waterfalls, maybe scenic areas."

"There are plenty of wooded areas around here," she said with a sheepish grin.

As Mona continued to talk I was amazed how the court-appointed psychiatrist could have found her incompetent to stand trial. Today, she was articulate, her thinking was organized and she was animated. A few short weeks ago she had an OxyContin affect, thorizine shuffle, and hardly knew her name.

"I've lost you, haven't I?" Mona picked up on my trancelike state.

"Oh, ah, I was just thinking how lost a city boy could get out there. I mean, I'm used to street signs and maps, not dirt roads, trees, and riverbeds."

She was quick to respond, "Silly, I wasn't talking about you going alone."

"I'm game, let's go."

Mona smiled and replied, "I'll show you one of my favorite waterfalls if you like. It's only an hour away."

"I'd like that, maybe get some pictures there too."

This was uncharted territory for me. I had planned to kill Mona in her apartment, but opportunity might prevail. Although convenient and only a small change in plans, it was risky—changing plans spontaneously was always risky. It was impossible to calculate all the things that could go wrong even when you'd planned everything and followed your plan to the letter—the possibility of something going wrong increased when you changed horses in midstream.

Mona and I chatted casually as we made our way north on Interstate 5. I was never more thankful the Avenger had bucket seats than on this trip. It kept some distance between us. As we drove she would occasionally run her hand up the inside of my thigh and back down to my knee, I suppose in some sort of preview of the command performance she was planning. Frankly, it was giving me the willies.

Dillon Falls on the Rouge River was closer than she thought. It was only a thirty minute drive. We were heading for Sam's Valley Road when Mona suggested we try the Upper River Road. It was everything she said it would be. This was a truly riparian environment with a mix of Brumitt firs standing alongside ponderosa pines and deciduous trees. As we proceeded east we rounded a large butte with grass-covered steep ridges to our south side, the river on our left.

I spotted a well-maintained dirt road off to the left that led down to the river's edge. The riverbank was covered with trees and underbrush, making it a perfect hiding place.

"I'd like to get a couple pictures, then we can get back in the car." Mona, smiling, replied, "Sure, whatever you want," slipping her hand up the inside of my leg. I waited to hear what additional cost she'd confer to this little venture.

The dirt road led to a turnaround that appeared to be the hub for a spiderweb of four-wheel-drive trails. I parked the car and told Mona I'd only be a few minutes. Mona said, "Take all the time you like, it'll be dark soon."

From the trunk I removed a black canvas bag containing my equipment. Mona accompanied me through the bushy terrain to the lava outcroppings over the river. I sat my bag down unzipping the top fold. Looking around I tried to give the appearance of setting up for a proper photo shoot. In reality I was checking to see if the area was conducive to completing my project.

Mona unbuttoned her shirt, exposing her braless breasts for a few seconds; I surmise she intended it as a preview of what she had planned for later. She gave me a come-hither smile while teasingly tying her shirt into a midriff fashion. She probably thought the photo shoot would feature her, maybe in a sexy position with nature as the backdrop. She was right to some extent. She was caught up in the moment as she pointed downriver. "This would make a beautiful picture." She gestured with a sweep of her hand, "I'd love to spend the rest of my life right here."

Once again, she hit the nail on the head. I softly added, "Today is your lucky day." Mona smiled as she turned back in my direction. Her expression changed abruptly as she focused on the barrel of my Glock pointing at her cleavage.

"The courts did you a disservice and I've come to correct that mistake. You let your child be abused. You aided and abetted in her torture and destruction. You covered it up and you are as guilty as you claim he is." I expected some argument, but that flat affect returned; only this time it was sincere. She was voiceless, her eyes stared into mine.

With that I squeezed the trigger, Thuup. Thuup. Her body hurled backward and down over the natural rock jetty on which she'd stood. Her body rolled in the current of the Rogue. I fired a series of shots to insure she was dead. Where I struck her at this point didn't make any difference. In fact, if there were multiple gunshot wounds it might appear personal, someone who knew her, someone who was angry with her. It would be to my advantage.

I scanned the hillside for any onlookers who might have seen me. Suddenly it dawned on me, I'm all alone. It was unusual not to have voices or apparitions, not even Destiny. I was all alone, was I wrong about this kill? I placed my equipment back in the bag and returned to the Avenger. I didn't worry about covering up my footprints or checking to see if there was blood splatter on the rocks, depending on how far the body drifted it was nearly impossible for searchers to find the crime scene. From the number of tracks on the ground in the parking area and the nearby four-wheeler trails, the indication was this area saw a lot of activity. Any tracks I might have left would be concealed within a few days.

After a comfortable night's sleep in Medford, I decided to spend the rest of the week sightseeing in the area. A day trip to Crater Lake was awesome and refreshing. A last-day visit to the Jacksonville Museum before heading back to Portland rounded out my few days of rest and relaxation.

I followed the local news to see if Mona was discovered. A report of an unidentified female body at Foot's Creek surfaced four days after Mona's disappearance. The location was significant. It was only a few miles from where Mona had fallen into the river. In a candid acknowledgement, the police spokeswoman commented, "Investigators are not releasing additional details at this time." So for now the wait-and-see continued.

Mona would not fit into the puzzle for Detective Ware, who seemed interested primarily in dead or missing sex offenders. Unlike TV shows that solve complex forensic problems in fifty minutes, give or take a couple of commercial breaks, it was much more difficult in real life. Police relied heavily on theory, profiles, and breaks in a case when they didn't have a suspect. Forensic evidence gathered at crime scenes would support their case, when the time came, but it was not going to identify a suspect.

Mona's killing did not significantly impact the local community. Police were releasing only necessary information to the public. With the cops being tight-lipped, public pressure to make an arrest was nil. The local media was on board with police to preserve the integrity of the investigation. But in the absence of factual information they were quick to fill in the gaps with their own rendition. Mona had friends and acquaintances, people who could add information and value to their stories, and that's what they focused on. If not for freelance writer Anna Sasins, Mona's name might never have been mentioned again. Not surprising, Medford news outlets did not carry Sasins' story. However, her article was widely distributed throughout metro areas of the Pacific Northwest.

Sasins focused her article on domestic violence. The inclusion of Vanessa's story set the stage for an alarming set of statistics concerning violence toward children in the home. She pointed out data identifying mothers as abusing children more frequently than fathers did, although it was frequently thought opposite. She laid out the facts and they were chilling. She used Mona's legal case to focus on aspects of criminal parenting. The article concluded more like an epitaph touching briefly on Mona's death. Sasins wrote, "Lott may have fell victim to her own drug-infested lifestyle." She didn't exactly strike oil with that one but it would be helpful if the police bought it.

Sasins was correct though. Mona was a victim of her lifestyle. She was executed for what she didn't do as much as for what she did. "Mona, Sasins wrote, was shot repeatedly and her body dumped in the river." Wait a minute! How did she know Mona had multiple gunshot wounds? She had information that was not publicly released. What else did she know and how did she know it? She obviously had an inside track on privileged information.

I had grown to respect Sasins as I had Horn. In a half dozen articles I'd read written by her, she had advocated greater punishment for the offenders. She expressed her concerns about law enforcement not following up on domestic violence when it was reported to community services. She spoke for the people, perhaps from the perspective of a victim, I don't know. In any case, she seemed to be following my work closely, although perhaps unintentionally. I got a sense from her writings that she knew I existed—just not my identity. She clearly understood someone was extracting vengeance on a specific criminal element. She had previously cited Deed's killing and wrote, "There exists a likelihood other vigilantes may be intent on doing the same thing. Not so haphazard but as dedicated to the same cause." In her profile attached to each article was a picture of Sasins and a simple email address Archangel@ccm.com. Could it be possible I had an unintentional ally in this quest after all?

I went to the library and opened up a free email account under the name "Scythian." It was traceable to some degree although not easily since I was able to use it from a number of public locations. The email account did not require any personal information and since I was accessing from public terminals, tracing would be difficult. I sent a simple message.

Archangel,

I admire the opinions you put forth in many of your recent articles. I would have you know you have included some of my work in your writings. Your conclusions are not far from the truth. I work alone. I have chosen this life because it is necessary. Someone must right the wrong violent predators do. Since the judicial system is lacking in its ability to punish, I have accepted the responsibility. I hope in future articles any reference to my work will be made with understanding and not a shot in the dark as to why. I make myself available to you for this purpose.

Scythian

I debated sending the email for some time. I questioned myself repeatedly. This might not be a smart move. However, there might come a time in the near future I wanted someone to tell my story; what I did and why. If she was agreeable I could trust her to present my thoughts and feelings to the public.

Predator, hear me! My advice to you is this: kill yourself and save me the time and effort. If not, I will come looking and when I find you I will show you the same mercy you showed your victim—none. It may be tomorrow, next week, or next year but I will come with a vengeance or my name isn't Walter E Goe.

Chapter 11

I have come to resurrect justice; it is my destiny.
—Walter

Ever since I came to the realization there are some really sick individuals in this world, I have believed in the death penalty. I don't mean sick in a medical sense but with a depravity that mankind tolerates because they cannot come to grips with the fact they need to be extirpated. These depraved individuals attack the dignity of humanity and just locking them up for a while solves nothing. Every violent sexual predator's conviction, release, and subsequent offense reinforce my belief that they should be put down. I would call them animals but that description doesn't fit. Animals are far better than the likes of these monsters.

While I awaited a response from Archangel to my rather nebulous email, I busied myself with another project. Regardless of whether Sasins contacted me or not, I needed to continue my quest. Going through files and scanning news articles from dozens of sources was keeping my nose to the grindstone. What I was looking for I wasn't seeing. No vibes, no sensory perceptions, it was as if something was blocking the development of a project. Was it me, was I looking in the wrong place for the lead? I am capable of carrying out a project without all the bells and whistles that usually accompany the development. I have no problem deciding who dies without help from mortals or the supernatural—ethereal beings only serve to validate my personal convictions and sanction my call to action.

After a couple of exhausting weeks searching, I spotted a small news piece in an eastern Oregon newspaper. A story buried on the third page of the *Pendleton Chronicle* carried a tidbit about a sex offender of a whole different nature. It was neither an April Fools' Day joke nor a laughing matter. It was a current event and as sick as they come. I was surprised when I checked my files I had no historical documents on this perp, just an instant connection commanding me to pursue.

Willard (Willie) B. Hartigan was an Idahoan sex offender according to the Thursday newspaper account. Some eleven years earlier he had earned his offender status as a seventeen-year-old juvenile. The victim was a six-year-old boy with the bad luck to live next door to Willie. The article outlined Hartigan's payment to society confined to a Rebar Hotel in Caldwell, Idaho. I can only imagine how horrific juvenile detention might be. But he survived until his release at the ripe old age of nineteen. Somehow it didn't seem sufficient.

Upon discharge he was considered a danger to the community and required by law to register his residence. That was the one thing Idaho did right because Willie was still a danger. Hartigan moved frequently, mostly finding refuge in small rural communities. He failed occasionally to comply with the registry law and authorities eventually caught up with him. The reporter elaborated on a few historical facts from Hartigan's past he thought readers would find interesting. Hartigan, twice since his release from incarceration in Idaho, had short stays in county jails for parole violations. It was, according to Hartigan, just an oversight on his behalf. It was certainly a believable story. Anyone might fail to register if they were moving into another state. In fact it might even be the reason to move to another state. In the second go-around he was jailed at Powder River Correctional Center because of another error, at least one of judgment, if you believe it was unintentional. Anyone might wander too near a grade school unknowingly if you were a convicted child rapist. The fact that he had in his possession duct tape and a small spool of rope in a brown paper bag was probably coincidental. The newest headline on Willie took a bizarre twist for the people of Baker City, Oregon, to consider.

It had been nearly a month since I emailed Archangel. I'd resisted the impulse to check my email. The noose tightened with frequent exposure; something I couldn't afford. In the public library I found it best to become Walter. Most cameras in public facilities are easily noticed, hence a valuable deterrence to criminal behavior. They could also be used to identify me if the police ran a trace on my email to Anna. No sense letting down my guard; besides, I liked being Walter, it felt comfortable. I slipped on the latex gloves and entered my information. The site box popped up revealing what I was hoping to see.

Scythian,

I am not sure what you are referring to as "work" that I've cited in my articles? Tell me a little more about yourself and maybe then I'll understand your reference.

Archangel

Reporters and writers are great when it comes to letting the faucet drip. They never shut them off. It didn't seem like much, just a drip, but it was an opportunity to finally relate my feelings as to why I do what I do, yet remain anonymous. I guess I've wanted to tell someone from day one of this journey. Secrets are hard to keep; we all have a need to share the things we know. I was of the opinion I would someday be caught and tried for murder. When that day came, I wanted to take the stand and tell them all, "I killed them for being what they are, but you are on trial, not me. You are why I'm standing before you today. You liberal judges, unscrupulous lawyers, and cowardly jurors are all guilty of the murders I've committed; you didn't do your job and I had to do it for you. You claim to stand for justice; you are all frauds; I'm the only one in this room standing for justice."

I thought for a while about my response to Archangel. What was her real question? Perhaps some confirmation I wasn't a crackpot yahoo I suppose. I don't imagine she gets correspondence from serial killers every day. In fact with her points of view, I doubt any would contact her. I decided the straight-up approach with her would be to my advantage. Something she would recognize.

Archangel,

Owen "Icky" Moore, the subject of your recent article, is a vicious man who enjoys inflicting pain. For a short while his life is spared. He longs for his freedom from incarceration but on that day, if our paths cross, he will surely die.

Mona was not innocent of wrongdoing. She aided and abetted her man in the brutal assault and torture of their daughter.

Vanessa will never fully recover. How could she? She bears the scars in both body and soul. Sure, she's in state custody for now, but the damage is done. Maybe she will learn to cope, maybe not. Maybe she'll be a ward of the state for the rest of her life or maybe she will end the nightmares and torment once and for all by suicide. Many do and I really don't blame them.

I have come to resurrect justice; it is my destiny. You won't necessarily agree with what I do, but I exist because the times demand it. For too long the liberal courts have violated the victims and shown favor to the criminals.

I will soon send an undeniable confirmation of what I am. All I ask for is an opportunity to communicate the truth to someone who might be able to understand a lone voice crying out in the wilderness.

Scythian

It was time to send it and leave it alone. I needed to get on with the current project. Hartigan was up against charges that weren't going to net him a lot of time. Willie was accused of cruelty to animals, criminal mischief, theft, and bestiality, but these types of charges are frequently boiled down to one or two charges by court time. A couple of witnesses watched Willie skillfully tie a small cord or rope around a sheep in a pasture and abscond with it. The witnesses pursued Willie and caught up with him not far from the fence line. According to the witnesses they observed Hartigan tie the sheep to a tree and then bend down behind the helpless animal and execute a sexual act. At twenty-eight years of age, Willie B. Hartigan was once again caught with his pants down, literally.

Baker City is small-town USA. It was once a major hub during the westward expansion along the Oregon Trail, now relegated to mostly small farms and ranches. I located a nice campground only twenty miles southwest of Baker City on Phillips Lake in the Willawa-Whitman National Forest. To me it seemed very remote but as I recall it was the largest campground in the area.

I decided to arrive in town only as Walter E. Goe, Freelance writer–reporter. Since I had plenty of business cards to choose from, it was wise not to use the same one I did in Medford. No sense making a simple connection for the cops.

Once in Baker City I made the local greasy spoon my hangout and it didn't take long to catch the drift among the townspeople. Locals were furious and vocal. Willie B. was already out on bail. He had served his time on parole and finished it. Now he was out on bail while he awaited trial. My immediate thoughts were who would bail out this sick pervert? According to the townsfolk, Hartigan had moved here to live with or off his cousins. They now served as third-party custodians with the courts.

Asking upset people stupid questions about a perverse crime does provoke unique responses. Just the sort of thing I wanted. A good ol' boy named

Bootleg invited himself to sit at my table and keep me company. He wasn't a typical Baker City resident but a home-grown Oregon hillbilly. He didn't say much at first but eventually warmed to the idea of a conversation. It took a little getting used to Bootleg to understand his speech. Leaning in my direction, Bootleg whispered in a gravelly tone. "Yes'em, tha' steali'n youngin better high 'n tailer out'a he-ere or we'd be's to hangin'em." Bootleg paused to cough up some phlegm before continuing, "You'd think wee'se don't noed where he'd been liven'. He'd need a posse pertectin' him if'a he'd thinks he'sa gonna liven're. He'd done wored out he's we'come." Somehow it all made sense when he said it.

I acted surprised by what he said. "He's staying with family here?"

Bootleg laughed, "You's noed he are, right next to-dah farm he'd stoled datta sheep from."

"Where's that?"

"Bout'in mile er-so's out'er town on Seven."

I took this to mean Highway 7 and continued to chat with other folks as they became available. Some had questions for me, mostly curious of particular stories I'd covered. A few folks had heard of some of the people I referred to, others I probably just thought they had.

I visited the county courthouse daily to read the calendar call for circuit court cases posted in the hallway. I wouldn't have to wait long to see action here. Within the first week of monitoring, Hartigan's name was posted with a motion to change counsel. If granted, and no reason to believe it would not be, Hartigan would be represented by a new attorney to the case. Ruben Darroe, an unheard-of name in these parts perhaps but one I readily recognized as my nemesis. Further, Darroe and Hartigan were two peas in a pod—amorality and iniquity.

Counsel for the defense wasted no time filing motions with the circuit court. I attended court to see Willie B. Hartigan, I couldn't care less about the motions. You can always tell who's who at the defense table. One person is dressed up nicely. That's the defendant. The bearded guy with the ponytail and sandals is the defense attorney.

Darroe was first to enter the nostalgic-looking old courtroom. I remember him well; he fits my perception of a criminal defense attorney perfectly. Hartigan strolled in a few minutes later with his third-party custodian in tow. He was casually dressed, not overdone, with cheap slacks and button-down shirt. His hair cut short, neatly trimmed, and he sported extended lamb-chop sideburns with a soul patch for facial hair. He sat down at the defense table with a self-satisfied smirk on his face and began to converse with his attorney, or should I say rehearse the script for the opening act.

The bailiff commanded, "All rise." I whispered under my breath, "And let the games begin!" The prosecutor opened with a few known basics concerning the charges. Darroe countered with motions to dismiss the specific charges of bestiality and suppress evidence obtained, according to Darroe, unlawfully by the sheriff's department. Darroe's focus was clear and clever from the beginning. He wanted the human-animal sexual interaction out of the jury's mind. Darroe knew it was reprehensible behavior to most people. It was more apt to trigger a harsh reaction to Hartigan at jury deliberation. He provided a long list of documentation from researchers and renowned professors acknowledging the cultural perspectives of westerners,

"It is nothing more than a culture of unfounded fear. It's a Salem-style witch hunt of those with a different sexual orientation," Darroe clamored.

The defense provided document after document reflecting negatively on the taboo based ancient Judeo-Christian beliefs and a throwback to pseudosciences of the Dark Ages. Unfortunately, for the prosecution, there were landmark cases where morality was not sufficient justification for law. Darroe with his courtroom dynamics, "That's all this is, is someone's ancient moral views made into law" gained momentum.

I couldn't help my thoughts rebutting everything Darroe said. If I had been the prosecutor maybe I'd have played into Darroe's hand, but at least I'd have had my say. The more I listened to him the more difficult it was not to shoot Darroe and let Willie dance from Bootleg's barn rafter.

As I sit listening to this diatribe about zoosexual activity being natural and enjoyed by many, animals and humans alike, I'm thinking about how normal it is to kill something that is vile and repulsive, like animal rapists.

Darroe went after the animal cruelty charge with fervor. Legal terminology was vague. The law could not conclude whether or not sexual activity can be proven to be cruel or abusive. You would think so but sadly it's not an open and shut book. What Darroe wanted to do was create doubt in the prosecutor's mind as to whether or not they had an ironclad case. The fact was they didn't have it in the bag. Ultimately, Darroe would succeed in creating wiggle room for some old-fashioned plea bargaining. Something he's notorious for.

Could prosecutors prove without a reasonable doubt penetration had occurred? Bestiality hinged on that issue. The animal was examined according to documents, but only the trauma of being tied to the tree could be validated. "Is it abuse when a veterinarian artificially inseminates a cow?" Darroe roared. "Did the cow ask for the veterinarian to violate her clear up to his shoulder?" Darroe paused. "Animal husbandry is practiced every day in America and it's not illegal."

Darroe again offered various opinions from "experts" with supporting documents proving there was no evidence animals were injured by the sexual interaction with humans and in fact may actually enjoy it—that did it, I'm killing Darroe.

Lastly, he addressed the actions of Hartigan as someone who had successfully dealt with the issue of sexuality and impulsivity by using an animal that he had not harmed for sex. It was by no way an admission of guilt. "As distasteful as it may seem, my client was trying to walk the straight and narrow," Darroe said passionately. I didn't see it that way. Looking around the courtroom, Darroe surmised, "This is a nonissue issue in this case." It was becoming clear this case would be disposed of by the prosecutors. After all, they're just lawyers too.

The day ended and Darroe had the upper hand. His client would probably have at least some of the charges dismissed and without being on parole, would probably only see a short stint in the hoosegow. Since Hartigan was out on bail in third-party custody of a family member I decided to loosely tail his coming and going to court.

It was less than a month after Darroe began his court motions that the plea bargain came down. It was clear the prosecutors wanted to move on quickly. There would be at least one more court appearance for Hartigan. All parties would have to accept the terms of the agreement and the judge pronounce his blessing on the deal. The court date was set for the announcement but local reporters had little intention of waiting for the official rendition. Terms of the plea bargain were speedily broadcast. It was the talk of the town.

Early in the morning I drove a two-and-a-half-hour stretch to Boise, Idaho. It was time to make contact with Archangel. I could have used a computer in Baker City but being removed a good distance seemed more sensible. I arrived at the library and logged into my email.

> Archangel,
>
> You will soon hear of a sex offender's death in eastern Oregon. If you choose to cover this with an article, take into consideration the nature of the crimes he has committed in the past as well as the nature of his current crime.
>
> I will be in contact.
>
> Scythian

I now had to make quick work of taking out the target. In someone's book he was only guilty of committing a couple of misdemeanors. By Oregon's standards I guess that was the way the law crumbled. The prosecutors might not have been able to match wits with Darroe, but none of that persuaded me to a different course of action. He might have acted out some sexual fantasy with the sheep but that wasn't the sum total of his crimes; he was a convicted child rapist and he would be back for more.

Back in Baker City the town was abuzz. It was the nastiest newsworthy thing to happen in a decade. People were discussing the case openly and few townsfolk were without an opinion.

Willie B. rode with his cousin to a local grocery store. It was only a few minutes' drive from their little farm on the south side of town. Traffic provided cover and concealment in most cities but out here you could see for a country mile, which coincidentally was about the distance I tailed from. You couldn't miss the old canary-yellow International Scout in the Mom and Pop's parking lot. Here was a challenge. A little corner store with a small lot and few cars. My only advantage as far as I could see was that Hartigan's ride found the only handicapped sign to park in front of. I wondered what handicap the cousin had besides stupidity.

I was parked only a few minutes when Hartigan emerged from the store. He was already in violation of the court orders. A stipulation of his release was to be in sight of his third-party custodian at all times. Seemingly, with the plea deal pending, he took on an air of laxity. He strolled to the yellow beater of a vehicle, briefly leaned in, then stood up and looked about. Hartigan walked to the outside corner of the store glancing back as he rounded the corner. He remained unaccompanied.

I had kept my Glock ready to rock 'n roll for the past few days of observation. Quickly I attached the moderator and jacked a round into the chamber. Stepping from the car I slipped the weapon under my lightweight windbreaker and proceeded to the back corner of the store. Hartigan appeared relaxed, standing in plain view, smoking a cigarette. The lot behind the store was an undeveloped parcel covered with mounds of dirt and trash strewn about. Rooftops could be seen of single-level homes in the distance but a six-foot wood fence separated the housing from the vacant lot. I walked toward Willie.

He turned toward me, making direct eye contact, with a rude response full of expletives, he inquired of my purpose for following him.

I wanted to respond but a horrid vision immobilized me. This visualization was more like a flashback that included a level of reality I had never experienced before. Pain penetrated my consciousness. I felt violated.

"Hey, I'm talking to you dude!"

Dressed like Clark Kent and impersonating a mental ward escapee, I suspect I wasn't too intimidating but I had something that was.

"What is your problem?" His voice now increased with intensity.

I saw him rile, his chest puffed up as he aggressively flexed toward me. He flicked his cigarette in my direction, he was ready to rumble. My Glock presented like a well-oiled piece of machinery. It and I were becoming one. This little bantam rooster relaxed his stance like a deflated balloon. Willie, who liked to dominate little boys and small farm animals for his personal gratification had the shoe on the other foot now. I knew he got his jollies from pain—others' pain—and I was made privy to it. I was about to find out if he enjoyed his own pain as much as I was going to.

"Go on. Get out of here," Hartigan said, taking a few steps backward. His voice now constrained. I recognized his behavior, I'd seen it before. It was fear and I liked it. Next would come crying big ol' crocodile tears followed by begging for another chance but I didn't have time for all that.

Thuup! Thuup! Willie fell to the ground. I could see he was still alive and conscious. My shots had hit in the lower stomach area and ribcage. Did I need to get in some target practice? Nah, I don't know what came over me but I wanted him to feel pain for a minute. I stepped closer and fired two more rounds into his chest.

Willie now lay motionless. Any pain he felt was likely gone. I concealed my weapon, looked about, policed my brass and strolled to my Avenger.

I really hated to go but certain necessities forced my hand to load my trailer and leave the campsite for my old stomping grounds on the Deschutes River. After a week on the Deschutes I made a run to Sherman County library to check email. I wasn't necessarily surprised to see a message in my in-box from Archangel since I had put her on notice of what to watch for.

Scythian,

A sexual offender was murdered in Baker City, Oregon. What is it you want from me?

Archangel

She was apprehensive and maybe frightened, it was understandable. She saw the monster in me. Somehow I must win her trust so she might see me for who I was. Then again, who was I?

In response I wrote,

Archangel,

I am not asking for involvement, just a fair representation if you cover the story. I'd like you to know the inside scoop of why I do what I do. I think you are a good candidate to understand my passion.

More people will die. Guilty people; guilty of inhuman acts to those weaker, smaller, younger, and innocent. It is the natural law of humanity; those guilty of violent and sexual assaults will be punished severely. That is my part. You know more about my cause than any other person. All I ask is that you give your coverage of my work a fair and honest appraisal. If I am apprehended I would like you to have exclusive rights to my story

Scythian

After sending the email, I took the opportunity to check up on happenings with the Hartigan killing. Neighboring towns all carried a piece of the action. Even larger cities like Pendleton.

A few things struck me after perusing the articles. No mention of someone of my description or persons of interest. Either they were being extremely guarded or they didn't have a real lead. Reporters interviewed local townsfolk and all were quoted as being very negative about the Hartigan plea deal. Not one person condemned the killer. I was practically a hero to those folks and probably the livestock too.

The plea deal was another waste of taxpayer money! Darroe said Hartigan had had counseling, which was part of the reason given for why he abused the sheep. Aha, counseling was to blame for that poor sheep being sexually assaulted! I think not! Hartigan had a wiring problem. The only cure was death. For Walter it was never about the sheep; it was always the little boy Willie raped.

I read and reread the local townsfolk's comments in the newspaper. They were inspiring in a morbid way. Through their comments I felt the impact of their anger. All the printed comments carried a central theme; we don't want these kinds of people living in our midst. To Walter, they were all missing the real picture. Seemingly forgotten was Hartigan's past. He was a predator who preyed on children. Had he had the opportunity with a child in the same way he did the sheep, another child would have been notched on his belt. The people of Baker City weren't overcome with fear there was a killer on the loose, they practically welcomed him into their midst.

I had the distinct impression from the locals that they suspected the killer was one of their own. A neighbor, perhaps even someone they knew personally. The comments clearly indicated they believed this murder to be an isolated incident. What about the sheriff's department's investigation? I hesitated to say they were joking, but the sheriff put the number of suspects in the case at around six thousand people. Was it a nice round figure or a figurative guess that just happened to correspond to the resident population of Baker City?

Sasins ran a feature article on the Hartigan case. After interviewing Darroe she drew her conclusions. Darroe was not presented in a positive light. He was livid about the killing of his client. He insisted it was a local vigilante who was incensed by the nature of the crime. Playing devil's advocate, Sasins alluded to the killing having as much to do with his theft and sexual abuse of the animal as it did with his previous child rape offense. "Fate has a way of rolling forward to finally catch those who continue to violate the natural laws of a society" she said. I had to consider that statement applicable to me as well.

Some weeks passed and the local news died off. Checking email, Sasins sent me a message.

> Scythian,
>
> Are you aware of a task force assembled to investigate vigilante activity against paroled felons? Forensic evidence indicates two or more murders being investigated are linked.
>
> I would like to talk sometime, call me on my cell phone. You'll find the number in my electronic signature block.
>
> Archangel

This was positive. Sasins was evidently willing to stay in contact. Further, she was probing by putting information out to evoke a response. I already had my suspicions about some sort of task force. But, being good-natured as I am I was willing to help Detective Ware by adding more statistics for his team to work with. It was the least I could do.

Chapter 12

He was a lot like me; a façade that took on reality.
—Walter

I've never trusted lawyers. Why should I, it's a dishonest trade. Law school is an oxymoron; on the one hand they teach constitutional law, on the other hand they teach how to manipulate those laws by misrepresenting, omitting, and out-and-out lying. We see it all the time. Skewing facts are forms of lying in Walter's book. Their goals are winning at all costs, the truth be damned.

Defendants with cash, have attorneys stacked up like a pro football team roster. When the courts declared everyone has a right to an attorney it provided a vehicle for unscrupulous lawyers to reach into the deep pockets of the taxpayer via government edict. They can file appeal after appeal after appeal. They will bleed the prosecutor's budget dry.

The answer, cut a deal. Plea deals, if accepted by all parties, come with a clause prohibiting appeal and carry a lesser sentence for the guilty. It's a win-win. The victims don't have to endure a trial. Without a trial there is less expense to the taxpayer and the prosecutors still score a victory. The criminal will serve less time, have a reduced fine, or whatever the deal. Defense attorneys consider it a win because they won a reduced sentence for their client. To me they're all just hired guns driven by fame, greed, and self-interest. They are no better than politicians; everybody knows politicians are nothing but scoundrels and liars. Lawyers broker deals, coddle the wicked, and contaminate others. When a victim or a victim's family enters the realm of the judicial system seeking justice, they are little better off than Dorothy was in the Wizard of Oz. Only, instead of, "lions, tigers, and bears" presenting danger at every bend in the road—it's a trial lawyer. The tune repeated countless times in my thoughts, only the words to the song changed, "Liars, scoundrels, and thieves—oh my!" I couldn't shake it.

I was bothered more by Darroe's recent shenanigans than those of the past. Bothered was probably a mild understatement. I concluded after my first encounter with Darroe and considerable research into a list of his clients, he needed to die for using his position to aid and abet countless numbers of sex offenders. He has repeated his performance so many times he delivers his courtroom sermons more like a Pentecostal preacher than a lawyer—it was his specialty. I've watched him perform in court and followed his career long enough to know Darroe was the epitome of scum-sucking attorneys.

I was off to a little camping area northwest of Spokane, Washington. I had visited the Okanogan Range when I was much younger and enjoyed the cascading beauty of the steep mountains and lush green firs. It was a few hundred miles but I was well equipped with travel trailer and supplies. I could grow my goatee, sip some fine Irish whiskey, do a little trout fishing, and give Walter a well-deserved break.

I arrived at my campsite, backed the trailer into an isolated spot near a stand of trees and pursued my objective—to relax and enjoy the out-of-doors. As I sat in one of the most scenic places I can remember, the haunting tune played over and over again, "Liars, scoundrels, and thieves—oh my!" These were not the same sensory perceptions I had become accustomed to, nor the same feelings that accompanied my previous projects, yet there were similarities inasmuch as they kept a steady stream of thoughts flooding my consciousness. Any semblances of a relaxing vacation were fleeting.

As I sat secluded in the mountainous terrain I recalled watching a television show many, many years ago, with a high-profile defense attorney who had written a book on his courtroom successes. He was very proud of his exploits and demonstrated in his book an example of one of his maneuvers that had brought him fame. He described how he would go about getting a date-rapist off. With the victim on the stand he would ask "Did you tell him to stop?" She would reply "Yes." He then asked her, "Did you tell him, Don't" and she would answer in the affirmative. He repeated his question in essence asking her if she said, "Stop." "Yes!" she retorted. Then with a tinge of theatrics on this attorney's part, he picked up the pace, "Did you say, 'Don't,' Did you say, 'Stop,' did you say it over and over so he heard you?" The victim gave a frustrated "Yes" to each statement. Then the boom was lowered in his rapid attack, "So you said, 'Stop, Don't, Stop, Don't Stop Don't Stop, Don't Stop,

Don't Stop, Don't Stop.' " The victim sat speechless at how he twisted the truth and spun doubt in the jurors mind as to what actually took place. The audience uproariously laughed, and I guess it would be funny if it weren't true. The big-shot lawyer had no concern for the victim or truth, not even for defending his client, only for winning.

Ruben Darroe was such a lawyer. I'd watched him defending his clients' already bad names. Thankfully, there were no attendance sheets in court. In most cases I was just an unknown entity watching the proceedings from the sidelines. I've read several transcripts, all from his cases that were of special interest to me. A few of the cases dated back eight or ten years. It was clear, Darroe made a career out of mocking the judicial system and revictimizing the victims of violent and sexual crimes. Having watched his cocky walk and arrogant behavior, I knew it was more than ensuring his client was being treated justly—he had a mission to fulfill.

Darroe wasn't much to look at, his physical stature was unimpressive and I had difficulty guesstimating his age. He was in his midforties or early fifties, slender build, and John-Lennon-style wire-rim glasses stylish in the '70s. His slightly retreating hairline coupled with a tiny nub of a pony tail and graying beard gave the impression of a homeless hippie. His choice of clothing was similar to that of a street urchin, but in court he dressed up for the occasion. Levis, turtleneck T-shirt, sport jacket with multicolored preppie socks and well-worn sandals. I came to realize he was a lot like me; a façade that took on reality.

I was sick of all the slimy defense lawyers who were giving their own sleazy occupation a bad name. It bothered me that law and truth were so easily separated from each other in a courtroom. I knew it wasn't the responsibility of the defense to make sure the truth came out; that was the job of the prosecutors. It was the defense's job to defend their client despite what might actually be true. I understood the adversarial role of prosecution and defense. What I had a hard time understanding was why the courts allowed ridiculous defenses, the badgering of witnesses and victims, and allowed defense attorneys to make false insinuations of exculpatory evidence and misconduct by authorities when they were baseless. It was a flawed system and devoid of common sense.

Darroe was culpable in rapes, murders, and other violent crimes; at least that's the way I saw it. I had no qualms with lawyers who challenged facts in a case, but that wasn't Darroe's style. His verbal assaults on a victim's testimony were all too common. Throw in a dash of Hollywood theatrics, accusations of wrongdoing on the police's or victim's part, and change the meaning of a few terms; presto, the truth was manipulated. The trial would gain momentum with the intent to convince jurors there was a reasonable doubt on one or all of the charges. One jury member was all it would take and another criminal benefitted from his command courtroom performance. That made him responsible for their freedom to reoffend. And they did.

What was puzzling to me in Darroe's case was why? Why the fervency and passion to get sexual predators off the hook at all costs? What was in it for him? Was it personal? I wanted to know what his motivation was. Certainly not money—for the most part his clients were indigent, yet he ran an upscale law office. How was he able to finance his operation? He had defended high-profile sex cases in the past that had brought him notoriety. Maybe it had been a cash cow as well. Regardless, I held him responsible for crimes committed by offenders he got off the hook.

It was time to pack up and leave. Darroe was a project that had to happen. I had second thoughts about what I felt needed to be done, yet Darroe had to be stopped. This project would be riskier. I stood the chance of alienating my newfound friend, Anna Sasins. She might not understand my reasons and see it as a vicious criminal act. Maybe even worse, contacting Detective Ware with information she had acquired from me.

Ware was not likely to respond to the killing of a high-profile lawyer like Darroe unless forensics found a connection. If so, the heat would be dramatically increased. Killing sex offenders and perverts caused concern for the police but would be nothing compared to the panic amongst law enforcement agencies should the killing of a big-time defense lawyer be connected to a vigilante. This would be especially true for an attorney successful in defending sex offenders who had already died at the hands of a vigilante.

Admittedly, I had focused on lower-level criminals but there were plenty of richer, high-profile types that were just as guilty. On the flip side, there were plenty of victims and victims' families with resources enough to hire a professional to make the hit. Nevertheless, law enforcement, fearing where such vigilantism might lead, couldn't afford to allow it to continue. The business executives, politicians, and Hollywood producers were no better than any others if they committed the same crimes. In many cases their money bought their way out and that didn't sit well with Walter. But for now, I settled for the ones I could get.

Darroe's law office was located in Salem, Oregon. He advertised extensively and was easy to track. From sitting in the courtroom when he was performing I knew exactly what he looked like and would recognize him in any situation. I knew at least one car he drove. I knew he worked all over Oregon and was frequently on the road. It would take time to map out this very special project. Unlike others, I had questions I wanted answers to. Responses that could only be discovered face to face, at the point of death.

First order of business upon my return was checking email. I was surprised to see an email from Sasins. In the past I had initiated the contact.

Scythian,

It has been a few weeks since we last corresponded. MCSD task force that I mentioned before has released information from profilers assigned to the force. They believe evidence suggests an evolving criminal complexity. Profilers have identified the person of interest as middle-aged male, religious, lives alone, and probably a victim or a close family member of a victim of a violent sexual crime. I thought you might find it interesting.

Archangel

I didn't find it especially interesting. The more I killed and the more dots they connected the closer the profile would resemble me. Yet, I found myself thankful Sasins was willing to provide me with information she felt I needed to know.

Archangel,

Profilers play percentages based on collective evidence. As far as some greater complexity to what I do, I don't know about that. I would say they have a ways to go to paint a clear picture of who I am. Thank you for your input. I will finish a project very soon and will explain my actions in the aftermath. You will have the scoop.

Scythian

The planning stages for this project would come after considerable reconnaissance. I devoted the first week to observing the law office in the North Lancaster area, learning who the employees were. It also revealed when Darroe visited the office and that wasn't often. I didn't know what to expect from an attorney's schedule. During that week he visited his office once or twice a day. His stays were usually short, less than an hour in most cases. He had two females employed. Few other people visited the office. Darroe's residence was originally unknown to me. His frequent comings and goings at the office gave opportunity to follow him until I was able to locate his house southeast of Salem. A two-story upper-end cedar home nestled back from the frontage road in a stand of trees.

The second week I set up observation on his home. There was no evidence anyone lived with Darroe, although he could have private security or a paralegal employee. I had caught glimpses of a silver Lexus with tinted windows near Darroe's place. I felt they might be aware of my presence as well, perhaps even had me under loose surveillance.

Within a few days I was able to confidently say Darroe lived alone. He stayed at his residence a great deal of the time and appeared to leave only when he went to the office. Occasionally he stopped by a store on his trips to work or back; otherwise, he stayed at home.

A man in his position I suspect had few real friends and fewer people he could trust. Penetrating his home to take care of business was too risky. He had the resources to have security systems in place and there was the issue of the unusual vehicle traffic in the area. Killing him would not be the difficult part. Finding the right place was more complicated. I'd have to wait it out for a better opportunity.

Three weeks into this cat-and-mouse game, Darroe was out front of his home loading his older Volvo 240 wagon with suitcases. I felt encouraged. This was exactly what needed to happen. I needed him exposed.

Darroe pulled out early in the morning and instead of heading north toward his law office, he turned south. I lay back a short distance and cruised the frontage road until reaching Interstate 5. As we pulled into the heavy traffic I was amped with excitement.

As I adjusted my rear view mirror I caught a glimpse of what appeared to be a gray or silver sedan behind me. I tried to slow my Avenger and force the car to pass but heavy morning traffic compelled me to stay in line, keep up my speed, and go with the flow. People riding up on my bumper and honking their horns took away from the idea of stealth pretty quickly. Now, to complicate my tail on Darroe, I had lost sight of his car. I was going to have to step on it and regain my positioning.

The traffic on Interstate 5 had its advantages. I could tail at a relatively short distance behind Darroe and yet stay hidden. After passing through Grants Pass and onto Highway 199 all that changed. There was the occasional vehicle, more semi-trucks hauling logs and freight than automobile traffic. We dropped down into Northern California as we made our way toward the coastline. We passed through the Six Rivers National Forest; it had been a long time since I was in the midst of the giant redwoods.

A road sign indicated the next gas station on this route was Smith River, a likely place for Darroe to pull over I thought. I'd lost sight of his wagon again. It was sometimes necessary in the hilly area we came through to back off farther than I'd like to. Now I was tasked with locating him, again. Twenty miles or so south of Smith River a rest area came into view. The Volvo Darroe was driving was parked near the restrooms. As I pulled into the rest area he was out of his car and nowhere in sight. I stopped short of the rest area highway return ramp and watched the parking area with my mirrors. A couple of large trucks pulled in behind me blocking much of my rear view.

I waited for a few minutes but when he had not shown, I exited my Avenger. I was becoming antsy. In front of the restrooms a small footbridge crossed a creek and led to a series of scenic trails going in different directions. I could see signage marking trails and someone walking along one of the trails. That someone was possibly Darroe. My binoculars confirmed my target was moving away from the rest area signifying to me this remote spot alongside the road was as opportunistic as it got.

Quickly, I pulled out the case containing my AR15, and headed down to the bridge. After crossing the footbridge the trail separated into three paths. One headed south along the river embankment, another traveled west with a warning sign of a rocky incline to a saddle between two peaks and the last went north westerly around the base of the peak. I chose the peak. It was a climb onto the rocky crags, but from the top I could see areas along all three paths intermittently.

As I moved from side to side of the rock outcroppings, Darroe came into view. He was sauntering. Absent was his cocky walk and arrogant appearance. Maybe he was thinking about his destination or a defense strategy he would use in the next trial. I had no idea and it really didn't matter. My plan was to interrupt the thought process permanently.

Darroe slowed his gait and looked in my direction, it was less than a 100 meters but I doubt he could see me. I was slightly above his position, prone; my AR15 resting on its bipod stand aimed in his direction. As I looked into the face of a different type of evil my thoughts were conflicted. I couldn't explain it, but now it felt wrong to kill him. I was in position, all I had to do was pull the trigger, but once I did, there was no changing the outcome.

Besides, Darroe owed me something. I wanted a face-to-face encounter to ask him one question, why he did what he did. Until he answered I wouldn't be satisfied killing him. Maybe that was the reason I couldn't justify the shot.

Destiny had not accompanied me on this trip. I felt very much alone. No glimpses of chaotic visual perceptions or pain resided with my intentions. I only felt a strong prompting of my heart to kill. That wasn't enough.

I kept my scope trained in Darroe's direction as he made his way back toward the rest area, but I continued to struggle with the idea of killing him. This was easy to do. Pull the trigger! Pull the trigger! I kept telling myself. Do it! Alas, I could not. I packed up the rifle and headed for my car.

As I approached the footbridge, I watched Darroe as he slithered into his Volvo. Minutes later he drove away in the direction of Smith River. I sat quietly in my car, a bit dazed. The two parked trucks fired up and pulled out together onto the highway. A vehicle had been parked between the trucks was now exposed to my view. Moments later, the silver sedan pulled out in the same direction as Darroe and was soon out of sight.

This whole trip had taken on an eerie, uncanny nature. What seemingly should have been a simple task had resulted in confusion for me. I needed time to reflect. Darroe went about his business and I was headed home. I'd relegated Darroe to a meaningful part of the game. He was a star performer; through his efforts he put targets back on the street. Then it was my turn. It was in my estimation our cycle of life. Perhaps the sequence cannot be interrupted.

After a few days back home I started my routine again. Part of it now included checking email. I wasn't expecting anything but wasn't overly surprised to see an email from Sasins. She no doubt wondered what became of her scoop I had promised.

> Scythian,
>
> I am concerned. I haven't heard from you. You identified Hartigan as your work and I have no reason to think differently, but was his attorney, Ruben Darroe, your work as well?
>
> Archangel

Darroe! What does she know about Darroe? Why would she refer to him as my work? If it had been my work, he would be dead. It didn't make sense.

Archangel,

I believe Darroe is as guilty as his clients and deserves to die for his part. But with that said, he's no different than a hundred other defense attorneys. It's true I don't like his courtroom antics but it's the way it is. Look at his record, do some digging, use your resources and you will have plenty for a scoop.

Scythian

With that I hoped she would once again bring to light in her article the kind of low life he really was. I wanted her to use her resources to paint an ugly picture of Darroe; especially if it was the truth.

I didn't have to wait for Sasins to respond to my email to find out why she was asking about Darroe. It was all over the news. Evidently, Darroe was shot and killed north of Brookings, Oregon, on Highway 101. According to authorities Darroe's destination was Gold Beach, Oregon, where he was scheduled to meet with a client in police custody. Oregon state troopers were still in the beginning stages of their investigation and little else was released on the event.

Wow! It was only hours after I was tailing him that he was killed. Was this a sign to me? It was a question that would remain unanswered. It clearly wasn't his day.

Now that I knew what Sasins was talking about I needed to get back to her and clear up any miscommunication on the issue. Pulling up email I found Sasins was quick to respond to my last note.

Scythian,

My sources have revealed information I plan to use in a feature article on Attorney Darroe. I have been told child pornography was recovered from his home. I don't have a clear picture of what the contents may have been but it is clearly videos and photographs of underage foreign children of Latin descent. Police are also investigating financial deposits from one or more pedophile organizations advocating legalization of children's rights to choose consensual sex with adults. Evidently, police have been sitting on this lead for a while and haven't done anything with it. I will keep you informed. Watch for the article.

Archangel

While Sasins was working on Darroe's posthumous feature article, I was rifling through my files looking for a new project. Oregon state troopers were likewise busy, hypothesizing what transpired with Darroe. The current rumor circling about a mob hit was exactly that, a rumor. In his profession he may have been in cahoots with organized crime, who knows the truth. In Walter's book the issue had been settled.

Chapter 13

Darkness had become my friend.
I honed my skills to take advantage of the night.
—Walter

I love the night—more than that, I love the darkness the night brings. It is a natural cover and concealment for the kind of work I find most appealing. I remember as a youngster I was deathly afraid of the dark. Not that fear of the dark is uncommon, it is an instinctive trait connected to our survival response, but it can be overcome. Any response trigger can be conquered. Finding value in the darkness was my first step in this quest. Value dispels misunderstandings associated with fear. A lesson I would learn.

I was like most ranch kids of the day, we didn't have handheld game consoles and computers, we played hide 'n seek in the barn when friends visited. It was in this setting I learned to overcome my scary surroundings in order to have fun. It was during these times of play I found darkness to be an ally. My friends could be concealed but so could I.

A lesson of this nature takes time to develop. There are applications of pressure you can choose to bend, or allow to temper your mettle. At the homestead, creatures of the night, such as bears and cougars roamed through the woods and would be dangerous if by chance I encountered one. Honestly, I don't think I thought about them. It was mythical creatures brought to life in my imagination that haunted my darkness.

> I grew up during the dawning of horror movies and TV shows that imbedded thoughts in my mind only to pop out when I least wanted or expected them. Werewolves, vampires, mummies, and the headless horseman weren't real and I knew it but it didn't stop the imagination from working against common sense. As well as I knew these things were

phony, they became real to the point of my being able to feel the threat in my emotions. Then I'd run like the dickens until I got to the house.

Thinking back, the headless horseman was one of my favorites. During the summer months one of my ranch chores was to turn on the field irrigation system at night. Around ten o'clock, I made my way out to a valve located in the center of the alfalfa field. When the moon was full and the sky cloudy and windy, the field took on a life of its own. The swaying alfalfa made it hard to identify shapes and the trees moaned from the blustery winds. A skunk light mounted on a line pole usually helped illuminate a portion of the field, but added confusion to the night. Its light dancing about through two large pine trees cast eerie shadows to further stimulate my creative imagination.

Toward the end of my senior year in high school and for a few months after I graduated, I worked for a wildlife conservation society. I was a camp hand with various duties of assisting visitors with setting up tents, gathering firewood, and packing equipment as needed. It was interesting to watch these city slickers fumble their way around in the darkness. They literally understood nothing about the night. Sitting around the campfire you could hear the natural sound of the woods. A bull elk would bellow in the distance and everyone would be quiet as a mouse. Coyotes would begin their song and again the people would grow quiet, not to appreciate the singing but in concern for their safety. Birds, bugs and frogs were all lending their voices to the fireside symphony and the people expressed their fears of all of them. Abruptly, when every creature of the night went silent, an eerie chill could be felt. The visitors would relax in the quiet, thinking everything was now safe while I kept a close eye out. Something was out there and had disrupted the serenade. I realized my comfort was in the natural understanding of the dark.

Soon afterward I enlisted in the military. In Air Base Ground Defense School I found reconnaissance missions carried out more easily in the dark of night. During search-and-destroy missions, a dawn raid carried out more precisely if we moved into our positions under the cover of night before executing our mission.

Now, I employed these things learned in a new mode. I engaged the dark rather than shunned it. Darkness had become my friend. I honed my skills to take advantage of the night. I had become the predator hunter and protector of the prey.

Portland weather could be downright hot in the dog days of August. It was not humid, just hot, and it stayed hot until the early hours of the mornings. My stakeout had begun a few weeks before, during the dark of night, and had proven profitable. The late summer heat was a viable factor in my success. Phillip Graves, West River Heights Mortuary, was going about his custodial work; it was disturbing to say the least.

The mortuary basement contained corpses awaiting cremation and embalming. The basement windows were tinted, slightly inset, and approximately a foot above ground level. They opened only a few inches at the top to a maximum width of about four inches but enough to see through. Using the cover of night and the tree-lined yard I moved about freely observing my target's activity.

Phillip's employment began a couple hours after the funeral staff left for the day. As the only janitor he had free run of the place. He began in the upstairs lobby, working his way through the chapel, viewing room, offices, and then downstairs to the basement work areas. If it had not been for the hot summer the basement windows might not have been open; but they were. Peeking through the basement windows I could see Graves picking up trash cans and emptying them into a large garbage bag.

On Friday nights, Graves's janitorial routine changed. Through the window I caught a glimpse of a naked male torso laid out on a table. This followed the pattern I'd watched three times now. On Fridays he wheeled out a corpse to satisfy his lusts. At West River Heights Mortuary bodies were generally refrigerated to prevent deterioration after being picked up by funerary staff. For a traditional burial, the body was embalmed at the funeral home soon after it arrived. The daylong process preserved the body by replacing bodily fluids with embalming fluid and was completed the day it arrived. With cremation the body was refrigerated when it arrived. It remained there until the funeral director obtained the permits necessary for cremation.

Allegations of funeral home misconduct were nothing new and Graves was an added complaint. Most often it involved the mishandling of the corpse; it wasn't an epidemic problem but it could happen anywhere in the nation, not just Oregon. However, what I'd been witness to these past few weeks constituted a crime far worse than mishandling—this was clear-cut perversion.

Graves's gravitation to this work environment was no accident of employment, it was with purpose. He was a people person, he just preferred them stone cold and freshly refrigerated. My gravitation to him was likewise no accident. My intent was to show him the access route to the people he enjoyed being with the most; I had to make him dead first.

In the early nineties, Graves, then a nineteen-year-old teenager, had wrapped himself in one of the growing fads of the day, the Gothic lifestyle. He claimed his attraction was the music genre known as death metal punk, a music style common to explorers of the darker aspects of human nature. His chosen pursuit of the macabre and preoccupation with death and sensuality combined with the pale-face makeup, black eyeliner, nail polish, and black clothing appealed to his obsession with death. Only he was more of a believer in the lifestyle than most of his friends, and he proved it on his twenty-first birthday.

Graves celebrated his birthday long into the night. What exactly happened would forever remain a mystery. According to Graves he found a female dead in the cellar of an old abandoned house. He contacted friends that were of like mind and showed them the body. He talked several of his friends into masturbating on the corpse. However, one of his visitors wanted no part and alerted authorities to the location of the body.

According to witnesses for the prosecution, Graves told them he had lured the woman to the cellar with the promise of drugs. There he killed her by striking her in the head and had sex with the body. Graves was arrested on murder charges. Much of the forensic evidence was tampered with by friends who joined him in masturbating on the body and disturbing the crime scene over a five-day period prior to the police involvement. Two of Graves's friends that were identified as having participated with him agreed to testify for the prosecution. DNA evidence however, determined more people, unknown and unidentified, were involved. Those persons might have provided a toxic solution that rendered the victim unconscious; Graves denied having provided the substance. The unknown people added to the difficulty the prosecution faced with the murder charge. Graves did not deny the claim to his friends that he killed the woman, but insisted he was only bragging to impress them.

The trial proceeded but problems arose with the witnesses. Their evidence tampering and participation made them targets for the defense. They proved to be unreliable witnesses. An autopsy performed by the State of Oregon medical examiner's office confirmed the cause of death and the toxic substance overdose, none of which could be linked directly to Graves.

A reasonable doubt lingered in the minds of the jury, who found him not guilty on the murder charge. He was, however, convicted on lesser charges of abuse of a corpse and tampering with evidence. Necrophilia, sex without consent of the dead body, would be Phillip Graves' lifelong haunting. When paroled after a five-year hitch at the Rebar Hotel, Graves returned to society. His crime was vague history in most people's minds. Walter, however, was not most people.

Graves was not considered a predator or sex offender under Oregon law and wasn't required to register. My hunch was he wasn't required to change either. He was predatory in his own special way, evidence of which I have seen firsthand and wanted exposed to the news media and authorities. A simple arrest would not do justice.

The mortuary was a comfortable setting for a person of his caliber. He seemed almost at home. I can't understand his infatuation with dead bodies. No normal person can. I work in the industry too, so to speak, but I have no such affinity for corpses. The only time I handle a corpse is in an attempt to hide it and I still don't like touching it. Having sex with a dead body, something Graves seemed to enjoy, was even further from my comprehension.

I parked my Avenger along the curb adjoining the acre-size front yard. A cloudy night made a dark night and an extra layer of comfort for me. My AR15 was fully assembled and ready for action. I charged the bolt. There was no sound so sweet as the bolt driving a cartridge into the chamber. No sooner had I left the car than I noticed I was not alone along the tree line. Destiny was with me. She hadn't accompanied me here before. I had to assume she was here for the finale.

Graves was partially naked on top of a male corpse when my AR15 slipped through the open basement window. I saw no reason to dawdle. All I came to do was give him what was rightfully his. Shurrrp! Shurrrp! Graves rolled onto the floor and bled heavily from his back wounds. There was no hiding what had happened here. Slugs penetrated his back and entered the torso of the corpse. There would be no escaping the conclusion I wanted investigators to see. Graves was engaged in a sex act with the corpse, and two, Graves was murdered while in the act. My interest was piqued as I speculated how police and media would handle this case. The next morning I sent Sasins an email,

Archangel,

I recently completed a project I've been working on over the past month. Police investigators are not likely to release much information due to the nature of evidence at the scene. I'm giving you a heads-up on this one. The victim was a pervert engaged in a sex act with a corpse when he met his end. I would like to see the media incriminate him to the fullest for his history of perversion.

It wasn't his first go-around. The adage, "he got away with murder" may be old but applicable. Jurors may not have convicted him at the time based on admissible evidence but he is still the killer. His repulsive, twisted acts of perversion have now caught up with him. He has been judged, found guilty, and the sentence carried out.

Scythian

Officially, at what is commonly referred to as the "press release" nothing concrete was given except the name of the victim, employment at the mortuary, and method of killing. Unofficially, sources close to the case reported police believed this was an isolated event and possibly a revenge murder. Ballistics, however, could identify my AR 15 as the same weapon that killed Pohle. The question was not if, but when would Detective Ware be able to connect the dots? When would they engage in this investigation? Graves was not a sex offender but he was a bizarre felon with a unique history. I feel Ware, being old school as he is, will make the connection and expand his efforts rapidly.

Archangel's quick reply confused me. A one-liner, "I'll check into it," was not very reassuring. News agencies across the Northwest were running stories on this murder, emphasizing it took place in a mortuary. There was no mention of Graves and his involvement with one of the cadavers. You would think some connection to his name and history would have been made after the initial story was released but sadly, all seemed either forgiven or forgotten, maybe both.

Anna Sasins, true to form, came out of left field with a stinging historical account of Graves' macabre lifestyle and a solid rehash of his felony conviction. Her emphasis on his sex acts with his first known victim caused considerable stir among other news agencies. Reporters began posing difficult questions in their articles. "Why was someone with his history allowed to be employed at a mortuary?" "Are background checks of funeral employees a requirement for employment?" The mortuary staff and police were ducking questions and trying to avoid additional publicity, but there was always someone ready to divulge what they knew for fame or fortune. Usually it was the money that talked loudest.

The police catered to none of the questions. "No comment" became a standard answer. Sasins sent an email letting me know she had far more information than what had been released. "As for the news story, I'm feeding bits and pieces to other reporters, friends of mine, letting them run with it." She assured me the best way to get the information out was piecemeal.

Unfortunately for police, they had leaks in their departments as well. Regardless of how tight-lipped they were officially, details continued to slip from their grip to the media. Something I'd learned about reporters, they had to be treated with a degree of respect. They were ruthless interrogators, devoid of the legal restraints hampering police. They were a strange mixture of clergy and black ops. They could talk to victims, witnesses, or the accused from a theoretical neutral position. They could draw on resources, pay them off in cash, and never have to reveal their sources.

More information leaked, finally making the big splash with what really happened that night with Graves. My old friend Harold Horn put two and two together; although tempered, it was the ugly truth. No emphasis on who killed Graves now. It was all about the juicy story. For once in my killing career I was relegated to the mundane. It was especially true since the killer wasn't on the prowl for just anyone; a fact not overlooked by the media's presentation. Could it be, as much as I disdained reporters, I had found value in them?

Sasins sent another email:

> Scythian,
>
> I attended the MCSD briefing early this morning. A spokesperson for the Felony Task Force chastised reporters for causing what they referred to as, "a Chicken Little effect." They are downplaying the significance of this recent murder in connection with other murder investigations they are conducting. My sources outside the Task Force circle are telling me Detective Ware has brought on board more assistance and financing. I will keep you posted on any developments.
>
> Archangel

The police were facing a new problem from all the recent news coverage, an uptake of criticism. What they referred to at the press release as "a Chicken Little effect" was a point of contention with the news agencies. It seemed parolees and registered sex offenders were turning up missing, a lot of them! As much as I'd like to take credit for a permanent absence on their part; I had nothing directly to do with it. I don't know where they went but the reporters were speculating they were on the lam because of the recent murder victims. This was a frightening prospect for Oregonians who were under the impression these criminals were being watched by authorities.

Secondary to the general public's concerns about the whereabouts of felony predators was the cops' concerns with the parole and registration violations. These were criminal events that required time-consuming investigation. Police were now tasked with finding these felons to put to rest the public outcry for safety and to ensure they didn't have a slew of felons that had met with foul play.

If the Felony Task Force was looking for a reason to exist, they had now found it. I was giving them a little business from a couple of known kills but that paled in comparison with the amount of business I was sending to them through the fallout. Detective Ware would have preferred to put his efforts into narrowing down the suspect field, but now he dealt with the exponential curve of new cases. Personally, I liked Ware busy, busy, busy, and if one of these offenders turned up dead by some means other than my achievement, it only helped to confuse the picture for my pursuer.

Local residents filled the ranks of their community watch programs. Citizens were expressing themselves semi-vigilante-style or at least putting themselves in situations that might bring about a vigilante response. A group of young people formed a Yellow T-shirt brigade whose mission was to patrol parks with the express purpose to interrupt illegal activity. The police dispatchers were getting an increased call log of "Good Samaritans" reporting suspicious activities and gang-related crimes. The people were increasing their vigilance; they were reporting more activity, and the police were working overtime to address the public's concerns. My view was probably different from most. I saw it as a good thing; in fact, I felt people were now doing what they should have been doing all along. Being vigilant and taking a stand against criminals in their neighborhoods.

The great fear that a society would take the rule of law into their own hands and deprive someone of their civil rights was a real threat. When the rule of law failed to provide security through justice, society was left defenseless and to their own means. They would find a way to insure a secure environment.

It was inevitable, if the public actively denounced criminal behavior, the lid would blow off a situation. The Yellow T-shirt squad received the first black eye from the liberal left-leaning media. They were already previously labeled and presented by the press as Gestapo Hitler youths; they were at the disadvantage in the public's view. Now, the media had labeled them vigilantes.

Yellow T's were on patrol in one of the many Portland parks to add a degree of security for others. As the newspaper accounts all pointed out, they engaged in a verbal exchange with a group of anarchists that were displaying an American flag upside down and chanting anti-American slogans. On the surface it was not a terrible situation and the police should have been contacted to break up the anarchists' illegal protest. Instead, a clash followed. No clear picture emerged as to who was at fault for the melee but the Yellow T's caught the brunt of the media. Why? Yellow T's represented citizens taking the law into their own hands. Whatever the facts of the case were, it was lost in the term Vigilante. The anarchists evidently were clear of any wrongdoing, at least according to the press. In any case, it hardly seemed like real vigilantism to Walter. Media exploited the first situation they found; it was a mountain out of a molehill.

Sometimes I'd like to respond to some of these so-called reporters. They had people make a statement so they could quote them to present their point of view. One doctor of something-or-other was quoted concerning a mother's pain after the kidnapping and murder of her six-year-old daughter. She was livid with the justice system that allowed a perp out on early release because he was a perfect candidate for their program. The doctor concluded, "Giving the mother any platform to speak is ridiculous. She is too personally involved. What society should do is treat this mother with compassion and provide professional treatment and emotional support. To address crime and punishment because something of this nature has occurred should be resisted; it is simply hysterical nonsense."

Now here was a guy that didn't understand jack! That an over-burdened prison system was looking for "candidates" for early release didn't make it a right decision. Furthermore, anyone, like this doctor, who promoted their own businesslike "treatment" for the victim's families, was just filling his own coffers. He would say the same thing for the criminal. "He needs treatment." I guess I was out of sync with society. The treatment for the victim and family was to know the perp was dead, not that the sex offender was getting treatment so they could be assimilated back into society as a well-adjusted killer and live a long and prosperous life. The whole argument was overrated by the doctors. I, Walter, could guarantee a level of satisfaction that treatment could only hope to achieve.

Sifting through project files I once again felt the presence of apparitions, a signal I welcomed. Some names received more urging from my ghostly audience than others. I was uncertain which to choose next. All of them would be nice but unrealistic. What I did understand was the need of speeding up the process.

While I diligently looked for the next project, reporters were busy trying to identify any and all acts of vigilantism or at least anything they could label that way. My take on these articles was summed up in one word—bravo. What I saw was common, ordinary people protecting themselves or intervening in criminal events they observed. Something I believed should happen regardless of my influence. These vigilante acts weren't newsworthy until they came into vogue. Now it was the talk of the town. The police spokespeople were making public announcements in an effort to dissuade the good citizens not to overreact and aggressively confront dangerous situations. Call 911—sounds good, but .40-caliber will protect or save you. The citizens were reacting right. I remember in high school when the girls were being taught not to resist sexual assault because it might expose them to a greater danger than the rapist had planned. I thought that was the dumbest advice I had ever heard but it was the thinking of the day. Next came along the advice to yell "Fire!" The idea was spread around; never shout "Help!" Someone is more likely to respond to fire than help. I preferred what we had taught in jujitsu—always resist. We worked the self-defense class in real-life scenarios, emphasizing readiness to engage at all times. They learned to position keys in their hands to use as weapons, to never turn their backs on their assailants, where to stomp or kick, and many other viable tools to combat an attacker. Surprise was the element and maybe, just maybe, the perp would be screaming "Fire!" before it was over.

These are things that may help an adult, but a small child is just easy prey. That's why I'm needed. I'm a necessary evil in some books and yet, a godsend to others. Predators should beware; go, run, and hide under a rock. I am coming with judgment and I will discover your whereabouts. I will kill you. I have no qualms in so doing.

I'd grown accustomed to receiving emails from Sasins and looked forward to them. I'd begun using my computer more from home with the most sophisticated IP blockers on the market. Yet, I continued to access my email moving to different locations. A couple of weeks had passed since I had shot Graves and finally I had centered my attention on a new target. Destiny's eyes flared red when I read the name aloud. A sea of voices reached a crescendo as I openly declared he would be next. I sat back wondering if this sexual deviate had any idea apparitions followed his every move. There was no hiding.

Sasins had been busy too, her email was revealing.

Scythian,

The latest updates through my sources are saying the Task Force criminologist believes he has identified the signature of the killer. A modus operandi was identified through three or more murders that are linked through architecture of the crime and tools used. Based on crime scene analysis the killer is well organized. The emotional core component of the signature is the killings are likely based on gratification and not revenge. These are the most recent conclusions by the Task Force and are not made public at this time. Keep me up on what's happening.

Archangel

Reflecting on the "signature" the criminologist was addressing caused me to ponder the ideas. I had a hard time identifying the feeling I got when I took a life. Thinking on those that I had sent on their way I felt nothing for the individuals, only a sense of satisfaction in doing so. I suppose that equals gratification. I personally like to think of it like a calling a religious zealot would experience when he exercised his faith. Well, maybe this criminologist has nailed this concept correctly because I do feel gratified.

Sasins deserved a response. That was kind of the unwritten deal we'd happened upon. She fed me current information and I gave her the heads-up on my next kill with a little history to understand why. It seemed to be working.

Archangel,

My motive for my actions is this: I believe. It would not be so if the punishment fit the crime but no such confidence by the people exists. The doctors and lawyers line up in opposition to the law of nature that directs us to rid our society of those that will not live civilized within its confines; the confines of security. I make this world a safer place, not for the uncivilized, but for those that desire peace of mind. Violent sexual predators, pedophiles and the lot have lost their place in such a society. They are untrusted and unwanted vagabonds in our world. This I believe.

Scythian

Sasins responded.

Scythian,

We should talk sometime. I have questions I would like to ask that cannot be addressed in email. Please consider it. You have my phone number.

Archangel

A meeting is out. I would like to express myself in a more personal way but I'm not interested in showing my identity to anyone. I know she wants the scoop on a killer as much as I want her to present an accurate account of what I've done. I really don't want any more than that from her. I'll keep her phone number but for now, email will have to do.

Pulling into the drive where my trailer sat, I saw two cop cars parked alongside a string of mailboxes and another black unmarked car across the street from them. I tried to look nonchalant as I drove past them looking for a way to pass by my home. If I continued through to the other exit I ran the risk of drawing attention to myself; something I didn't want to do. If I pulled into my driveway, they'd know it was me. In my rearview mirror another cop car had come up on me quickly. I had to consider, the game might be over. I pulled into my driveway. The cop car continued past my position to an unknown destination. I sat quietly for a moment then proceeded into my house.

Peeking through my window curtain I could see the two cop cars by the mailboxes. The officers remained in their cars waiting, I assumed, to spring the trap. I could feel the rush of adrenaline, my heart pounded against the wall of my chest. Officers dismounted and walked to the black car. A moment later they entered a nearby mobile home. I watched as they brought a handcuffed man from the residence. As I've said, you never know how far from evil you might be. If nothing else it made for an exciting end of the day. It was time to get back to the project.

Chapter 14

It is an arduous war for justice; I will not recant or vacillate.
—Walter

Just north of Skidmore Street, the cheap little run-down house was nestled away amidst a sea of identical-looking World War II–built homes in the Albina district of Portland. During the seventies, this area was considered "the projects" as older housing was demolished to make room for lower-income apartment dwellings. Housing tracts not part of the agenda remained and were populated with tree-hugging, dope-smoking, communal-living hippies who thought they'd found a haven in the Northwest. They were successful in escaping the crime-laden Haight-Ashbury scene in California, only to discover their lifestyle brought with it a decadent crime wave to Albina. Many of the educated hippies moved on to more capitalistic futures in the alfalfa sprout business. Other visionaries opened health food and café stores while a few made Picasso pottery or engaged in body painting, calling it the "arts." Skidmore and the surrounding area fell into deeper ruin. Rampant crime continued to spread throughout the district. No one felt safe and only the oldest and poorest residents remained.

Here I focused my attention on Stewart Pidd, a thirty-seven-year-old convicted child molester from a neighboring state. He had done a couple years' stretch for his involvement as a rising porn star after copping a plea to sexual assault of a minor in the second degree. In reality, he had committed far worse. You'd have thought a video of repeated sexual penetration of a minor in various orifices would bring a first-degree conviction, but plea bargains saved the victims and their families the humiliation of court exposure. At least that was the prosecutor's perspective. In reality it saved the courts time and money while still scoring a conviction on the attorney's report card.

Fortunately, his twelve-year-old niece, the unwilling costar, was saved from the embarrassment of the video being distributed only because she committed suicide. Her parents said she killed herself after hearing her uncle received the light sentence.

I first became aware of Pidd through an article Anna Sasins published on fast-food chains where many young kids got their first jobs. It might appear to be a casual human-interest feature to the untrained eye, but its contents were telling and startling. According to Sasins, fast-food joints were employing many sex offenders in the Portland area. In fact, it left some question in my mind whether these so-called restaurants screened applicants at all. Just by reading the article I thought the problem was obvious, but Sasins spelled it out. "Kids are at risk working in an environment where sex offenders work. Some measures should be taken to limit exposure." I love that style of reporting. It was a beeline for the jugular. Sasins went on to name more than a dozen fast-food businesses in the Portland area where child sex offenders worked.

My interest was piqued. I wrote Sasins, requested her sources and explained to her how much I appreciated her writing. I too had noticed people of interest working in these places. Maybe they couldn't find better employment or maybe they had a more sinister purpose. My assumption was you could find some of both where easy prey was available.

Sasins responded with the previously undisclosed names to the corresponding fast-food restaurants that were in her article. I don't know what she thought I was going to do with the information but then again, maybe she did. I checked through my files and came across only one name that matched–Stewart Pidd. Seven years had passed since he went to jail in California, now he was working in my city. He was not registered in Oregon as a Class III sex offender, yet his crime should have qualified him. He evidently was not categorized to likely reoffend or he was in violation of the Oregon registry. I really didn't care one way or the other.

Learning your prey's behavior was a valuable hunting skill. Trust me when I say, hunting is hunting, regardless of the prey. When it's a rabbit or quail, you can be haphazard. The risk to the hunter is negligible. When you set out to kill something that can do the same to you, the risk must be taken into consideration.

I found tracking Pidd to be difficult. Portland is a maze of freeways and turnpikes that lead into the boondocks. Pidd seemingly liked to cruise them all. To make things more difficult, Stewart or Stew as he preferred to be called, worked varying shifts in Lake Oswego, a suburb community of Portland's south side.

He was disgustingly unkempt, roly-poly, with bulging, bloodshot eyes. My guess was he cleared six feet and weighed easily in excess of 300 pounds. He was chief fry cook and griller, which added a daily layer of lubricant to his diaphoretic Neanderthal appearance. His hair was straggly long and dripped with perspiration as he slaved over the fryer. After his shift he disrobed to a well-soiled wife beater T-shirt. When the breeze was right, his pungent body odor drifted across the parking lot.

His ride was a ratty-looking, washed-out light blue Ford Pinto. It wasn't the kind of car that stuck out in the crowd, at least not in the Skidmore area. Picking him up when he left work was not difficult; tailing him was. Inevitably, I would lose sight of Pidd between where he worked and where he lived. It took me a few days to figure out why. He wasn't heading straight home after work. He was cruising. His routes varied through Gresham, Aloha, Wilsonville, Tigard, and Hillsboro. It wasn't his skill that shook me off his tail, he had no idea I existed. In all likelihood, I lost him because I wasn't tailing him tight enough.

It wasn't until I picked him up at the restaurant during a morning shift that I was successful in finding his house. When the shift ended he made a beeline to his house on Skidmore. I wasn't comfortable trying to set up an observation on his house from any angle on the street. The area was intimidating and unfriendly, not an environment where you'd want to mingle with the neighbors. I would wait for him to show up for work and then do a recon on his home. It would be a bit chancy, there might be others living with him, he could have house guests, or a guard dog penned up inside. It was a chance I would have to take.

He didn't show at work the next day, maybe it was a day off. Waiting was tough, my trigger finger was itching. Two days passed and still no sign of Pidd. I did a little cruising myself, driving by his home. The Pinto was parked in his driveway and no one was in sight.

I sent Sasins an email, something I'd become comfortable doing. I believed we had developed a quasi-working relationship. She had given me information that I'd acted upon. I did my best to return the favor.

Archangel,

I have great respect for your work. I understand your passion to side with victims and defend those that are weaker. It has been said the pen is mightier than the sword. I postulate swords provide pens with power and vice versa. We use might for right and seek justice in our own way. This is our relationship.

You may not agree with the method I've chosen to deliver the penalties, but the punishment is deserved and long overdue. Until the legal system realizes the severity of their passive approach to justice, I will continue to deliver on my promise. It is an arduous war for justice; I will not recant or vacillate. More treatment or education will only produce well-adjusted, smarter criminals. A greater understanding by society will only lead to acceptance, which is pretty much where we've arrived today. You and I are two lights within the same spectrum.

Scythian

The nights were wearing on me. One nightmare after another besieged me to find Pidd before it was too late. Too late for what, I wondered? Was he planning to move away and unknowingly escape Walter's justice?

On the third day Pidd showed up for work. I waited until he was busy grilling before heading to Skidmore. I felt good about the time frames; he had consistently worked eight-hour shifts. In the Albina district not many people were up early. Those that were out and about were generally on their way to work, the rest were more like blood-suckers, venturing out once darkness embraced the neighborhood.

Nothing appeared out of the ordinary at Pidd's house. His backyard bordered an old church parking lot. The church was abandoned and boarded up. I pulled my Avenger up next to his unfenced lot and watched. After half an hour's observation I was still uncomfortable with the situation, but having seen nothing out of the ordinary I determined it was time to act. I stealthily made my way around to the front door. I knocked and listened; it was quiet. I knocked a second time, nothing. My preferred way of entry was the back door, but in this case the front door was well hidden from view. The wood-framed screen door hung partially open. Using bump keys the lock opened in seconds and I was in.

The stench filled my nostrils immediately. I walked slowly through the house trying to hold my breath. My hopes were to set up an ambush but that seemed less likely now—I couldn't hold my breath that long. Bang, bang, and it would be over, that's all the time I needed and his debt would be paid. The innocent niece he abused and exploited to be a porn star would finally have justice.

The home was a single-level two-bedroom box. The front door opened into a small living room that was adjacent to the hallway, an easy ambush. The kitchen and dining room were one and the same leading to a laundry room by the back door. Any place in here would work if I knew which door he would use. The putrid smell of body odor from the bathroom to the bedrooms was so bad I'd have to use one of the other rooms.

A hall closet sat at the end of the hallway and was bolted with three bolts, top, middle and near the bottom. Why would anyone need three bolt locks on the outside of a closet door? My curiosity got the best of me and I began with the top bolt sliding it slowly out of the hasp. I slipped the bottom bolt out next, and then with Glock in hand, released the middle bolt. I turned the knob and opened the door. Movement in a back corner stood my hair on end as I retreated a few steps. My Glock responded automatically to a dead-on firing position. In the dim light it took a moment to focus on the young girl that was bound and gagged. I slipped my weapon into my belt and froze in place. Now what do I do? Squinting as her sight adjusted from the closet darkness she waited for my next move. I dropped to one knee and leaned toward her. With both hands I pulled her from captivity. I wrestled the gag from around her head releasing a torrent of sobs and uttering of unintelligible words. As the girl cried her heart out I heard Destiny speak, "take her from here." When Destiny touched my back I understood why the dreams had pressed me into acting.

I was faced with a new dilemma, one that I hadn't planned for. She was clothed in an oversized T shirt that reeked of Pidd. I cut the duct tape from her wrists and ankles and helped her to her feet. She continued to sob and try to speak; I knew I had to get her out of the house right away. Unlike any other rescuer, I couldn't bring myself to call 911. We headed for the back door. If Pidd had showed up then and there, I'd have taken my knife and skinned him alive. I would have enjoyed every minute of it, in fact hours of it. I would not have been quick.

I'll admit, when it comes to building a rapport or talking with kids, I'm at a loss. "What's your name?" I asked. It was a slow process. She made multiple attempts to speak but had difficulty forming words. I was becoming a mixed bag of emotions as I waited. Anxiety loomed. Finally, I was able to understand her to say "Helen."

"Helen you are going to be safe; you're safe with me." Helen nodded her head as she held back the tears.

I helped Helen into the passenger side of my car as I tried to figure out what to do with her. I knew what I had to do, but how?

"Helen, I need to call someone," Helen nodded between sobs. "I need to know your last name?" She paused briefly as if trying to remember, "Beck, Helen Beck," she answered.

I've kept Sasins phone number with me since she invited me to contact her, never really expecting to actually call. In my bug-out bag I kept a prepaid mobile phone. I had intentionally loaded it with only twenty-five minutes' air time intended for a one-time use and then into the river with it. A couple of blocks away stood a Mom and Pop's grocery that catered to an older crowd. This was a good place to stop and make the call. It was my best hope.

I pulled into a parking spot near the end of the building, excused myself from Helen, and placed the call from in front of my car. I was relieved when I heard a female answer.

"Anna Sasins."

"This is Wal-ah, Scythian."

Sasins was silent for several seconds.

"I didn't expect to hear from you."

"I need your help, Anna."

Anna replied in a startled and high-pitched tone, "With what?" I knew she didn't want to be involved in anything I was doing; she had made that clear enough early on. Now the inflection in her voice reinforced her notable concern. From my perspective, I wasn't all that jazzed about her involvement either, but I needed her to make an exception.

"I have rescued a young girl from a sex offender; I need to turn her over to you."

Anna, with a whispering sigh, asked the million-dollar question, "Why me?"

"She was a hostage. She needs transport to a hospital. They will contact the police. I need someone I can trust and you're the only one that can do it. I will give you the address where she was being kept for the police."

There was a short pause before I asked again, "Anna I need your help on this; I can't take her myself and I don't have friends I can call on."

"Okay, okay, do you know the girl's name?"

"Helen Beck."

"Helen Beck!" Anna exclaimed. "She's been missing for the past four days. She was kidnapped on her way home from school in Aloha."

"Well, she's not missing anymore. Where can we meet?"

Helen was watching me; I couldn't help but feel the poor little thing was becoming more frightened by my actions. She wanted to go home, that was the only thing on her mind. "Anna, hang on a minute, I want you to talk with Helen and reassure her that she is safe with me and will be safe with you."

I handed Helen the phone through the passenger side window. The conversation was short with a couple of uh-huh's before she handed the phone back. I could see a relief in Helen's face but it wouldn't last long.

"Where to?"

"What part of town are you in?"

"Albina, do you know it?"

"Yes, let's meet at the Multnomah County Library in Grant Park off Tillamook St. I'm at the Lloyd Center right now. It'll take me maybe a half hour to get there."

"We'll be there."

The Avenger cranked up and we started in that direction. Helen was still crying occasionally but for the most part she sat quietly. I told her I was taking her to a nice lady that would reunite her with her family. By now, Helen would be able to provide police with at least some description of Walter and my Avenger. This good deed might cost me my freedom but with some luck it wouldn't be before I paid Pidd a visit.

We arrived before Sasins and backed into the first slot in the rear parking area. Helen was getting anxious and I wasn't doing much better. I was concerned for her health after having been in Pidd's custody. Whatever she had gone through, I didn't want to ask. I didn't need to. There was nothing further I could help her with and it didn't change what I was planning.

I didn't know what type car I would be looking for or for that matter what Sasins really looked like. Her photo accompanied her articles, but it could have been taken twenty years ago.

After a long ten minutes, a silver Lexus pulled up directly to my Avenger. There was something oddly familiar about this car, I couldn't put my finger on it; my thoughts were focused on getting rid of Helen. A fortyish-looking redhead stepped out. Her newspaper photo did her a disservice. She was beautiful and generously constructed.

"Scythian?"

Without answering, I stepped from my Avenger taking Helen by the hand and assisted her across the bucket seats and out the driver's door.

"This is Helen," I said.

Anna immediately took Helen by the hand pulling her into an embrace as if they were mother and daughter.

"I'll give you the address, Anna, but I want you to write it on something of yours."

I read off the address as she copied it onto a steno pad.

"Thank you, Anna. I need to hurry. Pidd will be off work soon and I intend to finish what I've started. I need some time, a couple hours at least and I need you to buy it for me."

Anna assisted Helen into the Lexus, fastened the seatbelt for her and shut the door. "How do you want me to present this to the authorities, Scythian?"

"You don't know anything other than I called your number from the newspaper. To your knowledge it was a random selection. Take her to the hospital. When police arrive give them the address, but wait as long as you can before giving it to them. When they get to Pidd's house, they'll find everthing taken care of."

I waited for Anna to drive from the lot before hitting the Avenger's ignition. Sasins had seen my car and maybe took note of my license plate number; I needed to swap them out with another set of phony plates. My plan was simple, go to Pidd's home, set the ambush and get out of Dodge before the cops arrive. Shoot, kill, and be gone. Nothing could be simpler.

It was a frustrating drive through congested traffic back to the target site. I could feel the strange mixture of anxiety and anticipation, nervousness, and excitement. I liked it.

Finally, behind the abandoned church again, I pulled up to the edge of Pidd's backyard. I sat quietly for a moment checking my watch and looking at the back door. Something was amiss. I was trying to recall if I shut the door or left it ajar. I questioned myself but it was an exercise in futility, I couldn't remember. The only thing that was clear was leaving with Helen.

I was choosing a few items from my bug-out bag needed to complete the project when the back door burst open. Pidd rushed frantically from the house toward a vehicle canopy in his driveway. I ran to the corner of the house; I knew at that distance I could make the shot if an opportunity existed. I peeked around the corner just in time to get a glimpse of Pidd's Pinto backing from the driveway. I ran back to my car, hit the ignition, dropped it in gear and fishtailed onto the street. It was a couple blocks before I had good visual on his car. The chase was on, only Pidd didn't know we were playing cat and mouse.

I followed at a distance as we headed south. I was comfortable behind him: it was not likely he would expect me to be there or that I existed. He drove erratically, zipping in and out of lanes but rarely passing any vehicles.

I had no doubt he was making a run for it. His flight was briefly interrupted when he pulled into his place of employment. I found a good place to observe the door Pidd had disappeared through. I knew he would not be long, he left the Pinto engine running. Fewer than five minutes passed before he reappeared with what looked like a large white bag used for "take out" family dinners. Back on the road we continued south. I didn't know where he was going and I doubted he had friends. Nevertheless we were on our way someplace as fast as his car would roll. Obviously, it wasn't very fast; it was a Pinto.

Dead-heading south on the I-5 Corridor led straight into Mexico. It was a long haul I preferred not to make. If Mexico was his destination we would need gas, food and maybe even a catnap along the way. Best-case scenario for me would be to have him pull off the main drag onto a quiet and remote little side road to rest his eyes for a while. I would make it a long while.

If he made it to the Mexifornia border there was a 99 percent chance he'd cross without getting caught. Even if they were notified with a BOLO, Cali is lax, too lax. You would have to be stupid to get caught. A good reason I needed to get him before he got stopped at the border.

We traveled for hours reaching the Oregon–California border late in the evening. I would have preferred to take care of this project in Oregon. Killing across a state line guaranteed the FBI would be involved, something I didn't need.

On the south side of Redding, Pidd pulled off the road into an economy motel parking lot. A few minutes after our arrival, he reentered his Ford and moved it to the end of one of the two-story complexes.

I continued to watch from my car while Pidd settled into his room. As the night wore on the realization set in, he was snug and comfortable in his motel room; TV, shower—which I doubted he would use—and bed, while I sat crunched up behind the steering wheel with nothing to do besides watch and wait.

It was after midnight and activity around the motel had slowed considerably—nothing had moved in the last half hour. The parking area was well lit; any attempt to sabotage his car was out of the question. The room access was likewise well lit; there might be little time to force entry without creating noise and being seen. Adjacent motel rooms on either side of his were occupied as well. On the back side of the building was a small sliding-glass window that appeared to be positioned in the bathroom; much too small to gain access through. As I weighed the options, it was beginning to look dismal to finish up here. He was a lucky man for now but the cat-and-mouse game was still in play.

My eyelids grew heavy and from time to time would shut for a minute or two, maybe longer. The pulse of my heart was slowing and I could hear the quietness of the night humming in my inner ears. All bad signs I was losing the battle to stay awake

It was midmorning before Pidd ventured out of his hole and loaded his car with what few belongings he had brought into his motel unit. He refueled at a large gas station providing me an opportunity to do the same. Pidd pulled out of the gas station and headed south on Interstate 5 again. I was close behind.

A few hours later we pulled into Sacramento. I figured he had probably devoured the bag of sweets he had bought at the gas station and now it was time for a full-course meal. We passed through an older neighborhood to a small dimly lit tavern. It was a shabby place on the outside with visible plywood patches on the exterior siding. The name was partially illuminated, making it difficult to read, "El Diablo Club." The parking lot was full of cheap, older-model cars; it looked like a busy place. Why was he here? He drove directly to this sleazy watering hole; my guess was, it was not his first time here. Pidd must have a connection, someone who could help him out of his predicament. The possibilities were endless.

I was amazed at the lack of people coming and going with the number of cars in the lot. Something wasn't right. Darkness was setting in. We had gotten such a late start out of Redding I had to believe this was Pidd's intended destination, at least for this day. More than an hour passed before he reappeared on the front porch landing. He was deeply engaged in conversation with a Hispanic male. Both men talked and pointed in the direction of the Pinto, followed by circling gestures with their hands. Pidd and his Latino buddy shook hands as they separated. Stew made a beeline for his car while the other man walked around behind the tavern. Moments later the Pinto was inching along behind El Diablo with its headlights off. I wasn't worried about following him; it was obvious he was hiding his car from view, not sneaking away.

Fatigue was setting in; a good leg stretch was called for. Using a hedgerow I was able to stay concealed as I looked over the area behind the bar. A one-story house adjoined the old dilapidated bar along with a few more cars and a bus parked in what used to be a yard.

Hippie flophouses were all too common throughout the 1960s and '70s in California. The communal-living free-love generation had moved on but the flophouses remained with a new clientele. Transients and illegal aliens now dominated the old flophouse scene. I could see people, mostly young Latino males, strewn about on old couches and bench car seats near the front of the house. A fat English doughboy like Pidd didn't fit in here. The only thing he might have in common was a felony record. He was a man on the lam; a liability, not an asset, and it was impossible for him to blend into his new ethnic environment.

Pidd unloaded the suitcase from his car and followed the cantina attendant through the front door of the house. The negatives became apparent. I would have to wade past a small army of witnesses to get my target. I could undoubtedly yell, "Police raid" and all those fine folks would scramble like cockroaches but Pidd might run as well. My luck, he'd have a heart attack and die of natural causes. That was too good for him.

I could see Stew through a bedroom window. Without drapes in the way it was an easy shot from the hedge but the muzzle blast in the dark of night would still be visible even muted by the flash suppressor. A longer shot would have to wait for daylight.

While I was busy chasing doughboy around, news headlines were starting to break. The radio carried a ghastly commentary on the recovery of Helen. A not-so-factual report seasoned by the lack of police comment made for a tasteless superficial newscast. What it did tell me was that Anna had successfully delivered Helen to the authorities. With that I was pleased.

My concerns were mounting. What kind of chain reaction had this calamity set in motion? Could Sasins be trusted with what she knew or would she reveal what she knew to one of her inside sources? Had Aloha police alerted the task force? Why should they, they were looking for Stewart Pidd, child molester, not me. Detective Ware was old-school and cunning in his own right. He had intuition and used it like a crystal ball. He would put two and two together and be involved as soon as he heard of Pidd's death. With the kidnapping in one district and the sexual assault in another, it could work in my favor. With prosecutors and police agencies from different districts, trying to work together, it would be a time-consuming process. Time I planned to use to make this kill and get away.

I moved my car out of the parking area and onto the street just off the lot with a partial view of the back. With one eye open, I cat-napped through the night, getting as much rest as was possible in the front seat of my Avenger.

Early in the morning I caught a glimpse of Pidd climbing on board the rickety old bus with about a dozen Hispanic males. I followed the cantina crew down back alleys and side streets across Sacramento to a deserted-looking warehouse complex. The bus parked with its door emptying out to the complex's entrance. I set up visual on the opposite side of the roadway behind an old concrete bridge abutment. As much as I would have liked to have had the bus doors open in my direction, it would have to do for now.

About ten o'clock Pidd and others were milling around the entrance to the largest facility in the complex. My target was a pasty white blimp standing next to these dark-brown smaller figures. If I had to make a long shot with my AR, it would be easy to distinguish which one to shoot.

As noon approached I retrieved my rifle from the trunk and put finishing touches on its assembly. I decided the long shot was the best idea. As I anticipated, Pidd and others walked out of the building and outside the gated entrance of the facility. They boarded the bus and took seats, but no driver. I scanned the windows with my scope but the sun's reflection made it impossible to pick out my target. As the break finished I could see people moving at the doorway of the bus.

With bipod fixed and sights leveled I waited to squeeze the trigger. Pidd filled the doorway above the steps leading off the bus for only a second when my weapon fired. Shurrp! My sights held firm on the doorway as the first round blasted through the driver's side window, Pidd went down. People were crouching, others made a run for the warehouse; the target was nowhere in sight. I could see heads bobbing and weaving trying to find a safe way to see what was happening. I waited but I couldn't wait long.

Sweeping my scope left to right and back left again, I could not see Pidd. I was guessing he had taken the blunt of the bullet. I never like to leave a person with only one hole in them; they might live and defeat the whole purpose of shooting them in the first place. In this case, I might just have to hope he would bleed out. My thoughts shifted to bugging out before all the sirens and lights rolled in. I pulled my AR down and began the disassembly before slipping over to the Avenger. I glanced up as I pulled the bipod off in time to see my target running from the bus toward the gated entrance. I'd missed him completely. I pulled my AR back up but too late to make a shot. Pidd had momentarily escaped.

The direction he ran was away from his newfound friends, rounding the nearest corner of the warehouse and almost totally concealed by the bus. Quickly I tossed the AR into the trunk and strapped up my .40-caliber. I drove forward in his direction trying not to draw attention to my vehicle. Skirting the outside of the fenced area I could see the fence line end as did the parking lot. Pidd was still moving toward the back of the warehouse trying doors as he went. As of yet, no sirens were wailing in the distance.

Parking the Avenger at the end of the corner parking lot I sprinted across an arid clearing toward the facility. I crossed over the fence on a mashed down corner and proceeded toward the rear of the warehouse. Multiple outbuildings stretched across the rear of the compound; Pidd had, no doubt, made it into one of these. I opened the first storage shed, it was pitch black inside other than the light I was now shedding with a partially open door. It was clear immediately he had not chosen this first building, it was jammed full of wood pallets. One by one I entered these windowless wood structures in search of my prey. Opening the door to the fourth building a kaleidoscope of images appeared before me. They were the faces of many looking for revenge. They may not have been Pidd's victims, past or future but violated souls of the living dead and I their weapon. The outside light now announced my presence and the sound of heavy breathing somewhere down the narrow corridor made me acutely aware the search for Pidd's whereabouts had come to an end.

The wood floor creaked about every other step as I moved slowly down the darkened corridor. The entrance door had closed to a fraction of an inch allowing only a sliver of light to penetrate the darkness behind me. I kept an eye open for movement but my eyes had not adjusted to the darkness. I continued to advance in the direction of the labored breathing. Whap! Pain surged through my skull from being struck in the head with something. My equilibrium spun in circles as I crashed backwards into the hallway wall. Before I could gain my balance Pidd rammed into me loosening the Glock from my grip and collapsing me to the floor under him. I could hear my weapon bouncing off the wood floor but was unable to see it in the dark; Pidd scrambled to reach it. Our hands banged into each other as we wildly searched. My adversary crawled forward partially freeing me from underneath him as he tried to locate the gun. I reached for my Buck knife. He continued forward allowing me to thrust the six-inch blade into his lower back. He wailed like a banshee.

He was still frantically searching for my Glock when I pulled myself from underneath him. Reaching forward I found his greasy hair and yanked it backwards. "Ah, ah, ah, yaaah," he cried out. My knife plunged into the side of his neck. Where I hit I didn't care. His body went rigid. I thrust the knife repeatedly into his throat; blood spurted with every heartbeat. I could feel his warm blood soaking my hand. Pidd gurgled; no longer able to form words. His movement slowed, finally ceasing; silence followed.

My heart continued to pound and I shook from the adrenaline rush. It was different from anything I had experienced before. I located my Glock and kept it close to my side like a security blanket. Pulling my thoughts back together an inescapable fact occurred to me—the forensic evidence was spread out all along this crime scene. It was time for a barbecue.

These storage sheds were all wood construction. What I needed was a way to ignite it. This unit contained packing material and I was never without my Zippo. It was going to be a scorcher! I glanced back to see the boxes in flames as I made my way toward the light of day.

Once outside I began working my way back to the Avenger. I couldn't help speculating as to why the cops had not shown up yet. I don't know what was going on in the warehouse but whatever it was kept the others from calling the police. As I pulled out on the commercial drive, I noticed the bus was gone and the front gate closed. Odd, yes, but the world Pidd had brought me to, was a criminal world, one that I was beginning to understand and hate.

My clothes and gloves were covered in blood that stuck to everything I touched. I peeled off the gloves and broke out my supply of disposable baby wipes and bottled water I kept in my bug out bag. About a mile from the warehouse I stopped at a roadside turnout to clean up. After my hands and face were scrubbed, I stripped off outer layers of clothing and put on a jogging suit, stepped into a pair of tennis shoes, and laced them up tight. This was comfortable, casual, and clean. I bagged my clothes, shoes, and proceeded to wipe down the interior of the Avenger, for any trace of blood. Minutes later I was on the road looking for a spider hole.

On the northern outskirts of Sacramento I pulled into a motel to get a shower and much-needed sleep. It was chancy to stay in the area. The license plate numbers or my vehicle make and model might be reported to the police. It was a chance I had to take. I didn't have extra plates with me.

I crossed the border into Oregon just after four o'clock the next afternoon. I stopped by a diner to enjoy a quiet meal and scan the daily newspaper. "Kidnap Victim Rescued by Good Samaritan" the headline story read. That wouldn't last long when they found Pidd murdered. Lots of hoopla leading the public to believe something great and wonderful was done but I didn't feel that way. Sure, Helen didn't die. Pidd had been saving that for last but I could only imagine how he had violated her innocence. I didn't really know what torment and trauma he put her through and I didn't want to know. I didn't live for the details; I lived to execute. That was my passion and my desire. In Helen's case I had stumbled across her accidentally. It was too little, too late, to save her from the likes of Pidd as far as I was concerned. Too little on the part of the judicial system in allowing this predatory animal back into society and too late for the prosecutors to promise Stewart Pidd would remain behind bars for the rest of his life. Besides, I'd made the prosecutor's usual promise a moot point.

I was eager to contact Sasins to see how it went when she turned Helen over to the authorities. My hope was the police didn't put her through the wringer. My experience with the Estelle Hertz case had taught me witnesses got the brunt of the interrogation while criminals lawyered up and went unscathed.

Anna, however, was not Hertz and was well skilled in police interrogation and tactics. If Sasins broke and rolled over on me, I might have company awaiting my return. I didn't like the thought of the police as my enemies, I would have liked to think we were on the same team but I knew we couldn't be.

Chapter 15

DNA matches have changed the face of guilt;
It has made those at fault guiltier.
—Walter

My immediate concerns were put to rest when I pulled into my driveway at home without being arrested. Foremost on my agenda was communication with Anna. There were questions I needed to ask, her answers could give me insight to what the future held for me. To clear my guilty conscience required that I apologize for getting her mixed up in the rescue.

Archangel,

Thank you seems shallow for your help with Helen. I found myself wedged between a rock and a hard place. On the one hand, I had to get her out of the situation; on the other, I could not reveal myself as the rescuer. Too much would have to be explained. You saved the day. Helen was reunited with her parents and the police knew little, if anything about me and my involvement. Again, thanks.

Scythian

A week after Helen's rescue the kidnapping was no longer the lead story and the media were looking for another story of atrocious criminal behavior to sensationalize. There was little in the news of interest to me. Short snippets appeared showing Pidd's photo and asking the public for help in locating him. The Aloha police department was broadcasting a Crimestoppers advertisement looking for any information on the alleged kidnapping. I could give 'em a tip on where to find him but why spoil their fun.

Anna's response went a long way toward putting my mind at ease. She had informed the police a man had called her and said he had information pertaining to Helen Beck, but would not give his name. The man refused to give any details over the phone and demanded a face-to-face meeting—it wasn't the first time she had received anonymous information this way. Anna didn't know why he selected her as a go-between. Anna told investigators she was totally blown away when the man opened his car door and pulled the little girl out. Before she could ask any questions the man recited an address then jumped into the car and drove away. She didn't get a license number and was too distracted by the turn of events to give an accurate detailed description of the man or his car. Anna's inside sources revealed authorities were satisfied with the information given to them. She believed there was little reason to be concerned about anything Helen might recall from her rescue. She was emotionally compromised. It might be years before she was able to provide details about her time in captivity or the man who rescued her. Anna ended on a positive note to keep me informed on any developments in the case. I would later learn Anna's resources reached into areas I would never have imagined and would prove valuable in keeping my neck out of the noose.

I couldn't help thinking Anna was aware of her part in my quest; regardless, she asked nothing of me and I was comfortable with that. Receiving frequent updates from Sasins became the norm. Sometimes it was the press release, info passed out to all news agencies. At other times it was a tidbit from one of her sources passed to me by email. She assumed I'd taken care of Pidd although it had never been discussed.

Anna's next email contained both good and bad news.

> Scythian,
>
> Hot off the Sacramento wire, "Police say, fire not cause of death in warehouse blaze." My source tells me Stewart Pidd's remains were identified and the state medical examiner's office has made the final identification and classified it as a homicide. His name is being withheld at this time. Investigators are not elaborating on the case except that his badly burned body was discovered by firefighters as they finished extinguishing hotspots in the warehouse complex fire. Local police confirmed the fire was intentionally set and there is a homicide investigation in progress. Detective Ware and task force members have been in contact with local authorities in Sacramento and are expected to arrive there soon. I doubt

all this is news to you but I wanted you to know Pidd was located. My source will continue to feed information as the case progresses.

Archangel

Pidd's body had been found and the authorities knew he was murdered. The most likely suspect would be the unidentified and unaccounted-for Good Samaritan, who for unknown reasons had been digging around Stew's house. This was the foundation cornerstone Ware and posse was looking for. This would be critical to the construction of the case, not against Pidd but against a murdering entity—me.

Email from Anna was becoming more and more frequent.

Scythian,

It is important I talk with you. Call me.

Archangel

Well, I liked the straight-up approach. Beating around the bush tires me out—this was as direct as communication got. I owed her this one. Throwaway cell phones were going to get expensive. I made the call.

"Anna Sasins."

"This is Scythian."

Anna paused momentarily and then whispered, "I picked up reliable information on the task force. Detective Ware is setting up a sting operation, code name Vigilant Response, in hopes of snaring the culprit they believe responsible for as many as five murders. Ware is convinced the killer is targeting sex offenders. He believes the victims have something more in common than their felonies. Possibly a link to some sort of media attention."

"I think he's barking up the wrong tree on media attention, Anna. Is Ware prepared for a large scale operation?"

"He has the full weight and resource of MCSD behind it."

"What do you mean 'full weight and resource'?"

"The task force will augment from regular patrols and off duty officers to man it around the clock."

"Where are they planning to run this sting?"

"I don't know, but I understand it is set to go active this coming Monday. It'll be a high-profile case with plenty of media coverage for sure. Task force members are counting on the defendant fitting the criteria of a potential victim."

"Have you heard of any cases coming up that would make good bait?"

"Seymour Johnson."

Seymour had been in the news. The adult son of prominent Portland businessman, Richard Johnson, also known as Biggie D, appeared to be a chip off the old block. Richard had been photographed with high-end escorts for years and was well known to the Portland swinger scene. He slung a lot of power around locally and reportedly was well known in the world of organized crime as a connected man. The unfounded rumor about Biggie was he bought whatever he wanted. When his money wasn't good enough to make a deal, he paid the right people to procure it for him. Money always talked one way or another.

Seymour was alleged to have promoted and distributed pornography, some of which included underage girls. The task force would ensure it had media coverage, providing it was the bait. Ware would not be setting this guy up, but monitoring the case closely hoping to catch a break if the hitter exposed him- or herself by the lure of Seymour.

"I know the name, thanks for the heads up, Anna."

"Scythian, do you play chess?"

"Ah," I muttered into silence.

What kind of left-field question was this? Did she want to get together, now we are acquainted, for a game of chess? Finally the words formed I was looking for. "I've played, but it's not something that really interests me."

"Oh, I think it would," Anna quietly responded.

"Thanks again," I said as I hung up the phone. I wasn't really sure if it was time to hang up or what courtesy was expected but I didn't want to engage in casual conversation with Anna. All the pertinent information was delivered and that was all I had called for. Now it was time to think through a strategy on how to handle the information.

On the one hand, it was a challenge. The gauntlet had been tossed down and a game of sorts, them against me, was expected. If I could pluck this bait out from under their noses, I could essentially win but there was nothing to win. If anything, it would prove Detective Ware's theory right. Something I was not in a hurry to confirm. Besides, if Seymour caught the rap, he'd be locked up for a while. I could always kill him later. On the other hand, while the task force was tied up with around-the-clock coverage of this trial, the rest of the field was wide open for play. Maybe that was what Anna had alluded to by chess. Strategy.

Seymour's trial began without incident, at least without any interruption from me. Biggie D was boisterous and condescending concerning the police and the prosecutor's case—the reporter's ate it up. Seymour had a stack of defense attorneys at his disposal. The trial was short and the jury deliberation long—too long. Not a good sign for the prosecution. A week into deliberation the jury announced it was unable to reach a verdict.

I watched the proceedings in the media, resisting the urge to personally attend. Based on the coverage, I was sure it was an attempt to draw me out. I was further tempted to drive around Biggie D's place to see if I could spot the task force members. Pure curiosity was consuming me.

After the hung verdict, life resumed as normal. Seymour was free pending review of the charges. Prosecutors would have to determine if the case was viable and under the circumstances, it would probably never fly. Not because there was a lack of evidence to bring justice, but because there was a lack of integrity in the legal system. It was a big con.

Another month passed; things quieted down between Anna and me. There wasn't much to talk about. The task force hadn't been heard from since the sting had been ineffective at flushing out a serial killer. I kept myself busy working on a project. I would act on it soon. Destiny was guiding my hand.

Anna continued to puzzle me. I didn't understand what she wanted. I was not interested in becoming emotionally involved but she seemed to want some level of personal relationship. I couldn't get a handle on it. Her most recent email perplexed me.

> Scythian,
>
> What is your favorite chess piece?
>
> Archangel

I was never a fan of small talk. How did I skillfully tell her I didn't care about chess? If she was trying to make a point, that was fine, make it. She insisted on this social discourse but I was accustomed to life in the shadows. I was a mystery to everyone I crossed paths with and I was comfortable to exist in that manner. Even the profilers had taken notice—the person they sought was an introvert who existed on the outskirts of humanity.

Anna was a great person to know for a resource, but my interest was strictly business. I could invite more dialogue by responding to her with some corny answer about queen's rook or some other time-wasting discourse but what was the point. I needed to be straight with her.

Archangel,

I'm not really a chess player, I've played but I'm a coffeehouse player and will never be taken seriously. Different pieces don't mean much to me and I'm not into competition. Sorry, if I seem short on this subject but I have a myriad of things demanding my time and attention.

Scythian

Anna was quick to respond.

Scythian,

You may not see yourself as a chess player but I do. You play a very dangerous game of chess; winner takes all. You employ strategies and move aggressively to a checkmate; your ultimate reason for the play.

I imagine your chess piece as a Knight. You move unlike other pieces on the field of play. Your approach is the least detectable on the board; you attack at will. It fits you.

Archangel

Anna passed along a few tidbits she had picked up on, but that had dwindled away. I didn't think Anna was holding anything back, although that was always possible. Nothing new from her as of late, even the media had slowed its antivigilante rhetoric as it searched for another soapbox it could use. Quiet was good, but I was about ready to liven it up a bit.

Jack Cass was another run-of-the-mill rapist, sort of. He was a middle-aged truck driver, never married, and maintained a low profile. According to Cass he was a closet homosexual who had a lot of one-night stands but no serious relationships. He liked to party, drink heavily, and dabbled in whatever drugs were available.

His trouble came when he offered a thirteen-year-old boy a ride home from such a party. According to the victim, Cass attacked him in the car and forced him into anal sex. The victim admitted he was too inebriated to fight Cass off. Cass also admitted to being high on a mixture of alcohol and morphine, did not remember what led up to the sex, but insisted the boy asked for sex. The victim insisted he never consented to the act and that he was hetrosexual. Cass maintained his innocence but was convicted. Justice was served.

In days gone by, guilt was more questionable but DNA matches have changed the face of guilt; it's made those at fault guiltier. Following closely on the heels of DNA was the resurrection of the popular game show "Let's Make A Deal," only this time prosecutors were the emcees. But it was still just a game until Walter came into play. I changed the rules.

After a brief introduction at gunpoint as to why I was at Jack's residence, he spun and ran a few feet. I didn't like shooting people in the back but sometimes you had to do what you had to do. I punched his ticket for the next life; whatever it might bring.

I didn't mention this project to Anna. Why should I, I didn't have to prove anything to her. It was across the state line in Washington and as far as I knew, didn't involve her sources. If she heard something, I had no doubt she would be quick to let me know.

A couple months crept by while I laid the foundation for my next project. When I finally got around to checking my email I found a message from Anna in my inbox.

Scythian,

Detective B. A. Ware has hung up his shield. FBI Agent Loren Odar has taken over the Pidd case. Sources have it Vigilant Response was Ware's last bid to get the job done before FBI assumed responsibility. It is not clear as of yet whether they disbanded the task force or have designated a new one. Detective Ware made it indisputably clear he wasn't playing second fiddle to any new academy grad, especially one who is arrogant and egotistical. I've met Agent Odar at a press conference. He appears very confident and is a five-year veteran of the Bureau. He boasts a small army of profilers and forensic investigators to help him crack the case. He jokes saying his biggest challenge will be getting to know the Pacific Northwest having lived his entire life on the East Coast. Although he did not address his transfer to the Portland office, it is his first lead position.

Archangel

Well, if Agent Odar had been working the case as Anna said, he had either managed to put a cork in the information leaks or there was no new information to be had. In any case, so far, it hadn't impeded my progress. I'd chosen and closed in on my next project; I was just a few days away from another road trip.

September was one of my favorite months in Oregon. Coolness had returned to the mornings and I actually felt like getting up earlier than normal to enjoy a cup of coffee and smell the fresh air. I was finishing up with plans for my upcoming trip. This one was different from previous projects in a variety of ways. My target, Carlena Okie, was a fifty-year-old female whose flair for the entrepreneurial lifestyle had landed her a few years in the slammer.

Carlena, or Carrie as she prefers to be called, caught my eye because she confronted my thinking. Most of my life I had believed young teen girls were being kidnapped in America, taken across the Mexican border and sold into the sex slave trade. Now, before me, was the opposite scenario. Okie had been involved as the house mother where underage Mexican girls were transported to the United States and housed for the purpose of sex. Some of these girls were victims of lies whereas others were sold into slavery to pay off family debts. Regardless of how the girls were trapped in the trade, Okie was guilty of operating a lucrative sex-slave operation. When authorities pinched her in a sting, the Oregon native began to sing like a bird to get immunity from charges. She named Mexican suppliers and local johns in exchange for a sweet deal. She was the government's star witness. She had to do time but not a lot. It turned out she was guilty of some human rights violations but the feds were able to mitigate her incarceration. Society was paid in full in no time. In my view, a short tour behind bars paid nothing for the pain she brought to dozens of girls.

Okie was an easy target. She managed to get on the con speaking circuit where she was paid to tell her story of vice and how communities could protect themselves from this type of criminal behavior. Her website had the whole circuit laid out. Why some felon had to explain what was wrong with kidnapping young girls and enslaving them in the sex trade and then get paid for her wealth of knowledge was pure bull and I wasn't buying it. She was guilty, just as guilty as every one of those she fingered in the deal and I was a fixin' to bring that to her remembrance.

I arose that Tuesday morning with the prospect of a little drive to meet Carrie. I ground the coffee beans and flipped on the TV as was my routine. I wasn't paying much attention to what was being broadcast; my mind was elsewhere when my eye caught a glimpse of one of the Twin Towers of the World Trade Center on fire. I was stunned with disbelief. All news channels were carrying the tragedy unfolding live from New York. Throughout the day and for days following I was riveted to my TV as government and news agencies pieced the puzzle together. Carrie Okie would have to wait.

Anna contacted me via email as the events of 9/11 unfolded. I didn't have any answers that made sense and I knew it, although I tried to explain these acts of terror in a rational way.

Anna continued daily contact after 9/11, mostly just trying to understand why these rag-head Islamikazis felt the need to attack innocent American civilians. She readily professed herself to be busy with her writing but I didn't see any articles being published from her desk. In the wake of the terrorist attacks a great deal of scrutiny was placed on the Islamic community by police and media. Oregon, with its liberal laws, was heavily populated with Muslims. Perhaps not all Muslims were terrorists but all 9/11 suicide hijackers were Muslim. A concern not easily overlooked by all law enforcement agencies, especially the Feds.

Anna's sources paid off once again.

Scythian,

As you are aware a national situation has evolved with Muslim "Cells". What you may not be aware of is the scenario has pulled most of Agent Odar's finances and manpower to be used elsewhere. At this point in time he essentially is working alone. My sources tell me MCSD is concentrating their efforts likewise on local investigations of Muslim activity. Terror threats to the nation take precedence and might as well be called the FBI's only priority now. If you've been following the news, and I'm sure you have, Anthrax attacks over the past few days have the U.S. Postal Service ground to a halt. This is devastating to our national security and has stretched all law enforcement resources to their breaking point. My sources tell me Agent Odar is despondent over the changes and wants reassignment to one of the terrorist task forces. He's made the statement, "That's where the action is" and he feels he's missing the opportunity of a lifetime.

Archangel

Agent Odar's dilemma was to my benefit. This would be the first break I've had since the bloodhounds started tracking me. Muslim hijackers followed by Anthrax attacks—the FBI had to throw everything they had at this problem, and it was likely to last a long time. I'm not so foolish as to think any law enforcement agency was going to give me carte blanche but I'd be on the back burner for now and I could become a cold case file if I quit. What an opportunity to get out alive in one piece. But it was not going to happen. My goal meant too much to me.

Road trip time! Carrie Okie was appearing on stage in Kelso, Washington. It was a hop, skip, and jump from my house. The Community Center engagement was slated to let out about 9 p.m. and she'd make her way from there to wherever she was staying. I was confident I could identify her easily and intervene. Her website and brochures plastered her face all over.

I arrived early enough to get a seat near the back. A few officers in uniform were attending the conference and a couple of others were identified from the podium. It was psychobabble at its best. A pack of unskilled wannabe therapists wallowing in the aroma of this flatulence spewed out as "real life experience." I was becoming ill. To me, it was nothing more than confessions of a con artist and making money off being a criminal.

I struggled through the extensive cerebral pain caused by Okie. I felt like driving to the nearest bar and drowning myself in cheap beer, but first I needed to play the last tune for her.

She exited the front doors of the Community Center and proceeded to her car. By this time most of the folks had left the parking area but it was still chancy. I had parked the Avenger in the rear of the parking lot nearest the roadway. One thing I like about community centers in small cities was that they tended to be located in isolated areas, like this one. I couldn't make a decent shot from here but I had a good visual over the lot.

I was in a good position to control the outcome at this point. Okie would have to pass by me during her exit. She was alone as she climbed behind the wheel of her car. She pulled forward toward my position. Having noted that she was an egocentric person at the podium, I grasped a brochure in my left hand and began to wave it at her. The Glock I kept concealed by my right side. She pulled to a stop while rolling down her driver's side window. I introduced myself as a reporter and inquired if she was interested in feature coverage with the magazine I represented. She slipped the car into park, replying with an immediate "Yes." Okie continued, "I have a phone number on my business card you can contact me at."

"That would be great," I said enthusiastically and began my threat scan of the parking lot. While Okie dug in a bag for a business card I placed the Glock next to the back of her head and fired. The moderator blocked the flash and muffled the sound perfectly. A quick scan and second round insured she was dead.

Back in the Avenger, I saw Destiny sitting quietly with me. I had not seen her arrive but evidently it was in time for the finale. Her eyes were aglow as she nodded to me her satisfaction. She looked in the direction of Okie's car as we pulled out of the lot and headed toward Oregon.

I don't know how many young girls' lives Okie or others like her have destroyed in their brothels but one is too many and too many of these remain in operation. During her presentation, Okie gave all the excuses of doing her part to feed and house the kids and help them all she could—but it rang hollow. She talked about being sorry for the girls, but her sorrow was a veneer; she was sorry she got caught, not sorry for what she had done. She rolled on the others to protect her own butt, which was her only concern.

As I relaxed with Destiny as my passenger in the Avenger I opened the window a sliver, allowing a stream of fresh air to whistle through. Wafting within the artificial breeze were the sounds of many voices full of exuberant joy. I was satisfied.

With Detective Ware out of the picture and Agent Odar wanting to fight terrorism I felt the field opening up more advantageously. Destiny was a great accomplice. She represented a legion of spirit-beings that sought vengeance without mercy. Sasins also played an integral part in fulfilling my quest. I had distanced myself from her and felt the need to reconnect. I wanted to work in absolute isolation but I understood the value of a companion like Anna. I couldn't help but wonder if what bothered me the most was that she was not only intelligent and resourceful but a beautiful and desirable woman. At times I found her dominating my subconscious and I feared a relationship might form. I fear I desired it.

Chapter 16

Time had a habit of being slow when there was plenty of it
and fast when there was too little.
—Walter

Religious cults have plagued societies since the dawn of man. Whether people realize it or not, all branches of religion started out as cults. For the most part I couldn't care less about them, but on rare occasions one of these strikes a chord with me. It especially bothers me when they sexually abuse children under the guise of a mandate for sexual exploitation of minors sanctioned by a religious order. Of course they don't see it that way; it's a revelation from God. It was wrong; ask Walter.

I find it difficult to understand how educated people "believe" these self-appointed prophets that give any god a bad name. Most of these so-called prophets are nonconformists to their own religion and are frequently off-shoots of an offshoot of an offshoot prophet who was supposed to be inspired by a revelation. God help us!

Reverend Tom Katt was the fifty-one-year-old prophet in a sect called "God's Chosen Salvation." He launched out on his own after a falling-out with his church organization over interpretations of their variety of Holy Script. Following him were three elders and the devout. Most of the sect was a typical mix of city folk, mostly middle class and high school educated products of broken homes and divorces with little stability in their lives. They looked and longed for something with meaning and purpose, which Katt provided.

The sect raised money and bought a small township in southern Oregon. This desolate area located just north of the Nevada border was hardly suited for a commune. Living off the land, farming, and so forth was a difficult cross to bear for the experienced in this remote and arid desert. Pair inexperience with lack of resources and you had a recipe for disaster. That was the course God's Chosen Salvation was directed to follow.

Recruitment was slow for the sect in the early '90s. Some of the folks had left with a couple of them telling their stories to reporters. This type of juicy stuff was what media thrived on. Authorities became aware of alleged underage marriages being arranged and performed, but with no complainant and a lack of evidence God's Chosen Salvation continued on their course.

Katt was himself a believer in polygamous marriages, having four wives. This prophet of God had no civil documentation and did not recognize the government mandates of legal marriage. Two of his wives came into union with him under fourteen years of age through divine revelation. The purposes of such early marriages were procreation and training in servitude to the husband. All God's chosen elders had likewise engaged in plural marriage as did other males in lesser positions in the sect.

With losses occurring in their ranks the sect set out to recruit followers. They canvassed homeless shelters for runaway teens or young independent mothers. The sect offered stability, security, and unconditional love. No more sleeping on benches or going hungry. It was the ticket a few looked for and accepted.

Opening up the commune to so many brought trouble of its own. Eventually, a fourteen-year-old escaped the compound and fingered Katt as the one responsible for arranging her marriage to a fifty-eight-year-old elder of the sect. She was sexually assaulted the day of her marriage and continuously for the following year prior to her escape.

What appeared to be the end of Katt's reign as a prophet backfired as he transformed into a martyr amongst his followers. Presentations to the grand jury for indictments found flimsy grounds for the case to rest on. The problem was witnesses. Runaway kids had a credibility issue. The commune became restricted to avoid contact with the outside world. By 2001 prosecutors had decided not to pursue the criminal charges against Katt and settled for a lesser charge against the fifty-eight-year-old husband of the victim. That didn't make Katt innocent; it only made him successful in dodging the bullet.

I contacted Anna. Her response to my request for all the information she had on Katt was, "We need to schedule a face-to-face."

She had followed this case through its roller-coaster ride of ups and downs. As we discussed the material she'd compiled she provided me a glimpse into a secretive society I'd heard referenced, but considered nothing more than a myth. The more time we spent together, the more she referenced this mystical society. Did she believe it really existed? Did it exist? I was too focused on Katt and his followers to consider it one way or another.

Anna referred to the compound of God's Chosen Salvation as more of a fortress than a commune. "It is a restricted compound," said Anna. Reports from police sources told of a withdrawal by these members from society as a whole. No TV, radio, or music were allowed. More recently, Katt had called for celibacy on the families part except when Katt announced he'd had a vision revealing it was time for "the seed of God" to be passed. Katt was now the only person in the sect who could arrange marriages within the commune. All matrimonial unions were required to take place in the "faith." Women were not allowed to talk except in a common room such as a kitchen. The supposed utopia of God's Chosen was nothing more than a Gestapo death camp. It was ruthlessly suppressed by stringent rules and penalties that succeeded to cover their abuse of children. One last oddity about this cult kept nagging me and probing my consciousness for an answer. I sat back and looked over the situation; the question came to me, how is it so many female babies are born into this commune and so few males? The ratio of boys to girls was questionable. Coincidence? Walter didn't think so.

My suspicions were nourished by bits and pieces of depravity exposed by Anna's research into the history on the cult. Over the next couple of weeks Anna and I met many times to discuss Katt and his flock. The reverend was not the original prophet. He had ascended to the position when the original leader disappeared. During grand-jury indictment hearings an attempt to locate the original leader was made, to no avail. His disappearance and whereabouts continued to be a mystery. Walter suspected foul play. This was his inveterate tendency when foul people were involved.

Katt was entirely a self-proclaimed prophet. His message was salvation of God's chosen people through divine intervention by the "seed of God." This mystical seed was passed through his followers during the "end times" to repopulate Earth. He claimed the "end times" were here and the "seed bearers" would be persecuted by the unholy. Walter called it horse droppings. The bigger the lie the easier it was to swallow.

According to Anna, the sect originated in Idaho as an offshoot of a polygamist religious sect, which was the offshoot of another supposed Christian denomination, which derived from another and so on, and so on. Probably more important was the fact that Katt had originally come in contact with the sect in Idaho through a prison ministry. Tom Katt was incarcerated at twenty-one for sex with a fifteen-year-old minor. It appeared to Walter that the revelation came before the religion.

Anna was clearly coming ever so close to being involved in what she knew would inevitably transpire. For someone who didn't want to become involved she was practically leading the way to the crime scene. Maybe she was living out her fantasies through me. Something she would do if she could but didn't have the cahonies to do. Personally, I didn't want Anna involved beyond her present role of providing information. Over time my thinking might change; perhaps a lot of things would change, but for the moment I preferred things to stay the same. I welcomed every moment we spent putting this project together. I had grown to trust her and her judgment, but I didn't want her incarcerated should the mission fail. I concerned myself for her safety; I was aware my concern for her might cause me to overlook something vital to the success of the operation.

You had to consider Katt a lucky man. He found people who believed in the same rubbish as he did and then called it "religion." From my years on the ranch I understood what I saw to be "herd" mentality. Maybe that's why Christians were commonly referred to as sheep. They behaved like herd animals. They were easily driven from watering hole to bountiful pastures by a shepherd. Unfortunately, in God's Chosen Salvation, the watering hole was dry and the pastures weed infested. Thus, the herd became hopeless victims in the harrowing of hell.

Walter, being Walter, saw the whole picture differently. Instead of victims he saw those responsible for the cultic revelations as guilty participants who had willfully violated the law of humanity. With FBI Agent Loren Odar wallowing in self-pity over missing the big terrorist ticket there was little to get in Walter's way.

Anna and I met at a little diner to go over material she had compiled. I sensed she knew I was very close to taking matters to the next level; one she had not been involved with previously. That might well be the reason she exposed the cult's weakness at this meeting. Anna reported, "God's Chosen Salvation makes a yearly pilgrimage to a secluded mountainous hot springs near Estacada, Oregon. They do this around Thanksgiving, so you have a little time to prepare if you're interested in seeing them outside their compound." Was this a question or a suggestion?

It was a lengthy road trip to southern Oregon with my trailer in tow. I made a couple of general passes by the commune to get an idea of the layout. The community consisted of a few homes along the paved road and a couple of houses on either side of two adjacent gravel roads. A small grocery store and gas station sat at the westernmost border of the town and existed more as a convenience to the commune than as a for-profit business. At the end of the southernmost gravel road was a large, square, three-story building enclosed by a chain-link fence eight feet high with concertina wire around the top. Floodlights lit up the building and compound like a prison; I had no doubt there were intrusion alarms. It wasn't going to be easy to breach security.

I'd pulled hundreds of observations and to my recollection none were as protected as this fortress. One of the benefits of having all the time I needed was being able to wait for an opportunity and the right moment. The only negative I could see, I'd have to watch with binoculars. I couldn't afford to have contact with the townsfolk; they all knew one another. An outsider hanging around or asking questions would only serve to alert the clan to someone spying on them and result in their kicking security up a notch. Nevertheless, there was always something to be learned through observation, even from a distance.

There was very little traffic or movement around the compound area. Vehicles that did exit were SUVs with tinted windows. Vehicles traveled in pairs when they entered or exited and it was clear to see they had security on the compound gate. I couldn't take a shot if I couldn't see my target. I would have to explore the hot springs pilgrimage as Anna had suggested.

I needed help with more information. History on the clan's hot springs trips to Estacada, photos of the main players, and a topographical map of the hot springs, basically everything Anna had. Time had a habit of being slow when there was plenty of it and fast when there was too little. Time was picking up speed on this project and the window of opportunity would open and close quickly. I had to be in place and ready to make it happen.

Anna seemed eager to respond to my requests for more, more, more—culminating in a gesture of help, "I'll bring it with me."

Whoa, I thought, this is not written in the stars. "Anna, I don't think you should get involved."

"I'm already involved. You involved me the moment you dropped Helen Beck in my lap. I want to be a part of this."

I didn't know what to say or do. I was bound with anxiety.

Calmly, Anna broke the tension, "I'm not asking to pull the trigger or be there when you do. I just want to be more involved. I need this for me."

That I understood from a personal perspective. What can I say besides okay?

I gave Anna directions to my campsite and began preparations for her arrival. It would be another day before we had face time to iron out our goals and concerns. It was clear we needed to talk. What better setting than the remote high desert of southern Oregon?

Anna arrived around two in the afternoon the following day. I gave her the two minute camper tour along with the sleeping arrangements, then invited her to relax. It must have been apparent I was spazzed out or Anna would not have brought up my weird actions. I was in a tizzy and even I recognized it. I asked Anna if she was up to it, maybe we could sit and talk for a little bit. She agreed it was needed.

"So, what's your story, Anna?"

Anna must have had a question on her mind as well, "Your name is not Scythian. I find it cumbersome and uncomfortable to continue to use it. What is your name?"

This was touchy; I have gone so long as Walter, I don't see myself as anyone else, although I know I was born under another name. What good would it do to tell her my real name; she has never known that person, only Walter the Scythian.

"My name is Walter."

"Walter—sure, I can see that," Anna said nodding her head in acknowledgment.

"I want to know about you, Anna. It's apparent from your articles you're on some sort of crusade to punish the guilty."

"Perceptive and true," Anna said, "I am a crusader. Perhaps more than you realize."

"Why, what is your motivation?"

Her body language spoke volumes as she adjusted her posture, leaning back from me and crossing her arms. "I am a victim," Anna paused, "it was when I was a young girl. In those days support for victims was nonexistent. I'm sure if my father had had his way, the man who attacked me would have paid a heavy price, but that's not the way it was and it hasn't improved enough." Anna relaxed back into her chair, "What about you, Walter?"

"My reasons are my own. I don't mean to sound rude or insensitive, but it's complicated. I wasn't a victim. I was predestined. I don't have a rational reason. That is what makes it difficult to explain."

Silence followed as we sat looking into each other's eyes searching for answers to the unasked questions of our thoughts.

"Anna, do you have dreams or nightmares that haunt you?"

"All victims do, Walter, do you?"

"Sometimes I feel sensory perceptions of pain and fear, maybe in some sense having a bond with victims of violent crimes. At other times it comes to me in dreams and more recently like a flashback. I don't know what to make of it other than I feel I have a close relationship with an ethereal world."

There was a long pause in the conversation as we detoured into territory rough to negotiate. If Anna was struggling at all with the flow of our chat, my last statement wasn't going to make it any smoother. I might have made myself out to be unstable and dangerous or at least a weirdo. If she will someday relate my story, she had to know the truth.

Anna reached out with both hands taking one of my hands in her embrace. Her eyes welled up with a tear followed by a soft tone of voice. "I think we all have some form of haunting."

I had a few days to review Anna's materials before heading to Estacada. My preference was to leave Anna at the trailer but she wasn't having any of it. She did buy off on the idea of staying with the vehicle while I did what I do best. It would be impromptu, but some plan was better than none.

The natural hot springs had been the destination for the scheduled bathing rituals since before the southern Oregon compound was built. The purpose and importance were unknown to Anna and me but they were strictly adhered to by all members. The hot springs was a heavily forested region in the Bull of the Woods wilderness area, deeply entrenched in the heart of the Cascade Mountains. God's Chosen Salvation was not the first to adopt these springs for ritualistic purposes. It was a favorite site of Native Americans for centuries before the white settlers reached Oregon.

The springs were improved in recent years when a bathhouse and communal tub were added. The springs were popular tourist sites. By Thanksgiving it often turned bitterly cold in the area and few people visited the hot springs in winter. This made it an ideal time for the religious sect to make their annual pilgrimage.

The hot springs were open twenty-four hours a day but camping was prohibited. A trail system connected three separate springs along with some minor outlets. I ran over to scout out the area before solidifying our plans. All the major outlets had soaking tubs made from cedar; I chose a remote minor outlet in the river and burned my buns on the first rock I touched. Man, it was hot. Someone had made a rock wall in the river causing a pool to form; it was almost too hot for comfort at first but after about ten minutes in the pool I never wanted to get out. There were postings indicating game wardens or park rangers patrolled the area regularly but I didn't see any.

On Monday, November 19, 2001 Anna and I did our first road trip together. Anna believed God's Chosen Elders would make the trip on the first day of their ritual bathing. I wasn't convinced, but gave her benefit of the doubt. My experience had shown stakeouts to be time-consuming ventures usually requiring a lot of coffee and doughnuts to get through them. With Anna along at least there would be someone to pass the boredom with other than Destiny. While Anna and I settled into a routine of chiding each other about who was right or wrong about everything, two SUVs and a bus without markings pulled into the Forest Service parking area. Although visitors were not allowed to camp overnight, parking was designed to accommodate RVs giving us the opportunity to be tucked away at the far end of the lot.

I recognized immediately the bus as one of God's Chosen fleet parked at the compound. The SUVs unloaded first, twelve men in all, dressed casually, huddled together at the rear of the vehicles. From the bus poured out a couple of dozen women and children. The kids group, made up entirely of girls, lined up to hike the mile and a half to the hot springs. Neither Katt nor the elders had arrived.

It was still early but we were drawing the conclusion that the cult might run in shifts. Maybe driven by religious protocol or some wacky revelation by Katt but the likelihood was that tomorrow another group would show. It was too far for them to run all the way back and make it back again while it was daylight. As I was bragging to Anna about how right I'd been in proclaiming Katt would not show up on the first day, another set of SUVs followed by a another bus pulled in and began unloading. Again, I recognized the bus from the compound. The group moved off together on the trail while both bus drivers carried on a conversation under a 10-by-10 pop-up tent they had erected. I made a sandwich and settled back for a long day. I wished Destiny would show. That would be a good indicator it was show time.

Three SUVs pulled into the parking area and rolled up to the tent. Two men were in the lead vehicle and two in the last. The middle SUV had a driver and four additional passengers. The drivers of all three SUVs stayed in the tented area while two worked point and rear guard for the four passengers as they approached the trailhead. I could see Katt was one of the four being escorted; Anna confirmed the other three were elders. I wanted to ask her how she knew these were elders but there was no time. I had to spring into action.

With guitar case housing my Rock River AR 15 I skirted the parking area and made my way to a hillside above the bathhouse. The hillside was in the shadow of higher surrounding peaks and was frosty cold like an icebox. I concealed myself behind a brush pile and assembled my rifle. By resting my weapon on a bipod I was able to get a close-up view through the scope. Katt and the elders were sprawled in a soaking tub by the time I secured the silencer in place. With the weapon locked and loaded, all that was left to do was pull the trigger and my finger was itching.

Katt's escorts walked down the hill to the river and joined with other cult members at the water's edge. Another group composed of women and children were seventy-five yards or more upriver from the escorts. Katt and his elder crew were alone. It was going to be like shooting fish in a barrel.

The noise from the kids grew louder as they sang hymns and bathed in the hot springs. The muffled shuups from my AR 15 firing through a silencer in rapid sequence was scarcely audible as I emptied the twenty-round clip. I loaded my weapon with a fresh clip and watched the tub as it ran red with blood. I could not distinguish if those by the riverside were singing a religious hymn in unison or were joined by the sound of a heavenly choir singing praises. A beautiful and bright crimson pool formed, with the sun adding to its hue. Before the first shot was fired, I'm not sure my intentions were to kill them all. But after the first trigger pull, it never crossed my mind to stop shooting. They all shared in the blame. They all shared in the penalty.

With my Glock as backup, I broke down my rifle into its carrying case. With no sign of life at the bathhouse I turned my attention to the others, watching closely to see if anyone was aware of the shooting. If any of the elders I shot had cried out for help, I didn't hear them, neither had anyone else. Undoubtedly they plunged into shock at the sight of the first one shot, and died soon after themselves.

Katt and elders had planned to enjoy their version of God's creation, specifically, little girls. Unfortunately for them, Walter plotted a different future for them or lack thereof. I mused over the possibility of there being a special hell for religious people who violate the good intentions of religion. If hell doesn't exist for them, it should.

Back in my Avenger, Anna was behind the wheel and ready to drive. I didn't see the need to discuss it, just go. Anna was composed. No sign of any emotional distress. Then again, she hadn't seen the pool of blood. The visual of killing might have been too much for her to embrace. We pulled away from the parking area as if nothing happened. The drivers were still gathered at their tent and seemingly paid no attention to us as we left.

We cruised back to the trailer where Anna's Lexus was parked; Anna scarcely uttering a word. Her calmness bothered me. She seemed bottled up inside. It was either that or she was a little too well-adjusted for what had just transpired. Anna and I made plans to touch bases in a couple days. I would initiate the contact. Anna left early the next morning; I broke camp and traveled to my home.

News reports were breaking nationwide. Reports centered on the unusual place where the murders occurred and the religious order of the cult. It would be media free-for-all. The personalities of those killed would garner the greatest attention.

I was growing eager to talk with Anna. After a short conversation on the phone we agreed to meet. Malls were great meeting places. Inside the Clackamas County Mall there were seating arrangements alongside plants in the center of the main floor aisle where we could talk and not be bothered by eavesdroppers. I was waiting for Anna when she arrived. I was worried she would appear disheveled after the lengthy ordeal; not to mention the news broadcasts referring to "the hot springs slaughter" not sitting very well with her. It was a pleasant surprise to see Anna as she walked down the mall looking relaxed, composed, and radiant. This killing thing didn't seem to have any ill effect on her at all.

I stood to greet Anna as she approached the seating area. To my surprise she embraced me with a hug. "How are you doing?"

"Fine, how 'bout you?"

"Never better—I have some information for you."

We sat down close to each other. Anna began immediately, "Warrants were issued to allow FBI investigators inside the compound in southern Oregon. Agent Loren Odar is on site at the commune and is looking at what a spokesperson called, 'the bigger picture.' My sources have not made mention of a serial killer at this point."

"That's great news. The FBI should be looking in the compound. I have a hunch Agent Odar will develop more questions than answers for the religious sect. Are you able to drop a hint through your sources?"

"I have reliable resources that can input when and where needed. What is it?"

"I believe something more sinister is happening at the commune. I don't know why the birth rate for the cult is about 90 percent female. Where are the male children that are born into their cult?"

"You think they are killing them?"

"Killing them, selling them in Mexico, whatever . . . something is wrong with the picture. I need your source to put a bug in the FBI's ear."

Anna agreed to make contact. If this cracked the door open for the FBI a little, all the better for me. It would keep the agents busy for a long time and finally give Agent Odar some sense of purpose.

The stage was set through these killings to discover the truth behind the scenes at the compound. It wouldn't excuse the murders; however, it didn't paint a clear picture of a suspect either. If my suspicions were right there might be dozens of little motives buried out there somewhere. The more motives the more suspects, and the more hidden I remained. Ballistics, however, might be my Achilles heel.

Anna and I began meeting regularly every other day. Anna was trying to sell me on some of her cockamamie ideas to pursue as projects but they seemed too far-fetched. I knew child sex slave operations existed, I just didn't see myself being a world traveler. Anna looked at the broader spectrum. I saw the local field and there was plenty to do here in Oregon.

Nearly a month after the hot springs murders, Anna related the FBI investigators unearthed bodies at the southern Oregon compound. Anna used the media leaks to alert the general population to the grisly discovery of both male and female children at the religious sect compound. Downplayed was the part about Katt and the elders being shot and killed. I saw it as a positive. Anna found it a bit more restrictive. She knew more and had a corner on the story, but wasn't in position to publish it. She was involved.

Uncovering a buried body is always big news. Reporters loved it. It was even bigger news when it was a baby or a young child. In this case, it was many more than I suspected. Katt's cult was keeping all levels of law enforcement busy. Forensics was busy establishing the victims' identities and determining cause of death. According to Anna's sources, it would be some time before they would have the remains sorted out. Would they ever connect me to this? I felt forgotten. It didn't seem like they were looking for the shooter now.

A new year dawned and already I had three projects to act on. Back to basic killing and enjoying it more. The nation's security condition was working in my favor; lawmakers were tightening the reign on bad guys, mostly out of fear for their own lives. With legislation being passed for longer sentences and mandatory jail time to be served I would have more time to act on past offenders and clean out the rat nest embedded in America's society. The foul stench of violent sex offenders would not dissipate because of lawmakers, but those that made news today would be incarcerated longer, giving me time to catch up a bit with correction's revolving door.

Crime fighting was catching on. TV media found a new gold mine with real-life cop shows and cold-case shows asking for the public's help. TV news agencies were expanding their investigative powers to turn the table on the bad guys and air the results on national television. I remember one such TV documentary that uncovered Americans traveling overseas in third-world nations exploiting children and sex slavery. I was stunned. Brazenly, Westerners traveled abroad to practice their perversions at the cost of a few dollars. It wasn't lawful in any of these countries any more than it was in the United States but it was tolerated because of the economic value it brought to their countries.

According to this TV reporter, foreign money was at the root of this evil. He identified doctors, lawyers, and business executives who traveled to and from poverty-stricken areas capitalizing on the lack of enforcement of their laws. Entrepreneurs exported their goods on cheap videotapes for private consumption on a global level. It made me sick. I didn't have to see more, it was exactly what Anna had focused on.

Disturbed by the images from this documentary I sat back in contemplation. What could Walter do to make a difference? It would be an overwhelming task to take on. I couldn't keep up with one state's criminal population. My finances might seem plentiful at this point but such a venture would undoubtedly run me dry quickly.

During one of our regular meetings, Anna and I rehashed the TV documentary.

"I know the documentary too well," Anna said. "One of the cameramen is an acquaintance of mine."

"Did he tell you about it?"

Anna replied, "No, I saw it some months ago. He had more than twelve hours tape-recorded; most cannot be shown on TV in America."

"Maybe that's what should happen. These were Americans, our own people."

I shook my head in dismay as Anna continued to talk about striking at the root of the problem. She kept repeating the words—sex industry. That's what it was; a business. There was a market. There were buyers and sellers. This was a whole new playing field from the individual perps I had gone after previously.

I was vaguely aware of child exploitation in the sex industry. I was naïve as to how prevalent it was. But, I have awakened to the reality. I think about it daily; all day long. I dream of extirpating this sex slavery with my lance. It consumes my nights and I treasure it. My only relief, however, is found in the recoil of my weapon and the smell of fresh-burnt gun powder. Only then is the burden tolerable.

Chapter 17

There are no innocent participants
—Walter

I arrived early at the mall to meet Anna. She said it was important. She had provided so many viable inputs I could scarcely think of doing what I did without her. If she said it was important then it unquestionably was.

Anna had a way of making a grand entry and today was no different. Her long-red-flowing hair against the backdrop of a black and white suit added to her professional demeanor. Her swank leather satchel added an aura of mystique. She was the quintessence of elegance and sophistication.

Making eye contact with Anna was an enjoyable and refreshing experience. They were a beautiful bright blue that expressed cheerfulness and comfort. I looked forward to gazing into them at every opportunity. Today, however, they were notably a steel blue, cold and piercing. I immediately felt something was terribly wrong. Without hesitation we sat next to each other and leaned close so that we could speak softly and not be heard by passersby.

"Do you remember the TV documentary you saw on sexual exploitation in Thailand?"

"How could I forget."

"The judicial system is powerless to do anything to these rich globetrotters. They travel as tourists to many of these destinations from Europe, Japan, and America to spend a lot of money for hotels, dining, and nightlife. In some cases their money goes to whet their sexual appetite."

I listened intently. Anna wasn't defending their behavior, she was motivating me; she knew what to do and how to do it. Money didn't buy a special brand of rights to prey upon the weak and young; if it did, it shouldn't. These globetrotters might not be convicted criminals, but they knew right from wrong, evidenced by their travel to countries where they fed their cravings without penalty. In Walter's book it was downright criminal.

Anna casually glanced about the mall before continuing. I knew her behavior well enough now to see we were approaching the real reason for the steely blue eyes.

"One of the five men profiled in the documentary is a doctor from Oregon. Do you know which one?"

"No, they didn't mention names or indicate where any of these degenerates lived."

Anna whispered a name, pronouncing each syllable slowly with a peculiar emphasis, "Rich-ard Fell-er."

"How do you know his name?"

"Let's just say I know—and leave it at that. The question I have—are you the right person?" As I mulled over the question, Anna continued, "I have something I think you'll find interesting. Hours of uncut film from the documentary that provides, shall we say, insight into Feller's perverted lifestyle?" Anna paused while moving her satchel close to my leg.

"I've got to go, Walter. I'll call you tomorrow."

"Okay, I'll go through the material tonight."

Standing together, Anna embraced me with a quick hug and smile

"Walter, have you given much thought to our discussions on chess?"

"Not really, I haven't been able to find the time."

Anna nodded her head in acceptance. Not wanting to be ill-mannered, I quickly made an offer, "Maybe we can get together and play a game one of these days?" Her response was cool and indifferent. "I don't play chess, but, maybe we'll play soon."

What the—my mind raced back through the questions she had asked about chess, and now she didn't play! What was her point about chess and chess pieces? What type of game does she want to play? Too many questions, I thought. My puzzled thoughts were momentarily interrupted as I watched Anna slip from view. Absolutely beautiful, I thought as I stood mesmerized.

For the rest of the day and well into the night I watched the uncut footage from the documentary. The film, transferred to VHS, made segments easy to review and saved time when gleaning details. It was easy to see why the film was edited. I had never seen anything so graphic in nature as the sex abuse committed on these young victims; it was distressing.

Walter, being criminal himself by nature, noticed something in the unedited material that many others might have missed because of the shocking display of sex acts. Feller participated in sex acts but he wasn't purchasing the services. The transactions Walter saw were the sale of children to others. Feller was involved in human trafficking. Doctor or not, convicted criminal or not, Walter had his number.

I lay in bed tossing and turning for hours. When sleep came it was interrupted by screams of banshees. Although I was cognizant I was in a dream I could feel a scythe in my hands and the motion of reaping. One moment I could feel resistance from the shafts of grain as I swept the blade through the harvest, the next moment it was the scythe decapitating Feller.

In the morning I once again pored over the material. I shouldn't have. I felt a boiling sensation that was unappeasable. I felt rage that only blood would vanquish. Anna had asked if I was the "right person." I didn't know any person more right for this kind of information than Walter but Thailand was a long way from Oregon?

I was finishing up my third cup of coffee when my cell phone rang.

"Do you trust me, Walter?"

I was speechless. I knew it was Anna, but I didn't know the answer. I wanted my reply to be yes, but the question lingered in my thoughts too long.

"Do you trust me?"

I thought it too late not to, so I answered, "Yes."

"Are you the right person?"

Again I responded, "Yes," only this time with less certainty than before. What was I the right person for? I didn't have a clue!

"Let's get together." Anna was clearly calling the shots on this. She followed up with a time and location for the meeting. I agreed to be there.

Berardino's was a quaint, well-established pub and diner in the Portland area. Anna was aware of my preference for meeting in public places. Casual conversation should not call attention to those meeting as long as it did not take on an air of secrecy. We met on the outdoor deck at the beginning of what was commonly referred to as happy hour. It suited me fine.

"What did you think of the documentary footage?"

"You know what I thought of it. I think there is more there than meets the eye." I felt Anna was baiting me and she had me pegged well enough. Sure, I wanted to kill him, but then again, I had a rather large list that fits into this category.

"What can I do about him unless you know he's here in Oregon?"

Anna replied, "He's not in Oregon."

"Well, there you go! Nothing I can do about it."

Anna was quiet. I couldn't tell if she was disappointed in my response or my lack of adventurism. When she continued her dialogue I would know the answer.

Anna looked out over the landscaped backdrop of the deck then toward where I was sitting, "Ever been to Pattaya?" A shimmering gleam in her eye and sinister smile revealed the thickening plot; I was digging it.

Sitting back in my chair I entertained an awkward pause before replying nonchalantly, "Where in the world is—Pat-tay-yar?" I knew this was going to be a doozy.

"Thailand," Anna sighed. She gave me a "Am I going to have to teach you everything" look and then continued. "I've compiled information on Pattaya for you. Oh, incidentally, Rich Feller has a bungalow there."

Before I could ask a single question, our conversation took a sharp turn to more delightful subjects. Anna spoke briefly about horses and her desire to have acreage to raise them. I related a few stories from my days on the ranch. She asked what I thought the future held for me. I was candid with my response, but reserved to the point of not being overly fatalistic. A few hours lapsed quickly, dinner, drinks and a few stories; it was time to go. We walked to her Lexus where she retrieved a 10-by-13-inch packet and held it out to me. I took the large mailer envelope and tucked it under my arm.

Anna said, I'll get back to you in a couple days, okay?"

She embraced me with a hug and a kiss on the cheek. I liked our meetings more and more. I held the door open as she slipped into the driver's seat. When I closed the door she flashed me a smile and waved as she drove away.

Something continued to trouble me about her car but I couldn't put my finger on it. The more I saw her car the harder it was for me to align my thoughts as to what I knew and what my subconscious was trying to tell me; it was becoming a blur. There was a connection here, I could sense it.

The material in Anna's packet was well organized and comprehensive, it was also time consuming. Since my earliest association with Harold Horn, I had held the notion that reporters and detectives came from the same mold. Anna was a prime example.

Mr. Feller was the focus of Anna's research. This was not a surprise. I knew what it was to target someone and she noticeably had him in her sights. I studied his personal background hoping to find keys to his personality. The psychobabblers said personalities were formed in the first five years of our lives. When I looked at someone's personal history I looked for behavioral signs that provided insight into who I was dealing with. Nothing in his case stuck out as unusual.

Feller was born and raised in Hollywood, California. His family life appeared stable with both parents employed in the cinema industry. The Fellers earned incomes sufficient to allow them to live in a ritzy neighborhood and their children to attend what is commonly referred to as "better schools." Richard was a high achiever in school. He was popular, elected student body vice-president two consecutive years, lettered in baseball and was president of the Letterman's Club his senior year. If anything was unusual about Feller it was the lack of behavioral problems. Tinsel town had a notorious reputation for its wild life and I'm not talking about four-footed critters. It wasn't unusual for kids living in a high-roller environment to get snared in its pitfalls. He had the money for drugs, booze, and any vice he cared to engage in but nothing here suggested he was ever in trouble. He was a mystery of sorts.

Richard matured and embarked on a medical career, specializing in podiatry. By all counts he seemed destined to be a valuable contributor to society. Soon after his graduation he volunteered his services to Global Center Alliance, a pseudo world peace health organization, destined to provide a form of socialized medicine to the world community. Now, a dozen years later, he still volunteered for "missions" instead of holding down a lucrative practice. If I had known nothing more of Feller's existence, I would have dismissed the notion he was evil, but, there was more.

The file contained official documents from Brazilian government sources on Feller's activities while "volunteering" to help the poor in their country. These documents painted a different portrait of the good doctor, one more in line with the documentary. Feller's Brazilian tour under Global Center Alliance's banner was cut short. Suspicious? Absolutely! For a government to intercede and take away free help for the poor was a strong indicator something was rotten in Denmark or, in this case, Brazil. Embedded were government documents referring to Feller's expulsion on the grounds of "questionable moral integrity." Here was a government that harbored Nazi war criminals and allowed mini-concentration camps to operate within its borders that was kicking a doctor out of their country for questionable moral integrity? It didn't make sense.

Three months after his return from Brazil, Global Center Alliance reassigned him to a year's contract in Indonesia. Things seemed to go okay for him there and then it was off to Thailand for a year's tour. Richard continued to volunteer in Thailand and resided in Pattaya.

Anna had an Oregon residential address for him but there was no indication he had ever lived there. He had never hung a shingle for his practice, assisted another doctor's business, or served on staff at any hospital. He was an Oregonian without roots; a Podiatrist without a footprint. He was, indeed, a mystery.

The kill was needed, but catching up with him would be a nightmare. Five days passed before I heard from Anna. "Meet me at Multnomah Falls tomorrow at 10 a.m. I'd like to hike to the upper bridge and feel the mist from the Punch Bowl."

"I'll be there." Nothing coded about this message. Anna wanted to go over the material. The Falls were a good idea. It had its share of tourists and got busy occasionally in the afternoons but a morning meeting would have few interruptions from people walking by. I was game.

The meeting went off as planned. The parking lot spread out over a couple of acres, but with only a few cars closely packed at the trailhead it was easy to find Anna. She was dressed casually for the trek. Black jeans with a red and black windbreaker went well with her long red hair tucked under a black knit cap. Her informal elegance caught me off guard.

At the upper bridge we watched the water cascade hundreds of feet before crashing into a pool dug out by centuries of repetition. The resulting mist saturated the air, adding an extra freshness to the already chilly morning. I waited for Anna to come forth with her proposal. Small talk and casual chat finally took on a serious tone as Anna pitched her idea.

"Walter, you said you trust me. I want you to accompany me overseas."

I already knew the answers to the questions I would ask, but I wanted to hear it from her. "Where to and what for?"

"Thailand—the 'what' will be up to you."

"You have my attention."

Anna and I moved to a nearby felled tree taking seats on the rotting bark. Anna wasted no time before launching into the details of her plan. I was to travel as her companion and cameraman for a feature she was writing. We would fly into Bangkok for her human-interest story, but as I'd already hypothesized, it was cover for our true destination and purpose. Our objective lay 100 miles south in Pattaya. It was a no-cost scenario to me. I was along for the ride and maybe some trigger time. The idea of a full-fledged partner was new to me. It would take time to get comfortable with the idea. Anna was trying to be helpful and she had put together what sounded like a first-rate project for a person relatively new to the game, but there were still issues to discuss.

"I don't have a passport and I'm not wild about exposing myself to risks in an unfamiliar arena."

Anna was quick to reply, "This is the part where you have to trust me."

"Okay, what hoops do I have to jump through to get the documents I need and how do I go about preparing for the trip?"

"I'll handle the legal requirements associated with getting your passport, visas, and corresponding identification. I have a contact that will take your photo and produce a set of high-quality forged documents. You will need to provide him with information you want on the documents. It is more difficult since 9/11 to forge identification but my contact will provide computer support for our entry. If everything goes well we'll be leaving in a couple weeks."

"What about weapons?"

"You won't be bringing weapons with you. I'll take care of all the things you'll need." I was hoping she was referring to more than weapons, but I knew I was dreaming. Nevertheless, I responded with a smirk and a statement I hoped would alert her to my fantasy.

"Great, all I have to do is pull the trigger."

Over the next few days I called Anna with questions as I thought of them. I felt my concerns were legitimate but she tired of my badgering. Finally, after a multi-call day, she told me to quit being "pesky" and reiterated, "Trust me." It was not reassuring.

Anna called, "It's time."

Dr. Richard Feller had no idea that 7,500 miles away Walter was boarding a plane with the intention of terminating his life. Anna had my forged passport, visas, and press pass in hand when I arrived at the terminal. It was official; my name was Walter Eloy Goe and I had documents that proved it. The prospects of sitting in a cramped cattle car for a sixteen-hour flight was less than appealing, but to accomplish what was necessary one must do what must be done. This trip would prove to be a learning experience in more ways than one.

Unlike me, Anna was at ease in any setting. I was a bit insecure outside my realm, and although polite and considerate of others, I was not ashamed of who I was and apologized to no one. I looked out of place sitting beside Anna in first class. Other passengers surely wondered about us. What was such a classy woman doing with a simple-looking guy like me? Yeah, I knew they were considering various scenarios, but it would never cross their minds I was a cold-blooded killer who enjoyed his work and she my enabler.

My mind processed what information I'd been given, but I didn't know how my cameo role would play out on stage in Thailand until the closing curtain fell. For me this was nothing more than a one-act play; just another chapter in my life. A life and lifestyle I had chosen.

We arrived at Don Mueang Airport as planned and processed through customs. I suspected Anna was a world traveler, and my suspicions were confirmed when the customs agent flipped through her passport looking for the correct page to place his seal; every page had multiple stamps.

Anna hailed a cab at the airport, haggled with him over a price to a destination, and then slipped him some American currency. I didn't know the Thai custom on payment or tipping, but he was all smiles. Miles south from the airport we entered the city of Bang Saen. A few left turns and a couple of right turns found us in the driveway of a getaway resort overlooking the Gulf of Thailand—an arm of the South China Sea. The area was touristy and a great place to blend in. We would be one of many nondescript foreigners spending our loot and taking in the sights.

Once in the room Anna suggested we take some time to freshen up. For me it was the beach followed by the Jacuzzi and maybe a nap. Anna retired to her bed area and shut the door. I had questions, but I had trust too, and it was growing in leaps and bounds.

Suddenly there came a tap, tap, tap of gentle rapping on the chamber door. My mind was slow to rouse my body as the tapping continued. Sporting a bad case of jet lag I stumbled to my feet to answer the door. Anna swept past me in a blaze arriving at the door well ahead of me. While the haze cleared Anna opened the door to a small-framed Asian man. Anna made customary introductions. "Walter, I'd like you to meet Nontawat, he will be our driver. Nontawat, this is Walter." With a smile he extended his hand and repeated my name or something similar, "Wah-ter." Anna began a dialogue with our visitor outlining our intended travels. When our driver left, Anna turned her attention to me, "Be ready to go in the morning by eight."

The rest of the afternoon we spent on the beach followed by cocktails and dinner at the hotel. Before turning in for bed I asked what our travel plans were for the next morning. "Pattaya," Anna responded, "We will acquire our target then put a plan in place."

Nontawat was an early riser, or he didn't know where Mickey's hands were supposed to be at eight o'clock. Regardless, he was knocking on the door before seven. I offered him a chair but in his broken English he responded, "I stand." Nontawat was clearly antsy. Was he anxious about what we were doing or was he eager to get it on? It was catching. Hurrying dominated my thoughts. Life was much easier when I worked alone.

Finally loaded into our driver's sedan we made our way south to Pattaya. Anna and I rode in the back, Nontawat was alone up front. On the seat between Anna and me was a black leather bag. As we traveled south, Anna unzipped the top of the bag revealing a variety of handguns, "Take your pick" Anna whispered. I wanted something I could rock Feller's world with. The Charter Arms .44 Special "Bulldog" would work for my intentions. None of the weapons were semiautos like I was used to. There were no moderators or silencers of any type. When that "Bulldog" barked, there would be no silent kill.

Loaded and ready, Anna filled me in on the recon. Richard Feller conducted his trade for the health organization out of an office near the central business district but lived a few miles south of Pattaya in Na Jotiem. He lived alone, drove a new Mitsubishi sports car, and had a modest single-dwelling bungalow. Nontawat drove straight to Feller's place indicating to me he'd been there before. The Mitsubishi was gone as expected and so was Feller.

Anna directed my attention to a map with her finger pointing to a street called Walking Street. "That's a red-light district where the doctor frequents."

"How do we know he hangs-out in this area?"

"Nontawat has been watching him for some time." I caught a glimpse of our driver's eyes staring in the rearview mirror. When we made eye contact his eyes were galvanized with resolve. He was just like me, a man on a mission. Someone was going to pay for the hurt he knew. It was the only way the pain subsided for a short while. Unfortunately, it always came back. You could never kill enough for it to vanish entirely.

"We'll go to Walking Street later this afternoon, for now I want to see the Global Center Alliance's layout." We circled the blocks where Feller had his practice and continued to cruise the streets to get a feel for the city. Nontawat, who had not spoken, broke his silence, "Doctor go to Walking Street club in afternoon." Anna nodded, "Let's go!"

I considered myself a seasoned veteran of the dark and seedy underworld but it paled in comparison to Pattaya's Walking Street in broad daylight and in clear view. This was a phantasmagoria of neon lights advertising sex shops, nightclubs, and exotic bars. Hookers galore, homosexuals, lesbians, transsexuals, and transgenders all wrapped up in one Walter nightmare.

Hundreds of thousands of children were coerced, forced, kidnapped, and sold to sex traffickers for the sex tourism trade. Some of these young girls undoubtedly were a product of such circumstance. I was taken aback by the sheer numbers of Europeans and Americans I saw shelling out big bucks to support this 100-billion-dollar-a-year business. Walter concluded rightly, those that fronted the capital created the market where children were enslaved to make their masters rich. There were no innocent participants.

The glare of streetlights and the cover of palm trees could not hide what was going on here. Organized crime and politicians were at the root of the business end. They were, in fact, the same thing. Russian prostitutes, tall and fair skinned, stood out among their Asian counterparts. The Russian Mafia, known for kidnapping, imported these young girls and forced them to hustle or die. Young Asian men in white shirts and ties hand out flyers advertising sex while police in helmets patrolled Pattaya's carnival atmosphere to keep a lid on crime. What crime? The kind government didn't get a cut of.

Nontawat brought our attention to one sex shop, "Here, in back, he here." The shop was considerably smaller than many around it. A middle-aged man stood quietly by a counter near a curtain. On the street, hookers were trying to engage us as we passed by—500 Baht for a quickie, 1,000 Baht if you wanted to take your time. At this quiet little shop, whatever he was selling in the back room wasn't being flaunted.

Nontawat spoke with the man and brokered a deal for Anna and me to go behind the curtain for 1,000 Baht. Nontawat stayed outside while Anna and I entered a very dark room; the show was already in progress. An adult Asian man and a young Asian teenage girl of maybe thirteen years of age engaged in sex acts. When that show concluded another man entered the stage and continued the sexual assault on the same young teen.

In the audience of a half-dozen men only one was clearly of European descent. We suspected he was our target. No need to stay in the tented showroom—we had front-row seats to the exit from outside. An hour passed before Feller emerged; he was not alone. The young stage girl was being led away to some unknown destination. Anna and I followed.

A few blocks south, Feller with girl in tow turned into an alley. We continued to watch falling back to a safe distance. Not far down the alley Feller took the little girl into a bar. Minutes later he reappeared, alone, and walked back from the direction he came. Walter, once again, put two and two together. It was his contention the girl was Feller's property. As a sex slave, she was sold to the highest bidder or in this case to make money on a stage. Who could argue with Walter, it was the most probable scenario.

Feller walked a couple of blocks north to an off-street parking area. He was relaxed, comfortable in his surroundings, and unaware he was targeted. I was closing the distance when Anna took me by the arm, saying, "Not now," and led me from my prey. Feller escaped Walter's clutches, momentarily.

Nontawat dropped us off at the resort with a plan in place to return the next afternoon. The plan would be, according to Anna, a "live take." This was news to me—confusing news. I thought I was going to shoot the slime and call it good. Anna explained Feller might be the tip of an iceberg and we wanted to know what he knew. It was an admirable idea but hugely risky. I'd rather kill than talk, but Anna had a point, I conjectured.

Once inside our suite, I asked Anna, "What is Nontawat's story?"

"He is what we refer to as a pawn."

There was that word "we" again. Who is "we?" I know Anna doesn't care for all my questions but I want to know about Nontawat. After all he will be privy to my involvement in Feller's execution. "I don't know a whole lot about chess but the pawn is the weakest piece on the board and pretty much useless."

"Not at all," Anna replied. "Pawns have limitations, not weaknesses. They are key factors in a solid defense, probing, and imperative in endgame strategy."

"Okay, so I don't understand pawns real well, what's up with this guy?"

Anna thought for a minute before she answered, "When he was a young child, he was kidnapped and sold into slavery. He was one of the more fortunate—it was a sweat shop, not the sex industry."

"What about his family?"

"He was too young to remember, he doesn't know who they are."

"So what did he do, escape finally?"

"A man called Maximillian rescued him. How or why, I really can't say. What I can tell you is this: you can trust Nontawat to support your next move."

As I turned in for the night I thought to myself, I hope Anna's right about this guy. He knows way more than I'm comfortable with. My thoughts coupled with jet lag were keeping me from a desired sound sleep. While busy tossing and turning, I slipped into a cognizant dream world. The windswept plains and thunderous dark clouds were giving way to a spectacular sunrise. As the sun shown above the horizon, the fields brought forth life, green and lush. My horse stood tall and I upon the saddle. An apparition appeared next to me dressed in glowing white. She was familiar to me and I welcomed her company. Destiny spoke serenely, "Let not your heart be troubled and be not afraid; place your faith in me and I will guide your steps. The path before you leads to all that you have asked for and sought after. Your destiny will be fulfilled."

I felt strangely rejuvenated in the morning and decided to approach this undertaking with a new fervor. Locating Feller's vehicle was easy. We were creatures of habit. In an environment where almost anything goes he had no reason to be bashful about parking in the open. What Feller could not realize was how dangerous a parking lot can be. After dark this was Walter's domain and he intended to rule it.

Nontawat stayed with his car just in case we required a speedy getaway. Our plan was sketchy at best. If opportunity prevailed we would catch him in the parking lot and whisk him away to some remote spot our driver had picked out. If we had to wait and take him at his house, we would, and then interrogate him. One way or the other he was going to tell us everything he knew.

Anna took up position on Walking Street. Her setup was simple; she would identify Feller and relay his movement to me via radio. Time was irrelevant now; it was just the wait that got to you. The crackle of the radio interrupted my concerns, bringing my full attention to bear. The noise of Walking Street almost completely drowned out the transmission. I listened more intently as Anna attempted to transmit again. I barely could distinguish it as her voice. I waited as instructed expecting to see Feller enter the parking area but the next transmission sounded weaker and less audible. I was troubled; Anna might be on the move away from my location. The radio crackled again and I began moving toward the hustle and bustle of Walking Street.

My fears worsened when I was unable to see Anna anywhere on the street. I was torn between getting Nontawat to aid me in my search or to hurry down the street with some hope of getting close enough to hear Anna's voice again. I hurried a couple of blocks south. It was a fifty-fifty chance it was the direction she had gone. I radioed Anna but there was no response. In a quandary I continued south. The radio crackled, it was Anna. The transmissions were garbled but I was able to tell her my location.

Anna replied, "Stay there, I will meet you."

A couple of minutes passed before Anna showed. "There is so much electrical interference these radios are useless," Anna spouted, rather frustrated.

"Why did you take off?"

"Follow me!"

We hurriedly rounded the corner and down an alley that was filled with smaller shops. It was the same location as the previous day. The lack of neon lights didn't seem to hinder the busy atmosphere. Anna came to an abrupt halt, "This is it!"

A bland wood-framed building with only a lit entrance stood before us. No windows were on the street level giving it the appearance more of a prison than a bar. From the door a staircase was visible leading to a landing above street level. "Feller's in here, we need to find out what kind of place this is and what he's doing." This was the kind of setup that makes me apprehensive. Spontaneity is a dangerous road map.

While I was mulling over what Anna was saying, Nontawat came from the shadows of the alley. It was unnerving. He explained he had seen my panicked reaction and followed me to see what had gone wrong. He was still spooky.

Nontawat was quick to volunteer to enter the establishment. As he entered the lower level Anna and I drifted back into the darkness of an alleyway cubbyhole. In a matter of fifteen minutes Nontawat rejoined us outside. He reported seeing young Asian girls; some as young as ten in his estimation. He couldn't tell how many were being held there, but more than a dozen, he thought. He excused himself from the bartender to go get money. They were all available for sex. Feller was nowhere in sight.

We discussed calling in the Thai police version of a task force, but what was the use? If they arrived it would be days from now and these sex slave owners would have been tipped off and gone already. Walter was still holding to the idea that Feller was involved in the trafficking. No sense ruining a good thing by calling in the cops when we could take care of business ourselves.

Nontawat suggested he contact a friend from a worldwide religious organization that took in runaways. "They able take kids from here," he said.

Finally, something churchgoers were good for. The idea had my vote.

"Do it," Anna commanded.

I monitored the entrance for any sign of Feller. If he showed, it was understood, game on. Any way I could make it happen was the new rule of thumb. Anna was keeping track of clientele coming and going. Maybe it was a slow night, but not many showed up, and fewer stayed. Nontawat returned with good news. The Christian group would be here shortly and would smuggle the children out of Pattaya. He urged Anna and me to do whatever it was we had planned to do. He looked up to Anna, literally and with great respect and admiration. I didn't have the heart to tell him we were fresh out of plans. Whatever was going to happen would happen; it was just a matter of time.

From the entrance we could see the tall figure of a white man talking with a much smaller Asian man behind the makeshift bar. From my vantage point I would swear I was looking at business partners chatting, not a customer relationship. Nontawat wanted a closer look, so back inside he went. This was getting more risky. The sex-slave merchants weren't known for being peaceful types. If they thought Nontawat was snooping around, they might get nasty.

Nontawat engaged the bartender, who responded with gestures indicating he needed to leave. Evidently our pawn made a sizable play and now was refusing to follow the rules of the game. Had Anna and I not made our appearance at the entry, something bad might have happened. I had a feeling something bad was still going to happen, but to whom was the question.

The bartender gestured with his hand for us to enter, followed by his invitation, "Come, come," which told me he didn't connect Nontawat and us. At least not fast enough. I'm sure he thought we were well-paying Caucasian customers. A tune he would not sing for long. As I brandished my firearm he had a sudden realization—checkmate!

Anna ordered Feller and the bartender to the back room. Nontawat stayed in the bar area, closed the entrance door and slipped the lock in place. Once in back I ordered both men to lie face down on the floor with their hands behind their backs. Anna did the honors by binding and gagging our captives.

Anna stepped out of the room briefly to solidify our intentions with Nontawat. No sooner had Anna reentered the room than she drew a black tactical folding knife from her handbag. She made eye contact with me, placed her handbag down, and took up a position kneeling on the Asian man's back.

Interrupting the flow of things, I said, "Hey, I can take care of this."

"The gun is too noisy. Think about it, it will alert too many people. It's better to ask our questions quietly." With that she stuck the knife blade in the right side of the bartender's carotid, puncturing the artery. I was shocked. I had not expected such a cold-blooded display. Without hesitation she kneeled on Feller's back, this time removing the gag. Anna didn't mince any words with Feller, "You have one chance to come clean. I want to know everything about your operation. Who brings in the kids, where do they get them, how large is the organization you're part of, everything?"

I thought he would divulge everything he knew to buy time or barter his way out but he made the wrong move and it cost him the game. Anna quickly pulled the gag back in place and repeated the process she had used on the first victim. Feller struggled momentarily as his life passed into oblivion. My concerns for protecting Anna on a project or getting her involved in murders faded away rapidly. She had the necessary disconnect for the job. Anna was stone-cold.

While Anna washed up at the bar she directed Nontawat and me to get the kids together and ready to move out. We went to the second floor where the children were housed. Nontawat was able to communicate with them and hurried them down the stairs. They might not have understood much about what was going on but they understood we were springing them, which seemed to suffice.

Anna joined me upstairs while Nontawat and the children waited in the bar. "Let's check each room again," Anna said. We started down the short hall that had only six visible doors. We cleared each room one by one until we were satisfied no johns or other children were there. Back downstairs Anna rifled through a makeshift office adjacent to the lounge area of the bar. She placed all the documents in her handbag. Large amounts of cash in various currencies were in the office. She collected the money from there and the bar placing it in a paper bag. Handing the bag of money to Nontawat she instructed him that the money was to be given to the church folks to be divided equally between the girls. He nodded.

Anna thought it best for Nontawat to wait alone with the girls. The religious folks already knew him, no reason to expose ourselves. Back in our streetside cubbyhole we watched the pickup unfold. Anna explained the church folks were very active and well versed in smuggling kids out of harm's way. "They will take care of them, they have before." I looked at her in disbelief. This was clearly not her first rodeo.

The kids quietly moved to a pair of vans parked in the alley and were gone. Nontawat stayed behind to tidy up a couple of things before catching up with Anna and me. As we walked together, Anna put her arm beneath mine and with a big smile said, "Let's take a little stroll." We had almost reached our destination when policemen ran by and the sounds of emergency vehicle sirens were coming closer. I wondered if the grisly killing had been discovered. Anna looked at Nontawat, who smiled and said, "I think it on fire." It was a dry wood structure. Undoubtedly extremely flammable, creating an intensely hot fire, and it would be gone in minutes. There would be no saving the structure or preserving the crime scene.

We didn't dally on Walking Street; there was nothing there for us. We arrived back at the resort and Nontawat was invited to stay. He declined, saying, "I have work to do at doctor's home." We still had a couple of days on our suite reservations and we made the best of it.

I rehashed some of the boondoggle effect, but Anna disagreed and felt it went smoothly. "How many times have you done something like this?" I asked. Her answer provided a lot of wiggle room. "Never," she replied, "Nothing is ever the same. It was an answer within a reply that didn't reveal anything. I felt other questions would receive similar responses so I put a sock in it.

Over the next couple of days I watched Anna pore over the documents she had gathered from the bar. I sucked down some fruity libations and caught a few rays. The morning arrived for us to catch our flight. Things progressed as they had for the entire trip; Anna had taken care of everything. All I needed to do was board the plane, except my ticket was wrong.

"Anna, my ticket says my flight is to Leonardo da Vinci airport; that's in Rome."

Anna responded as if she were surprised. "So it does!"

Anna looked at her ticket and exclaimed, "Mine does too—I guess we're going to Italy!"

I saw the smirk, but it wasn't that funny.

In a more serious tone Anna said, "I have someone I'd like you to meet. His name is Maximillian. I think you'll find him interesting." Anna paused, "No more questions for now."

That was easier said than done. I closed my eyes, leaned my head back, and waited to see what tomorrow would bring.

Chapter 18

It was a new dawn
—Walter

Anna and I sat quietly on the plane from Thailand to Rome. I occasionally interrupted her silence with idle chatter about anything that came to mind but my travel companion was not buying in. This was out of character for her. She was a warm-hearted individual with an outgoing and friendly personality. She liked to talk and carried a conversation even when I wasn't interested and less than receptive to discourse. Now, the shoe was on the other foot. It felt like we were breaking the ice all over again. Anna's focus was clearly on something else. I sensed whatever it was directly involved me and the outcome would either be a deal clincher or deal breaker as far as our relationship went.

In fairness, I was preoccupied as well. Anna was not the person she appeared to be. I had thought of her as a fragile socialite journalist seeking adventure close up and personal. The emerging truth was quite different. She was a well-connected professional killer. The knife work in Pattaya spoke loudly; she was cold, smooth, and deliberate.

As we deplaned at Leonardo da Vinci–Fiumicino Airport, Anna once again led the way through the processing maze of customs. I decided to pamper myself with a local beverage while Anna busied herself securing our in-country travel arrangements. I was in Rome or at least close to Rome. The history I'd read about in school was all around me. I wanted to see it for myself, but when Anna returned with more tickets in hand, the bombshell followed, "We have about an hour before we board the flight, Walter."

"Where to now?" I asked in a whiny tone. "I thought we were visiting Rome."

"Have you ever heard of Bellagio?"

Thinking for a moment I responded matter-of-factly, "Yeah, In Vegas."

Anna frowned and hesitated before continuing. I surmised she was trying to figure out if I was being sarcastic or if I was indeed ignorant of northern Italy. Her response indicated she had settled for the latter. "It's a beautiful village on Lake Como. You'll love it; it's nestled in the foothills of the Alps near the border of Switzerland."

"How long is this trip going to take?" I was back to whining again.

Anna responded tersely, "Get used to the idea—Bellagio is where we will be staying for the next few days."

It was about an hour's flight to Milan on a twin-engine puddle jumper. From there we hopped a train to Como, which was another half hour's trip on public transportation. By this point we had been traveling or waiting on the next connection to travel for nearly thirty hours. I found myself willing to settle for a hammock and a couple of trees, but there was no stopping Anna. She was bound and determined to reach Bellagio before nightfall. It wasn't clear to which day's end she was referring.

Arriving at Como, Anna and I took the covered escalators down to the piazza level, where she quickly acquired more tickets. With the fare paid, Anna snagged my arm and gently coerced my compliance to walk across the piazza to the pier on Lake Como and the awaiting hydrofoil. Seated on the foil, sarcasm slipped past my better judgment. "When we get off the boat, we don't have to ride a mule to a hilltop, do we?" She dismissed my remark without comment.

Passengers, most of whom had been with us on the train, loaded onto the boat and we were soon underway. The trip was incredibly scenic and relaxing. So much so, I napped most of the way. I thought hydrofoils were really fast boats but when they stop every ten minutes at some little lakeside village port on the way to Bellagio, it seemed like a long time. About an hour later we reached our destination. "We will catch a taxi to the villa where we are staying," Anna said. That was music to my ears.

Grand Hotel Villa Serbelloni, a five-star luxury hotel, was without doubt the most elegant accommodations I'd ever seen, not to mention stayed in. It appeared a little too upscale for the likes of me. I was comfortable with the pools and spas, even the ritzy restaurant and bar, but the clientele was a bit cultured for my blood. I had an immediate distrust for the lot of them.

Additionally troubling was the necessity to meet in such a place. Although I was not flipping the bill for this shindig, I questioned the reasons why someone might pay for this hoopla just for the sake of a meeting. If they thought there was a need to impress me, this was not it.

Evening descended into nightfall by the time we were escorted to a luxurious two-bedroom suite. It had been two long days of continuous travel without rest and we were dead tired. A bath and bed seemed in order. My head no sooner hit the pillow than I was cast into a desolate dream world. Before me I saw a cave with a large stone lying against it. A light shown deep within the cavern and I was profoundly moved within. A familiar figure emerged as a brilliant light and a voice spoke to me. "Your path of fulfillment lies before you. You will achieve your destiny."

I spoke to my spirit guide, "Why did you leave me on my own in Thailand? I looked for your presence and you were nowhere to be found."

"Scythian, you have never been alone in your quest. As for me, I will abide in your heart and dwell with you always." At that moment, Destiny stretched forth her hands from the light and we became as one. A burning in my bosom spoke to me of her dwelling within.

The next morning I arose prepared to embrace my calling. Anna's plan for the day was a sightseeing tour of Bellagio. That sounded really great, except it avoided the purpose of our visit. I was psyched for action. Anna's plan seemed more like a chore than a pleasure. Anna tried to excite me about the village with talk of climbing stairs and visiting souvenir shops—at least that was all I heard and it wasn't working for me.

Bellagio, settled snugly on a peninsula separating two legs of Lake Como, was a majestic union of land, water and sky. The hilly, picturesque landscape topped with snow-capped alpine peaks and a cool, brisk northern wind offered up a level of comfort only Mother Nature can provide.

We spent the afternoon hiking staircase alleyways and visiting pastry shops. I was taken in more by the Romanesque architecture, ornamental flowerbeds and century-old parks, than the touristy shops. It was a step back in time and a refreshing experience. Anna promised we would have time to visit the villas, palazzos, and chapels dotted around the lake, but first there was an agenda we could not ignore. She didn't come right out and say it that way but then again, she hadn't made plans for tomorrow.

Later in the evening Anna and I dined at the Grand Hotel. I decided on a taste of local cuisine, Risotto al Pesce Persico while Anna went a bit more Mediterranean. The atmosphere was romantic and our conversation was flowing smoothly. I had something I wanted to talk about with Anna, but I didn't know how to bring up the subject of our relationship. Before

I was able to articulate my thoughts, Anna brought up the reason we were here—business.

"We won't make plans for tomorrow. Maximillian will be here and he insists on meeting you."

"Why am I meeting him, Anna, who is he?"

"I'll let him explain tomorrow. He is a wonderful man with a big heart. I think you will like him. He is your type of people."

My type of people—what is my type of people? I didn't know I had a type. Her words were intended to disarm my concerns, but they did little to alleviate my apprehensions. I'd learned not to question Anna. She was tight-lipped with a poker face. I couldn't read her expressions, mood, or get anything out of her if she was not willing to divulge it. When she did answer a question, it usually led to more questions that she wouldn't answer.

I was up early the next morning anxiously awaiting Max's arrival. Around noon Anna prepared to leave the suite with a briefcase. She was dressed to kill, very sophisticated and professional in appearance.

"Be a dear and stay here, Walter; I want to be able to reach you when I need to."

A couple of hours passed without contact with Anna. A curious mixture of concern and boredom was setting in and my mood was souring. When the call came in from Anna my countenance immediately rebounded. She was short and to the point, "I'll be there soon."

Minutes later I heard a knock at the door. Not expecting anyone knocking at my suite, I opened the door slowly in such a way as to block the door swing with my foot. To my surprise it was Anna accompanied by an elderly gentleman, tall, with a slender build and wide bright smile.

"Come in, uh, come right on in." I hated using "uh" but sometimes it slipped out. In the days of debating with Teddy Bear at the factory, he would make fun of me by saying, uh, uh, uh, like I was stuttering, although I had uttered "uh" only once. Now I'm self-conscious about saying it, so as soon as I did, my thought process froze up and I couldn't think of anything appropriate to say. Anna sensed I was embarrassed; she lifted her hand and touched my cheek as she passed by me on her way into the room. The elderly man walking with the assistance of a cane stopped abruptly in front of me, extending his right hand while introducing himself.

"Ello, I'm Maximillian Karnage, pleased to meet you finally."

"Pleasure is mine, sir, I'm Walter."

With a sparkling in his eyes, he stated rather emphatically, "Yes, of course you are," as if he knew differently. He proceeded to lay his overcoat and hat on a chair by the entry and made his way into the parlor. Some might not have noticed, but Walter picked up on it right away, Max already knew the way to the parlor. He had been in this room before. Anna joined us in the parlor a few minutes later. She placed a call to room service ordering hors d'oeuvres and wine. My best guess was this wasn't her first time hosting a meeting with our guest either.

Maximillian impressed me as a traditional English noble or at least what I thought one would be like. He was stylish in appearance and his manners were dignified. He acted like a blue-blooded aristocrat, but then again, don't we all act?

"Anna tells me you have a particular niche that I find fascinating."

"I'm not sure I know what you're referring to."

"Well, Anna has kept me well informed of your—shall we say—activities. Let's not be shy, we likely have many of the same goals."

Thinking for a moment and watching Anna's head nodding yes in response to his question, I felt assured I could talk freely, "I hunt and kill bad people. It's that simple." Such a proclamation with most people would have a shocking effect. I didn't see it in his face.

Maximillian, leaning forward in a rosewood Victorian parlor chair, both hands clasped on the top of his cane, "Yes, tell me, is it a personal vendetta? Do you kill for revenge? Tell me man, which is it?"

"I wouldn't call it personal. Revenge is not the motivator for me. I am called to intercede for the victims. I do what they can't do for themselves. I avenge in their stead."

Max was digesting how I saw myself. He sat quietly with a distant look in his eyes.

I continued, "The people I kill are guilty of unspeakable atrocities and deserve nothing less than death. I'm at odds with the justice system and have made myself an enemy of law enforcement. I've been accused by the media for masquerading as an angel while doing the devil's work.

Neither is true, yet, both are; it is a matter of perspective."

"You undoubtedly have a set of guiding principles."

"My crusade is against those who violently assault and abuse the innocent, weak, young, or elderly. I have no remorse for my actions."

Maximillian, in a loud, sturdy voice said, "Marvelous, that is, simply splendid! I want you to consider a proposal, Walter. I want you to consider a more epic adventure than that which you have been undertaking. Are you game?"

"Absolutely." I've never thought of executing people as an adventure, but I was all ears.

"Alright then, let's have a listen to what Anna has." Leaning back in the lounge chair, I listened intently while Anna conducted her review of the Thailand escapade. She laid out the papers from her briefcase in a few small stacks. Feller's involvement in the child sex industry was clearly revealed. "He was a minor league player," Anna said, "looking to move into the majors." According to the documents, he was an importer, buying children on the black market like a cattle buyer purchasing livestock for a feeder lot. Anyone who bankrolled an operation like he had, expected a handsome return on their investment. This required a clientele willing to pay top dollar for the services he had to offer. The papers in Anna's possession were confirmations of his connection with prominent business professionals from around the globe. When Anna concluded her presentation, Maximillian exclaimed angrily, "Ruddy beggar!" He shook his head saying, "He was a blighter—well, good show then, the network is interrupted for now."

"Isn't someone else just going to fill the void?" I asked of whoever might answer.

Maximillian turned his attention toward me. "Yes, I suppose so. All the same, we won't be deterred from this course of action. With godspeed we will disrupt these beasts' abilities to continue their diabolical businesses."

Turning his attention back to Anna, he thanked her for the evening and bid her adieu. "I'll contact Nontawat concerning the names you have here," Max said, "It's likely they will look for another source in his country. We may be able to make a real mess of things yet."

Anna replied, "I'll make sure the others have the client names as well. They may be able to turn the tables on them in their own countries."

"Right then, it's nearly eight o'clock." Maximillian rose from his chair and finished his glass of wine. "Walter, walk with me to the door, if you will."

The elderly gentleman paused by the door to pick up his overcoat and hat. "I'll leave you in Anna's company. We do not offer fame or fortune, just opportunity."

"Who is 'we'?"

"Yes, well Anna will have to mentor you. I'm sure she can answer all your questions. Till tomorrow then."

I opened the door to the hall before saying goodbye.

"Thank you Max—May I call you Max?"

"I prefer Maxmillian if you will." He smiled and proceeded slowly down the hallway.

Returning to the parlor, Anna was waiting for me. "Now you can ask questions. You probably have a lot of them." She sighed. Oddly, for the moment, only one question came vividly to mind, "Who are you?"

For the next few hours, Anna opened doors of understanding into her life. "I belong to an organization, some would call it a secret society but that sounds so medieval. We are a select group with a unique mission. Our order is modeled after the Palatini Knighthood. The name means freelancers. In the earlier centuries during the height of Italian nobility and aristocracy, Knights took on roles of protection and guardianship for their country. Palatini were champions of the people. They were paragons of virtue, chivalrous, and heroic, with a bond of righteous principles."

"So you're knights?"

"The original Palatini took the Praetorian Guards' place in Rome and were absorbed into the Vatican. We are the resurrection of the order. We respect our oath of guardianship and much like you; we are professional freelance assassins who bring righteous judgment on the guilty. Our society is well organized and well financed for our missions. We simply refer to ourselves as Palatini."

"Is your name really Anna?" She probably didn't think my question was sincere from the grimace on her face, but I really wanted to know. "Yes and you know my Palatini name as well, Archangel. Now, let's move on."

"So—how does it work—does someone call the shots of who gets zapped next or tells you who to kill like 'Have gun will travel'?" My reference to the old Richard Boone TV shows "Paladin" didn't go unnoticed.

"It doesn't work like that and you're not Paladin. We are freelancers. We are offered opportunities, broader in spectrum, than what most Palatini could do on their own, or afford. We often work alone and at times we are asked to help each other. That is what the Society is about."

As Anna spoke, flashbacks permeated my consciousness. I recalled many dreams from the past few years of me upon a fiery warhorse draped in armor and charging into battle against apparitions of evil. Destiny herself had said this was my purpose. Somehow I believed it was ordained. Anna paused as if she were waiting for me to finish my thoughts. I didn't feel free to question Max as to what part in the scheme he played but the etched lines on his face were verification of untold battles against injustice. He was a man of sophistication and grit; a man I wanted to know more about.

"Who Is Max?"

"Maximillian is Grand Master of Society Palatini. He was selected by a vote of the Society to coordinate efforts worldwide. Unlike your efforts of selecting one person, stalking and killing them for their crimes against humanity, we target organizations who are engaged in child exploitation and abuse. Think about it Walter, it's the bigger picture you have dreamed about."

Anna paused for a moment then continued, "Maximillian is a clearinghouse for information and very ubiquitous when we have a need. He has a long history of taking care of business in the UK, much the same way as we have done in the US. In what the European courts have failed to do in their lapse of judgment, he has set the standard for righteousness. He executed those who profited from abuses to children. He operated much like you did when he started out. He had no idea others felt the same way or where to find them if they did. He also shares in being a product of child slavery. His rescue came at the hands of a British military officer who adopted him and bestowed upon him education and wealth. He served in the military and afterwards set a course to apply what he had learned through revenge."

"So how many Palatini are we talking about?"

"There are too few!" Anna's eyes welled up with tears, "There are perhaps half a million child abusers actively engaged in the world. They have websites overseas and pedophile associations that laws do not ban. If there were thousands of us, it would be too few."

"Is Nontawat a Knight?"

"No, he is what we refer to as a resource. In his case, he does a lot of leg work or facilitates an operation. He has a miniscule vision of what we do. What he sees is what is important to him—the children in Thailand."

For every question Anna answered, two more popped into my head. My sarcasm was gone and I was interested in righting the wrongs of which she spoke.

"How is it organized to work together?"

"Much of our work is by networking information. Leads come through continuous gathering of information from sources we have developed. When we need further assistance, we contact Maximillian with those needs. It is not complex, really."

"So—why me?"

"That's easy; you were already freelancing. One normally thinks of a freelancer as a person with a service to sell. You, like the Palatini, provide a service, but ask for nothing in return. Maximillian and I thought it best we work together and perhaps accomplish more."

"Yeah, but I found you, you didn't find me."

"Really—my police sources initially brought to light the likelihood of a serial killer preying on felony sex offenders. I didn't know who you were personally when you contacted me through email but you confirmed who you were when tailing Darroe."

"How's that?"

"Do you remember following Darroe to his office, and subsequent stops at the grocery store when he returned to his house?"

"Sure, I was on him like white on rice."

"Yes you were, and I surmise you thought your strategy very clever, but to the trained eye your intentions were obvious. I wouldn't go so far as to say your methods were amateurish, but your techniques lacked professionalism."

"Maybe I'm not as good as you, but I still get the job done." I was incensed by what she said, but she spoke the truth. Everything I'd learned I'd picked up on my own. I'd found applications from my time in the military and lessons learned growing up on the ranch, but there were no other teachers.

"Don't get all uppity and defensive. It was only noticeable because I was trailing Darroe too. I don't know if you remember, but you went into the store to keep an eye on Darroe, I took a picture of your VIN number and ran it through my source. It's easily visible through the windshield and they are located in the same place on all cars, bottom driver's side of the dash. If you want to stay undetected cover the VIN with a sunglass case or other item you might normally have on your dash."

"So what did you find out from the VIN?"

"I know who you are. Who you really are, or were, however you want to say it. I know where you were born, raised, and additional background information. I also know where your vehicle registered address is. I did my homework before we met."

It was an epiphany, "You killed Darroe!"

"That's right. When I saw you back off the shot at the rest area, I finished it."

"I couldn't justify killing him. He may have gotten dirtbags off, but he did it legally."

"Remember, I told you the police uncovered child porn in his house?"

"Yes, I remember thinking I wasn't wrong after all; I should have followed my instincts and popped him."

"I knew it was there. It's been a time-consuming operation to nail him. I ensured my sources discovered the porn he had when they were looking for a possible motive. The child porn was Brazilian made. Feller's first hitch was in Brazil before he was kicked out of the country for dabbling in the pornography. That game is still in play. A Palatini is in Brazil as we speak searching for the source. When he finds it, he will disrupt their reign of terror."

I muttered under my breath, maybe there really is a God. In my wildest dreams I could never have imagined an organization of vigilantes aimed at protecting and preserving civilization from an onslaught of decadence.

"I am willing to give it a try but I want it understood if I don't like the way things operate, I'm free to return to what I was doing without any complications.

"Fair enough" Anna quickly added. "I will contact Maximillian and we can arrange another get-together."

"Don't worry about it; he plans on seeing me tomorrow."

The next morning Max was at the door bright and early. Anna let him in and ordered a pot of tea with the appropriate complements and then woke me. I shaved, showered, dressed, and joined them in the parlor. Not wanting to offend our guest I tried a cup of tea, confirming, once again, I am a coffee drinker. Maximillian went straight to the point, "Walter, now that you've had some time to consider our proposal, have you come to a decision?"

"Honestly, I have reservations, but I'm willing to be part of the order, society, whatever as long as the condition I've given Anna is agreed to."

"Stand then, man, and swear an oath of allegiance to the cause."

He delivered the solemn oath of the Palatini and knighted me, "Scythian." I took orders from no one, but made myself available to assist other Palatini in their endeavors and likewise they would be there for me. Max spent the rest of the day explaining how I might contact other Society members through him and interact with them. "Sources are never divulged," Max said. "They are developed by Palatini for gathering information and are not passed around." If I needed assistance I was to contact Max and he would put me in contact with a Palatini who might have the source I needed. If they obtained information that might be valuable, the Knight would pass it on.

Max was clear on one thing; his primary mission was high rollers with global influence. People making a buck off the child slavery and sex industry were his main targets. Whether they were involved making porn, acting in the films, kidnapping, or distributing the product—they were targets. I could still pursue my targets as before, but I was now able to look at the bigger picture and move against it in ways I could only have dreamed about before.

Anna and I stayed on in Bellagio for a few more days. Frequently we walked the streets arm in arm, visiting the tourist attractions. Anna seemed affectionately closer now than ever before. I felt we had a deep bond between us; one that had potential to flourish. The last night was considerably awkward for me. As we finished up our evening meal, I felt the timing right for a little beating around the bush. "What are our plans next?"

Anna seemed prepared for the question, "We go back to doing what we did before."

"Are we going to continue to work together as a team or what?" It seemed to be the worst possible question I could ask at the moment.

"We are Palatini—by definition we are freelancers. We work independently unless we need assistance."

"I, uh, thought we had, uh, were a good team is all." I felt myself backing away from what I wanted to say.

Anna gazed at me with her bright blue eyes. I was tripping all over my words. What made it worse was I knew she was aware of my struggle. Anna more than once had rescued me from myself in conversation. It didn't appear she was mindful to do it this time until she cracked a slight smile.

"I would like very much to work together again but we are first and foremost Palatini. If our paths cross in work, and I'm sure they will, we'll see each other there."

"I would like that." Thataboy, I thought, what a manly response. I can kill people but I can't talk to women.

After dinner, Anna and I returned to our suite. Before retiring to our separate bedrooms Anna initiated a very long passionate kiss and embrace followed by a "Good night." Wow! My emotions were tingling. It had been many years since I'd felt what came over me at that moment. Whether she knew it or not, and I suspect she did, my night was now more difficult. Lying there alone in bed with only an unlocked door between us my mind was going a thousand miles an hour. I had visions of her opening the door and walking into my arms. I couldn't get through a whole thought before being bombarded by another and another. I was on overload; Palatini, Anna, bad guys, Anna, Destiny, Anna, who, what, where—it was chaos. Thoughts kept rushing at me with one not necessarily related to another. Often they collided, resulting in one beginning before the last one ended. The final results of my mental gymnastics; nothing made sense. At some point sleep came; otherwise I would have ended up a raving loony.

A week passed uneventfully. Anna and I talked daily on the phone, but work, the kind the newspapers paid her to do, had taken her "in the field." We made plans, but dreams and reality rarely merged.

I was starting to get the itch again. A couple of newspaper headlines about bad guys and I was back in the swing of things digging through old records for a likely candidate. Apparitions, visions, and voices no longer directed me. Yet, somewhere within, Destiny dwelt. I could feel her presence. But, with Anna gone on assignment I never felt more alone.

After a few days of contemplation I finally accepted the change in my life. It would not be the same anymore. I didn't have people in my life before, now I would. By involving myself with Anna and the Palatini I had accepted a responsibility to have others in my life. Before my association with the Society, I didn't feel anything and I was alone. Now, I felt lonely in their absence. It was a new dawn.

Max called to say hi, or so he said, but then related the real reason for calling. "There is a piece of mail due to arrive soon. If things aren't pressing I'd like you to attend." I watched for the postman the next day and soon after his delivery I made my way to the trailer park box and retrieved a six-by-nine-inch padded picture mailer. Inside the envelope was a first-class round-trip airline ticket to Houston, Texas. Hotel accommodations booked in my name and a single sheet of paper with the name of my contact, Seymour Bludd.

This was the adventure part Max had spoken of. From the hours spent together in Bellagio I understood the meaning of this rendezvous. My assistance was being requested. No weapons were necessary, only my attendance.

I called Anna that evening to see if she too received such an invitation. She had not. "Don't worry," she said, "I know you well enough, you like being involved. Besides I'm knee-deep in something too."

My flight was scheduled to depart in three days. It was a much shorter trip than the last series of fights but I was still hesitant to get back on a plane so quickly. Nevertheless, I hadn't decided on a project of my own, so I figured I might as well see how my Palatini counterparts got the job done. If I kept my eyes, ears, and most importantly my mind open, I could always learn something to adapt to my trade.

Chapter 19

. . . the greatest fault lay with those who created the market; the buyer of child porn"
—Walter

The phone rang catching me by surprise. I'd arrived only hours earlier and hadn't contacted anyone since checking into the hotel. "Giddaymate," the male voice said while sporting a chipper twang. "How are you this fine day?"

Despite his optimism for a quick response, his call begged the question, "Who is this?"

"It's Bludd; Captain Seymour Bludd, mate. Did you have a good flight?"

I really didn't have any complaints about the flight, it was smooth and uneventful. Not having met Mr. Bludd previously, I doubted he wanted to hear about my disdain for air travel, especially since he called the meeting, "It was fine, thanks."

"Yes, well then, Maximillian and some other lads are in the bistro. Why don't you join us for a cup? Whaddayah say, mate?"

Not yet oriented to the hotel or for that matter what a bistro was. I said, "Can you tell me how to find this place?"

"It's the hotel pub on the second floor. Easy to find; she's at the top of the foyer stairs where you registered."

"Give me about ten minutes or so and I'll be there."

"Alright mate, ten minutes it is."

At midafternoon the restaurant was virtually empty of patrons, allowing me to easily locate my host. Rather than clustering in a corner and appearing secretive, the men had chosen a strategically located table at the center axis of the bistro. This might appear meaningless to some, but I recognized it as a deliberate security precaution. The potential dangers to Palatini members at this clandestine meeting were many. The four men rose from their chairs as I approached.

One man stepped forward offering his hand in alliance, "Seymour Bludd is the name, mate." Bludd was a robust fortyish looking fellow with a large barrel chest, bald and wearing coveralls, T-shirt, and deck shoes. Gesturing in the direction of the man standing to his left, he said, "Of course you've met Maximillian?" Max extended his hand to greet me, "Happy to see you could make it."

Bludd continued his introduction, "Russell Gunn," gesturing to the man next to Max. "Call me Rusty," said the tall, lanky man. I utilize immediate impressions of strangers to judge how to best converse with them. Gunn appeared friendly; his body posture told me this was a deception intended to disarm the unsuspecting and a front for a man far more defensive and reserved. I extended my hand to Gunn, who looked at it before making the mental connection to respond with a handshake. Gunn broke eye contact looking past me toward the entryway, giving me the impression he was looking at someone other than me. Resisting the urge to turn and look for myself I relied on the others, who were not looking behind me. It was a defensive posture. Rusty was notably American, midthirties, and casually dressed in slacks and polo shirt.

Bludd turned his attention to the remaining man and with a slight hand gesture, said, "Donnie Brook." The man stretched out his hand to greet me, "Pleased to meet you, sir." This gentleman struck me as refined in manners and appearance. He had a notable foreign accent, sounding like Bela Lugosi in the old Dracula movie yet looking like Tab Hunter with wavy blonde hair. His bronze suntan gave him a youthful look for a man I put in his forties. Judging from my own height, Donnie was six feet tall and of average weight.

"Yes, well then, let's sit," Max said.

Max started the round-robin off providing a short personal history of himself followed by Bludd. Captain Seymour Bludd was Australian by birth but at an early age had decided on a life of adventure upon the high seas. Although he admitted his employment, piloting tugboats was far from glamorous, it had made substantial provision for his lifestyle and provided him a view of the world not seen by many. As he described it most people would prefer never to see it or acknowledge its existence. He was actively recruited by Max more than ten years ago and had been instrumental in "taking out" objectives. Max asked Rusty to weigh in next.

Russell Gunn grew up in Clearwater, Florida and followed his dad into a machinist trade in avionics. He was now independently employed. No one talked numbers, but Rusty made his first "target" on a personal response to a family situation. It wasn't enough for him and he soon found a second target, then a third. He had a run-in with the law on the third occasion where he was a person of interest—a fancy term for suspect—in the murder. An informant provided Max with details. Max provided Rusty with a top-notch legal team and finances. The prosecutors never made the case. Rusty was brought on board three years ago.

Donnie Brook was an actor in European pornography. In some sense it explained his shorter-haired Fabio appearance. I had difficulty listening to him at first; it seemed he was part of the problem, not the solution. As a young man he had bought into the allure of the sex stage and the money being made available. He traveled from Yorkshire to Hungary and Portugal at the whim of producers and distributors. While in Hungary he refused to "act" with a young girl who was being forced into the business by Serbian Mafioso. After receiving threats for his defiance he returned to England. The producers again wanted Donnie to engage with a girl who was playing the part of a fifteen-year-old, but was reportedly nineteen. He met with the so-called agents from the Czech Republic and decided against the project. The agents turned gangsters on him. After a little roughing up they let him know he was selected to do this project. If it was a problem with this girl they had many others.

Donnie met with the girl, who told him she had been kidnapped along with others in the Czech Republic and they were prostituting to pay off their captures. In a not-so-proud moment in his life he filled the obligation his producers had put him in and broke contract with them. After realizing they were directly involved with these criminals, he systematically set out to assassinate his producers and directors.

Through a contact he was introduced to Max a dozen years ago and had worked in Sweden, Finland, Czech Republic, Bosnia, and a half dozen other European countries. His primary targets were gangs operating in kidnapping schemes and child porn rings.

Max called on me next. Reflecting on what the others had said, I wondered what I could bring to the table. We were all different with different stories, but with the same objective. I was silent for several seconds as I looked around the table, gazing, in turn, deep into the eyes of these men before speaking.

"I don't know the exact time I came to the realization society betrays us with false hopes and the conviction that superheroes are coming to the rescue of the weak, the young, the elderly and the innocent. There are no superheroes. No one is coming to their aid. It is incumbent upon us. From the religious faithful, to the Hollywood scammers, evil is portrayed as manifestations of demonic ghostly figures, night-stocking vampires and flesh-eating zombies. In reality, evil lurks in our neighborhoods, workplaces, and even in our own family members—left to natural progression, only morals stand between good and evil. The embodiment of evil is in all of humankind. When sadistic crimes are perpetrated on the innocent and vulnerable, by cruel and inhuman individuals or organized criminals, no sense of justice prevails. Mankind cheers in the fairy tales as the demons are cast out and vampires eradicated with a stake. Yet, when faced with the opportunity to destroy real evil, they lament and coddle the sexual predator with light punishment and attempts to understand and explain their aberrant behavior. Judicial liberals can join the psychobabblers in the netherworld as far as I'm concerned. It is nothing more than a Band-Aid over a terminal cancer. Cast out the demon, drive the stake, but shoot the bullet at the real evil. I have joined you, the Palatini, for one reason only. I will seek out those worthy of death and ensure it is administered properly and timely. I am not new to killing. Adjustments to our system of punishment were in order; I've made long-overdue modifications. As I applied these revisions, I caught the attention of Archangel; she brought me to Maximillian. I became convinced I could better serve as a member of the Society Palatini than as a lone crusader; so here I am."

The men were quiet. Max was first to speak. He began by passing out directions for each of us to review. It was the basics of any operation. In the military we had what was referred to as situation reports. The documents were an overview of what had been discovered and confirmed. In this case, each of us could choose to participate or not.

The mission was a multipronged operation. If successful we would disrupt a child-porn production and distribution ring—an organization kidnapping and forcing poverty-stricken children into despicable acts against their will. Max would control central communications, logistics, and finances. Bludd, point man for the Op, has been on location in Port of Rio Grande, Brazil, for more than a year. He had located the group producing the child porn and relayed the message to Max. He had the names of producers and a local distributor for an overseas market. Max asked Rusty to work with Bludd. In Max's view, due to Gunn's previous circumstances with police, he would be better off out of country. Additionally the strike would require simultaneous hits on the two known entities in Brazil. While Bluud took down the producers, Rusty was the chosen asset for the distributor. Bludd acknowledged his appreciation, "Welcome aboard, mate, we'll be staying on my boat *The Hazard* docked at the Porto Novo wharf'."

Next on the distribution trail were importers. Max provided Donnie with information needed to research and locate the source of circulation in the United Kingdom. He was provided a short list of potential names. Donnie was headed to Switzerland; one of several known destinations of the Brazilian DVDs.

Max saved me for last. For a brief moment I thought and hoped to assist Donnie. He was a seasoned veteran of Palatini field work, an area I lacked. I could pull a trigger and not blink an eye, but an organized strike was beyond my current comprehension. My greatest fear was sitting in a cloistered little room waiting to be called into service. In the military we used to call it, "in the rear with the gear." As important as reinforcements could be to an operation it was not for me. I had an itch and I needed it scratched.

Max handed me my directions. A quick scan assured me of action. I was likewise on the distribution trail, right here in my own backyard.

"America is one of the largest importers of child pornography," Max said. "This industry exists because of consumers. They are no less guilty than those kidnapping or committing the atrocities we see on the DVDs. They all share equally in the responsibility." I had to agree. Bludd didn't spend much time looking over the documents; he had assisted Max in their preparation. This was his operation; he and Rusty were point of the spear. If all else failed the Brazilian leg of the operation had to go off without a flaw.

Max dismissed us, "Shall we retire for the evening and meet tomorrow after we've had a good look at the paperwork?" Each of us received info on a specific target. In the reference material it was apparent the common denominator was pornography. With the exception of those in Brazil, these were not people who normally associated with one another. Although my and Donnie's operations were on different continents, a measure of coordination had to occur. The last thing we wanted was a disruption on the distribution legs without getting the source. The action was more than an interruption of the industry. This was intended to be an out-and-out extermination.

My American target, Lou Cypher, was a second-generation millionaire a couple of times over. For his daddy's business sake, after the old man died, Lou had sold his interest in the company to the board of directors. At forty-two-years-old and with no apparent ambition, he cruised about in the Gulf of Mexico on his 103-foot Broward motor yacht. Max included recent photos of both Cypher and his boat, *Thai Tannic*.

The profile showed his vessel, when in port, was tied up in the Galveston Bay marina. It was also apparent that the likelihood of making a hit at the marina was slim at best. He was rarely there. Over the past year, Cypher had moored his boat as far south as Aruba, but more frequently was tracked from Cozumel north along the coastline to Galveston Bay. His current location along the barrier islands appeared to suit his needs. He lived alone on his yacht, employing a small crew only when he docked or traveled out of the Gulf area. His crew consisted of a pilot, mechanic, and dock hand who worked out of the Galveston marina.

By all accounts, Cypher was heterosexual with a preference for petite Latina women. He appeared to be more of a recluse than socialite. There was no indication his interest in child pornography was anything other than for distribution. He was known to distribute Ecstasy in small quantities, probably from a Mexican source. Financial needs were not likely a motivating factor for Cypher. He was a risk taker for the thrill of it.

The next morning at the Palatini meeting we rehearsed our options. It was a great feeling to once again enjoy the camaraderie I'd known in the military. We were instructed, once in place with our targets and a solution determined, to contact Max. As point of contact, he would initiate the "Go" order at the appropriate time. The dominos had to fall in order. Bludd had primary responsibility for first strike in the mission. If Donnie or I jumped the gun, word might trickle back to the source making Bludd and Rusty's job more difficult. Unlike my earliest days of hunting prey on my own, this was taking on considerably complexity. The part that motivated me most was the finale, where I busted a cap on my target. It was always my favorite part.

We continued our cohesion the remainder of the day, dwelling mostly on the mission options. It felt good to talk through the scenarios and listen to inputs. Before leaving, Max asked all of us to check in daily with updates. Back in my suite, I called Anna, "How are things in your neck of the woods?"

"I've been busy. There is a lot of information, not privy to the general public, becoming available. I think it will interest you."

"What's up?"

"Remember Brandon A. Ware, the retired MCSD Detective?"

"Sure, of course, how could I forget?"

"He is now a self-employed private investigator. My source was unusually direct with the impression Ware gave him. Ware had a score to settle. He was disgruntled over the FBI's handling of one of his cases. He believes he holds the answer and intends to finish what he started."

"Okay, I hate to tell him he's going to have to wait if it's me he wants. I have other business of my own to take care of."

"Walter—I'm going to be incommunicado for a bit. I will be traveling to help out a source search through some material."

"Same for me, I'll touch base with you when I can."

There was more I wanted to say or should have said, something deeper or more meaningful, but the timing wasn't right—it never seemed to be right. I went to bed thinking about Anna and Ware. It was an odd combination of thoughts to sort through.

Max provided a last known location on the *Thai Tannic*. He had filed a float plan for the waters of Corpus Christi about a week before. From Cypher's profile, there was nothing unusual about him remaining adrift in an area for weeks at a time. When he moved to a new area, customarily, he filed float plans with the U.S. Coast Guard. Unusual was a recent case of his boat appearing off the northern coast of Aruba having failed to follow his normal pattern of filing.

Max offered to assist with arrangements for my stay in Texas. I gave him my druthers for a rental vehicle and the Galveston area to stay in. He promptly provided both. Before saying goodbye, Max had the vehicle rental delivered to the hotel. The gray four-door Chevy Blazer was the type vehicle I had asked for. It wasn't fancy, but it had air-conditioning. If you're a northerner visiting the south, you appreciate the option.

The Galveston waterfront hotel overlooked the marina where *Thai Tannic* berthed. In the event he headed for port I wanted to be close enough to capitalize on the opportunity. Otherwise, it was a four-hour drive south from Galveston to the general vicinity Cypher was believed to be in.

Padre Island was long and touristy with more than one motor yacht in the waters. The open seas presented an entirely new challenge. Getting close to my target on his yacht without cover and concealment would be awkward. I am an ambush predator. I like to remain hidden until I strike.

I made calls the first evening to locate a private charter vessel. Money was no object. I needed an inconspicuous boat that would not bring attention to my activities. I found such a craft in Port Lavaca. The twenty-one-foot 1970s model Bayliner was well maintained, unlike Captain Crusty, the salty old sailor piloting it. His name wasn't really Crusty; I just called 'em like I saw 'em.

At my initial meeting with Crusty, I quickly learned how to read him. What he thought of me was written all over his face. It was clear he found me a nerdy nitwit probably incapable of tying my own shoes and I was okay with it.

"You say you want to do some sightseeing, mister?"

"Yes sir, I'm a writer, here's my card." I presented him with one of my many bogus business cards. "I'd like to locate some really big yachts in the Gulf, take pictures, that sort of thing."

Crusty thought for a minute before answering, "Usually a few down along Matagorda and Padre Island. We'll go on the Gulf side of the barrier islands and see what we can find. The bigger yachts cruise out there."

I leaned back in the quarter bench and let my hair blow in the wind. Padre Island is part of a long land mass referred to as the barrier islands along the coast of Texas and Mexico. We cast off at Port Lavaca and headed south for about an hour before coming up on a mega-yacht. We circled around it a couple times while I took pictures and scratched notes from Captain Crusty's repertoire. We traveled south for another hour before we came upon another yacht. This vessel was anchored with a number of smaller crafts around it. With all the activity going on it was easy to slip in close. Crusty said she was over 150 foot in length with the name "*Poor Boy*" etched into the bow on both sides. After a few photos it was time to leave the party-goers to themselves. Crusty asked, "If you don't mind I'd like a couple of those pictures?"

"Do you like the yacht?"

"I like the girls trying for a suntan without lines. Whoooaaahhh," Crusty hooted, followed by a raucous laugh.

We traveled farther south, and came across another yacht. As we pulled close to it, Crusty slowed the engines, saying, "Here's a smaller one about hundred-footer." As we slowed to a drift fifty yards away from the craft the name was easily identifiable, *Thai Tannic*. I pulled my camera out to take pictures as we slowly circled the boat.

The decks were almost fully enclosed by windows except on the bridge level and a small section on the afterdeck. I took pictures and made notes before giving Crusty a nod to continue on our way south along the coastline. When we completed our tour for the day I made sure Crusty was able to transport me every other day in search of additional yachts, a primary feature in furthering my plans.

Back in Galveston I reviewed the photo images taken with my digital camera. From my perspective, the most vulnerable area was the stern. Two decks were accessible from the entry point. The main level had a set of double ladders on either side of the stern from the swim deck to the afterdeck. The upper deck next to the bridge was a weather deck and would be accessed by ladders amidships. The craft appeared anchored about a mile from shoreline off Padre Island. The area had a lot of activity on the inter-coastal side, but considerably less on the Gulf side where Cypher moored. As my plans advanced I realized the need for a skiff to reach my target. I set out to find suitable sources.

Locating armament for the operation was first on my agenda. Houston newspaper classified advertisement sections were full of guns for sale. No identification, ATF forms, or questions—just cold hard cash and walk. What more could you ask for.

I located an accumulation of weapons for sale in the Gulf Gate area. I was suspicious of the ad, but decided it couldn't hurt to look; in the end it turned out to be a private collection. I purchased from the assortment an older model 870 Remington pump action 12-gauge shotgun and a mint condition 9mm Model 17 Glock without any modifications. Sure, I paid top dollar but they were worth every penny. I followed up by purchasing buckshot and hallow points at a local retail store.

Every other day for the past week and a half I'd had Crusty cruise the Padre Island coastline in search of yachts. By doing so, I was able to keep an eye on Cypher's whereabouts. Soon Crusty and I would part company.

I discussed my options with Max during the evening call. As I discussed my next move, he related the other Palatini were a "go." Donnie was "eyes on" target, meaning he was ready to take out his assigned target anytime the word came down. Bludd indicated he and Rusty were twenty-four hours from takedown. Essentially it meant they needed a little time to coordinate their efforts on a local level. With one day's notification they could set the domino effect into motion. Max concluded, "We are ready."

I knew he wasn't including me in the picture. If Bludd determined he would lose the opportunity he would call it into action. Donnie would more than likely get his target and I would make it happen on my end—I was confident I could carry it out efficiently. I was ready; all I needed was the word to proceed. I would promptly dispatch my target and disappear. Except for blood trails on an abandoned yacht, it would be as though I never existed. As eager as I might be, I had to keep in mind Lou Cypher was a target of secondary importance.

During my travels with Crusty I frequently spotted boats for sale in the marinas. I exercised diligence recording boat types, prices, and phone numbers of all likely candidates for future use. There was never a doubt I would need to secure a vessel of my own and move Crusty out of the picture. Being an avid outdoorsman I had operated various small craft in lakes and rivers. I had a good idea of what I was looking for.

Phone calls turned up a prospective purchase meeting my criteria. The seller of the fourteen-foot Zodiac was located on the outskirts of Port Aransas. This was an area north of Padre Island and not far from the *Thai Tannic*. On the phone the seller stated that his craft, boat trailer and a pair of older 25hp Johnson outboard motors went as a package. I had to be prepared for the what-ifs; two motors would minimize the possibilities of a single larger motor failing during the operation. It would be difficult to explain to the Coast Guard why I was drifting aimlessly near a murder scene. Two outboard motors were necessary.

We set a time and location to meet. He chose the Port Aransas marina. I was waiting when he pulled in with the Zodiac in tow. We dickered over the price and eventually settled on the asking price. I outfitted the Blazer for towing and picked up a trolling motor. The electric MotorGuide unit was an inexpensive accessory to what I perceived would come in handy. Approaching the yacht in the dark of night with a 25hp motor running defeated the purpose of sneaking in under cover of night. I preferred the inaudible hum of a trolling motor for the final assault; if I kept the revs low there would not be any noise from the propeller cutting through the water. My approach would be silent. Like many of the other items on my list I doubled up on what I could. If one fully charged deep-cycle marine battery was good for trolling, two was a better idea. While I was thinking in pairs, I added two extra gas tanks to my list.

I put the Zodiac in the water south of Galveston—a considerable distance from my prey—so that I might become familiar with the capabilities of the motors and any navigational quirks the little boat might have. Also, I needed to practice a stealth approach. One of the little things I had learned in the military; drill, drill, drill, made for successful operations.

I put out a cheap buoy and practiced floating up to it from different distances, checking the time it took and how much power I could keep on the electric motor while maintaining silent running. I placed a one-gallon water jug on top of the buoy and practiced making a shot from the boat.

My plan was ready. I picked up a tent, food and other supplies for a campout. Rounding out my list were two extra fully charged cell phone batteries for my Motorola Flip phone and a waterproof container for the phone and batteries. A relatively secure pay-and-park boat launch on the Gulf side of

Port Aransas was my initial destination. The *Thai Tannic* was slowly moving north. I was in a good position to intercept her and thrust Lou Cypher back to the abyss he came from. With the supplies loaded and the boat motors wailing away I kept a watchful eye out for my target.

From the shoreline where I set up a primitive camp, Cypher's location in the Gulf was nearly a mile away. By using binoculars to check his position I could keep a close eye on any movement and watch for visitors.

I had hoped for a quiet area where I could keep a close visual on the boat, but the southern tip of Mustang Island was a high-traffic beach area at times. Bird watchers, beachcombers, small boats, and water sport enthusiasts accounted for most of the passersby. Once again I found the openness and activity a perfect concealment. I would not be remembered by anyone.

I placed the call to Max, "I have eyes on."

Max fired back, "Capital!"

I don't always understand every colloquialism Max uses, but the tone was clear. The last domino was in place.

Short, sweet, and to the point. Just the way I like business conversations. I expected the next time would be shorter. If Max and Bludd decided to initiate the operation, I'd still be in a holding pattern. The down-channel "go" for Donnie and me would be after Max received confirmation from Brazil.

I was anxious. It was hard to control my temptation to hurry now that I was on target. Bludd, if successful, would soon eradicate the source of misery for dozens of Brazilian kids. As much as I blamed these scumbags who produced and promoted child exploitation, the greatest fault lay with those who created the market; the buyer of child porn. Bludd's target might be a simple case of economics, someone trying to make a buck at another's expense. The buyers, however, were perverse monsters who hid the depth of their filth behind a curtain of virtue. They were worthy of death.

I waited and dozed knowing the call could come at any moment. Around three in the morning I was awakened unexpectedly, not by the ring of my phone, but by the sound of voices in the darkness. I crawled from my pup tent as the sounds of laughter and loud talk grew closer. The beach was unlit; a quarter-moon was not much help in figuring out what my visitors were doing.

My Zodiac was beached fifteen yards from the water; my tent set on a brushy mound of sand near the Zodiac. My position provided a view of the *Thai Tannic*, my boat, and a wide expanse of beach. As the shadowy outlines drew closer, my concern heightened. I exited the tent with my shotgun in hand.

The shadow figures stopped by the Zodiac and their voices quieted to a whisper.

"Move on," I shouted.

"Just looking at your boat, man," one said.

"Thought maybe it washed up here," another alleged.

From the slurring of their words I supposed they were not in full control of their faculties. The more they talked the more my suspicion was confirmed. As they engaged in conversation I noted a couple of the group attempting to flank my position. I didn't know their intention, but it was time to elevate my concern.

It was commonly said, a picture is worth a thousand words; well, I was fresh out of pictures. I racked the shotgun slide chambering a round. It just so happened, the sound generated when you worked the slide of a 12-gauge shotgun was also worth a thousand words. The last I saw of those young men, they were traveling rapidly north along the beach, a little more sober than when they stopped to visit.

The sunrise illuminated the *Thai Tannic* against the blue sky and ocean. I had not detected any vessels coming or going from the yacht. However, the unknown was always the most haunting. There was the possibility that other people were on board—I'd work with whatever situation I found.

Max called shortly after seven in the evening. It was the call I'd waited for. It was simple, "Proceed." Bludd and Gunn had evidently been successful. Now it was my and Donnie's turn to cut the industry legs off. I made preparations to launch the Zodiac at nightfall. With weapons, a two-gallon gas can filled with kerosene and some additional combustible accelerants I had picked up, loaded on board, I was ready to do the deed.

A spectacular display of fireworks, like a yacht on fire, would catch the attention of everyone in the area. Not something I was hoping for while taking care of business. If I had to ignite it, I would. My intentions were in and out undetected with a dead body thrown to the sharks.

It was just after midnight and I had been ready to launch for hours. I gave Cypher sufficient time to bed down for the night then throttled the Johnson horses forward to break through the barrier waves. Thirty yards from shore I calmed the motor to a low roar as I made my way to the target vessel. When the dimly lit yacht became clearly visible I shut down the motors and drifted silently toward the stern. The warm and sunny day had given way to the cool air temperature of night and a light breeze. A mist formed creating an eerie glow around the yacht. I searched the deck with binoculars looking for signs of life. It appeared empty. There was no hurry now, the night was mine; so was Cypher.

I scanned the boat continuously for the better part of an hour with no sign of Lou Cypher on deck. A slight chop to the water would make my approach slower than anticipated. I pulled a black ski mask down over my face and donned a set of black leather search gloves. I turned the trolling motor on and advanced on the stern where two flights of steps emptied onto a swim platform just above the waterline. The Zodiac drifted up next to the stern, I threw the bowline around a cleat provided for that purpose and tied off with a standard cleat hitch. With a second line I secured the Zodiac to a cleat on the opposite side of the twin ladders and took out the slack so as to snug the Zodiac up against the ship's stern.

The yacht's aft lights were off, making the area dark. I climbed aboard, taking care not to make noise or cause any shifting of the boat. I drew the 9mm and stood poised to shoot if need be. I began to move slowly up the starboard semicircular steps to the aft deck. On the weather deck above, a series of running lights faintly illuminated the covered area below; this was equally good and bad.

I made my way slowly forward. I stopped momentarily to listen to an indistinguishable sound coming from the deck above me. As I listened, the sounds became more distinct. They were human sounds; the sounds of shuffling footsteps. I continued listening. A ladder amidships led to the deck above and the raised pilot house. I continued forward until I felt the upper deck handrail. I turned into the passageway and began my ascent to the next level. The top of the passage came into view; illuminated by the running lights of the upper deck I could see a silhouette approaching the ladder. I backed down the ladder into the darkness of the covered deck.

Objects were now identifiable. I kept my weapon trained in the direction of the approaching target. Adrenaline shot through my veins—twelve feet, eleven feet, ten feet, my heart continued to pound—seven feet, six feet, five, I didn't want to push the envelope. I could hear my heart beating in my ears, I had to act now.

"Don't move," I ordered. I purposely controlled the tone and inflection to not startle him more than was necessary. I repeated the command, "Don't move." The man lunged in my direction to which I responded to with a sharp blow with my 9mm against his head.

Now with the muzzle pressed against his temple, I repeated my command. "Don't move; don't even twitch a muscle, understand."

"Okay, okay—take whatever you want and leave."

"Where is Cypher?"

"What do you want with me?"

By this time I could see him well enough to be absolutely certain he was my target and I didn't like his attitude. The sound of his voice was "cocky" and he was in no position to be. "Who else is on board?"

"I have an army down below, but you probably know that already don't you?"

Dominance is best initiated through violence and I intended to have the upper hand in our conversation. I repeated my question with the added emphasis of my gun barrel across the back of his head. "Who's on board?" Now, seemingly more compliant with my request, he answered, "No one." I didn't wholeheartedly believe him, but thought we should move forward with our relationship. "Okay, let's try it again. Lou, can I call you Lou." I paused for his response, but there was none so I continued, "I'm going to ask a question and you are going to answer. Is that clear?" My captive audience started to mumble something under his breath but stopped midsentence; meeting the muzzle of my Nine on his face just under the cheek bone. I repositioned my weapon then remarked, "You're gonna have to get better at this or we're going to be here a long time."

Cypher cautiously responded, "I asked you already, what do you want—money?"

That's what I like, noncompliance. I'm supposed to ask the questions but as long as he's talking I'll let him talk and act surprised. "You have money on board? How much?"

"Look, I have some cash, not a lot, maybe a couple grand. It's yours, if you want it, take it and go."

"I appreciate the offer, Lou, but that seems a little light."

"What then? Tell me what you want?" His voice was cracking from a combination of strain and anger; he was no longer sarcastic, but frightened, and his nerves were on the verge of failing him altogether.

"You have ecstasy. I want it and any other drugs you have."

"Yeah, I get it. I get it now. That's what this is all about—well you're too late pal. I don't know where you get your information, but it's already gone. What I have left you can put in one pocket."

"So, you don't have much cash and you're out of drugs?"

"That's right."

"You're still light on the giving end, Lou. I'm going to give you one more chance. Don't fail me this time."

"I want all your DVDs, you know, the stuff with the kids on it."

Cypher was silent. The wheels were turning. If I gave him enough time he would come up with some nonsense line to feed me, so I interrupted.

"Turn on the deck lights." Pushing the muzzle into the middle of his shoulder blades as he moved toward the wall and light switch. "One more time," I said, "Where are they?"

"In the galley."

"Where in the galley?" I paused and waited for him to reply. The silence on his part spoke volumes. He was not going to be cooperative. "You are not very forthcoming with what I want to hear, where in the galley?"

"In a storage area behind a false front in the breakfast island, I have a couple hundred DVDs there. Take them all and go."

"If you're lying to me I'm going to be upset."

"I don't care about them. They don't mean anything to me."

"Tell me, Lou, are you into porn? Is that your sort of thing?"

"No."

"Do you get some sort of thrill out of watching little kids in porn, is that it?"

"What are you—my therapist?"

The reemergence of his cocky statement reminded me why I didn't carry on conversations with those I plan to kill. He's right; I'm not his doctor although I intended to cure his problem, "Let's go find the porn." Cypher, reluctant to move at first, responded nicely to the gentle persuasion of my 9mm. I kept prodding him with the muzzle, until he finally opened the secret hatch and exposed the DVDs. I pointed aft with my weapon and commanded, "Let's go." As we approached the stern, Cypher said, "Now what? You have what you came for." He mistook me for a petty thief and not one of grander purpose. His sudden show of arrogance was intended as a demonstration of his confidence and meant to disarm me. It wasn't working. "Down to the swim platform, Lou." Cypher started down the ladder leading to the swim platform. My weapon belched flame and a deafening noise. I heard the sound of tumbling followed by moaning from the platform area. I pulled out my flashlight and lit up the area. Cypher was still very much alive. With his back to me and an apparent shoulder wound he was pulling himself up to his feet. I quietly climbed down the ladder and fired a head shot at point blank range. Head wounds bleed profusely, especially when the heart is still beating. I decided to let him bleed out before I dealt with the mess. A minute or two passed, the bleeding slowed and the twitching stopped. I went scavenging for supplies.

Topside in the aft deck storage I found four block and tackle steel hoist pulleys, poly rope, chains, and steel cable. I chained the pulleys to the body and wrapped him in steel cable for a finishing touch. I rolled the body off the platform and sank it into the ocean.

There was blood, lots of it. No hiding it and trying to clean up the mess was useless. My shoe tracks were in blood and I left plenty of them around the boat. I opened every cabinet, pulled beds apart and opened up anything with a lid. I wanted to give the impression the motive was theft. I left the stash of drugs and child porn to be discovered by authorities. The cash was a different story. Lou had lied to me. He had bundles of cash hidden with the DVDs. It could be recycled to a worthy cause; one which helped kids, not hurt them. I hoisted anchor on the *Thai Tannic* and left her adrift.

I untied the Zodiac and hit the starter switches; the Johnsons roared to life. I sank my shoes and pointed the Zodiac toward shore. I didn't know how long it would be before the yacht would drift into an area endangering other boaters, and someone would board her or she would run aground, but I imagined it would be soon enough. If I was lucky it would be a few days before the alarm was sounded. By then, crab, snails and other crustaceans would be enjoying an ecosystem meal, compliments of Cypher.

I deadheaded toward land and then followed the coastline south. Along the route I dropped the Glock into the salty brine. I spotted my campsite and decided to take a dip to wash off any blood splatter. I've always felt there's nothing more refreshing than a skinny dip early in the morning.

Once on the beach I donned fresh clothes and slipped on a pair of tennis shoes, grabbed a snack and broke camp. I took one last look toward *Thai Tannic* as she floated aimlessly on a rising tide. I was moved. She was the first legitimate ghost ship I had ever seen. With my shotgun and gear stored in the Zodiac I headed for Port Aransas. Along the way I contacted Max by cellphone with the report.

Max had further instructions for me. "Drive to Corsicana, Texas. Check in at the Court Life Motel. You have a room already booked. A man will contact you by telephone and make arrangements to pick up the boat. Stay at this location until I contact you again. I want to go over the details with you."

Corsicana was a small town and easy to navigate. Once in my motel room I relaxed and placed a call to Anna. There was no answer. I wanted to catch up on local news with a special emphasis on B.A. Ware's whereabouts. It would have to wait. The following day I drove around the countryside as a way to wind down and regroup my thoughts. I had spent a lot of time on Cypher and I was still focused on what I could have done better or different. I supposed it was the nature of any business to go over decisions again, sort of quality assurance.

Max contacted me later that evening, "I'll be there tomorrow in the afternoon." I was still unable to get in touch with Anna. Why was she unable to take a call?

Max arrived promptly at one o'clock. I greeted him and filled him in on the success of my part in the mission. I was excited it had gone so smoothly. I was finally feeling like I was making a difference going after the root of the problem. Max briefed me on Bludd's operation. He was delighted with the outcome, but his face showed him to be troubled and concerned. Bludd had managed to free a child and killed two brothers who were engaged in sex trafficking and filming. With the "producers" out of the picture, Rusty had used an old .38-caliber Colt Army Special to take the distributor out. Rusty was conflicted by the fact his target was a family man with children of his own. In my book there was nothing redeeming about the target. He didn't care about the children who were being abused; and he should have.

Max grew quiet for a moment before he revealed the rest. Donnie was dead. The UK takedown had been too large for one person to handle effectively. Donnie engaged in a shootout with a gang of importers, leaving two dead and two hospitalized. They were Russian gangsters, part of an organized mob and heavily armed. Donnie died at the scene with multiple gunshot wounds. It was a success which cost too much. I cataloged it away in the recesses of my mind. One day I would finish what Donnie had begun. Their names were on record and they could be found when they least expected it.

Max sat back and silently looked out the window for a lengthy period of time. It was a time of reflection. I didn't have the right, nor was I interested in interrupting his moment. As for me, I was angry. I had only met Donnie, yet I felt a kinship with him. As I challenged my thoughts the ultimate question surfaced, Was Donnie's sacrifice worth his life? There are evil people among us and there always will be. They are broken vessels. What abides within them is a want to inflict atrocities on the innocent. No amount of counseling or punishment will dissuade them. There is no cure save one—death—that is their destiny. If required, will my sacrifice be worth my life? For the sake of the weak, elderly, young and innocent, I would answer yes. What more can a person ask for out of life than to give their life for another? It is the highest of all callings and I accept.

My thoughts raced, as they often did. I recognize that I have chosen my destiny as much as it has chosen me.

In time, Max reengaged in conversation. I was glad when he did.

"Scythian, an infiltration operation is in progress, are you interested?"

"I'm interested." I knew I had to get back into play.

"Excellent. A Palatini has penetrated a kidnapping ring operated across the borders of New York and Canada. Our asset is currently working alone. From the position they are in, they are at great risk. The asset has decided to go after the foreign elements. A Palatini is needed for the stateside operation. Scythian, this operation is extremely dangerous."

"Sounds like my kind of job." I couldn't identify my feelings but I craved the excitement of danger coupled with the sense of justice.

Max smiled, "I will count on you then."

Max gave a quick overview of the operation. "The Abbandanza crime family in Toronto and their American counterparts are the targets. They are politically connected and have a lot of protection on both sides of the border."

"Who is the asset I will be working with?"

"Anna Sasins; I hope you don't mind diversity in the work place."

I was stunned.

Max smiled, "Anna says she already has your phone number and will call you tomorrow."

"I always look forward to hearing from Anna."

An excerpt from *Lawless Measures*,
Lyle's next book, begins on the following page.

Lawless Measures

Chapter 1

Buffalo, New York
September 2002

I craved the arousal I felt as I lined up my shot. My trigger finger poised to unleash hell from my .223-caliber semi-auto AR-15. My weapon spoke twice, Shuup . . . Shuup, as the GemTech Halo Suppressor belched a puff of fiery smoke with each round. My target wobbled to the ground, struck in the back, center of mass. Giuseppe "Pepe" Pelosi, aka the Pimp, laid face down in the alleyway. I watched for signs of movement, but the only observable motion was that of blood as it pooled around the body. I concluded my target was eliminated.

I am a proud member of a secret society known as Palatini. We are an ancient knighthood, resurrected as an Order of freelance assassins. We are, as were our medieval predecessors, champions of the people, paragons of virtue, chivalrous, and heroic, with righteous principles as our bond. We espouse our oath to deliver a less imperiled world through our personal judgment. Our mission is one of guardianship of the people, for the people, and by the people. More simply put, we don't exactly call 911 in the face of heinous criminal events.

Not only was I proud to claim my allegiance to the Palatini, I was satisfied to claim the double tap as my signature. I was willing, however, to add a few extra slugs for good measure when needed. In this present situation it appeared two rounds were sufficient.

Pepe got shot square in the back. To some people, killing him this way might be viewed as a cowardly act, but I would disagree. It was an execution. Pepe was assassinated. There are no rules for murder, even a righteous murder. I didn't care if he had no chance to defend himself. My one and only concern was that he was dead.

Pepe had not only been a pimp and street hustler, but a soldier for the Abbandanza crime syndicate. I surmised he was of no great loss or importance as a person to Domenic Bacca, the ruthless Caporegime of the Buffalo and Niagara Falls faction. However, Pelosi did have a certain flair for the creation of finances. Pepe's premature death would be disruptive to the syndicate business, but not devastating. More of Bacca's soldiers had to die to shatter his illegal immigration stronghold. Their deaths had to resemble dominos falling in rapid succession to be effective and cause the level of confusion I hoped to achieve. I had to move fast.

Why was Society Palatini interested in the crime family's involvement in illegal immigration? The Abbandanza syndicate was not the run-of-the-mill coyotes. The pictures broadcast on television of foreigners huddled in box vans being snuck across United States southern borders, was not the business the syndicate was engaged in. Rather, they lured, tricked, or otherwise acquired underage girls with a belief they could obtain residency and nationality in America. Health, wealth, and happiness could be theirs for a small price. It was the answer to prayers for many third world inhabitants. But with the mob there was no path to citizenship, only a lifetime of slavery.

Pimp was more than a nickname for Pelosi; he was one of these facilitators. Anna Sasins, lead Palatini asset on this project, completed an extensive work-up on the crime family. As a result of her findings, Pepe was selected as a priority target to eliminate. Why Pepe first? He made the "arrangements." He was tasked with logistics for moving underage girls across the Canadian border between New York and Ontario. Taking him out early disrupted the flow of girls in and out of the country and presented a greater calamity to the entire criminal structure.

The Abbandanza mobsters were involved at many levels of organized crime. They ran the gambit from gambling to cybercrime. However, the Palatini interest with the syndicate's criminal venture was restricted to their underage sex rackets. Kidnapping and human trafficking were hallmarks of their illegal immigration enterprise. It was all too common and lucrative of a practice, and grossly overlooked by Federal Law Enforcement, who appeared to avoid any aspect of illegal immigration as if it were a hot potato.

Pepe, along with a couple of his minions, scratched out a scanty living on the streets of Buffalo's Lower West Side, seemingly on the lowest rung of the family's structure. His niche as it were, was to place girls in "service" at whorehouses to work off their indebtedness to the Abbandanza's Freedom Underground program. Realistically it was the lowest of the scams; "freedom" was a goal never to be achieved. These girls were doomed to a life of prostitution.